THE COMPASSIONATE TIGER

THE COMPASSIONATE TIGER

HUNTON DOWNS

CUTTING EDGE

ISBN-13: 978-1-957868-12-7

Published by
Cutting Edge Books
PO Box 8212
Calabasas, CA 91372
www.cuttingedgebooks.com

To M.D.
Who doctored both the manuscript and
the author during two years' residence in
Saigon, the city referred to—in alternating
breaths—as the "Pearl of the Orient" and
the "Yellow Hell of the East."

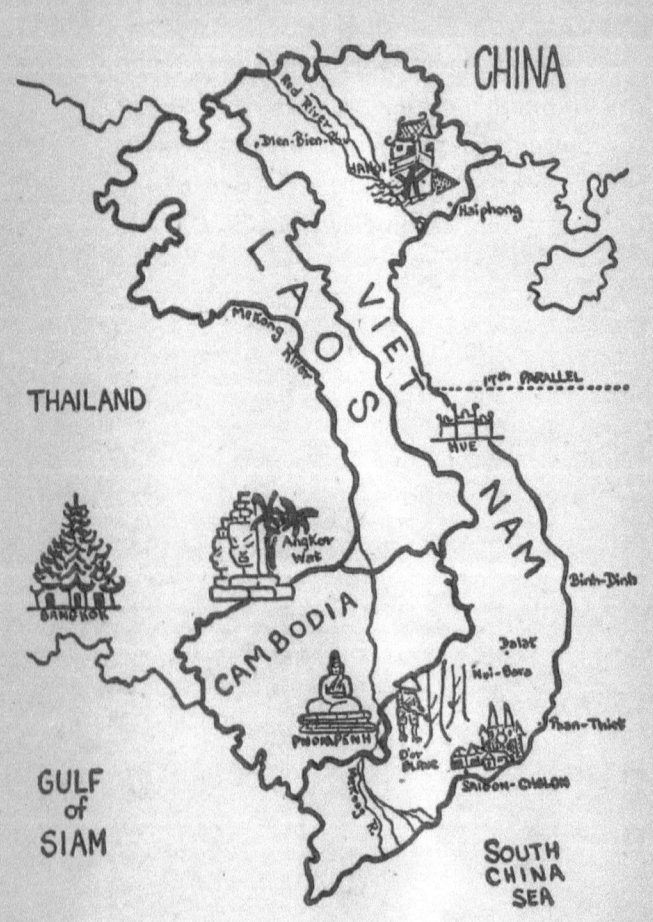

THE WARRING SECTS OF SOUTH VIET NAM

CAO-DAI—(cow-die) Religious fanatics of Viet Nam and Cambodia, worshiping Mohammed, Sun Yatsen, Jesus Christ, and Victor Hugo by means of ouija boards and dragon temples. Led by a self-styled "Pope," commanding fully equipped modern infantry divisions.

HOA-HAO—(wa-how) Blood-worshiping guerrillas, marked by the brutality of consecration rites and long hair—to grow until the Premier-President of Viet Nam, Ngo-dinh-Diem, is murdered.

BINH XUYEN—(bin-zwin) A pirate business syndicate controlling the city of Saigon's Port Authority, police and "Four Vices"—prostitution, gambling, opium and alcohol. Politically connected with Vietnamese interests in France. Supported by private army and navy.

VIETMINH—(vee-et-ming) Ho Chi Minh guerrillas. Formerly rice farmers and fishermen, armed by the Red Chinese. Bunkered strategically along the coast and interior of South Viet Nam.

PART ONE

CHAPTER ONE

I felt his presence in the room before I saw him.

With an effort, I smiled at my dinner partner and, giving her the cleft-chin profile which the Agency used in its brochure, told her in French that of course I wanted to hear about her experiences on the *Ile de France*. So she would understand, I told her in English.

Maxim's was as disorganized at this moment as it ever got. There was a whisper of feet—the cessation of tinkling crystal. Waiters paused in their serving. That's how I knew he had arrived.

Guillaume Mossard … adventurer … millionaire … planter … colonialist. One of the legendary Frenchmen of the twentieth century … King of Rubber in the Far East. I had never met him—nor he me.

As he passed our table, I could see that he was slightly built, fiftyish, ruddy, with an iron-gray shock of hair. His tuxedo was an immaculate fit.

My paying companion, Mrs. Beulah Steedman, prattled away about the wonder of pancakes fired with brandy, the squall that made all the other passengers squeamish except her—who was used to Texas horses—and the blue mink coat worn by some French actress she had never heard of. My eyes were on Guillaume Mossard as I nodded with pretended interest.

She was my client for the evening—courtesy of the Tailleur Escort Agency. If I had sunk low in standards of manhood for an ex-U. S. Army officer, it at least paid the rent on my Montmartre flat. And as jobs go in Paris for expatriate Americans, being a *compagnon de nuit* was not the worst. I knew.

In the Agency's confidential brochure, I was Daniel King. I passed as being half-French because the American dowagers who called the service mostly wanted French gigolos. Using and translating the language gave me a certain air, the romance that they were looking for. Whatever it was, my tuxedo was paid for ... out of tips.

The rubber planter was seated alone at a table for four. Ordering swiftly, he began to survey the room. I turned full attention to my client.

"... and she didn't seem to care who saw her," Mrs. Steedman finished breathlessly, face tinged with scarlet. "My ... oh, my. ..."

Knowing in general what she was referring to, I said with hard sophistication, "This is France, madame. The ... physical impulses are considered quite natural."

Then I smiled. "You will just have to get used to them."

"I suppose that's true." Her eyes sparkled after a moment. "It is ... sort of ... exciting. Are you going to take me to any of those wicked Paris places?"

"As you like."

Giggling, she whispered, "I want to see every one of them."

This was the point where I usually suggested a tour to embrace several nights. I said nothing.

Mrs. Steedman leaned forward confidentially.

"Cabel ... my husband ... was my husband ... wouldn't have approved. But then he wouldn't even have thought of coming to Paris, and eating this French food."

She clucked with what was meant to indicate utter futility.

"I'm so glad you brought me to Maxim's. I can hardly wait to tell everybody."

I got to my feet.

"Excusez-moi un moment? C'est un de mes amis." I indicated Mossard. "He is an old friend. Would you mind if I spoke to him?"

"Pa ... de ... too," she replied, pleased at the opportunity of practicing her guidebook phrases.

Bowing low, I touched my lips to her wrist.

She simpered and I strode to the table of Guillaume Mossard.

He was ringed with the accouterments of Escargots de Bourguinon—the dish Americans irreverently call snails. As he was commencing the gourmet ritual, I waited. His left hand snared a shell from the escalloped *panette* and canted its sauce into a spongy crust of bread. His other hand expertly extracted the snail. With a flash of silver, everything but the shell disappeared.

"My name is King ... Dan King," I announced in French. "Answering your ad."

He laid down the escargot instruments and examined me searchingly.

"Please sit down, Mr. King. You may speak English."

His eyes were set deeply behind craggy brows that jutted untamed across a high, square forehead. A luxuriant, disciplined thatch of hair belied his years. His skin was red-bronze.

I took the seat opposite him.

"Do you practice the cult of escargot?" he asked.

"No, but I eat a hell of a hamburger at Pam-Pam's."

He laughed drily. Unused lines etched his lips.

"My name is Mossard."

"Yes, I know."

'You can fill the qualifications?"

My heart thumped.

"You advertised: 'Tough, physically fit, single applicant for dangerous assignment Indochina. High pay. Leave immediately. Apply M. Mossard at Maxim's 9-10 P.M. Friday.' Fortunately, I had a tuxedo."

"Dinner was not included," he said shortly. "I had not thought of an American for the job, especially one of the expatriates who hang around Paris. If they had any fortitude, they would go home."

I felt my face growing hot.

"I don't see any long line of French candidates."

"The job is to be my bodyguard. I am not sure an American would qualify."

"I think I could."

The eyes probed me coolly from their bastions.

"Why?"

"I was in the army—in Germany and then here in France."

"That makes neither a soldier nor a bodyguard out of you."

I must have wanted the job badly because I kept from saying what flashed across my mind.

Taking a deep breath, I replied, "I am expert in rifle and pistol, sharpshooter in carbine. I taught judo for a year at Metz, and I can fill the rest of your qualifications."

"Why did you leave the army?"

"I was riffed."

The tangled mats of his eyebrows lifted with incomprehension.

"Reduction In Force," I explained uncomfortably, "for budgetary reasons. I could have gone back as a sergeant, but hell, I was expecting a promotion to major and they handed me a pink slip. So … I thought I would try civilian life."

"I see."

A shell popped up from the *panette* and dropped back. Wiping his lips delicately, with a monogrammed napkin, he added, "And now, you are tired of dowagers?"

He was sharp—this planter. I nodded.

"The army and I worked out fine as long as there was a war going on. It's just that … well, I wasn't quite the peacetime gentleman the book calls for. I guess that's the reason."

Mossard seemed to relish his next snail.

"What do you know about Indochina?" he asked finally.

"Enough to know there's a war going on. I tried to join the Foreign Legion. That's the reason I came to Paris."

"And?"

"They wouldn't give me a commission."

He laughed drily.

"You are ambitious, Mr. King, if most unreasonable. Our officers not only must be French but graduates of St. Cyr."

"Maybe that's part of the trouble out there."

A flush came barely noticeable to the bronze of his skin. The movements of his hands continued.

"Why do you say that?"

Realizing that I was on tender ground, I tried to match the quiet of his tone.

"From what I read of the campaign, you are trying to win by fighting from bunkers ... drawing the flies to the sugar, so to speak. That may be in the best Legion tradition, but it won't win a war. You have to find the enemy, close with him and destroy him."

"That is exactly what General Tassigny is doing. At Dien-Bien-Phu he is greatly outnumbered."

"He should try fire and movement," I said stubbornly.

"Fire and movement, as you call it, require more support and reserve than the Legion has available."

"That's what the Americans thought two hundred years ago when the Indians ran circles around us."

"You defeated them, did you not?"

"When we adopted their tactics."

The colonialist's hands picked up speed.

"King, neither you nor I are military experts on the situation in North Viet Nam. I am a rubber planter; you, a bodyguard— that is, if you meet the rest of my conditions. I do not intend to have my entire dinner spoiled so I shall pass to those conditions quickly. I am impressed with your military qualifications in that a good bodyguard, I should think, should not only be able to handle himself in close quarters but should be able to ferret out attempted traps or ambushes. Your tactical knowledge should be helpful in this respect in country as wild as Viet Nam. Your loyalty, however, is open to question. I have no way at this time to determine it. I shall be frank. If there were a French candidate with half your qualifications, I should choose him. But time does not allow the proper search. The deteriorating situation of Dien-Bien-Phu and the Communist threat to my plantation dictates that I return to Saigon tomorrow. Now, as to salary. I propose to pay you, so long as you perform to my satisfaction, the sum of ten thousand dollars a year. Living expenses and transportation furnished. Is that agreeable?"

Stunned at the figure, I could only nod.

"You are surprised at the generous arrangement. Perhaps I would not pay a Frenchman so much, but you Americans, I have heard, are loyal to your dollar. As it is my life to protect, I only hope that this is true."

He scrambled the empty shells in the *panette*. Waiters swooped from all directions. Plates disappeared and appeared.

"You are prepared to leave at three o'clock tomorrow?"

For the first time in months, it seemed, I grinned.

"Now ... if you say. I'm your man."

Mossard ignored my remark.

"In the time that remains, I shall have you investigated—at least to verify the statements you have given me tonight. If any have not been true, our arrangement is, of course, voided. If you have lied—and wish to back out gracefully—there is a bottle of champagne to continue your ... *nuit d'amour.*"

There was a touch of irony in his gesture toward Mrs. Steedman.

I turned and saw her fidgeting angrily. She pointed violently at her wrist watch and beckoned me.

"Three o'clock tomorrow afternoon," I said.

"At Orly Field. I shall have your contract there. Please give me your passport."

I handed it to him; he glanced at the photograph and slid it into his pocket.

The uniformed *sommelier* bent over his shoulder and offered a musty bottle of Vouvray for inspection. Mossard was absorbed at once in the label.

When he looked up, it was with surprise.

"Was there anything else?"

"No," I said getting up. "I guess that's all. *À demain*."

The good humor in his face was not altogether from the wine.

"Enjoy your last night in Paris," he said.

With the highly provoked Mrs. Steedman deposited in the Hotel Scribe lobby to await an American Express night club tour, I hurried to my apartment. Exhilaration accelerated my footsteps.

I was wanted—at last—and ten thousand dollars' worth. All of the knocks faded to insignificance. Remembering the poor jokes I had made about being riffed, I was able to laugh at them for the first time.

The playground of Paris opened before me as I ascended to Montmartre. The *tabarins* and jazz *bistros* gave way to narrow, winding streets cluttered with noise and people. The grimy pastel fronts, loud neons and cat-strewn garbage took on a new visage for me—like a Pigalle canvas. I felt strange, touristy and temporary. The girls, most of whom I knew, looked mysterious.

A tight-hipped *bouleuse* called me by name and dunned a cigarette. Lighting it for her, I stared into the mirror of a cheap fur shop. I wasn't in tip-top physical condition, but there was no slack. I could handle whatever was in store ... perhaps better. There were some different lines in my face ... wise lines.

As the soft round knobs of the Sacré-Coeur loomed above the candled chestnut tree in front of my apartment, I stopped and looked back. The Eiffel winked in red outline over a shimmering splash of light. Far off to the left two grotesque beams plowed through the sky. That would be Orly.

I debated whether to say good-by to the all-night waitress at La Sexy Boîte. Better to just fade away without a lot of talk. She wouldn't be hurt too much.

I went into the apartment, wrote a letter to the escort agency, finished off what was left in the Cinzano bottle, packed and went to bed.

CHAPTER TWO

Orly was bright with people in the afternoon sun. A tricolor snapped from a masthead. The Air France bus from the Invalides station lurched to a stop at the terminal entrance. The passengers—Orientals, red-hatted Legionnaires, a sprinkling of French civilians in white sharkskin and I—tumbled out.

Looking for Mossard and seeing no trace of him, I checked in at the desk, found a lounge seat nearby, and picked up a newspaper that was crumpled in the corner.

Dien-Bien-Phu was in the headlines. The French fortress in the mountain jungles was crumbling under the ferocious assault troops of Ho Chi Minh.

An editorialist gloomily gave it little hope.

I found a map on the inside pages. Viet Nam hugged the periphery of Indochina like a narrow scimitar. Dien-Bien-Phu was far to the north near Laos and the Great Wall of China. The fighting, indicated by dots on the map, was all in the north—from Hanoi and the Red River delta inland to Dien-Bien-Phu.

The rubber plantation area, marked *D'Or Blanc,* was about a thousand kilometers to the south, around Saigon, near the tip of the scimitar. *Or Blanc* translated was White Gold.

I was puzzled at why the colonialist was so concerned with the loss of a fort so remote from his interests.

The map was a good one. Quickly, I became fascinated with the names and landmarks of what for me was a little-known and exotic part of the world—Saigon, Bangkok, Phnom Penh, Angkor Wat....

A flurry of whipping blue shirts and gold braid churned through the lobby. Air France's reception committee was heading for the door. V.I.P. treatment coming up. I grabbed my bag.

Guillaume Mossard, in the center of the returning cordon, was immaculate in snowy Dacron. At his elbow was a tall, striking blonde, seemingly agitated, a mink stole flung carelessly about her shoulders. Reporters, photographers and secretaries with briefcases jostled in a knot behind. At a nod from the colonialist, the blue coats parted to let me in and I found myself being swept past counters piled high with baggage, a maze of unattended *contrôle* windows and out into the sun of Orly Field. The cordon disintegrated as we reached the steps of Super Constellation FBAZ-Y which apparently had been drawn up close to the terminal for the occasion.

I grinned sheepishly at a hostess whose *derrière* had enjoyed passing acquaintance with mine during the scramble. She snubbed me and pinned a carnation against Mossard's lapel. Flash bulbs exploded.

The backwash breeze stirred the planter's hair and brought his body into hard-rock outline. He was a good physical specimen for fifty. Better than good.

Surrendering my baggage, I selected the green and gold passport from a stack offered by a *douanier*. I noticed that the blonde wasn't going. She stood apart from the people surrounding Mossard, and a glint of moisture webbed the mascara of her lashes. Her hair was the smoky silver of a Mercedes sports car—her dress, under the mink, the shade *coutourier* ads called Harem Jade. She looked about thirty-five, but you would have to subtract ten years if she weren't crying. She carried herself like a Paris model—not the bone-thin type, but the kind that advertise Cordon Bleu and villas on the Riviera. I liked her wide-set eyes and the honest emotion. As she removed a glove to fumble through an orange-colored alligator bag, a blaze of diamonds lit up her hand.

"Madame Mossard?" I said, walking toward her.

She dabbed with a wisp of pale green lace that matched her dress and awarded me a wan smile. I spoke in French.

"My name is Daniel King."

"Oh yes, my husband told me about you."

"Then I guess that means I passed. Do you have any last-minute instructions like when he should take aspirins or wear overshoes?"

She trilled a forced laugh.

"I always cry when he leaves," she apologized. "It is a terrible moment for me. Our life used to be so marvelous. Nine months at the plantation, three months in Paris. Now—pouf! Nine months is a long time to be without a husband ... or children."

"If I were your husband, I would never leave you," I thought and was surprised that the words had come out.

Her expression clouded. She turned away.

While I was thinking of some way to recoup, Mossard strode out of the crowd.

"There ... there, no pouting!" He put his arm around her; then, seemingly conscious of the photographers, he released her and stepped away. I noticed that he was an inch or so shorter than she.

"You have your beloved Paris, and I have my duty to France. A soldier without uniform, but a soldier none the less."

She was silent.

I began to edge away, but Mossard caught me by the arm.

"We have another soldier in the D'Or Blanc family, my dear. May I present Mr. King, an American? Madame Mossard."

"*Enchanté,*" I murmured.

She repeated the acknowledgment.

He looked at his wife tenderly; their fingers intertwined. She bit her lip.

"Please, Guillaume," she said indistinctly. "I do not fear the danger. Let me go. Please. I can stay in Saigon and promise not to bother you. I promise. I promise."

Mossard looked stricken.

"Charlotte," he said in a low voice, "we have discussed all this a dozen times. You know that it is not safe. The north country is already untenable, and the south may explode at any time. You will not go, and that is final."

He stepped back from her and spoke with deliberate humor, "And now you are leaving me an ugly picture to take—tears and frowns."

There was a gentle sniffle. When Charlotte's face emerged from the handkerchief it was set in a frozen smile.

Mossard changed the subject.

"What do you know about rubber, Mr. King?" he asked.

"Only that it stretches," I said.

"Farther than you think." He glanced at the waiting press corps, walked to a "Follow Me" jeep and kicked the tire.

"There is one example. Where would the world be without rubber ... without wheels?"

His voice raised to attract attention.

"For another example, look at you."

Everybody turned obediently. I was in focus.

"Where would *you* be without rubber?" he demanded. "Your hair—you comb it with a rubber comb. Your back—you protect it with a raincoat. And, how do you keep your pants up?"

There was a hint of a smile from the Air France hostess who had been adjoined to me in the cordon.

"With a belt? With suspenders? Both rubber, Mr. King. The top of your shorts; the top of your socks; the bottom of your shoes."

Some of the press people began scribbling. This was obviously the farewell speech.

Mossard went on, "After a hard day's work, you go home. You wipe your feet on a rubber doormat; you walk on rubber flooring; your electricity is insulated by rubber; you fix a drink from a rubber ice tray; you feed the baby with a rubber nipple; store your food under rubber covers; and finally—if you have time—you go to sleep on a rubber mattress."

A polite titter crossed the assemblage.

"Sports? Golf balls...tennis balls...badminton...soccer. Do you go to the Tuileries? Balloons for the children; bathing suits; pneumatic boats. If you get sick, rubber gloves, hot water bottles, oxygen masks. Mr. King, there are over ten thousand products made of rubber and designed for the comfort of man. Where does this latex come from? From my world. The Far East. And there's plenty for all. Thousands upon thousands of miles of it. But, all rubber is not alike."

Dramatically, he pointed to the huge waiting plane.

"A transcontinental airliner. What happens when a tire blows out? When a battery fails, or electrical insulation cracks? Belts; hose; linings—a thousand pieces of rubber must be flawless.

"D'Or Blanc—my plantation—produces the toughest, most durable rubber in the world by scientific test in the laboratories of a dozen governments. That is why I am going back to Viet Nam at this critical hour.

"I built D'Or Blanc out of raw jungle. Eighty-five thousand acres, plowed into white gold, as we call it. I have swallowed more red dirt than I weigh, and I have been through more heat and hell than Dante. But, I built a new face on a piece of God's earth and it is producing for you and for us and for our friends."

The crowd was hushed.

"Now the Communists would like to have it to use on their planes and tanks and trucks. Be assured, my friends, that they will not get it so long as the tricolor flies and there is a drop of my blood left to protect it."

He pushed through the crowd to the plane.

Pencils flew furiously, and several people applauded.

Mossard mounted the high metal stairway and without looking back, disappeared into the plane.

I turned to Madame Mossard.

"Well, here goes for Lafayette."

She looked at the plane unbelievingly.

"My offer is still good," I said. "If there is anything you want me to do out there...."

She touched my arm.

"Mr. King," she said quietly, "tell me if... if there is another woman."

I looked at her closely. She was serious, intense.

"Please write and tell me. If you do not, I am coming to Saigon to find out for myself."

I laughed, but from the expression on her face it was no joke. The delicate features twisted until they were less than pretty. Tears sprang again.

"I will write you," I promised. "If things get... tough, maybe I will stick myself in the envelope."

Unsmiling, she handed me a scalloped gold-edged card.

"Charlotte... Charlotte Mossard."

"I know."

"My address."

I held the card in my hand and for some reason sniffed it. Shalimar.

The crowd had trickled away.

Looking into her eyes for an envious second, I said, "Please don't worry."

After the plane was sealed, I could see her standing. Mossard, sitting across the aisle from me, was reading.

The giant Constellation roared to life and trundled toward the runway. She slipped out of view waving her tiny handkerchief. The iron-haired planter never once looked up.

We were airborne and being served *apéritifs* before Mossard finally stirred. When he did, it was to turn the page of his magazine for the first time, get out a handkerchief and blow his nose.

At Rome, he passed me the contract.

"Your army in Orleans called Heidelberg this morning. This will make it legal."

It was a simple contract. I agreed to carry out implicitly and loyally whatever Mossard required me to do. I agreed to be waivered to French law and jurisdiction. The ten thousand dollars, or equivalent in francs, would be paid one year from today, May 14, 1955. Any breach of contract on my part, to be determined by Mossard, would nullify obligation of payment and return ticket. There was nothing about being returned other than alive. I signed.

Beirut was hotter than Rome; Karachi hotter still and humid.

Between Karachi and Calcutta, after dinner had been served, an ashen-faced steward brought the planter a telegram. He read it and passed it to me.

Dien-Bien-Phu had fallen.

Guillaume Mossard sat rigidly for almost an hour silhouetted against the dark porthole by the cone of overhead light, his only movement the rolling back and forth of a brandy snifter between his fingers. As sleepy as I was, the movement held me awake hypnotically.

Finally, he beckoned me to cross over and sit with him.

He unfolded an airline route chart from the elastic pouch of the seat.

In a low voice he said, "When we arrive in Saigon you will be issued protective weapons. Be on your guard from the moment we land. Do not let the languid tropical atmosphere of the city deceive you. The Vietminh has a price on my head."

Touching the map on the fat forepaw of Asia which was Indochina, I said, "The Vietminh is a long way from your plantation."

He grunted.

"The Vietminh is not only all around my plantation, but in it. The newspapers have had a tendency to ignore this fact and have attributed my apprehensions to mercenary interests. I am afraid the fall of Dien-Bien-Phu will spark these forces to revolution. If that happens, the finger is out of the dike in Asia. These revolutionary forces can spill over defenseless Cambodia, join the Ho Chi Minh forces coming down from Laos, overrun Thailand, and with the Red rebels already holding parts of the Malayan Peninsula, push on to block the Singapore Straits. They would have a foothold in Indonesia—could perhaps even threaten the Philippines.

"The consequences of such expansion are frightening. Neither France, Great Britain nor the United States could abide it. There would surely be a third world war."

Studying the map, I said, "To move that far that fast from South Viet Nam would take organized armies. A revolutionary mob is not an army."

His laughter was brittle.

"South Viet Nam is a honeycomb of armies—and organized."

He scribbled concentric circles over the map.

"West of Saigon to the Gulf of Siam there are Vietminh guerrillas armed and organized—waiting. Up the coast north of Saigon—more Vietminh armed and bunkered. Here," his pencil flew, "southwest of Saigon there is a private sect army under a chieftain named Ba-Cut. It is called the Hoa-Hao. Northwest of Saigon—another uncommitted army of two divisions run by a religious fanatic, a Pope who worships Christ, Sun Yat-sen and Victor Hugo. South of Saigon, along the river to the China Sea, there is another sect—the Binh Xuyen river pirates—with naval launches and modern infantry. And then there is the national army of the government itself which holds Saigon."

He scribbled an area which was about all that was left.

"D'Or Blanc."

"What about your army?"

"I am training a *gendarmerie* from among the rubber tappers to augment the Legion Detachment which we maintain for security. The native force is quite small, but if I increase it it has to be at the expense of reduced rubber production. And I am in business … not politics."

"You mentioned Vietminh on the plantation."

"Scratch a Viet," he said bitterly, "and you find a potential Communist. They think that it represents national freedom. One of my mandarins, Nguyen Cam, is the ringleader. I must have him on my side because he is the native chief of the plantation—the highest ranking in their feudal system. I have tried to compromise with him."

Mossard fell into heavy thought, his craggy eyebrows surging out from his forehead. His fingers closed around the brandy glass.

"What has kept these armies quiet up to now?" I asked finally.

He rang the service buzzer before answering.

"The French Foreign Legion, Paris thinks—but I disagree. A loser's head is quick to the guillotine in Indochina. The sect chieftains want to be sure they are on the winning side—and get their price for it. With Dien-Bien-Phu, we may be near the denouement."

"I hear there is an international conference in Geneva. Maybe that will solve the problem."

Mossard laughed contemptuously.

"The Four Power Conference? Great powers get together to compromise, but never to solve. When the West compromises, the Russians take advantage of them and then there has to be another conference. Ad infinitum. At Geneva the Russians will push for complete withdrawal of all French forces in Indochina."

"What would become of D'Or Blanc?"

He shrugged.

"I am what you Americans call a colonialist. Viet Nam is my country as well as France. I love it—perhaps even more than France—from the stinking sewers of Saigon to the jasmine of Dalat. Thirty years ago, when I came here, it was raw jungle— primitive and unconquerable—as your United States must have been a century ago. Rubber was growing wild on the plateaus—pods blown on the wind from Malaya. I brought in trucks and steam shovels. I tore hillsides of jungle away and planted trees.

"Do you know how long it takes for rubber trees to grow and produce latex? Years ... and without income. I went through blight, monsoons and pestilence, native indolence and superstition. Finally, I got sap, latex, rubber, money ... in that order. Then I was called a colonialist ... an imperialist ... a despoiler of men. Certainly, I benefited myself, but I deserved it. There are easier ways to accumulate wealth than by wading in mud and choking in red dust nine months a year. And that, Mr. King, is the thumbnail sketch of the twentieth century's most despised breed of man—the colonialist."

The stewardess brought Cordon Bleu. He nestled the new snifter in his palm, washed the amber liquid around the inside and inhaled the aroma. The cabin was dark except for our seats.

"In 1941 when the Germans overran France and we could no longer protect Indochina, I made the decision to leave rather than produce for the enemy. The Japanese took over ... and quite effectively. When I returned in 1945, France had lost Indochina irrevocably. We never again gained the respect we had known. Ho Chi Minh had replaced us.

"I had to fight D'Or Blanc into existence again, not physically but in the minds of men, and I think it taught me a lesson, King. If war or politics demand that I leave once more ... I shall not. I shall stay with my plantation, win or lose."

He sipped cognac.

"Do not think I am being overly dramatic—I intend to win."

"I see now why you left your wife in Paris," I said slowly.

A strange gentleness relaxed his face.

"Charlotte is a magnificent woman, but she thinks of plantation life as it used to be. Boudoir gossip across the continents, fashion shows flown in from Paris, weekends in Hong Kong or Penang, great parties with hundreds of guests. It is beyond her comprehension that times have changed. The harness of planta-tion life today would reduce her from a spirited filly to a plodding water buffalo.

"Do not misunderstand me, King, I am no sentimentalist in my business. I intend to keep my plantation through any means necessary—some of which you may not approve. That makes no difference. But this is as good a time as any to make one thing crystal clear. You know that I was hesitant in hiring you. The reason is that Americans tend to be imbued with the ideal of liberating the world's downtrodden. Well, if you have any such ideal, get rid of it now. The white man did not bring colonialism to Asia. The mandarins had a caste system in effect long before your America was discovered and while France was still in the Dark Ages. The system is just as rigid today and no white man will ever change it. Nor will the mandarins who benefit from our enterprises change it. The so-called white colonialists who intro-duced the twentieth century to Asia merely fitted themselves into the existing pattern and made arrangements with the manda-rins. They, in turn, used us not only to profit, but as scapegoats to blame for the people's ills. Now the mandarins see an opportu-nity to eliminate us completely and that is the seat of the trouble."

My face must have registered disbelief.

Mossard went on, "I'll give you an example of the manda-rin system. Last year, I gave one of my villages a bulldozer— something like your American aid program, on a minor scale. I showed them how to lay streets, dig garden paddies and pull roots. And what happened? The bulldozer disappeared and fifty Chinese coolies from Cholon—the Chinatown of Saigon— showed up with bamboo picks. I asked the village mandarin what had happened to the bulldozer. His answer was: 'Coolies more better—also not so hard work for Vietnamese.' The old fox had blackmarketed the bulldozer, hired coolies and had enough left over to buy a 1937 Peugeot sedan and a new wife."

I laughed.

"You laugh, Mr. King," the planter said, "but it was a delicate moment. I stood to lose face. I agreed with the 'great wisdom' of the old mandarin, but pointed out to him that the bulldozer had been a community gift. So, logically, the car and wife should be for the community also. Leaving the villagers to digest that bit of logic, I sat back to await developments. They were not long in coming. Fighting broke out over who was going to use the car and get the young wife—presumably she was virgin. Even the new Chinese coolies claimed rights as members of the village.

"So, I bought another bulldozer and this time I gave it to the Chinese who, with all the squabbling, were not getting very far with the village modernization. This settled the argument over the car and wife, and the old mandarin was very grateful. But, as time went on, the Chinese, who have a habit of segregating themselves, worked only on their end of the village, prospered, opened up shops and sidewalk inns in the Vietnamese section, and gained firm control over the whole village economy.

"Finally, the old mandarin came to visit me at the Château, my plantation house, and after hemming and hawing for an hour, asked for yet another bulldozer...for the Vietnamese. With seeming reluctance, I granted his request and his joy knew no bounds. Well, it cost me three bulldozers—so far—to bring progress to the village. But, do you think that settled the matter?"

Mossard sighed and shook his head.

"The Vietnamese, in order to prove their superiority over the Chinese, anchored the bulldozer on sacred ground, fenced it in, painted it to resemble a dragon with huge teeth on the blades, and mounted their ancestor worship altars around it. They pointed with scorn at the Chinese bulldozer and the 'coolies' who used it for labor. The Chinese, to save their pride and placate their own offended ancestors, were forced to do the same thing."

There was a touch of humor in Mossard's grave expression.

"You can understand, King, why that was my last attempt to raise the standard of living. Political platitudes about 'nationalism' sweeping across Asia—nonsense! It is the same old struggle for power that has been going on for three thousand years. Only now, it is being publicized. We are white men in a yellow land—respected, envied, emulated, hated. I advise you not to lose your perspective. Walk like a lord, talk like a king, act like a general. But, do not forget that *I* am your god."

His eyes were shaggy holes under the condensed light. He leaned forward, sipping brandy.

"Do as I say," he said calmly, "and there is every chance that we will be together on this plane again—going back."

It was three o'clock in the morning when we left Bangkok. The next stop was Saigon. The plane, after thirty hours in flight, was cluttered, stale. There was a new tenseness among the passengers that had not been evident before; somebody mentioned a Constellation that had gone down between Bangkok and Saigon several years before with all lost. Sabotage. I remembered reading about it. Our plane flew high and fast.

Three cups of coffee later, the sun burst over the horizon and the landscape below us flamed in a checkerboard of terrestial fire. Dawn was reflected in the sea of rice fields. This was Communist-held territory.

The intercom sounded and the plane dipped sharply downward to a green and ocher city, caught in the serpentine coils of a dozen muddy waterways.

We landed in Saigon, Viet Nam, Indochina.

Mossard woke up on the second bounce.

CHAPTER THREE

Sitting next to Mossard in the back seat of a highly polished black Citroën, I grunted with surprise as we moved around circles of flowering lawn leaving the airport and into an avenue of palatial villas.

The planter gave me a sharp look.

"What's the matter, King?"

"It looks like Paris."

"Wait," he said.

Trees lined the *rues,* the architecture was French, billboards advertised *apértifs* and Renaults. The tricolor hung limply atop tawny buildings and the street we sped along was rue de Gaulle.

"This is the dry season," Mossard commented, wiping his face.

The equatorial humidity soon seeped through my shirt and trousers.

The chauffeur, a spidery Vietnamese in shorts and T shirt, was glued against the steering wheel. Next to him sat a fat Chinese who almost obliterated my view. His bowling-pin figure, draped in an expanse of white linen, mushroomed from window to gear-shift. Mossard had greeted him warmly and called him Lien-Fat.

We were the center car in a convoy of five identical unmarked Citroëns.

A silver-helmeted, leather-girdled Legionnaire led us on a motorcycle, siren screaming. The streets were nearly deserted.

The upper body of the Chinese revolved in sections as he turned to speak to Mossard.

"Very glad you back, monsieur. Much trouble. Much big trouble. I very much to tell—"

His pidgin French was interrupted as the convoy swerved suddenly into an unpaved side street cluttered with buffalo carts and people.

Guillaume Mossard's fingers bit deeply into the mountainous blubber of Lien-Fat's arm.

"Where are we going?"

"Go to villa," the Chinese explained. "Much rubble on rue de Gaulle. Street all broken. We make detour."

The planter cursed and tossed himself back against the cushions.

The siren died to an apologetic growl, and the convoy slowed.

Both sides of the car became meshed with humanity—brown, taupe and apricot-colored bodies—wrestling to get out of the way. The hot breath of the crowd swept over us. I smelled decay, sweat, fish and incense. Faces, topped with conic straw hats, stared at us. They were curious, friendly, hostile, grinning, gaping or unconcerned. I saw no sign of the reputed implacability of the Orient. The convoy halted uncertainly. I fanned.

I heard clashing cymbals and weird monotonous flutes and string instruments.

Mossard swore again.

"Get out and see what is stopping us," he ordered Lien-Fat.

The folds of fat jellied in deference.

"No need, monsieur. Chinese funeral passing. One...two minutes maybe...that all." His tongue clucked as the funeral procession came in view, barely fifty feet in front of us.

Columns of white-clad mourners held aloft blue, red and orange scrolls. A small cart followed, bearing a smoking altar and a picture of the deceased. An elaborately gilded circus painted hearse came into sight, seemingly propelled by no human or mechanical power. The musicians, pouring out their plaintive melody, sat crouched along the edges.

Two bewhiskered ancients walked painfully at the rear of the hearse. They were followed at a respectful distance by a group of middle-aged men, then several columns of women and finally a host of children. All wore white mourning clothes and multicolored turbans.

"Very rich Chinese," Lien-Fat muttered, "to have such big funeral. Live very old."

The mass of natives around the cars paid slight attention to the passing funeral. Somebody spat lustily and jeered. The sound found echoes. A chorus lifted in unison.

"Roll up the windows," Mossard ordered.

A bicycle pedaled alongside and a boy thrust a large bouquet of fruit through the aperture.

"*Des fruits, monsieu?*" he singsonged. "*Sapotilles, pommes, pommes cannelle, pamplemousses, ananas…?*"

"*Allez-vous-en!*" Mossard snapped.

I almost amputated the youngster's hand as he withdrew the proffered package. As it was, a pineapple rolled out of the paper cone onto the floor of the car. We lurched forward and the sirenmounted.

I stared at the small, green, knobbed fruit. Diving for it, I crammed it out the side vent and fell over on top of Mossard. The grenade exploded just outside the window. Shattering glass flew through the car. The spiny Vietnamese fell to the floorboard. It must have been a plastic, I thought with grim consolation. If it had been steel encased, I wouldn't be conscious… or alive.

"*Nom de Dieu! Allez!*" Mossard roared from under me. "Drive! Get it out of here!"

He threw me off and vaulted into the front seat.

Lien-Fat was blubbering with pain and trying to lower his bulk below window level. His neck was flecked with red. The Vietnamese driver was curled on the floor in a shaking lump.

The angry hubbub outside was deafening. Brandished fists poked at us. I saw three bodies writhing on the ground and one still. I caught another glimpse of the would-be assassin, head lowered, peddling furiously.

Mossard threw gears wantonly and and slashed the Citroën into the crush of people. They separated like waves before a ship's prow. Moments later, we turned into a broad boulevard, passed the Chinese funeral procession and sped at full throttle. The driver sheepishly came to life, but dared not expand under Mossard's feet. Lien-Fat managed a wheezy chuckle after examining the dabs of. blood on his handkerchief.

I felt a stinging sensation against the seat. My trousers were burned. The powder of the plastic grenade had penetrated my skin. Nothing serious. No glass.

We swung between iron-grilled gates bearing a brass plate: *Villa d'Or Blanc.* A knot of Orientals stood waiting in the shade of the portico. The villa was a modern Corbusier-like creation with terraces encircling each of its three floors. A wide smooth lawn anchored tall coconut palms and scarlet-plumed flame trees. It seemed impossible that this setting was only minutes from the violence and squalor to which we had been exposed.

Mossard jumped out of the car. The Vietnamese chauffeur unwound and tumbled after him. The planter looked at him contemptuously.

"Pick up your pay. Be gone in fifteen minutes."

The Vietnamese bowed and stumbled toward the villa.

Lien-Fat, who was getting out on the other side, winced at Mossard's order, changed his mind and slammed the door. Jagged glass tinkled onto the drive.

Guillaume Mossard strolled past the stunned groups stumbling from the other cars to the cylindrical portico. I followed. The waiting men, obviously employees, retreated as he approached. He examined them closely and without comment.

Finally, he smiled broadly.

One by one, they responded, their teeth gleaming.

"More gold, I see. The best sign of trouble I know is when the wealth of the family goes portable. I shall have to look over your wives to see who is wearing 18-karat necklaces and bracelets. Then, I shall know who sold out my arrival time."

The golden crescents disappeared. Indignant protestations filled the air.

The colonialist raised his hand for silence.

"Never mind. If one of you is guilty, I shall know by tomorrow, and that one will know better than to come to work."

Extending his hand to them, he said, "I have missed you, and I am glad to see you again."

Greeting each one of them, he then turned to the French and Vietnamese V.I.P.s who had met us at the plane. "I apologize, gentlemen, for subjecting you to such a harrowing experience. But these are the days we may expect it. Step inside … all of you. It will be cooler, and a drink will calm your nerves. I shall join you in a moment."

As the crowd thinned, Mossard swung around looking for Lien-Fat.

"Get out of the car, you old fraud. I pay you for brains—not to sit there getting fatter."

The Chinese plopped out, hissing with relief.

"Thank you. Very good sir. Thank you."

The Frenchman turned to me.

"Good work, King. Were you cut?"

I bent to show the evidence.

He laughed heartily.

"We will fix that. Lien-Fat, call the nurse from the hospital. Neither one of you looks incapacitated. And while she is here, have her give Mr. King his inoculations—everything he will need for upcountry."

Lien-Fat bobbed his head.

"Yes sir. I call. Send nurse five minutes. But, monsieur, first must tell you plantation bad news. Everything not working on D'Or Blanc. I am afraid Communists make coup."

Mossard moved his head incredulously.

"What did you say?"

"Is true!" The Chinese nodded. "Tracks of railroad through forest broken. Train must stop. We send courier car, but car turn back from gunfire. I very much afraid plantation is finish."

I could see the pressure building in the planter's temples.

"When did this happen?"

"Near one week now. Yes ... five days ...."

"Did you cable me in Paris, or send a cable to the plane? I had no word."

"Not like spoil trip," Lien-Fat answered blithely. "We know you come soon. What you can do before reach Saigon anyhow? Is not so?" The Chinese waited.

Mossard sighed heavily.

"Is so," he said.

With an ironic glance at me, "Welcome to the Orient, Mr. King," he said.

CHAPTER FOUR

I woke up with an arm poking at me through the shroud of mosquito netting.

"Yes, what is it?" I demanded of the shadowy figure on the outside of the net.

"You sleep day and night now." Lien-Fat's moonface peered cheerfully through the mesh. "Monsieur Mossard no wait for you more." The fat man's English was as fluid and ungrammatical as his French.

I eased out of the netting. My arms ached as if they had been pounded with clubs.

"I hearby apologize to all G.I. medics around the world."

"Beg pardon?" Lien-Fat's brow wrinkled.

"Nothing. Private joke."

Looking at the unglassed window opening out on the terrace, I saw moonlight streaming in.

"What time is it?"

"Is two o'clock."

Despite a ceiling fan that whirred over the bed, the night air was sticky and stifling. I started to slip into my shoes.

"Oh-no ... no," Lien-Fat grinned. "Better you look first."

He leaned over exposing several Band-Aids across his neck, and overturned my shoes. A finger-long lizard skittered out and raced up the wall, where it paused, snapped its tail, and pounced on a hovering insect.

"*Margouilla*. He eat mosquitoes. Very good for house."

Suddenly, I noticed a metallic array of weapons on the French-style dresser. Lien-Fat followed my eyes and grinned.

"Very best American equipment. I buy for you. You no like, I get other."

There was a Colt forty-five, a Thompson submachine gun, a crate of grenades—fragmentation type—a grenade belt, and a box of ammunition clips.

"Is okay?" asked the Chinese.

"Where's the Sherman tank?"

His face fell.

"I go look, Ahhh ... you make joke. Never mind, I find if you want. Lien-Fat buy tank, or even fighter plane. Saigon very good market for arms. Just get Mossard okay. How your bottom is?"

I checked. It was better.

Coffee and a shower helped. When I reported to the colonialist's office, I was back to near normal.

Mossard's face in the light of the desk lamp was lined with fatigue. He looked as if he had not slept.

"D'Or Blanc is, in effect, cut off," he began abruptly. "We have no communication with the plantation—by radio or telephone—so there is no way to determine the extent of the insurgence, except by reconnaissance. Be ready to leave at six o'clock."

"Is the Legion sending out a column?"

"You and I are going alone."

His eyes bored into me.

I shrugged, but inside I began to tingle.

"You found your armament?"

"Yes ... but I should have ordered the Sherman tank when I had the chance."

"We shall see what you learned from your Indians," he said with relish, "in the way of fire and movement."

He poured coffee from a slender thermos and drank in a series of quick sips.

"News travels slowly in this part of the world, King. Even the fall of Dien-Bien-Phu is not yet known outside of official circles. The plantation coup—if it is that—occurred before the disaster in the north. So ... we cannot conclude that it is the result of any co-ordination with the Vietminh or indicative of any general uprising in the south. Actually, the sect armies appear uncommonly quiet at the moment. The commandant of the French Expeditionary Force here in Saigon is reluctant to mount a column northward for fear of igniting a full-scale conflagration. Of course, I defer to his judgment."

"What about the grenade attempt yesterday?"

Mossard grimaced.

"Such incidents are altogether too common in Saigon. A gamin is given a grenade and pedals around looking for a French car to dump it in. On the surface there would seem to be some connection with the plantation, but I doubt it."

"I thought you suspected one of your employees."

He grunted. "I was concerned with who was tongue-wagging in the market place. Three of my walking gold mines did not return to work after siesta yesterday."

"So we are going to visit your chief mandarin?"

Eying me with appreciation, he said, "Nguyen Cam has tremendous influence among the workers but he has never before had recourse to arms. Supply is no problem—there is more armament than food in Viet Nam. But to train a force during my short absence that could overrun both the Legion Detachment and my *gendarmerie,* I find difficult to believe. I suspect the rail severance and gunfire incidents are guerrilla actions that Cam may even deny knowledge of."

He held the coffee cup to his lips, contemplating me.

"But, I could be wrong," he said.

I slapped a mosquito and said, "Next time you buy weapons, let me go along. That Thompson is so rusty, it, can't shoot nails."

"You have two hours," he said curtly.

By five forty-five I had gotten a half shine in the bore, oiled and assembled the parts, loaded the gun and hoped it would work. The Colt was new. Slinging the grenade belt over my shoulder, I went down to the bar—a continuation of the portico—and looked for Mossard.

A black Citroën was waiting in the drive, white flags pinioned to each front fender. The villa seemed deserted. Only the Legionnaire patrolling the grilled gates was awake.

The sun broke over the horizon and stirred a horde of insects in the flame trees. They burst into a high ringing oscillation; the sound was deafening. Nature's alarm clock, I thought, and turned my attention to the mural above the bar. It depicted D'Or Blanc. The Plantation of White Gold was shaped like a tilting hourglass. The railroad and highway ran north from Saigon through the lower bell and on into the upper. The railroad terminated there at what was shown as the Château. The highway veered left into Cambodia. Villages were identified by name throughout the acreage. Tapper villages, I figured. The plantation was bordered on all sides by jungle, with symbolic pictures of a tiger, a waterfall marked *Nui-Bara,* and a brown-skinned savage holding a spear.

There was nothing to indicate where the French Legion was bastioned. Looking closer, I saw the mural as dated 1937.

"Let's go," Mossard said quietly at my back.

He drove as if the car had come equipped with him at the factory. Spinning the wheel incessantly, he weaved through barricades of straw-hatted humanity, overloaded oxcarts and coolies who trudged to market with weighted shoulder poles. Near the outskirts of the city, he indicated two Vietnamese walking leisurely, holding aloft umbrellas.

"Mandarins," he said. "Like Cam but not so high. You can tell from the robes they wear."

One was in black, the other white. Wispy beards hung from their chins.

"What color robe does Cam wear?"

"Blue…and sometimes purple. It is a capital offense to wear purple unless you are a member of the Emperor's family, so Cam finally devised a shade that is somewhere in between."

"Where did he get his rank?"

"The Royal Palace in Hue awards the mandarinates, much the same as degrees…but they are degrees in power. A blue mandarin is a little king."

He swerved to avoid hitting a screeching chicken, and I glanced into the rear of the Citroën. The Browning automatic rifle, sandbagged into position, had not jarred. This was the special car, Mossard had explained, used for diplomatic missions—false trunk, knocked-out back seat, spring catch to open the lid for the B.A.R., bulletproof, and white flags.

In an hour we were out of Saigon and beyond any traces of French civilization. The native huts close to the road were bamboo-sided and thatched with palm. Rough-hewn furniture of hand-wound rattan sat in steaming gardens or upon bamboo porches. Rice paddy embankments were everywhere. Buffalo, chickens, and people emerged from the same shelters. Brightly painted altars dotted the primitive roadside in bird-box dignity.

Ahead, alternating gabions blocked the highway. Mossard slowed and guided the Citroen around the cement-filled oil drums, coming to a halt before a striped-pole barrier. Two wine-complexioned Legionnaires sauntered out from a barbed-wire bunker.

They advised us to turn back, but on the basis of Mossard's indentification, let us through.

After four more Legion outposts, we passed the dusty village of Ben-Cat, and ran out of people. Miles of barren paddy land stretched on either side of the road, with only an occasional thatched shack or deserted temple. Bamboo bramble and flop-eared banana palms scarred the arid waste. Blue mountains loomed far in the distance.

Mossard idled the car to a stop, got out and pointed. I could see a low line of foliage—a light green brush stroke that extended completely across the horizon a mile or so ahead.

"D'Or Blanc." Mossard's voice held pride. "Let us see if our calling cards are in order."

I clambered in the back, hit the release spring and fingered off a round as the trunk flew open. Sighting on a low palm about five hundred yards down the road, I banked up the tripod, shifted the stock and tried a burst.

With less confidence, I got out and aimed the Thompson. The rattle of fire seemed to echo to the mountains and back. Patting the stock fondly, I carved a T in an eroding hillock fifty yards away. When the dust settled and the T appeared, I grinned at Mossard.

"Keep your guns down and windows up until we get there—then vice versa. Whatever happens, do not be lured out of the car. Keep me covered at all times and if you shoot … make it good."

As we roared into the arbor of rubber trees, it was like entering a cool tunnel. The gray-splotched trunks intertwined overhead in waxy foliage that extended without break in every direction. The rows shuttered past with dizzy monotony—flashing aisles of green. It seemed to me that it would have to end soon.

"How far does it go like this?" I asked.

"Oh, fifty miles or so." His face was radiant.

"When I enter my forest," he said quietly, "I share one of God's emotions. I have taken a clod of dust and brought to it order and refinement."

The radiance did not last long.

"These trees have not been touched for weeks." His voice was tight with rage. "Look at those scars. Shameful!"

All I could see were myriads of white cups, arranged in line along each row.

Mossard's face set in cold fury. He drove faster, then swerved abruptly, and went off the macadam. We jounced into a red dirt road cut between the trees.

Grasping the Thompson firmly, I scouted both sides of the road. In a few minutes a village grew in front of us. Mossard drove right into the middle of it. Rows of cottages, plastered neatly and covered with French tile, nestled in semicircles in a large clearing. It was more civilized than I expected, but with less signs of life. Only a group of boys were in the square playing quoits. The planter spun the car in a circle and stopped by the wall of a schoolhouse.

"Closer to the wall," I suggested, "with the back end out. That gives me leverage, seals off my flanks, and lets the B.A.R. command the square."

"Good idea," he said, and shifted the car quickly.

His fury was replaced by a detached calm as he climbed out over my side. I lowered the window and let the Thompson bristle out.

The hubbub wasn't long in coming. We had taken the village completely by surprise. Children erupted out of the houses, followed by women with drooping breasts shouting for them to come back, and finally men with rifles.

Mossard held out his hand in a peaceful gesture and the din ceased. Some of the scowling men pushed to the front. They hesitated when they saw my Tommy. Their guns were of a strange type—shorter and stockier than Garands.

"I mean no harm," Mossard spoke quietly in French. "I want to speak to Nguyen Cam."

The Vietnamese men looked at each other, jabbered and shook their heads.

"Your mandarin," Mossard continued, "has he fled from the village?"

They thought this was funny and laughed uproariously. One of the kids got down on his knees and urinated. His mother jerked him up and he stood regarding me stoically.

"Then … your mandarin is afraid to meet me," the planter said.

His remark threw the entire assemblage into a chatter. This was loss of face. Rifles were brandished; one was leveled.

I aimed. The warrior's gun lowered.

Mossard balanced delicately on his heels and nodded to himself as if the mandarin's fear to meet him were indeed the truth.

A spindle-legged boy was dispatched toward a central house of two stories, larger than the rest. Moments later Nguyen Cam emerged and strode unhesitatingly toward us.

A sigh of relief passed over the villagers.

Cam was tall and bronzed and could have passed for an American Indian, save for the long wisp of whiskers blowing from his chin. His near-purple tunic flowed about him with feathery grace, and he walked with a confidence that commanded respect. When he stood in front of Mossard, it was he who was taller.

"You are paying me a call, Monsieur Mossard?" His French was faultless.

"I am asking you the meaning of this insurgence, Father. Why are your men and women not out in the hevea collecting the white gold? Why are you flaunting these weapons at your friends?"

"I have so decreed it throughout the plantation," Cam replied with dignity.

Mossard studied the dust at his feet.

"What you do in your own infinite wisdom within your own village is a matter for your conscience and your ancestors' advice. But I must warn you, Father, that your authority does not extend over the plantation. The other villages are returning to work. I advise you to do the same. Otherwise, your women will go gaunt from squatting and your men will sneak away in the night to a village that prospers from honest work."

The tall mandarin spat on the ground.

"Your words sing in the sugar cane," he said with contempt. "This ground is not yours. It is Vietnamese. The trees, and the white gold from them, belong not to fat foreigners, but to the seed of our race. The sun of your day has set, monsieur."

The Frenchman reflected for a moment.

"The chaff of Ho Chi Minh blows through your ears and speaks of Viet Nam for the Vietnamese. Do you not know that behind the Uncle lies the crafty Chinese, your natural enemy, and the rude Mongolian who would chain your sons and fertilize your daughters?"

"The Uncle is for the Vietnamese," Nguyen Cam replied.

"I remember when you came from the Upper Mekong, Father, with your women pushing the wheels of your oxcarts. They had no gold in their ears and the coiled braids of their hair hung loose from vermin. I granted you this ground and had built for you this beautiful village. None of your wide family has gone wanting. Indeed they have found luxury. Your coffers are heavy. Is this not for the Vietnamese?"

"The plantation belongs to the Vietnamese," the mandarin muttered. "The French must go." He bent in thought, tugging at his whiskers.

Mossard stood quietly, waiting out the inner conflict.

Nguyen Cam straightened and looked squarely at the planter.

"We have listened too long to the French. You are the enemy to our progress. I am sorry. The answer is no."

He turned his back to us and retraced his steps to the house.

"Cam!" Mossard's voice cracked like a pistol shot and stopped the mandarin in his tracks.

"You are a traitor, Cam. A father not of your people but of insane folly. You no longer deserve the robe and respect of a mandarin. Unless the butterflies escape through your ears by tomorrow, I shall place you under sentence of death. Your body will be burned and your spirit choked in smoke. When your ashes are cast from my plane into the unwalked jungle, only the foxes and the serpents will bow."

An incredulous gasp rose from the group. Several faces blanched. One of the women pressed her hands into steeples and dipped them rapidly at the dirt. All eyes focused on the tall motionless mandarin.

He turned slowly and there was a fixed smile on his face.

"You cannot, monsieur," he said. "You have not the power." His shoulders stiffened arrogantly, he snapped an order in Vietnamese. The entire assemblage turned its back and followed him silently.

Mossard stood carved as from marble.

"Expect a trick," he shot out of the corner of his mouth. "Be ready with the B.A.R."

I scrambled into the back of the Citroën.

Mossard lit a cigar, waited a few moments, walked leisurely to the car, and got in.

Not a sound or movement came from the village.

As we turned out on the macadam road, I got back into the front seat. The planter frowned.

"It is more serious than I thought," he said. "Cam speaks from strength, and he has Chinese weapons."

The Legion Detachment outpost near the Hon-Quan railhead in the Lower Loop reported that there had been a strafing attack three days before. A weapons carrier had been destroyed by grenades. There had been no change of guard from Detachment Headquarters at the Château for over a week.

Mossard held the accelerator to the floor as we careened along the white ribbon northward through the eternal trees. We met no cars nor any sign of tapping. Hundreds of thousands of white clay cups had overflowed—the latex dried.

"Cam has organized it well," he said grimly. "I only hope to God…"

I could only guess at the base of Mossard's fear.

The rubber forest became hilly and the road snakier. We came to another red and white barrier. The huge block of cement that was the bunker tilted akimbo. It had been blown.

"*Allo!*" Mossard shouted. No answer.

The planter jumped out, untangled a field phone and cranked. It was dead.

He swore, elevated the barrier, and we drove on to Loc-Ninh.

"This is the Château," he said and cut sharply into a side paved road. We bounced over a single gauge railroad spur, and shot upgrade through an arcade of hibiscus trees.

"Thank God," he breathed with deep feeling.

We came to a high grilled fence, a gate boldly emblazoned in white letters with the words D'OR BLANC. Standing by a red, white and blue sentry box was a French Legionnaire, carbine ready. He waved us through.

The Château of White Gold appeared. It was a miniature Fontainebleau, dazzling white, cresting the rise of the hill a quarter of a mile away. The immaculate lawns leading up to it were terraced with flowers. Fan-shaped sultan palms arched along each side of the long, concave, white graveled driveway that terminated at the double-horseshoe Napoleon stairs.

I caught a glimpse of a swimming pool at the side, as we drove up to the front.

Mossard slammed the brakes and was out of the car before the shower of gravel touched ground. He bounded up the baroque stairs and was no sooner at the panoply of wrought iron surrounding the *porte d'entrée* than the double door opened and a tall Vietnamese girl appeared.

She was dressed as I had seen the women in Saigon dressed—tight silk pants, wide at the ankles, and a long, swirling double-apron tunic split to the waist. As the planter kissed her on the cheek, she dropped to one knee and embraced him perfunctorily.

A stream of people poured from the door. Braided Legionnaires, Frenchmen in Bermuda shorts and Orientals surrounded the planter, all talking at once in a brouhaha.

I went to join them.

"Later ... later ..." Mossard barked and turned to a pan-hatted officer.

"Captain, this is not Dien-Bien-Phu. Get a detail out to the Loc-Ninh bunker and lay some new wire. Push reconnaissance cars out into the rubber beyond the compound in all directions until they strike fire. Start a double guard with reinforcements toward the Lower Loop and report back to me when you have some intelligence."

The Legionnaire saluted and elbowed out of the group.

My eyes were irresistibly drawn to the Vietnamese girl who was standing quietly by. Pretty enough from a distance, close up she was breath-taking. Ebony hair cascaded over her shoulders. Her oriental face, more carved than molded, held arching eyes that glinted purple and were leaf-shaped. Her features were oddly familiar. As I stared, trying to place them, she caught me looking at her and a slight smile curved the pink mounts of her lips. She poked her hair—nervously it seemed—into already well-ordered place.

"Tuyet," Mossard called over the hubbub.

She glided toward him.

"Where is Roland d'Arbre?"

A hush blanketed the veranda.

"In his room, I think." Her voice revealed no emotion.

Everybody stared at the floor or ceiling.

The planter lowered his fist slowly into his palm.

"I had better talk to him privately. Come along, King."

As I swung into step beside him, he said, "Oh, by the way, this is Thi-Tuyet, my wife—my second wife."

My mouth must have dropped open, for his next words were sardonic. He spoke in French.

"If you are surprised, such an arrangement is quite common in Viet Nam—especially for business advantages. You have met her father … Nguyen Cam."

At his explanation, Tuyet's lashes fanned downward and a smudge of scarlet blurred her high cheekbones. When we left her on the veranda to enter the Château, I saw that she was barefoot—her toenails painted the same violet color as her eyes.

Green marble stairs mounted to the second floor where an outside terraced corridor ran the entire rear length of the Château; off this *couloir* were several apartments.

The swimming pool was in full view, set against the mountains—a kidney-shaped sapphire in the emerald lawn—edged by pineapple palms and pastel beach furniture.

Mossard stopped at the last door on the corridor and knocked.

"Roland d'Arbre is one of my foremen," he said. "My best rubber man, but weak. I probably should not have left him in charge."

He knocked again and tried the door. It swung open. The sound of heavy breathing fell on my ears.

The foreman lay stretched across the bed in a pool of sweat. He was fully clothed and badly in need of a shave. The air in the room was foul. Mossard sniffed, kicked open the window blinds and started the overhead fan.

"Exactly what I thought," the planter grunted and dug the toe of his shoe along the underside of the bed. A queer, bright object spun out into sight, resembling more than anything a musical kazoo.

"Get some water."

I went into the adjoining bathroom, found a wastepaper basket and filled it.

Mossard knelt over the prone body. He slapped first one cheek, then the other. The man on the bed groaned and licked his lips. Mossard paused long enough to roll up his sleeves and went back to work harder.

The foreman came up coughing, his face beet-red. That's when, on Mossard's signal, I doused him with the full bucket.

He sat up, saw the colonialist and shuddered.

"Mon Dieu," he said, voice quivering. He looked to be about thirty-five. Unkempt blond hair fell in a tangle over his pasty face.

The planter wiped his hands carefully on the gauze of the mosquito net.

"So, they got to you with opium?"

"My first pipe—so help me God, Guillaume, my first pipe," D'Arbre whimpered.

Mossard reached for a small glass lamp on the bedside table.

"First pipe?"

"I ... I ... well ..."

Mossard turned to me and said, "You see, King, opium lamps cake up like a tobacco pipe. First one ... he says."

"I ... it is a secondhand lamp, Guillaume."

"Who got you started?"

The foreman regarded him silently. Then he buried his head and sobbed.

Mossard's voice was ice. "You not only lie to me, Roland, you put a knife in my back. Do you realize what you have done?"

The dripping yellow head nodded feebly.

Mossard sat on the edge of the bed and placed his hand on the foreman's shoulder.

"All right. What happened?"

Roland d'Arbre got to his feet unsteadily and walked to a chair.

"Well, they—Cam, Thong, Ai and Qui—and the other mandarins brought a petition. They had formed a union they said ...."

"Who did the talking?"

"Cam."

"Go on."

"They asked three piasters more per hour for tappers and five for the specialists ... plus truck-out to truck-in pay. They also demanded the right to strike."

"Lien-Fat knows nothing of this."

"I ... I did not think it necessary to consult him. I stalled. I told them ... they must wait until your return."

"Then they told you they would strike immediately, if you did not sign."

D'Arbre showed signs of anger.

"*Fichtre*, Guillaume, you cannot deny them the need." He was breathing heavily. "They would be underpaid if you doubled their wages. These are not colonial times any longer. You have got to treat them like people."

"When the mandarins do, so will I."

"I ... I thought it would keep us out of trouble. When I signed ... then ... they went on strike. There was nothing I could do."

"What demands did they present this time?"

"Vietnamese management. They offered to keep me in an advisory capacity."

"Did you sign that one, too?"

"No ... of course not. Then they tore up the railroad."

"And the *gendarmerie?*"

"They deserted."

"Deserted?" Mossard repeated coldly.

D'Arbre's face was a mask of agony.

"The soldiers petitioned to return to their villages. They had good cause. They were being called traitors. One of them was shot. I ... I ... of course made them turn their arms over to the Legion."

Mossard stood up. His face was filled with the same detached calm I had noticed at Cam's village.

"Roland, I think you have a gun concealed on your person."

D'Arbre looked stunned.

"What did you say, Guillaume?"

"Would you say, King, that that is a pistol under his shirt?"

I could see nothing.

D'Arbre's eyes widened. He clutched himself nervously and fell back on the bed.

"I ... I ... what do you mean, Guillaume?"

"Mr. King is my new bodyguard. If anyone makes a suspicious move in my direction, he is prepared for action. King, stand by with your Thompson. I believe D'Arbre is reaching for his gun."

The significance of Mossard's words penetrated D'Arbre. Hands trembled violently, he cringed.

"No ... no, Guillaume ... I have no gun." He ripped off his shirt. "See?"

I lifted the submachine gun unsurely. I had no taste for killing a man in cold blood.

At the sight of the weapon pointed at him, D'Arbre screamed, "No gun ... no gun." Tearing off his pants, he dropped to his knees clad only in shorts, and appealed to me in frozen anguish.

"Well, Mr. King?" Mossard said quietly. I honestly do not think it would have mattered to him if I had pressed the trigger. I decided to wait until I was ordered.

Fully a minute passed. I could hear sweat falling to the floor and occasional bursts of D'Arbre's chattering teeth.

"Who gave you that pipe, Roland?" Mossard's voice was a whisper.

"I ... I ... I ..." The foreman's eyes rolled and he fell with a wet thud to the tiled floor.

The planter stepped over him, picked up the opium lamp from the table and hurled it against the wall. It smashed to splinters.

"There is an empty apartment next to this one, King. See Tuyet about servants, linen and meals. She functions as our housekeeper and, for all of her youth, is not inefficient. Conduct yourself on a stand-by basis. I shall perhaps need you on short notice."

Pocketing the opium pipe, he added, stepping once more over the unconscious D'Arbre, "It was important for me to know if you were a killer by instinct."

CHAPTER FIVE

The apartment next door was unlocked. When I walked in, Thi-Tuyet (Mossard had pronounced it Tee-Tooyet) was preening herself at a vanity.

"I beg your pardon," I spoke in French and retreated hastily. It was difficult to tell if she was wearing the Vietnamese costume or was *en négligée.*

"This is your apartment," she said, caressing her hair in a final approving fling.

I saw then that she was not alone.

"This is your *boyesse,* monsieur." She motioned to the elder of the two servants who were puttering with feather dusters. "Her name is Thi-Ba. You may have the other, if you like, too, but I think you will need only one."

The chosen one bowed and awarded me a golden smile.

"Do you want her to sleep here?" Thi-Tuyet asked matter-of-factly.

"Well, I . . . no, I hardly think so."

She appeared not to understand the inflection.

"There is a small room that connects to your closet. She can sleep there—or not—as you say. But, she is not to use your bath. We are very strict about that. If you find her doing so, please report it to me."

"As a matter of fact, I won't be needing Thi-Ba at all."

"But, monsieur"—she looked at me unbelievingly—"everybody has servants. I have two—a *boyesse* and a *femme de chambre.* If I have a baby, then I shall need three."

She could not be over nineteen, I thought.

She stood up but seemed in no mood to leave.

"Did you know her in Paris?"

"Who?"

"Madame Mossard ... Charlotte. The *patron's* first wife."

"I met ... her at the airport."

"I should like to meet her. The *patron* loves her very deeply. Why does she not return to Viet Nam?"

I swallowed and said nothing.

"I should like her, I think. I remember when I was small—she was so beautiful and had such elegant clothes. She was always kind to the Vietnamese. Once, I presented her with a garland of jungle flowers at the *Fête Champêtre* in Nui-Bara. She patted my head and said I was pretty. It would be better if the *patron* had an old wife here. I try to help, but so many things are beyond my knowledge. Also ... one should ask the first wife's permission to spend a night with the second wife. *Patron* assures me that it is not necessary."

The somber expression on her face clouded as if from inner doubt.

"Mossard ... *patron* ... said you would tell me about meals," I prompted.

She replied in a singsong manner, as if she had memorized the instructions and was bored with repeating them. "If you wish to eat in your room, Thi-Ba will bring you a tray. If not, the dining room is downstairs. A chef is always on duty. There are no fixed hours. Of course, if the *patron* wishes you to eat with him, you will be advised and will please be on time."

A tantalizing smile curved her lips. "You are not French?"

"No ... American."

"I can tell."

"How?"

I laid the Thompson on the bed, sat down and began to take off my shoes.

She pirouetted gaily and announced, "You have not tried to pinch me."

Both *boyesses* cackled with laughter.

Her trim figure was well proportioned in the tight-waisted oriental dress.

Tuyet whirled again. "Why did you look at me like that downstairs?"

Uncomfortably I asked, "Like what?"

"Like I was…shameful. Do not Americans have several wives?"

"No, only one—that is, one at a time."

"Oh." She appeared relieved. "I would not like to live in America then. France is more like Viet Nam. *Patron* says that in France it is customary to have several wives. They call them…mistresses I think he said."

I could not help smiling.

Unaware of the humor, she continued, "France is better than America. America is primitive like Viet Nam."

"Who told you that?"

"I see the cowboy pictures in our cinema room downstairs."

I laughed.

"That was America a hundred years ago. Nobody lives that way now. There are apartments. Like this one…or larger, and villas like the ones behind the Château."

"But you have no châteaux?"

"No," I admitted. "I have never seen anything quite like this."

"Then, I should not like America," she said and clapped her hands sharply.

The *boyesses*, who had stopped to listen, jumped. Thi-Ba, flustered, unleashed a stream of vituperation at the other girl, who bent silently to the floor. Both renewed their tasks with vigor.

The dallying seemed to remind Thi-Tuyet that she herself had been remiss.

"Your bedroom connects with a salon ... through here." She pointed at a draped doorway. "The bath is in between. The balcony outside also connects with the salon. It is nice to take breakfast there before the heat. Here is your key."

"Thank you very much. You are most efficient."

The compliment pleased her.

"I do not like to work, monsieur, but *patron* thinks I should set an example for the other women. By working I lose face, but then, I have my own apartment next to his." Her voice was filled with pride. "No other woman has an apartment in the Château—not even French—and it is just the same as yours. Well almost...." There was a touch of superiority in her tone. "You have no connecting door."

"No," I said, as discreetly as possible.

At the entrance to the *couloir*, Tuyet turned. The tempestuous adolescent qualities in her manner were gone. She examined me calculatingly and I could detect in her eyes the wily cunning of Cam.

"À *bientôt*, monsieur. We shall see much of each other."

Our eyes held for a brief moment and the hair on the back of my neck tingled.

She left, the aprons of her filmy tunic swirling high over rounded, silken hips.

Thoughtfully, I walked to the vanity where she had been sitting when I entered. After a few moments, I heard a fit of coughing and the sounds of Roland d'Arbre moving about in his room.

CHAPTER SIX

My tour of the Château grounds took more than two hours, but I formed what I thought was a reasonable defense, in case of attack. Mossard was planning to deploy the entire Legion Detachment on a specific mission, and I had been appointed captain of the home guards.

I was amazed to find that the Fontainebleau-type manor was only a fragment of the compound. I had seen the smaller houses, luxuriant with tropical cultivation, ranged in semicircle a few hundred feet behind the Château—they housed the French civilian technicians and Legion officers.

But behind this residential area, the compound stretched several kilometers. There were tennis courts, a hangar and airstrip, a complex of warehouses, a railroad spur and depot, a fifty-car garage, gas station, commissary, power plant, water tower, military barracks, a dispensary, a school, a fleet of cistern trucks, processing sheds, a laboratory, and rows of connecting houses for Vietnamese personnel. The entire area was landscaped, painted and scrubbed, and encircled by heavy cross-ribbed fencing. Beyond the wire in every direction was the rubber forest.

The vulnerable points to the estate were the exits. There were four altogether, including the front gate with the sentry box. The others—one for the railroad spur and two for trucks—were locked but unguarded.

If a would-be attacker had no mortars or tanks, the fencing could be held under a relatively light field of fire. Not so the exits. I debated if it would be wise to run security scouts into the rubber

51

and effect a main line of defense outside. I decided against such strategy, as the scouts would be caught against the fence when the enemy pressed forward and outlined against the intermittent spotlights along the balustrade.

I earmarked four buildings where second-floor windows gave fields of crossfire over the exits, and at the same time covered large stretches of the fencing. To protect the front of the Château, I thought that foxholes—with the advantage of rising round—would be more efficient than mountings in the Château itself.

Mossard bought my plan instantly and dispatched the Legionnaire captain—who I discovered occupied one of the apartments off the *couloir*—to set up the crossfire points and train volunteers. The entire rubber staff had "volunteered" for the home guards, Mossard told me, or would—whether they liked it or not.

No one apparently realized it yet, except Mossard, for when I left his suite, shouts and splashes drifted up from the swimming pool.

I gave up trying to sleep and told Thi-Ba to find swim trunks for me.

The sun had fallen below the crest of rubber trees and the sky was shot with ice-cream colors when I walked out to the pool. The May heat, beaten into layers by the torrid sun, lifted almost visibly in waves and created mirages of impossible fantasy among the flowers and foliage. Perfumes wafted strongly on the air.

Boys in starched whites circulated around the terrace by the pool, taking drink orders, Latin music filtered from a speaker hidden in one of the pineapple palms.

The tables were crowded with French—in bikinis and monsieur bikinis—sipping, chattering; one couple was dancing on the tiles. Roland d'Arbre, shaved and wearing a red sport shirt and shorts, was alone at a table.

I sat down beside him.

"Come to join the orgy?"

He was drinking a Citron-Vermouth. With *attention de toi-lette,* he looked older, more dignified.

"Not bad for the jungle," I said, answering in French. "Madame Pompadour would have appreciated it."

"Here she would have had more competition," he replied bitterly.

"Don't you believe in women?"

"Not on a rubber plantation. But, I recognize the facts of life, monsieur. To keep men in this isolated place, one must keep women as well—and, believe me, most of them are well kept."

He twirled the liquid in his glass.

"Do not misunderstand. These are nice girls from Saigon—fiancées or *invitées.* You see, Monsieur King, we do not allow prostitutes."

I ordered a Cinzano from a hovering boy.

"Unfortunately for me, there is one who interests me—the only one I would lift a finger for—but she is sealed. *Tant pis,* so much the worse. Ah ...."

His expression softened and I followed his glance.

Tuyet came across the grass from the Château, swinging a yellow terry-cloth robe. She wore a melon-beige bikini, which in the facing red sky, melted to the color of her skin. She walked, haughtily erect, to the springboard, poised and dived.

D'Arbre sighed as the lithe body split the surface of the water.

"Thi-Tuyet does not mix very much—nor is she particularly popular. So ... she swims."

"She must have been lonesome while Mossard was gone."

He glanced at me sharply.

'You pick up things fast for a newcomer. No, Tuyet does not smoke opium ... if that is what you meant."

"I meant being a wife without a husband."

His tense expression eased to a semblance of humor.

"I suppose it seems strange to you—second wife and all that. You met Charlotte in Paris?"

I nodded.

The humor broadened into a smile. "Mossard has latex in his veins instead of blood. He thought that if he cemented a family relationship with Cam that would eliminate the Vietminh infiltration. He was desperate at the time. Cam had stirred up a lot of hatred."

My *apértif* was served in chilled crystal.

"She was a long and gangly girl," D'Arbre continued, "too tall and sharp-nosed for Vietnamese tastes. Cam was having no luck with potential husbands, and she was fast developing a wandering eye for Frenchmen. Cam, who is no fool, decided to get his price before she disgraced him. 'A featherless turkey' he called her in Vietnamese."

"Didn't she have any say in the matter?"

The Frenchman snorted.

"Marriage out here is half-face, half-finance, and all arranged by the elders. There was a big native wedding. The two of them ran out into the woods and all that. I am sure he spent the prescribed time looking for wild rubber trees."

I laughed.

"It cost Guillaume a pretty piaster. He had to remodel Cam's entire village. Everything went fine for a while, but then there was no sign of pregnancy, and in Viet Nam that is an ill omen.

"Then, Thi-Tuyet blossomed into a stunning girl, the best-looking on the plantation ... and that infuriated Cam even more because a Frenchman owned her. *Voilà* ... ."

"And, tell me, where does Madame Mossard—Charlotte—fit into the picture?"

"Mother of God, she does not—and never mention it to the old man. It is a very sore point that he has to leave her in Paris. Charlotte Mossard would never understand. Would any woman ... after taking a look at Tuyet?"

D'Arbre sipped his drink thoughtfully and lit a cigarette.

"Does he...?" I paused, not knowing how to continue the question tactfully.

D'Arbre shrugged and answered, "What do you think? The nights are dull and nine months are a long time to sweat out celibacy."

"Well... I mean does he love her?"

"I think he hates her for what she makes him do. He is amazing, the old man, the most ruthless I have ever encountered. He would sell his soul—and Charlotte's as well—to hold on to D'Or Blanc. Actually, the liaison with Thi-Tuyet was brilliant... as much as I hate to admit it. It saved the plantation at the time, and ever since, Cam has had more trouble in creating disorder."

I grunted, "It looks like your theory has suddenly gone sour."

"No, the Viets are a very romantic race. They liked the idea of a 'royal wedding.' It was a sop to their national pride—which is fierce—and then, too, some of the mandarins who were tired of Cam's domination gained an arguing point. The old rallying cry of white supremacy lost its power. That is why I gave them as much help as I did. I did not realize that Cam would commandeer the *gendarmerie* and have access to outside weapons."

D'Arbre's voice trailed off. He pressed the heels of his hands to his temples and his expression was one of hellish pain.

"If you will excuse me now, monsieur," he mumbled hoarsely, "I must go... go to my room."

His hand trembled across dry lips. He stood up shakily.

"Sit down," I ordered and was surprised when he obeyed.

"You are in real trouble, Roland, if you try to find more opium. I do not know much about smokers, but I have had my hand with alcoholics in the army. The thing for you is to get busy... stay busy... and keep busy."

"There is nothing for me to do."

"There is plenty for you to do. First of all, the men have volunteered—Mossard fashion—to defend the Château grounds as home guards. Apparently, they do not know it yet. You can tell them and get them out of this Nero's Bath and over to the barracks for weapon familiarity. Secondly, the girls, if your story is straight, have probably had more than passing experience with bandages. It would not hurt your position with Mossard to get a class going. Force yourself to work. I will tell the old man that you got everybody under way."

He contemplated me dully. "You know, you sound just like him, but ... nicer ... somehow."

Thi-Tuyet finished her swim. Clad in the yellow robe, she walked back across the lawn.

"*Bonne chance,*" I said to him, dived and swam the length of the pool. Tracing her footsteps, I could hear grumbles and scraping chairs from behind as D'Arbre gave the word.

My eyes on the haughty figure of the girl ahead, I thought of Charlotte Mossard and my promise to write. Perhaps I would write later—not now.

CHAPTER SEVEN

Five of us sat around an oval table in the high-ceilinged dining room on the first floor. Despite candlelight, wine and delicious cuisine, it was an unpleasant dinner.

We had been silent through six courses, waiting for Mossard to divulge his reasons for ordering a "social evening" in the midst of military preparations.

The Legionnaire captain, in full-dress pomp, fidgeted—glanced openly at his wrist watch. Roland d'Arbe picked at his food and left most of it. His knee jarred in vibrations against the table leg.

Thi-Tuyet sat stiffly at Mossard's left, uncomfortable in European dress. She was in a sheath of purple lace and pearls.

Guillaume Mossard, in tuxedo, ate with debonair detachment.

The overhead fans were the only intruding sounds.

Two shoeless boys, wraithlike in the vaporous haze of mosquito coils, watched alertly for Mossard's every gesture.

I passed up the cheese course and concentrated on the fanciful flight of two lizards across the wall. One was trying to eat the other's tail.

"We are delighted to welcome Mr. King to our little group," the planter said, breaking the difficult silence. "The combination of rangy American, curly hair and dimpled chin should accelerate the heartbeats around our swimming pool!"

I nodded agreeably, but nobody responded.

Mossard's hand suddenly crashed down on the table. Porcelain and silver rattled.

"Mon Dieu!" he snapped. "Have you forgotten how to be Frenchmen?"

The table came to life with bows, smiles and fatuous grunts.

"I have often said," he grumbled, "that if I left D'Or Blanc for one year, nature would reclaim it. But it is worse than I thought. I leave for three months and find nothing but apes at the dining table when I return."

Each one looked around expectantly for somebody to speak. Nobody did.

The planter shook his head in disgust.

"I apologize, Mr. King. You can see that we have grown soft to the point where a minor crisis throws us into a panic of stupidity."

He finished a triangle of Port Salud, reached for a mango, sliced it expertly around the seed, and said, "I have examined the contract you signed, Roland. My lawyers in Paris could not have drawn a better one. It is airtight. You deserve congratulations … from the Vietnamese."

D'Arbre flushed. His knees stopped jarring the table.

"Well … I looked up—"

"We have no legal recourse," Mossard interrupted crisply. "They can sit on strike until Buddha's three-thousandth birthday. But, under the laws of this country, we can put down armed insurrection. And that I intend to do."

The French captain leaned forward.

"Captain DuPont thinks that Cam received the transfer of communist arms from Binh-Dinh province on the coast. There were enough arms to equip a good part of the *gendarmerie* but not more. If he had had more, he would have attacked the Château.

"But one thing is obvious—the more successful Cam is, the more arms he will receive. After Dien-Bien-Phu, the Vietminh may well be striving for an imbalance of power in the south to outweigh the noncommitted sects. The men of D'Or Blanc, under arms, would give them the edge."

Mossard sipped wine, glanced around the table and continued, "Tomorrow the Legion will deploy on a purely peaceful mission. You, Roland, will go with them to convince the village mandarins of my good intentions."

D'Arbre's brows knitted dubiously.

"I am willing to let them go back to work—without punishment or penalty in pay for time lost. That includes Cam. I want to talk to them. Invite them to a *fête champêtre*—here in the Château grounds—a feast in the tradition of their ancestors—tomorrow night."

The foreman studied the tablecloth.

"They will not come, Guillaume," he said quietly.

"Then it is up to you to convince them to come," Mossard replied. "They do not dare refuse to attend a Feast of the Ancestors—not if so much as one worshiper appears. I shall pay for everything, tell them—the joss sticks, pictures of the dead, paper offerings, the cards, food and entertainment. If they will not come, then … you have the Legion at your back. Bring them."

Roland d'Arbre held the napkin to his lips for a long moment.

"Guillaume," he said softly, "you do not seem to realize that the days of colonialism are over. You cannot order these people around like slaves, or frighten them with supernatural fakery. They are becoming educated. They realize it is their land and they want a voice in its development. I suggest you wait until they come to their senses. Then we can effect a compromise."

Mossard's face drained chalk-white.

"Your policy in my absence was soft," he said. "You let them believe they were people—not slaves—and where are we tonight? Defending our lives … while twenty million trees lie choking and the world screams for rubber. You speak of slaves. Yes, we must have slaves—who work for a pittance—who trudge through mosquitoes and red mud without question—who train their children to do the same thing."

Mossard's voice was cold as he continued, "You, Roland, you want to dress them in white sharkskin suits and give them a new car every year. Why, we couldn't afford to hire them. So...we tap by machines...is that it? Mr. King, you are an American. Can you, in America, invent a machine that will slide automatically down a trunk, judge the scar to see if it is ready, tear the strip, gouge to proper depth, respiral, dump the cup, scrape and repin?"

He paused, waiting. I said nothing.

"Perhaps you can...and how much will it cost? We have twenty million trees on D'Or Blanc. One tree gives a cup of latex every three days. That is a pack of rubber bands per day, per machine—barely a franc's profit—and we still have nobody to pick up and process the rubber. Ha!"

Mossard turned from me to the foreman.

"You surprise me, Roland. You are like the prating do-gooders all over the world. You cluck at the misery of the poor from a safe distance and do not get close enough to realize that they are happy the way they are. Not only happy, Roland...but necessary. For every luxury somebody enjoys, somebody else must suffer. That, my friend, is the law of human nature, and it has not changed in five thousand years."

D'Arbre's knee began to jiggle again. Mossard continued relentlessly.

"All political upheavals since the time of Moses have been mouthed for the sake of the people. And look at them today. No better off...and perhaps worse. I have no such delusions, my friends. I consign myself in honest bastardy which, at least, is stimulating and rewarding. When the bubbleheads die frothing with political frustration, I can face my Maker with gratification, knowing that my fruit will outlast theirs."

The planter turned a disarming smile around the silent group, dwelling finally on Tuyet. In a different voice he announced, "It is positively pagan to discuss philosophy without cognac."

At his gesture, a bottle of Bisquit Dubouchet materialized on a tray, along with engraved snifters.

"Captain DuPont, you will go to Cam's village last. I want to avoid conflict, if possible, and if he sees the other mandarins coming along peacefully, perhaps he will also. If not, and he arrays his forces, then the decision to fight is his, and you will accept it. Do you understand?"

"Yes, sir."

Mossard turned to his second wife and asked, "What will Cam do, Tuyet?"

"Cam will come," the girl announced. "To lose face is to lose power."

D'Arbre's head snapped as she spoke. Staring intently at her, his expression tightened visibly.

Mossard waved a long Philippine cigar and circled himself with rings of fragrant smoke.

"Well, Roland?" he demanded pleasantly.

The foreman cleared his throat.

"You win, Guillaume," he answered, rising from the table.

"You might be interested," the planter said, puffing on his cigar, "in the end of the line for men on opium. You know, they lie on hard wooden shelves in a cage, racking their scrawny chests desperately to draw one more cloud from a burnt-out shell. And … unless they have ten piasters for another ball, they are thrown out of the den and must lie in the gutter, live on dead rats, and beg for the price to get back into Paradise."

The lines of the devil were written across Mossard's face.

D'Arbre rocked slightly.

"I have had the servants clean your room. They have destroyed your supply. I warned them that if you are found with more, the whole lot of them is fired. Now sit down and finish your meal."

The foreman obeyed mechanically.

"Opium is nasty, King," Mossard said in English. "Fortunately, he has not gone too far. Notice his weight—still well distributed. He is just at the stage where he would rather dream of food than eat it."

"May I be excused, sir?" The captain scraped his chair.

Mossard nodded.

As the captain's heels dimmed down the corridor, Mossard swirled the snifter of cognac.

"Well, King," he said, "what do you think of Madame Mossard the Second?"

I thought of all sorts of things and finally answered, "Nice girl."

"A political property, one might call her, but very helpful on occasion, as you have just witnessed. I am sure you have heard the gossip surrounding her acquisition, so I will not bore you with further background. Such gossip, I might add, is abetted by the nimble tongues of jealousy—female and male. It will be wise for you not to discuss Thi-Tuyet—particularly off the plantation. That is understood?"

I nodded. It was understood ... only too well.

Mossard swallowed a generous amount of cognac and followed it with a deep puff on his cigar, all the while studying Roland d'Arbre. When he spoke again it was in French.

"Our colleague, Monsieur d'Arbre, suffers from a lack of enthusiasm over his assigned task tomorrow."

The foreman staring blankly at his fruit plate was fingering a papaya.

"Roland, I am going to be blunt. You got us into this situation. You will get us out. The incentive is your life. If you fail, I shall order your death, with no more mercy than I would give a lizard on the wall."

With a cool glance at me, Mossard added, "Mr. King, I am sure, would accept the chore with technological efficiency."

"If they come at all," D'Arbre said in a low voice, "it is because they trust *me*—not you."

"Of course."

"If you are planning some macabre trick, Guillaume..." the foreman burst out passionately.

"Perhaps I am." The planter's voice matched the steel of his eyes. "Does that change your mind?"

The foreman's knuckles dug into the papaya. Discarding it, he poured with trembling hands a half goblet of cognac and forced it down his throat.

Mossard stood up and yawned.

"Six o'clock in the morning, then. I suggest we get to bed."

Thi-Tuyet hastened to pull back his chair.

"Look at the color of her skin, King," he said in English. "Like an orange shielded from the bright sun. Why... I am darker than she is. As a matter of fact, the more I drink, the whiter she gets."

Draining the circlet of brandy, he turned and walked carefully to the door.

Thi-Tuyet, in high heels, followed clumsily. Their steps sounded briefly on the marble stair and a door handle banged. All was silent except the fans.

D'Arbre pounded his clenched fist onto the table... once, twice, again and again, until the silver danced and the amber liquor slopped on the snowy cloth.

CHAPTER EIGHT

The Legion Detachment decamped promptly at six in the morning. The armed half-tracks and 6-by-6 trucks, filled with disciplined Legionnaires, looked formidable.

I began to appreciate Mossard's logic. One could easily be swayed by such a bristling array appearing suddenly to extend an invitation.

My job for the day was routine. The defense bastions and foxholes had been well constructed. Aside from detecting smuggled wine bottles among the home guards, I had little to do but supervise.

Midmorning Mossard selected the center of the front lawn for the feast, saying that he wanted the guests within sight of the machine-gun emplacements. He demurred when workers began spading the velvet nap of the lawn and chopping into the symmetrical flower beds, but overcame his misgivings with a wry shrug and went to his room.

Late in the afternoon, a *troupeau* of elephants meandered up the gravel driveway, resplendent in silver trappings and dangling bells. Mossard met them at the Napoleon stairs and shook hands cordially with three black-bronze chieftains who, disdaining to force the elephants to kneel, leaped from their high perches with graceful fluidity.

These were the Moi from the blue mountains toward the sea where Mossard's vast cultivation had penetrated a lost civilization.

Colorful loincloths fell in folds to ankle length; their burnished mahogany breasts were studies in rippling sculpture.

Gold paillettes danced from the necks and ear lobes of the chieftains as they stood tall, conversing with dignity. They were a different race completely from the Vietnamese. The planter greeted them like old friends, and took them into the Château as the Moi attendants herded the elephants back toward the garage.

The evening sky was beginning to overflow with pastels when I heard the convoy approaching. The vehicles labored through the big front gate. I counted quickly. All personnel in place—all wheels in order. There had been no combat.

The mandarins tumbled out of the truck beds and swung down from the cabin doors. Far from being disgruntled, they gestured excitedly at the elaborate entrenchments of the feast site and walked quickly over to inspect. They could have been uniformed in the similarity of their robes, except for the variance of color. Black cloche turbans perched atop their heads. Umbrellas, small brass spittoons and reed pipes and scrolls jutted from under their arms.

Three of them remained by the trucks turning their backs to the feast area. Legionnaires quickly prodded them across the grass. I searched for but did not see Cam.

D'Arbre dismounted from the lead truck and came toward me.

"Where is Mossard?" he asked.

"With the three Moi chieftains—somewhere in the rear complex, I think."

"Cam made a clean getaway."

"So I gathered. What happened?"

"He must have gotten advance word that we were coming. He had 'left to consult his ancestors in the mountains,' they said at his village."

"Are you sure he was not there?"

"Ask DuPont—we searched the village."

"The rest of them are here, I take it."

He grimaced. "All here. If you see Guillaume, tell him. I want a shower before joining the feast. If Guillaume has ... some sort of revenge planned, at least I will be on hand to do what I can. Are you coming to the feast? The food is good."

"I doubt it," I said. "My ancestors never heard of Indochina."

When night folded over the Château, the front lawn came ablaze with dotted beds of fire, bouncing lanterns, and the glow-worms of lighted joss sticks. Frantic drums bit the air and a two-man dragon, its head a gigantic hideous mask, serpentined from corner to corner, purging evil spirits which might be lurking. Cook fires, tended by scurrying *boyesses,* materialized at the fringe. The pungency of burnt sugar, charcoal, roasted meat and fish sauce blended through the area.

The Moi chiefs joined the mandarins and found their marked places in the huge circle. The *Fête Champêtre* was on.

Guillaume Mossard was not in evidence. Knocking at the door of his suite, I was told by his *boyesse* that he and Captain DuPont were not to be disturbed.

Watching the festivities from my balcony, I was convinced that the blond foreman, Roland d'Arbre, had been born in the wrong hemisphere. With an olive skin he would have been an oriental leader. A cacophony of greetings overwhelmed him as he entered the circle; he was tugged from one mandarin to the other, pressed to take a coveted position. His dress was a tunic similar to theirs.

Plucked strings quavered over the babble of voices and a mournful flute commenced an aria that must have been written before Christ. I had the feeling that the time barrier was broken. I could have been looking down from a hill at the camp of Genghis Khan.

A noise from behind made me turn. Thi-Tuyet was standing in my room. Surprised, I walked in and closed the balcony door. She regarded me solemnly for a long moment, bit her lip, and tears flooded from the purple eyes.

"I had no one to come to but you," she sobbed.

As naturally as a father, I took her into my arms. But the thin, clinging silk and her body soon dispelled any paternal instinct. I led her to a chair.

"It is my father ... I am worried about my father," she faltered.

"Your father has escaped to the mountains, Tuyet," I consoled.

Her lips quivered as she fought to control herself.

I was aware of heated perspiration and a scent of Chanel Number Five.

"He made me tell him where he was," she said softly.

"Tell who ... what?"

"*Patron*. He made me tell where my father was."

"How would you know?"

"I do not know. I mean ... I only know where he used to go in the mountains for ancestor worship."

"Where was that?"

"Nui-Bara ... near the great waterfalls."

"Why did you tell Mossard?"

"He ... forced me. He knew I would know the place. I begged him not to make me tell, but ..." Fresh tears rushed from the agonized eyes.

"What do you want me to do?"

"I do not know. I am just afraid of what *patron* will do if he finds him. Perhaps you can ... cool his anger."

She was trembling.

"You are not afraid for your husband?"

She reflected for a long moment.

"No ... he has more machine guns."

"There is no need to worry, Tuyet. Mossard only wants Cam to have all of the mandarins together."

"You are sure?"

"I am almost sure," I told her.

"If you are right, I will kiss you."

"And … if I am wrong?"

She studied me.

"I think you are wrong. I had better kiss you now."

The scent of Chanel and her soft, moist lips left me breathless.

"Do you think I am a better qualified wife than Madame Charlotte?" she demanded.

"What one of you may lack the other certainly has," I replied with feeling. "You had better go now."

She glided reluctantly toward the door.

"You are a very strange man, King. You are the first to push me away. Roland never pushed me—I pushed him."

"Then, life at D'Or Blanc is not boring for you?"

"No." She was thoughtful. "I could have all the men I want, but I do not admire that—only cleverness."

She surveyed me openly.

"In many ways you are like *patron*. You are more clever but he is more cruel. You have the advantage, I think, because he cannot become more clever. But … you can become more cruel. You have not much time to make a success. Do not waste it."

She gave me a flat brilliant smile. The door clicked and she was gone.

A volley of shots shattered the night air.

In what seemed like one stretching moment, I extinguished the lights, picked up the Thompson and was on the balcony.

Shadowy figures moved around the fires below. The hum of conversation buzzed lazily. The whang-g-g of a lute thinned off into the *gecko* cry of a tree alligator, coming from the distance.

Scanning the grounds critically, I saw the spewing flashes of firecrackers and again heard the reports.

A *petit enfant* from the kitchens was trailing a tightly bound fascine around the fringe of the fires—more ammunition against evil spirits. Laughing at my pent-up nerves, I decided that what I needed was relaxation. My gun went back in the "hot closet"—a dehumidifying cabinet kept dry by a burning light bulb—and I descended to the front lawn.

La Fête des Ancêtres was a spectacle beyond imagination. Each mandarin had his own domain of ground around the vast circle, replete with candle lanterns, dragon heads, scroll pictures of his ancestors, spittoons for betel juice, vats of rice wine, a table full of *papier-mâché* offerings, an incense-shrouded altar, and a bevy of servants awaiting his call.

I watched the one nearest me. Squatting in the center of the impressive array of appurtenances, he selected a card from the table—somewhat larger than a playing card and decorated with oriental figurations. Bowing to the ground, he uttered singsong incantations as if calling for someone. He threw the card in the fire and then, as servants handed him the offerings, he prayed over each and tossed it after the card. An umbrella, shoe clogs, a pipe, a rice bowl, a turban—each went into the fire and was quickly consumed by the crackling flames. Another servant was ready with a bowl of real food. The mandarin offered it deferentially to the departed ancestor by touching each morsel at the end of his chopsticks lightly to the flame before devouring it. When he had finished with the course, two servants helped him to his feet and canted the huge upright wine vat while he drank.

I wondered how Mossard had prepared the infinite detail of the consecration with less than a day's notice.

Strolling past the bake pots, I lost whatever appetite the exotic smells had conjured up. Boiled rice and fish stomachs were being garnished with cut-up bat wings—and doused with a strong fish sauce. Curried shrimp paste, wrapped around sugar-cane popsickles, sizzled on the charcoal. Ginger, lotus seeds and scorched flowers were being ground for a later course.

Roland d'Arbre squatted, ate with his fingers, sipped wine through communal straws and moved casually from one chief to another. It was the first time I had heard him speak tonal Vietnamese.

The three Moi chieftains sat close together observing the rituals as deferentially as the others. The red fires reflected gold from their teeth. They ate gustily and moved often to the vats.

There was still no sign of Mossard.

I checked the emplacements of the home guards and promised relief as soon as the Legion rested up.

All of a sudden I was bone-tired from the day's activities. Entering the great doors of the Château, I lay down on the Louis XVI divan in the hall.

It was ten o'clock when he woke me.

"*Allons*, King," Mossard said jovially. "You do not want to miss the finale—although I must say you displayed discernment in sleeping through dinner."

The colonialist looked as if he had slept all evening. He was immaculate in a white silk sport shirt and tight-fitting sharkskin slacks.

"Better get your gun. The fireworks may not be over."

We joined the festivities.

Mossard shook hands as each mandarin rose to greet him, but there was a noticeable chill over the crowd.

The planter seated himself ostentatiously in the space reserved for Nguyen Cam.

Slipping off to the rear where I could cover the affair in the event hell started popping, I wedged my back against one of the sultan palms.

With a clashing of gongs, the entertainment commenced. The dancing for my taste was not inspired, although the audience applauded the stop-and-go movements with vigor. I began to get a headache from the same five notes of the orchestra.

A Legion truck with swathed headlights dazzled the scene briefly and rumbled on past the foxhole entrenchments to the front gate. Back on the job, I thought.

The games that followed the dance exhibitions excluded everything else from my mind.

Two shirtless men, faces painted, circled warily around the fires. Each parried a long bamboo pole—the butt end thick as a man's wrist and tapering to a savage lash. Suddenly, I heard a whistling sound as one of the antagonists hunched. There was a blur of wood and a brittle snap as the other successfully fenced the blow.

The circle of mandarins applauded noisily and coins twinkled in betting piles.

The two warriors wove through the fires, ballet-leaped, crossed, feinted and retreated. They wore no protection. It looked to me like a one-blow fight. Whoever connected first would be able to walk away.

Vicious swats split the stillness with bow-twang sound. The gladiators inched up on each other in a flurry of close combat.

The whiplashes became constant.

Then I heard the crack that was not bamboo—and the groan. The slighter of the two went squirming to the ground. Several of the mandarins shouted with exultation. The downed warrior got to his feet, limping badly, and pushed the length of bamboo into sparring position. Another slash caught him on the side of the head. He flip-flopped into a fire and lay there bleeding from the ears. The winner dragged him roughly from the coals, and dug the heavy butt end of the pole into his chest.

The audience shouted as Mossard counted out bills to the grinning victor.

Boyesses carried the unconscious competitor toward the Château.

Mossard took his seat again and the winner moved around the circle slowly, making strange menacing gestures and croaking sounds. He was greeted by jeers and laughter. This was part of the ritual, I gathered—a champion defending his crown.

A tall sinewy Moi—one of the elephant attendants—leaped from behind the wine vats to the center of the flame-strewn area. He was a panther of rippling satin and fought well, but suffered the fate of the first. He walked from the ring, one arm hanging useless and a raw bleeding cut across his cheek.

The panting, smoke-stained victor commenced his third round of mockery. He was a crowd pleaser for the Vietnamese, but the Moi were silent. No gold shown from their faces.

The warrior stood in front of Mossard, shook the bamboo pole perfunctorily and passed on to concentrate on the Moi chiefs.

The planter stood up and accepted the challenge.

In the stillness you could hear the faggots crackling and the far-off geckos from the rubber trees.

Mossard weighed the pole tentatively, swished it, motioned the fighter to rest, and strode to the center of the circle.

In a ringing voice he announced, "I am fighting in lieu of the bravest of all Vietnamese mandarins, Nguyen Cam, your spokesman and leader. He is the bravest among you—yet, he has profaned his ancestors and flown to the mountains as a chicken runs from a cook's knife. I fight in his place to defend his honor and yours."

Red gold gleamed from the mouths of the Moi.

"With the understanding that if I am the victor, he is no longer your chief mandarin, and by his public cowardice, justifies the condemnation that I have placed on his head."

Several angry voices were audible in the undertone that followed.

Mossard's voice cut through the buzz, "Is there one of you who will fight in my stead?"

Silence replaced the noise. Mossard began to walk slowly around the circle.

"While I was gone, you petitioned for several rights for your people. They were granted and you took advantage of them. I ask you now to consider what you have done. When you strike and join in arms against me, who will pay you? Will your fortune slowly wither away until your children slink from you in disrespect, or don the uniform of a sect to slit your throat unfeelingly? Will you finally be left alone to ramble through the ghost of your village, and to be picked at by wives who lack strength to climb the aracas for betel? Will you be reduced to squatting in spittle at the marketplace clutching for coins, or will you, sighing, stroke the neck of a cobra to join the spirits who dance at the tip of our flames?"

Mossard's French was crisp and delivered slowly so that all could understand. He continued around the circle, pausing before each mandarin.

"You disgust your ancestors, who are present at this sacred fire. Do you think Nguyen Cam dared come here tonight? Death would have stricken his tongue and sent his spirit... not to Paradise, but to the darkness that lies behind the moon."

His voice dropped almost to a whisper, but every ear could hear.

"I hold no grievance for what has passed. Tomorrow we will start anew. Your people may return to work at the new wage agreed in my absence. I shall ask your ancestors to lend me their skill in this fight. If they do, you shall see it and reckon its meaning."

His figure, etched bronze against the fires, bowed in prayer. The mandarins gaped.

"Let the spirits of the ancestors rule," the planter said as he turned to the champion. The fight was on.

Mossard seemed to shed years as he crouched and twitched the bamboo pole nervously. The Vietnamese, rested and confident, bore in.

The air was sliced. Mossard dodged nimbly. Another whish of air and Mossard short-stepped backwards. A button blew from his shirt. He had not parried or struck, but I had a growing feeling. Apparently, so did the Vietnamese warrior. His smile disappeared.

I caught the sound of coins clinking. One of the Moi chiefs upended his entire purse. A black-toothed mandarin hesitated, then equaled it.

The Frenchman took three short steps and went in with his wood. The two matched blow for blow. It was beautiful to watch, like a ballet. They leaned, knelt, pirouetted and jackknifed over the burning flames. The air rang with whistling lashes and the sharp breathing.

The spectators were carved in immobility.

The bamboo suddenly sailed from the hands of the Vietnamese. It arched end over end and knifed quivering into the grass.

The unbelieving champion retreated, seeking a path to retrieve his weapon. Mossard hopped, blocking his exit, at the same time dragging the tip of the pole through the fires. The green bamboo burst into flames. Then the planter went to work, cutting patterns of light around the warrior's body. He cross-marked his chest with two lines of burning soot and then with incredibly tiny figure-of-eight swirls, set fire to the warrior's hair.

The Vietnamese fell to the ground. Mossard walked away from him and faced his audience.

"It is late, my friends, and I am tired. We shall leave now and contemplate what we have seen. You will walk home to your villages."

Even in the stunned silence of the group, an undercurrent of protest was audible.

The planter was cold and unemotional.

"You came here tonight, hating the French—your souls filled with the venom of a serpent. Even as you mocked, you rode from French-built villages, on French-built roads, in French trucks, under the protection of French arms. Think well, as you walk home in footsteps honored many times by your ancestors, what your life would be without France—or without me."

Roland d'Arbre got unsteadily to his feet.

"Mossard … you bastard …."

The planter ignored him and nodded to me.

"Escort them past the main gate."

The Thompson slung under my arm, I brought up the rear as the file of mandarins moved like rustling locusts down the gravel drive.

D'Arbre, walking with us, started to apologize. One of the turbaned chiefs cut him off. I gathered that more than one of them felt that they deserved the long walk home.

The three Moi, scarcely able to conceal their exuberance disappeared with Mossard into the Château. I was betting that the live spirits of the three, sometime in the past, had had more to do with the planter's proficiency at tilting than all the dead ones put together.

Just short of the sentry box, the column halted raggedly and pressed back. A gasp crisped the air.

"Open up," I shouted at the Legionnaire ahead.

And then I saw that the wrought-iron paling across the road was open.

A few yards outside the gate, hanging from a tree upside down, was the executed body of Nguyen Cam.

One of the mandarins keeled over in a faint.

D'Arbre cursed.

Cam's ankle was tied high to a projecting limb. The other leg dangled loose. His arms were bound and he was gagged. Coal-black hair hung straight down and extended to within a few inches of the ground. Strings of blood ran out of cut nostrils, coursed through his eyes, and dripped along matted hair onto the ground.

I felt sick.

"Native execution," D'Arbre said, "arranged by the ancestors...*grâce à Mossard.* It takes about three hours to die this way."

He approached the slowly twisting body and rapped the unbound kneecap sharply with his hand. The leg reflexed.

"Still living," he muttered. "I will cut him down."

"You do," I said, and was surprised at the steel in my voice, "and I will do the same thing faster to you."

One by one the mandarins passed the body—eyes straight ahead—and were swallowed in the night of rubber trees. All had pronounced Nguyen Cam guilty.

"So...the Far East has gotten to you, Monsieur King?" D'Arbre sneered. "It usually takes a little longer. Far East Fever, they call it. Every man in this Godforsaken Asia goes crazy sooner or later. Either power-mad or weak. There is no in-between. You rule or you get ruled. Did you ever get salt in a cut?"

I did not acknowledge his question.

"That is what they do in these native executions. They cut a little slit across the nostril, and stuff it with salt. Then the victim is hung upside down. Not too big a slit—he is not supposed to die too fast."

My stomach started rolling.

The foreman grinned. "Why don't you do something about it?"

I tried not to look at the body of Cam.

"Big brave American. Just another wart on Mossard's ass."

"You had better leave," I said in a low voice.

"You know something? You are right. I am going where I can live with myself—but not that way." He gestured at the Château. "I would rather scratch lice and eat buffalo dung for the rest of my life than set foot in that transplanted monstrosity again. You can tell the great Mossard I said so—the bastard!"

He turned abruptly and, with loping, uneven strides, followed the mandarins.

I waited, expecting him to come back. He did not.

The body swung silently.

Beyond the fence lights, the Château squatted dark and majestic, a hazy outline. A square eye of light opened menacingly. Mossard was retiring.

I turned on the dying Cam, re-entered the estate and clanged the gate shut behind me.

CHAPTER NINE

As tired as I was, no sleep came. I tossed and turned under the stifling tent of mosquito netting.

I had seen my share of dead and dying men—some good friends. Cam meant nothing. Trying to fathom the haunting emotion that was disturbing me, I gave up trying to sleep and with a sigh pushed through the foods of the net.

Something moved beside my bed.

"He is dead," Thi-Tuyet whispered.

I should have released her and turned on the light, but with her trembling against me, I let her cry until the curves of her throbbing flesh bound me with such pressure that my hands moved on her irresistibly.

She became quiet, then still and finally tense.

Her rigidity brought me to my senses. Ashamed, I untangled and flicked on the small night lamp.

Tuyet's face was streaked with mascara. Panties and brassière were visible under the perspiration-soaked tunic.

"I am sorry..." I mumbled.

Her wet almond eyes were filled with terror.

"*Patron* has killed him," she whispered, "and I am to blame for his death. His spirit will seek its vengeance on me. I have no hope. I will surely die...."

She broke into a stream of singsong Vietnamese, writhed to a kneeling position, palms together, and bent until her head touched the floor.

"Tuyet!"

She raised her face and crept toward me, pleading, "Please, King, take his body home."

"What do you mean?"

"Take him to Cam-Xe…to my village…to my family for worship and burial. If his spirit is honored, it will not be so vengeful."

"You ask me to risk my job and maybe my neck to deliver a dead body?"

Tears filled her eyes again. She pleaded, "My people will believe that the White God has compassion. They will work willingly and with greater strength to produce the rubber."

"Did you tell that to Mossard?"

"He did not hear. His mind is as set as a coconut."

She hugged my knees tightly, pressing until her breasts flattened.

"King…if you will do this for me…I will do anything…."

Jerking away from her, I circled the room. I was angry because I could not resist her. What was it D'Arbre had said? Far East Fever…brought out the strength or the weakness in a man.

She watched me sorrowfully as I donned pants and shirt. The significance of my actions suddenly dawned on her.

"You are going?" She scrambled to her feet.

I nodded grimly.

"I shall wait for you here," she said, smoothing her hair.

"You will not."

Tuyet's tear-stained face was blank with surprise as I pushed her ahead of me to the door.

The sentinel at the front gate was absorbed in a French comic book.

"*Fini?*" he asked without interest.

"*C'est fini,*" I said, checking my watch. Cam had hung well over three hours.

The body came down easily. It could not have weighed over one hundred thirty pounds. Not bothering to untie the ropes, I dumped it into the back of a jeep drawn from the motor pool and started for Cam-Xe.

Along the way I looked for D'Arbre and the mandarins, but there was only the empty flutter of headlights against the trees. Probably they were sleeping in the forest.

I kept thinking about the dead man's eyes. As I had lifted him, they had stared accusingly at me, popped and crusted. I stole an uneasy glance over my shoulder. The open eyes blazed at me. A shudder rippled up my back. Grabbing the rope binding the ankle, I gave it a vicious jerk and the body toppled over on its back. At least, now, the eyes would be facing the sky.

As I swung around a curve south of the Hon-Quan bunker, the bound foot seemed to move. Slamming on the brakes, I stopped to get hold of myself. My nerves were ragged. The foot moved again. The mandarin's eyes were closed.

Nguyen Cam was still alive.

CHAPTER TEN

I was routed out of bed rudely by the *boyesse* Thi-Ba. In short breaths she reported that the *patron* was *en coleur*—very angry. He wanted to see me at once.

She had brought an omelette, *croissants* and *café au lait*. Ignoring the pitcher of hot milk, I scalded my stomach with the bitter black coffee and glanced at my watch.

It was not quite eight o'clock when I knocked on the door of the master suite. This would be the showdown, I thought. I would have to take the offensive.

The planter's face was glacial.

"Good morning," I said.

"I may have made a mistake in hiring you," he began abruptly. "I like men who mind their own business. What have you done with Nguyen Cam?"

"I buried him."

"You admit it?"

"I never tried to hide it. I drew the jeep in your name, got past the guard in your name, and cut Cam down in your name."

He studied me heavily for a few moments.

"Thi-Tuyet?"

"She pleaded with me to return the body to her village. I thought it was a good idea ... in line with that speech you made."

"How do you know Cam was dead when you cut him down, King?"

"He was not."

Mossard's powerful hand tightened on my shoulder.

"Talk... and make it accurate."

"I thought he was dead when I cut him down. En route to the village, he showed signs of life, so there was a little interlude in the forest. Under the jeep. I did not think it a good idea to present him to the family in that condition. I hope your wife will understand."

Guillaume Mossard lit a cigar and sat down.

"Why did you kill him?" he asked.

Surprised at the question, I answered, "I thought I had to."

He took his time surveying me.

"You could have thought that the other day... that I wanted you to kill D'Arbre."

My pulse was pounding as I said, "I had a choice then."

He seemed unimpressed.

"You are *sure* he is dead?"

I bowed my head slightly, imitating his stance in front of the mandarins at the feast, and answered reverently, "He died under the trees he loved so well—under the gum his ancestors hacked before him. And, as his spirit passed, he breathed the immortal phrase, 'God bless Mossard for showing us the way!' "

The cigar almost disappeared. When the planter removed it from his mouth, he was smiling.

"I think I can understand the success of you Americans. The French may be immoral—but you, *bigre,* you are amoral."

The smile did not last. He asked, "And D'Arbre—where is he?"

"Followed the mandarins. He left word for you about eating some unmentionables before he would ever set foot in the Château again."

The colonialist bit at the cigar. "He will be back. He loves his comfort—even more than opium. Now to the subject of my wife who, with her silly superstition, involved you in this affair."

Mossard settled comfortably into the chair.

"I have debated the necessity of keeping her on, now that her father is dead. I am convinced that I must. She will be even more valuable as a symbol of the French-Vietnamese 'marriage of endeavor'—D'Or Blanc. On the other hand, if I let her go, it would disturb the positive accomplishments of last evening— perhaps to the extent that a new canker would emerge from the ranks. God knows, in these troublesome times, I cannot afford that."

He gave me a long direct look and continued, "I tell you this so that there will be no doubt as to her importance to me. However, she has no voice in the management nor does she in any way have authority to speak for me as perhaps she led you to think last night."

I said nothing.

He leaned forward. "If your alacrity was, by chance, motivated by more basic instincts, I must warn you that second-wife status does not imply moral promiscuity. If I were to allow that, she would be scorned by the Vietnamese. Her value would be completely destroyed. I should have to deal with her and the offending accomplice in a manner which I would dislike."

I indicated two poles mounted crosswise on the wall. "Your swizzle sticks?"

He did not smile.

"It was a pleasant pastime in more peaceful days, when I hunted big game with the Moi. Last night was as appropriate an occasion as any to acquaint the Vietnamese with my prowess."

He produced a billow of fragrant cigar smoke.

"You have a disarming knack, King, developed no doubt through endless *soirées* with wealthy American widows and French *abandonées*. Exactly where did you bury Cam?"

His question threw me off balance, but I answered quickly, "In a patch of jungle that breaks the road between Hon-Quan and Cam-Xe."

"Ah yes," he said. "I would like to see the body."

"Any time you say."

"I shall let you know," he said, rising expansively. "We are re-establishing communications with Saigon. I shall have your luggage sent up with the first courier. If latex is collected normally from now on—and I expect it to be—you will have occasional free time. There are many lovely and reasonably moraled French girls in Saigon who enjoy the carefree plantation life. I have no objection to any arrangement you may wish to make...so long as you are discreet. You may consider that part of your logistical support."

"Thanks," I said. "It sounds interesting."

I went directly to my room, drained what was left of the cold coffee, and contemplated the ordeal facing me. If Nguyen Cam were still alive, I would have to murder him.

Where I had left him, partly covered with brush under the rubber trees, he would almost surely be discovered by the tappers as they returned to work.

I damned Tuyet for getting me involved and then damned myself for rising to the bait she offered. But the profanities did not solve the realities ahead. I was treading close to disaster and had no illusions as to Guillaume Mossard's actions if he discovered my deception.

Combat, I had discovered last night, was not the same as cold-blooded murder.

At noon when the relentless May sun drove every living thing to a sweat-soaked siesta, I left the Château unnoticed and checked out a vehicle.

In the Lower Loop where the ugly skid marks loomed on the pavement, I turned the jeep off the road and into the darkened lanes of heveas. I stopped at the rude pile of brush. Shoes extended from one end of the dead foliage.

Gripping the sweat-slick stock of the forty-five I had with me, I got out. Cam was not dead. Through the thin bramble, I saw him breathing irregularly. I pushed the safety off, raised the pistol and sighted. I felt sick.

If I could get him off the plantation, hide him somewhere until he were strong enough to walk, he would surely listen to logic—go into exile or into the mountains—rather than be hunted down like an animal and slaughtered. If he would not listen to reason then, I thought grimly, I would not be so reluctant in pulling the trigger.

CHAPTER ELEVEN

At an intersection with the Rubber Road, I saw a small, faded sign marked Nui-Bara that pointed toward rutted tire tracks. Steering into them, I drove for twenty minutes through the cool forest path and then emerged in the blazing sunlight. I was confronted by a bamboo wilderness into which a narrow roadway had been hacked. The jeep fought on into the jungle.

I closed my eyes to swab away the sweat and red dust. There was no shade. To turn around or back out was impossible. The jeep began to steam. I ducked to avoid a covey of wild parrots who, startled by the intrusion, dived at the car, crying discordantly. Huge trees loomed ahead, gaunt, white and without vegetation. These skeletons gave way gradually to camphor and ironwood. Fern took the place of bamboo and it felt cooler. The jeep lurched suddenly and tipped over the rim of a canyon. Pink rocks leapt as high as the trees and caught others to push them still higher.

The Nui-Bara Falls cascaded in the depths of the canyon.

When I reached the river, it looked deceitfully placid, like a vast fishpond crossed with steppingstones. But at the throat of the cascade, a fury of hidden current converged and crashed violently in a mighty arch that sprayed into a gorge below.

I turned to look at the mandarin in the back seat. The jouncing had brought him to consciousness.

"End of the line," I said in French.

He was slumped, his head against the isinglass.

"Nui-Bara," he whispered. *"Toi doi An ... toi doi ..."*

Cam kept repeating the Vietnamese words. Finally, he pointed to his mouth.

Propping him against a tree, I went to look for food. Papaya was within reach and I shot down a coconut. While he drank the gray milk and bit at the fruit, I scrambled down the slick mossy shale to the edge of the cataract. Wrestling loose an overhanging bamboo stripling I stabbed several times between the rocks and came up with a wriggling fish. The force of the undercurrent almost ripped the pole from my hands.

"Etes-vous communist?" the mandarin asked weakly, accepting the fish.

"No."

His eyes had gained enough strength to become shrewd.

"Then you want gold?"

I shook my head negatively. He said nothing else, but bit into the strugglish fish and devoured it to the skeleton.

"You are a weakling then," he said. "It is a sign of the times. The French crumble like rice cakes under foot. Get me some water."

My anger came suddenly.

"If you save your insults, maybe you will find enough strength to get it yourself."

He looked me over blandly.

"You are not French?"

"I am American."

He dropped his head with fatigue. The conversation was wearing him.

I thought he was asleep until his lips fluttered.

"Foreigners ... always foreigners. What do Americans want from Viet Nam? You race the sun to cover the moon, until your spirit is spun from this globe into emptiness. Confusing ...."

He seemed to sleep. Then, lapsing into heavy breathing, he went on.

"You...want not gold...not power...nor are you a slave. Ahhh...."

His eyes glittered and he sat upright with unexpected agility "The affectionate tiger kills with compassion."

I felt his forehead. There was no fever. He shook my hand away impatiently.

"You Westerners are like children in the innocence of your thoughts. You do not understand the truth of existence."

"The affectionate tiger kills with compassion?" I queried.

"An oriental parable—the aura of which surrounds you."

"What does it mean?"

"Ahhh...." His gold teeth glistened. "When you have brought me rice and clothes, I shall tell you."

"I will bring them," I said, "on condition that you leave D'Or Blanc permanently. You are not fool enough to tempt your gods twice, I think. I cut you down once, but if you come back, I will likely be in no position to help you. I might be hanging myself."

"I am grateful for your compassion," he said weakly, "but I am even more grateful to my ancestors."

His eyes turned across the cascade toward the hazy range of high mountains. "In ten days I shall join them beyond the river," he whispered.

"Good. I think your ancestors will advise you to stay."

A strange smile slid across the thin gray lips.

"The affectionate tiger kills with compassion. You are not angry now. You will bring the rice and clothes in ten days?"

I nodded.

He sighed, looked around and whispered, "Help me to a place safe from the night animals. I will sleep."

I carried him to a niche high in the rocks.

"I do not regret the execution," he said, breathing painfully. "To be tortured is good. It clears the mind."

Within seconds he was asleep.

I left him and drove to the triangular patch of jungle that I had described to Mossard. I camouflaged a mock grave that could be seen from the road.

I was back at the Château before sunset.

CHAPTER TWELVE

Guillaume Mossard dispensed smiles, cigars and confidence. He made quick inspection trips to the far ranges of the plantation and bubbled with general optimism. Fifteen thousand workers had returned to the job as he had predicted, and the rusting mechanism of the D'Or Blanc groaned into life.

Dripping milk, the snore of gouge tools, and the purple exhaust of cistern trucks filled the forest. The sheds for *feuilles fumées* boiled, the crepe tanks sloshed the acetic acid, the wash-dry machinery cranked incessantly, and the presses rolled and stamped. Latex gave birth to crude rubber which was stacked, sealed into bales, graded and stenciled. Boxcars creaked from the depot siding.

Tappers moved like combs through the forest—seven hundred trees a day per worker—repeating every third day. Frenchmen in shorts bustled and checked, marked and swore.

The Legion Detachment, reorganized, moved out from its roadside bastions and became roving patrols. Cam's village mourned in white for several days, then climbed with resignation into predawn trucks. The band of armed insurgents disappeared from the plantation. One of Nguyen Cam's relatives—a quiet, frowning brother-in-law—set himself up as the new mandarin, swore allegiance to Mossard and received the village rice dole and payroll without question.

A thousand tons of *fumée,* crepe, and flat bark moved to Saigon. The train came back with rice, gasoline and supplies. Mossard went to Saigon without me and flew back in his single-engine Piper. Everything was calm. Every evening the swimming pool was crowded with a gay group, sporting new bikinis and gossiping.

Colonialism had conquered.

I pretended eagerness to show Cam's "grave" to Mossard. He dismissed the idea—he had seen it. He handed me a packet of ten thousand piasters and encouraged me to go to Saigon. I told him that not only was it too hot to think of women, but it was too hot to think. He laughed. I kept the ten thousand.

Nguyen Cam became a legend of the past.

Thi-Tuyet had not been at the swimming pool since the execution, nor was she to be seen around the Château. I inquired discreetly. Thi-Ba, the *boyesse* who cleaned my quarters, told me that she had not left her rooms even to take meals. I learned from her that "Thi" meant woman. "Ba" stood for "two," her husband's second wife. "Tuyet" meant snow.

One of Lien-Fat's payroll clerks in the Saigon villa reported an incident from a tiny rubber village called Pham-Quan, near the Cambodian border. A European, named Roland d'Arbre, had asked for a laboring job as a tapper. The request was passed up through a dozen hands until it reached Mossard. Mossard grumbled and sent a personal courier to bring the foreman back. D'Arbre refused. Mossard forwarded him a contract as apprentice tapper, paying five hundred piasters per month plus rice. It figured out at seventeen dollars. The contract was returned signed. The planter washed his hands of the affair—Roland d'Arbre as a man no longer existed in his mind.

I was walking a tightrope charged with electricity, but no one realized it. I ate, slept, swam, tanned, and searched for an alternative to the grim reality that my life hung on the mandarin coattails of Nguyen Cam.

Nine days had passed.

The affectionate tiger kills with compassion. My mind revolved around the riddle—dissected it, analyzed it, swore at it, discarded it, and returned to it. I was as anxious to learn the meaning as I was to see Cam on his way to the mountains.

"Thi-Ba," I said, "the affectionate tiger kills with compassion."

"Pardon, monsieur?" The little *buoyesse* was frightened.

I repeated the phrase. She appeared relieved.

"Ah, monsieur, you have had bad dream."

"No. It is an old Vietnamese parable—a saying that has some significance. What does it mean?"

She shook her head, and in her crude French said, "I know not, monsieur. You must ask mandarin. They are only one who study words."

"You must have some idea."

She grinned widely, showing betel-stained teeth.

"Is good joke, I think. Tiger never affectionate. Kill everything. Deer, water buffalo, elephant. Foolish Vietnamese people also favorite food of tiger. Very bad."

She grimaced and began to raise dust with a wad of cock feathers fastened to the end of a short pole.

"Thi-Ba!"

She stiffened. "Monsieur?"

"Ask *Madame de la Maison*—Thi-Tuyet."

The *boyesse* regarded me unblinkingly.

"Cannot, monsieur. Madame very sick about father. See no person. Many yellow balls and much joss stick."

I meditated, gnawing my lip. "Ask her," I said. "It is very urgent."

With strong disapproval written on her face, she marched to the door and disappeared.

Momentarily, I discarded the parable and thought about Cam. How could I convince him to stay in exile? Was there any sure way? I decided to cross that bridge when I got to it. The mandarin knew as well as I did his life would be forfeit.

Thi-Ba came quickly into the room on silent barefeet.

"Madame very angry," she said. "I hope I not offend honored ancestors."

She made a surreptitious "sim-sim" with palms held together.

"What did Madame say?"

"Madame think you try to apologize for killing father. You the tiger. You kill father with no compassion. She cry. Say you bother her again, she tell *patron*."

The *boyesse* flounced the broom in sweeps of disapproval.

"For God's sake, Thi-Ba, there is enough dust in this damned country. Let it alone."

She looked at me obliquely, dropped the cock feathers and continued with a cloth. The dust rose again from the tiles. I went out on the balcony to escape. The little *boyesse* followed me.

"Monsieur... Thi-Ba understand. You like Madame. She likes you too. But it is too hot. Everybody feel bad. Monsoon come... maybe next week. Maybe today. Then... no more dust. Is nice. Is cool. Madame feel much better. Monsieur feel much better too. Maybe *patron* make visit to Saigon? Then...?"

I could not help laughing at the barefoot cupid and chucked her under the chin. She giggled and went back to her dusting.

"Wait a minute, Thi-Ba," I called. "Can you sew?"

"All Vietnamese women sew, monsieur."

"I would like something to wear around the apartment. Something cool. Maybe light silk... a kind of robe. Something like Madame wears... only for a man. Do you know what I mean?"

She giggled with delight.

"Ah, monsieur, I think you like Vietnamese custom. That is good. I sew for you beautiful robe and pants. Maybe purple. Highest mandarin wears purple. You like I make for you purple?"

"Purple would be fine," I replied slowly. "You make it by tomorrow."

CHAPTER THIRTEEN

The sky was angry yellow and shot through with black when my jeep lurched into the rim of Nui-Bara canyon. I was caked from dust that blasted across the bamboo jungle in the teeth of a violent wind that bent the strong canes like grass.

For the first time in Viet Nam, I felt cold. There was no sun. I heard the rasp of the falls only when I switched off the motor near the edge of the river. Tissues of spray whipped the windshield.

I hardly recognized the mandarin. He walked toward me with the strong, swinging stride of our first meeting. The scar under his nose had fully scabbed. His skin was clear and the long raven hair was carefully coiled.

"Come!" he shouted, waving at the length of the turbulent vista.

We carried the provisions up the slope to a small natural cavern in the rock. Inside, the sounds diminished and the fury broke beyond us.

A small fire smoldered at the opening of the cave, fed with chunks of natural peat.

"I stole matches from a sleeping Moi," Cam said proudly.

Tearing into the sack of rice grains I had bought in Loc-Ninh on the way to the falls, he scooped out several handfuls into a stubby section of green bamboo. I watched fascinated. Bamboo is a hollow wood but with a thin bulkhead at the joints.

When the piece of bamboo was brimming with rice kernels, Cam added water from a coconut and closed the open end with black mud. Placing the crude pressure cooker on the live coals, he explained in French, "The fire bakes the mud to clay, turns the water to steam and cooks the rice. Then, the steam blows out the clay stopper."

He motioned me to a seat of wild rattan and fern fronds.

"You have discovered this method of cooking in America just recently, I believe?"

I laughed. "We suffer from a lack of bamboo. We have to makeshift with aluminum and rubber."

"Both probably from Viet Nam." He scowled. "One of these days, you in America and France will discover our rice. You wonder why your bodies degenerate, your flesh becomes fat, and you are ridden with disease—when with your living standard, there should be no disease. Rice is the food of wisdom. If our people were not struck by plague and pest, they would live to a hundred years. Even so, they stay young and firm to beyond sixty."

He lapsed into brooding silence, watching the container of rice.

"What is the news from D'Or Blanc?" he asked.

"Everyone thinks you are dead and buried. The mandarins concurred in your execution. The tappers have the new wage increase and rubber is flowing again. If you returned now, it is not only the Legion you would have to fear."

He cleared his throat contemptuously. "We lost twenty of our patriots to every Westerner at Dien-Bien-Phu. Yet, our movement was victorious. The wisest French generals, the best German soldiers, and the finest American equipment could not stop us. The people of the south will rise when the time is right. But ... enough of politics. Let us speak of things agreed and agreeable. I thank you for your generosity of this rice and robe."

"What about the parable?"

Cam's brow knitted. "The affectionate tiger kills with compassion. That is true of you, but not important now that I am well. With the new strength of blood flowing through my brain, I have been able to deduce the dominant reason for your tenderness.

"The western mind sacrifices all considerations for a spiritual union between the sexes. Thi-Tuyet failed with the Frenchman called D'Arbre. Willing enough, he was too weak and foolish to benefit. I can see that my daughter has chosen more wisely."

I frowned.

"You are in luck, my son. You shall reap great fortune from the flower of her body and the perfume of her vigor. Welcome to our family and to our cause."

I sat stunned.

"We Vietnamese are not serpents, monsieur. I gave her to Mossard honestly with no tendrils dragging. A lotus transplanted and scalded with conjugal water may not sigh for the old shadow. But ever she becomes more pointed of breast, agonizing of hip, and flatter of stomach. There is no child. He plunders our race—takes but does not give."

When I said nothing, he continued, "No, my son. We Vietnamese do not award our clay for moonlight gyrations. My daughter is for a man of seed, of compassion. I have ordered her to depose Mossard by any means of feminine wile. If you are her chosen instrument, you will reflect in Buddha's smile."

The mud cork in the bamboo popped and while Cam extricated the smoldering piece, I gathered my thoughts.

So, Tuyet was playing the double game. I had half-suspected it, but the revelation came as a distinct shock. It all added up. The addiction of D'Arbre to opium during Mossard's absence could have been at Tuyet's provocation. His drug-soaked mind could have been influenced in the near giveway of the plantation. And, she had made *sure* that he would not tell. Listening that day at the vanity when D'Arbre fell from favor, it would have been natural for her to select a new tool—me. All the things she had said came back—the flattery. I was infuriated that I had been duped so easily.

Then, the image of her tortured face flashed at me, her stricken fear at divulging Cam's hideout. She need not have told Mossard the exact place, not if she were intriguing to the extent of overthrowing him. She could have indicated any one of a dozen deserted temples—would have guarded her father's secret at any cost. She was impetuous, opportunistic, spoiled—yes, but she was no actress. Cam's viewpoint, I was willing to bet, was largely colored by wishful thinking.

"Tuyet pleases me," I said lightly, "but why has she not followed your orders? It would have been easy for her to kill Mossard."

The mandarin banged out the steaming rice onto a banana leaf.

"Our women kill only with the kindness," he said. "Otherwise, what Vietnamese family could trust another?"

He began to eat, using his fingers.

"I was curious about the 'affectionate tiger' and asked Tuyet. She did not know."

Cam laughed. "She is not a mandarin, monsieur. To be learned, one must study not only the philosophy of nature, but the wisdom of centuries, passed in scrolls from our ancestors. The examinations are rigid and difficult…prescribed by the mandarinate in Hue…from the seals of the Emperor himself. One must read, write, keep columns, and prove himself artistically clever, before he may even apply. Thus…he who wears the cloak of learning is acknowledged as leader by all. Women are not considered."

He scooped up the remaining crumbs of rice with a curved fingernail and belched.

The wind outside had died, although the sky hung thunderous and black.

"The rain will not come today," Cam announced, rising and packing away the rice bag.

The words were scarcely out of his mouth when a torrent of water, with the force of a fire hose, stabbed the earth. The crack resounded the length of the canyon, and you could not see beyond the cave entrance. The fire sputtered out.

As I was smiling at Cam's poor prophecy, he pointed and I looked toward the cave entrance again.

The rain had stopped as suddenly as it started. If it were not for the inch of water on the ground, I might have thought the quick downpour an illusion.

"Indian monsoon," he said and spat. "Like spittle. In a few days, it will disgorge and men cannot stand under it."

The sun broke out in a blaze. Steam rose from the fern and rocks and the air was more sultry than before.

I saw that he was preparing to leave. Glancing at me quizzically as he bound the provisions inside the purple tunic—forming a crude shoulder sack—he said, "You are as a child hungering for a sticky-rice cake. I shall tell you the meaning of the parable.

"The tiger is affectionate when it nurses a cub. You are a soldier, are you not?"

"Yes."

"A tiger by nature. You were born with the thirst of blood on your lips. But you are an affectionate tiger. You have always nursed a 'cub'—not one of physical dimensions, but of spiritual. Let us call it a conscience. If you kill at all, it is to feed your cub—to satisfy your conscience."

I thought back to my combat experience and its motivation. Conscience.

Cam grasped a tall, slim pole of bamboo and strode out into the sun. He continued, "Eventually, the tiger teaches its cub to kill without mercy. If the cub is reluctant, the mother destroys it. She kills it with compassion, knowing instinctively that the cub will fall prey to a lesser beast of the jungle. Such will happen to your conscience if you do not teach it to kill for its existence. You will completely destroy it."

Glancing at me thoughtfully, he added, "It is fortunate that you were still affectionate when you found me alive."

He made his way nimbly down the rocks. I followed.

"There is another great truth of nature," I heard him saying more to himself than to me. "When one has an interminable task before him, he begins by conquering a thing he is deathly afraid of. If he succeeds in that, nothing can halt him."

We were close enough to the crescendo of the falls that he had to shout for his voice to reach me. "All my life I have watched the jumping water here at the crest and dared not cross so close to the gorge. Perhaps it cannot be done, but I will try. If my ancestors affirm my footing, nothing will stop my coming back to liberate my people."

The rocks at the nape of the gorge crossed the mouth of the river in jagged teeth. To leap from one to the other was possible, but they were slick from mossy slime. A misstep would be fatal.

"You are going to cross here?" I shouted back.

Adjusting his shoulder pack, he nodded. A hundred yards up the river there were flat stones where he would risk no more than a sprained ankle.

"Then, we can both stop worrying about your return."

Cam shook his head smiling. "I shall not worry, nor should you." His voice raised to pierce the roaring waters. "The jungle has no peer for the tiger who kills with compassion."

He gazed briefly across the chasm, folded his hands in a prayerful "sim-sim" and jumped.

Mist cloaked him from view. He wavered once and I thought he was gone, but he bounded again and was still upright. A racing stream, yards wide, separated him from a craggy rock that jutted in the center of the falls. If there were steppingstones between, they were under water.

The mandarin poked tentatively with his pole and the current thrashed it out of his hands. He set himself and jumped...his body twisting wildly. He went ankle-deep...then knee-deep. As I grimaced and waited, I saw him climbing up on the center rock. He turned and waved After resting a moment, he jumped again...stood still...and again. Finally, I could just make out his figure as his ran up to the rearing green wall of jungle on the other side and was swallowed up in the brush.

Walking slowly back to the jeep, I began to ponder the dubious future. I was as convinced now as he must be, that he would return.

CHAPTER FOURTEEN

With the rains came a new work schedule and skidding red mud to replace the dust. The tappers were picked up at four in the morning—two hours earlier—and collected latex until noon. I realized now why the heveas were planted so that their interweaving branches formed an endless umbrella. If the sun shone directly on the bleeding scars, they would dry up. The trees were spaced so that the *cueillettes du latex* were in eternal shade.

The rains always came in the afternoon. Workers' quotas had to be made by twelve-thirty.

Nguyen Cam had been right in his description of the monsoons. It was impossible to stand erect under the downpour. The torrent, although it lasted less than an hour, would rip off a jeep roof. All morning long, snowy thunderheads would puff into the bright sky and, almost precisely at two o'clock, converge.

Guillaume Mossard predicted that the rains would lighten and lengthen in about a month, settle to intermittent drizzles, and eventually stop. Then...the hot, dry season would start. The planter was glad to see the rains. They increased the flow of latex—production mounted steadily during the entire season. D'Or Blanc rubber, he said, was the best in the world because its cultivation was geared to climate.

Life continued its luxurious routine with even longer siestas.

Thi-Tuyet was still incommunicado, self-confined to her apartment. Mossard dismissed her prolonged absence as "some superstitious worship period."

A radio report announced the arrival in Saigon of a new Vietnamese premier. Several persons had heard of him. His name was Ngo-dinh-Diem. The radio broadcast a military review for him given by the French.

Mossard was deprecatory. If the French ran the country as he ran D'Or Blanc, he said, there would be no trouble, no Communists, nor any need for a premier. Nevertheless he flew to the capital to meet Diem. I suggested that if he were not too concerned with personal safety while in Saigon, it would be better if I kept an eye on the Château He agreed.

No sooner had the thin purr of the Piper faded into the distance than I counted off a thousand piasters from my wallet and went to Thi-Tuyet's apartment.

"*Madame partie!*" from two rows of black teeth clacking behind a crack in the door was my only answer to repeated knocks and calls. Madame was not in.

Shoving the piaster notes through the aperture, I demanded, "Where is she?"

The door inched, hesitated, then opened a bit wider. My hand became lighter by one thousand piasters.

"Madame go to altar of father ancestor," the crone told me.

"Where is the altar?"

"I not know, monsieur. Madame build altar. Please you go now."

The door slammed in my face.

The altar. Could it be where I had rigged the appearance of the grave? No…that was too close to the road, to public. Nui-Bara. It must be at Nui-Bara.

CHAPTER FIFTEEN

A plantation jeep protruded from the towering fern at the falls but she was not to be found. I searched the river edge and up on the rocks. Stepping gingerly out on a shoal well back of the cascade, I scanned the terrain. A pale wisp of smoke floated downstream.

The brush on the bank was too thick to push through The only way to get upstream was by rock-hopping. Leaping out on the stones, I curveted, sticking to the short brambles as closely as possible. Progress was slow but the drift of smoke thickened.

Unexpectedly, I came upon a tiny inlet, placid and cleared of underbrush.

Tuyet was kneeling in front of a bamboo-lashed altar, the cotton square of her mourning tunic spread neatly on the ground in front of her. Fragrant incense spiraled from josh sticks planted in the dirt.

"Thi-Tuyet?"

She whirled around as quickly as a cobra and rose with blazing eyes.

I splashed through the shallow inlet to the bank where frangipani gave off cloying perfume, and a banyan tree reared in ageless majesty.

"You profane the sacred ground of my father," she said, clenching her fists. "Go away."

"I am not going to profane you, your father or the ground. Sit down and be quiet."

With oriental resignation for the inescapable, she seated herself gracefully on one of the snaky roots of the banyan tree, folded her arms and looked in another direction.

"I see that your father's spirit has not taken its revenge," I said, not without sarcasm.

She lifted a slim arm and pointed to the altar. "If I want to live, I must worship each day. First in my room, then here. I must look not this way—not that way—and especially not at the man who murdered my father."

"If you believed that sincerely, Tuyet, you would leave Mossard."

The limpid depths of violet narrowed as they turned to me. Tears welled and spilled over.

"I am lonesome and afraid," she quavered. "I loved my father, but I am not meant to turn into a monk."

I sat down, took off my shoes and socks and placed them in the sun to dry.

"Let me tell you what you believe in," I said. "Security and luxury."

"I do," she acknowledged, her tears ebbing.

"You are here because of your guilty conscience. You did not do all that your father ordered in undermining the plantation."

She was studiously stern when she answered, "I do not mislead the *patron*."

"Roland d'Arbre was in love with you. He misled *patron*."

She looked at me searchingly, then transferred her gaze to folded ivory hands.

"It is very difficult," she said in a low voice, "for women to be their own masters. Men are strong like this banyan tree. It grows tall ... and alone, and plants itself by water that never runs dry. Its roots do not hide. They crawl in full sight, overrunning those trees which are not so strong. But, we women are the frangipani—guests in your garden. We cannot go near the water. We must nestle, bow and send perfumed blossoms for your pleasure. We cannot trust you, but must deceive you for life itself."

"A pretty parable, and so you are caught in the roots of two banyan trees."

She sighed.

"Why is it that Westerners are never content with less than the truth? All right. I admit. I helped my father a little bit ...." She bowed hurriedly at the altar. "... All that I could. I am no stupid lizard, King. If I disobeyed my father and he succeeded ..." She drew a forefinger significantly across her throat.

"And Mossard?" I asked ironically.

She shrugged slim shoulders. "He would not bother to save me."

"Very clever, Tuyet." I seated myself on the root beside her. "And very safe ... until Mossard finds out?"

"You will tell him?" Her body tensed, then relaxed. "I shall deny it. He will, of course, believe me."

"Not if I tell him something else I know."

She waved her hand scornfully, but curiosity finally triumphed.

"What else?" she demanded.

"Cam is still alive."

She stood up, the body under her skimpy tunic rigid as the banyan roots.

"You profane this ground, King." Her voice was contemptuous. "So, that is why you followed me ... to seduce me with words, so that I will remember the promise I made. Hot air from the back of an elephant! If you want a woman so badly, go to the House of Mirrors in Saigon. I am not so easily tricked."

"I am not lying, Tuyet. That grave on the Rubber Road is false. When I found Cam still alive, I brought him here to Nui-Bara. Ten days later I took him rice and a purple tunic. He crossed the stones at the top of the falls—to satisfy an inner challenge he said—and went to the mountains."

A glimmer of comprehension showed on her face.

"If that is true, why did you do it? You are *patron's* hired killer."

"I thought he would have enough sense to go into the mountains and stay there. But he would not listen to reason. He said that if he succeeded in crossing the rocks, nothing would prevent his return."

"And when *patron* finds out?" A slight smile curved Tuyet's lips. "You will say that you did it for me?"

I became angry. "I am not afraid of Mossard, Tuyet. But I am breaking a contract worth ten thousand dollars." I got to my feet. "I intend to tell him *everything* when he returns from Saigon."

Her look was cold. "He will kill you, King."

"Then I shall have to take my chances. I came here to ask you to warn me the next time Cam sends you a message. He will, I am sure. He is convinced you are giving your all for the glory of his cause. Now, I could not care less. I am sick of this whole double-dealing business."

Turning away, I splashed out into the inlet.

A warm softness lit on my back and I sank ankle-deep in the silt. She had jumped and wrapped her legs around my hips.

"You forgot your shoes." Her voice was low.

I turned and slogged back to the banyan tree.

She slid around in front of me, her hands digging across my chest until they met behind my neck.

"I will not let you be killed so stupidly. If this is the only way I can prevent it ... then ..."

The torpor of the hot air and her flaming passion made my senses reel. I pushed her from me.

"So you think Mossard might believe me?" I remarked caustically.

She sat down on the banyan root and crossed one trousered leg over the other. "How much money do you have?"

Surprised at her question, I said, "A few thousand piasters."

"That is nothing. Have you friends who would pay a ship for you?"

"No."

"Then I shall give you money. There is no time for you to lose. You have not lived with *patron* long. You are so very honest. Ha! You would tell him of Cam and of me. He would find the grave as empty as a nest of birds above an anthill—and be sour of speech and angry. But he would forgive you. Oh yes, he would forgive you! As you slept that night, with your clear conscience, the door would open. You would wake to look at the tiny hole of a gun in the hands of one of the large squat soldiers who carry the tattoos of lightning on their arm. The hole would become red and you would becoming nothing."

"Fantastic. He had much more reason to kill D'Arbre."

"Roland was French," Tuyet said simply. "*Patron* would not have to account for you."

In terms of cold logic, there was much in what she said.

"Then it must be your great love for me," I said with sarcasm, "that you would give money to get me out of the country."

Her bosom rose with emotion. "Go...go and tell *patron*. Perhaps he will believe you, not me. But he cannot afford to eliminate me. He needs me as the thread to bind him to the people. Perhaps I will be degraded and ignored by him, but when my father's message arrives, then I shall pass it to him. That will forever break his doubts."

"I believe you would," I said softly.

Tuyet stood up, pressed her hands down the full length of her body straightening the tunic. She moved close to me. Her hair was damp against my shoulder.

"When I kissed you in the Château," she whispered, "I did it to make you do what I wanted. That is what the women do in the French cinema. But I did not like it. Vietnamese women think kissing is vulgar—as if someone is going to eat you. But when you kissed me...just now..." She trembled slightly. The damson eyes closed. "Do not run away, King," she said. "I have the money and I will give it to you. But do not go. Stay with me …."

I felt her roundness through the silk. The buttons of my shirt ripped and her diaphanous costume offered no resistance.

"What is love, King?" she asked in a low voice.

I was startled. "Love is … well, it is … being together, wanting to be together …. something like that. I have never been in love, Tuyet, so I would not know exactly."

"We do not know the word love in Viet Nam, but it is used very often in the French cinema." She stretched her legs. "We have respect, admiration, consideration, passion … even ecstasy. Perhaps love is a combination of all. One would be very fortunate to experience them at the same time. I think to do so is impossible."

"Some people seem to."

"Who?"

I was thinking of Mossard and Charlotte. "Oh, just … people."

"See, you cannot think of examples. It is like I said—impossible. And a very good thing. To have all joys at once bring jealousy and suspicion. Buddha warns us against these."

She scrambled to her feet in panic and faced the altar. Her hands darted quickly as she bent to her knees and sang a weird incantation that repeated the same five notes. The incense fizzling at the bottom of a long ash smoked furiously and went out.

Rising to her feet, Tuyet said somberly, "I was suddenly suspicious that you had lied to me."

A clash of thunder smote the canyon.

"Come on," I shouted.

The sky over Nui-Bara was black and glowering.

Grabbing our clothes we skipped down the treacherous river shoals and barely reached the cavern niche. Everything flattened. Fern, bamboo, clumps of rattan and foliage were bent to the ground by the fury of the sudden storm. Lightning split the sky. The grotesque rock formations reverberated from the blast. The downpour sealed us in the cave with a solid curtain of glittering silver. It was stifling hot. She came toward me.

"My father is alive? You swear?"

My breath caught at the sheen of her hair.

"This is where he hid. See...his bamboo cooker...his bed...."

"You saved him because of me, King?"

I could not honestly answer her, nor did I try. Holding her in my arms, I sank slowly onto the cushion of palms.

CHAPTER SIXTEEN

Boredom settled like a fog. The pool, the dining room, the *salle de cinéma* and the library brought no relief. The conversations of the *apértif* hour were swirls of nonsense to which, at best, I could offer *oui* and *non*.

Tuyet's elusiveness aroused my desire more keenly. Our mating had not satiated me. Rather, it had opened the valves of some emotion I did not know I possessed. Our chance meetings around the Château were circumspect—even awkward. She appeared fearful that Mossard would get an inkling of what had transpired.

I felt the frustration that once seized Roland d'Arbre when she came to dive in the pool, swim for a few minutes and leave without so much as a glance.

Still, I had not gone to the planter with my knowledge. I kept waiting, postponing…planning for another rendezvous. The days passed….

During Mossard's quick trip, he had been in touch with Paris, had flown to Hanoi to inspect the Legion fortifications along the Red River delta.

"Dien-Bien-Phu was a blood bath and a press agent's dream," he said cynically. "We killed twenty thousand men and lost a general—a real-life Beau Geste—but, *mon Dieu*, it was only a battle. From the conference at Geneva, you would think we had lost the war."

But his worry was evident. "They want me to consider 'bleeding,' " he said without explaining and ordered me to stand by at five o'clock next morning.

I knew from experience that a seven-o'clock alert meant an upper loop inspection; six o'clock a southern loop; and five o'clock both.

I determined when I got the chance and we were alone in the car, I would tell him.

We turned out onto the Rubber Road promptly at five the next morning. Lights probed mysteriously through the forest as checkers, lab samplers, and estimators were already busy with their chores.

By sunup we were at the Cambodian border near Tay-Ninh. This was where the Pope of the Cao Dai Sect maintained a fearsome, ice-cream-parlor temple of snakes and dragons which magnetized the faithful—some of whom were on the plantation's payroll.

The Pope had two active divisions, I remembered Mossard saying. Lately it was rumored that he was anti-Diem. Mossard maintained good relations with the Pope—had even contributed to the temple.

I wheeled the black Citroën off the road and scraped to a halt. Mossard jumped out.

The trees were being worked like clocks. Shallow spiral wounds, topping a creamy-colored fluid, dripped in not-quite-tight faucets to an infinity of saucers. It was a familiar sight by now, but I never failed to be impressed.

Mossard stripped some gray-mottled gum from a tree that had yet to be tapped. He stretched it, sniffed it and scraped the bowl with his fingernail. Nodding, he walked straight on for a quarter of a mile, examining the baskets strapped to the backs of the tappers and caressing the scars of one tree after another. Finally, he paused before the splotched trunk of a thick, gnarled hevea that bore no cup.

"Age," he said sadly. "We wither together, my mistresses and I."

He slapped the rubber tree.

"Look at this old lady, King. I remember when they planted her twenty years ago. She was beautiful and as straight as bamboo. She should be worn out by now, but is she? My tappers think so—they have left her alone to shrivel and die. But, she is my mistress—not theirs. Let us see if she shows appreciation as a good mistress should."

He opened a penknife and scratched a line across the lower end of the scar. Thin milk appeared and gravitated toward the cup.

"Pretty close to joining her ancestors, would you say?"

He continued to stroke the trunk.

"But, mistresses can surprise you, King, especially the old ones. You must have learned that in Paris."

He circled the tree, scanning and sounding it. High over his head he slashed a long spiral marker.

"Scorn," he said, "inspires the old to the full fury of young love."

I watched the new cut. It gave nothing. Suddenly, a rich squirt bubbled into it, the color and thickness of tooth paste. The planter called for a pin and started the flow.

"You see? My mistresses do not easily die. As ripe virgins I woo and spoil them, piercing them callously, but with care. Then, as they age, I let them beg—occasionally hurt them savagely. When, like this one, they are wrinkled and ready to fall into humus, they will still be loyal."

He walked away from the tree.

Oddly, I wondered what Charlotte Mossard would have said to his speech.

Alongside a break in the foliage, Mossard stopped and looked at a cone-shaped mountain that rose in blue solitude from the earth floor. His face was drawn and old. I was on the verge of telling him about Cam when he burst out:

" 'Bleed' Saigon says... 'bleed' Paris says. Rather than let D'Or Blanc fall to the Communists ... bleed!"

He rubbed a hand over his face and through his hair.

"You do not know what that means, King. We strip the bark in rings all the way to the top … like a snake. We gush latex. Two trains a day. We can fill the bottoms of a hundred scows and bring them back for more. And the trees, my mistresses, will slowly give up their lives. In a year, D'Or Blanc from here to Nui-Bara will be dead. Stumps and chaparral. In five years … jungle."

He paused, then shot out, "What would you do, King?"

"If you told me to bleed, I would bleed."

He sneered. *"Pas tendresse.* The hired killer. You are well cast as a soldier of fortune. *Eh bien.* I thank you for your advice. You affirm my decision. The stupid Communists would not know what to do with my trees. They would milk the nodules as they do water buffalo—light a joss stick and expect the branches to turn into rubber tires. *Non!* I shall not bleed. I shall defend my mistresses."

He wiped perspiration from his face and continued walking. As I caught up with him, he spun in his tracks and stooped to peer through the gloom.

"Well … well," he said, "production must be booming in this tract."

Roland d'Arbre, in black calico trousers caked with mud, unshaven, was kneeling, wrestling with a trap cup that had been driven too deeply.

"This man is slow," the planter snapped at the fawning Vietnamese labor boss. "Is this the best help you can dig out of your mothy village?"

The Vietnamese appeared stunned.

"Yes sir … no sir," he stammered.

The kneeling D'Arbre lowered his head. His skin was tanned mahogany from the waist up.

"I do not allow pipe smoking on the job. You know the rules."

"He not smoke pipe." The foreman spoke anxiously in broken French. "He no smoke on job or in village. Sure, monsieur. I guarantee. Is very good worker."

"What is his name?" Mossard's voice was deadly.

The Viet's eyes rounded. He looked from Mossard to D'Arbre to his clipboard of papers.

"D'Arbre... Roland d'Arbre, monsieur. Apprentice."

"How many trees does he tap each day?"

"Five hundred, monsieur."

"Five hundred? The usual is seven hundred... you know that."

"But is apprentice, monsieur."

"Ah yes... of course." Mossard stabbed the kneeling D'Arbre with his forefinger. "But look at those shoulders. Good capability...."

"*Oui, oui,* monsieur. Good capable."

"We should give him more responsibility. Appoint him as a full-fledged tapper. Stand up, you." He prodded D'Arbre.

The flaxen-haired Frenchman got stiffly to his feet. His lips were drawn in a thin line.

"Are you ready to come home, Roland?" Mossard asked.

D'Arbre stared at the planter in silence.

Mossard pushed D'Arbre's lips back cruelly with a thumb.

"Open up." Running his finger over the gums, he peered into the gaping mouth. Then he stretched the blond Frenchman's eyelids.

"*Assez bonne santé,*" he commented casually.

"You cannot break me, Guillaume," D'Arbre muttered through clenched teeth.

"Speaks French too," Mossard said approvingly. "Gouge, fellow. Let us see the brand of your work."

D'Arbre took his knife, a stocky butt of bamboo couching a sharp blade, and droned the sloping tissue.

"Too slow," Mossard barked impatiently. "Here... this is the way it is done." Taking the tool, and in a motion defying the eye, he left a welt of white growing on the bark.

Handing the knife back, he said, "When he gets that fast, he can qualify as a tapper. Meanwhile, let him practice—on his knees—from tree to tree. When he is fast enough, increase him to seven hundred. But he is to be kept on his knees at all times from the moment he detrucks to the moment he is finished with his quota. That includes getting from tree to tree. If he falls behind the others, speed him up. I hold you personally responsible."

"*C'est ça!*" The Vietnamese foreman's heavy-lidded eyes glinted with understanding. The clipboard slapped against his thighs and the dawning of expression was drenched with bitterness of years under the white thumb.

"If he gives you any trouble," Mossard added, beckoning to me that he was ready to leave, "hang him."

For the rest of the tour, I weighed the fruits of integrity against the decided probability that Tuyet was right.

As we turned into the gravel drive of D'Or Blanc, I still had not told him.

CHAPTER SEVENTEEN

On July 20, 1954, I made up my mind. As we sat having coffee and cognac after dinner, Radio Saigon broadcast the stunning news.

The Geneva Accords had sliced Viet Nam into halves. The long curved scimitar diking the coast of Indochina was severed. To the Communists went the entire north—the port of Haiphong, the capital of Hanoi, the Red River delta and all Vietnamese territory between Laos and China to the seventeenth parallel. The French forces—north and south—were to pull out.

Mossard frantically spun the dial to get Paris on short wave. There were further details.

The entrenched Communists in the south were to regroup northward. The Vietnamese soldiers who had fought for the French were to come south and join Diem. Free movement across the parallel would be permitted for six months. An International Control Commission would then patrol north and south. Free elections would be held in two years' time.

The planter snapped the set to medium wave.

A wag on Radio Malaya sang, "You take the Thai Road, and I'll take the Lao Road, and I'll be in Bangkok before you!"

The starch in Guillaume Mossard's backbone wilted. He stood before the subdued assembly and spoke one word. "Bleed."

The command hit the tappers where it hurt—in their future. The next day a strange rash of sickness enveloped them. Trucks chugged through the acreage with one, two, and sometimes no workers. When the Legion went to investigate, the Vietnamese groaned, squirmed and flogged the floors of their shacks so unconvincingly that even the mandarins were forced to admit it was a farce. The contract D'Arbre had made in Mossard's absence gave the workers medical rights. In isolated areas, the Chinese and Moi methodically began the stripping.

I was sitting in my salon deciding on the most disarming way of breaking the unpleasant news of Cam to Mossard when Thi-Ba appeared in the doorway.

"Madame here for you," she whispered. She was jiggling with suppressed excitement. Pointing in wide sweeps over her shoulder, she said, "I tell her wait in bedroom."

I started to stride past the *boyesse* and thought better of it. Thi-Ba winced when I clamped her arm. "You tell one person she was here and I will have you sent back to your village."

The little *boyesse's* face seemed more hurt from my lack of trust than from my grip. "I tell no person," she protested. "She like you. You like her. Long time you wait. Is very nice. And now is cool."

"Ask her to come in here. You wait outside."

Bowing as she retreated, Thi-Ba glowed with romantic approval.

Tuyet appeared in the draped doorway, lovely in clinging rose silk. I took her silently and tightly in my arms. She responded, then placed finger tips between our lips.

"I have not long, King. I come to you because I have word from my father."

"He is on the plantation?"

She nodded calmly, disengaging herself. "He has a force of men and arms—five times more than the Legion. His plan is to strike the Château."

"Have you told Mossard?"

"No." Her voice was quiet, detached, deadly. "There is a message for you, King." A faint smile appeared. "You are to dispose of *patron*."

"What?" I stared at her. "Either you give that message to Mossard, or I will."

"I do not intend to," she replied. "You may do as you like."

My hands dropped from her arms as if they were stung.

"So ... the frangipani leans to the largest banyan root," I said bitterly.

She shrugged. "The *patron* cannot win. It is not pleasant to be on the losing side, if the Vietminh are the winners. This you will discover if you do not heed my father's instructions."

"Cam is exaggerating as usual. He could not get that many men on this plantation without being seen and reported."

"My messenger has seen his army." She looked at me inquiringly. "He is waiting—your answer."

"Tell him that I shall not kill Mossard."

Violet eyes widened. "Your refusal will not send me running to *patron,* King—if you expect that. My father does not need your help. He is giving you a chance, just as you gave him a chance."

Chance, I thought. Cam would have considered the parable: The affectionate tiger kills with compassion.

"Sorry," I said curtly.

She lifted her hands to my face. "King, *chéri,* I could have love for you. I have never met a man who ... made me feel like a parrot in a flame tree. I tell you this for I may not have the chance again. Do not expect me to help you when the plantation is crushed ... when you are in agony and your tongue is torn from your mouth. I shall turn my back."

"You know that I will warn Mossard."

"If it will make you feel more noble," she said, "please do."

Kissing me lightly, Tuyet glided from the room.

Guillaume Mossard was a defeated man. Sprawled in the desk chair before the double window, staring vacantly out at the lawn, he did not reply.

I spoke louder. "Cam is alive, Mossard."

The chair swung briskly. His eyebrows rose with the uncertainty of having misunderstood. "What is this you are saying, King?"

Taking a deep breath, I plunged. "I lied to you. Cam is not dead. I let him escape because I felt sorry for him and did not like to kill a defenseless man. I took him to the mountains and warned him to stay in exile. Unfortunately... he did not listen to me. He has assembled an army, reported to be five times as strong as the D'Or Blanc Legion force. He is on the plantation and is preparing to attack the Château."

The planter's face was white.

"I have not adhered strictly to my contract," I continued, "but at least I am telling you now. That shows a certain amount of loyalty."

I had expected an outburst. None came.

In a quieter voice, I went on, "I could have said nothing—let you be surprised—perhaps wiped out. Or I could have deserted to Saigon, left you without protection and hopped aboard a ship. Or... I could have taken my informant's advice and murdered you for my own protection."

His voice came thin and sharp, cutting as a razor's edge. "Who is your informant?"

"Thi-Tuyet."

Muscles flickered in his face.

"When did she tell you this?"

"Five minutes ago—not longer."

"We shall see," he said, springing from the chair and striding into an antechamber. I heard doors opening and slamming. He was gone barely a minute. When he returned, his step was measured. Reseating himself at the desk, he said dispassionately, "Tuyet is not in the Château. She took a jeep this morning to go worship at her father's shrine. She has not returned."

I realized then why the Vietnamese girl had not been concerned at my threat to tell Mossard. Her convenient alibi placed a double onus on my story, and she was probably on her way to join Cam.

"King, you are in a grave position. Your story smacks of collaboration for high stakes—behind my back. Your disarming manner and protestation of loyalty no doubt are insurance in the event Cam fails. Your 'alerting' me is ludicrous. If the story is true to the extent you paint it, the Legion is aware of it by now. Your sudden stricken conscience fails because it is late. So, too, does your attempt to involve Thi-Tuyet. You are under arrest. I would not hesitate using the pistol I have in this drawer … if you are rash."

Weeks of pent-up restraint exploded and I shouted, "Mossard, you deserve to lose … if for no other reason that you are so damned stupid. If you did not have so much rubber in your veins, you would see that other people have blood. D'Arbre sold you for opium. Tuyet sleeps behind your back and plots with whomever Cam says. Her *boyesses* lie through their teeth. The only one around here who is legitimate you put under arrest! I suggest you reach for that pistol and give me an excuse to take Tuyet's advice." I meant it.

Motionless, we glared at each other. A minute passed.

The roar of reconnaissance vehicles spewing gravel pell-mell sounded on the driveway. Hurrying boots clattered on the marble of the horseshoe stairs. Mossard expanded in the chair.

"Word of your accomplice's presence has reached us," he said and carefully lit a cigar.

From the malevolence in his face, I knew that my future would receive special attention.

CHAPTER EIGHTEEN

efore I was marched to my room, I had the satisfaction of seeing Mossard's lips pinching white around the clamped cigar.

Nguyen Cam, the Legionnaires reported volubly, was not only alive but arousing his villagers to vengeance. Spellbinding the tappers as being "reincarnated by the ancestors," he was passing out arms, chanting, "To the Château." Mossard's appointed mandarin, Cam's replacement, was now hanging upside down.

When the Legion patrol attempted to intervene, it was ambushed by grenade launchers and forced to retreat. Former *gendarmerie* soldiers were identified. One of the sergeants reported seeing a convoy of trucks loaded with weapons. Another hazarded that they were arms of the Vietminh Communists who were starting north to regroup. Cam could have brought them over the mountains from Binh-Dinh via the Dalat road.

The patrol was ambushed again north of Hon-Quan. One half-track was disabled and abandoned. A Legionnaire was killed.

The German guard who marched me lock-step left a bruise on my back from the snout of his carbine. Emptying my hot closet of armament, he bolted the balcony portico and lowered himself into a chair. The carbine was pointed firmly to my stomach.

There was a sour taste in my mouth and I wondered what date it was. Not that it made much difference ....

"Guten Tag," I tried on him.

His face was blank.

"Wie geht es Ihnen? Was gibt es mit der Legion?"

The *commerçant* shifted his cud and said nothing.

"Haben Sie eine Fräulein hier im Schloss?"

The former S.S. trooper sank the carbine into my flesh.

"Ruhig!" he growled.

Well . . . it was not going to be now. That was some—if little—consolation. Measuring the distance between us, I toyed with the idea of judo. Thinking better of it, I lay on the bed to encourage his relaxation—maybe he would nod. His vigil remained as monotonously alert as before. When it became dark and nothing more had occurred than the grind of vehicles back and forth on the front drive, I de-decided that I might as well sleep.

I was awakened by the sudden rattle of gunfire and started to spring up from the bed.

"Nein! Gehen Sie zurück." The Deutscher in French uniform shoved me back roughly with the carbine.

I looked at my watch—two in the morning. If I had overslept, at least I felt refreshed.

"Der Krieg . . . was ist los?" I asked.

Jiggling the carbine, the Legionnaire pointed to a tray of food on the floor. Everything was cold, including the coffee, but I downed it ravenously.

The house shuddered.

Cam was in strength—there was no doubt. This was the showdown. A wave of excitement flooded me.

Concentrating on the fire, I made out rifles, machine guns, mortars—light ones—and grenades. Straining, I could hear nothing heavier. The attack seemed to be from the forest on the swimming pool side. The cross volleys nearby led me to think that the Legion was using my defense plan, but the home guard fire points had not counted on mortars—nor on attack in strength.

Quickly I subtracted the maximum Legion firepower from the audible density. The answer gave Cam about a hundred men in the woods. This was not the vaunted five-times-as-much strength.

The interchange slackened. Minutes passed with only sporadic fire. Then, the bombardment started again, louder and closer.

With D'Or Blanc in Communist hands...I thought of the chain reaction.

"You sonofabitch," I said to my guard, "if I had that carbine in my hands..."

The German yawned, kept watching me.

Shattering glass overrode the tattoo of fire. The floor shook violently. That would be D'Arbre's old quarters. They had found the mortar range.

Mossard came about three o'clock. His iron-gray hair was frizzled, and there were powder burns on his chin. A pistol dangled from his drooping hand. I figured that this was where the road ran out for me. He needed the German's firepower.

"*Schnell...schnell!*" he gestured toward the battle. The Legionnaire hobnailed out on the double.

"I am going to pardon you," Mossard said with obvious distaste, "if you want to fight."

I controlled my eagerness.

"No...thanks."

He was too tired to be angry. Sitting himself heavily, he said, "You will not remain here to reap the rewards of treachery. Go at once to the firing line. There you will be forced to defend your life."

"I am getting paid to defend yours."

He examined me critically but his interest was evident.

"If you have some idea, out with it," he said.

"I do...but first things first. You pardon me? No little round holes in the dead of night in case we win?"

The planter's lips tightened. "That depends."

"Then I shall need more time to think."

As he surveyed me with undisguised hatred, a crevice leaped across the wall and the floor shook.

"All right, King, if what you have to suggest is worthwhile, I shall pardon you unequivocally. But to continue your contract, you will have to admit that you were lying about Thi-Tuyet."

Something in his face warned me.

"Oh, she is back?" I asked easily.

"Of course she is back. She returned shortly after you were confined. I confronted her with your preposterous allegations. She broke into tears and swore she knew nothing of Cam."

"Actually," I said with pretended rue, "I heard it from two Vietnamese who had just returned from Cam-Xe. Sorry to involve Tuyet, but with your suspicious mind, I figured you might delay my execution long enough to find out if she were guilty." Shrugging, I added, "Looks like I was right."

Mossard appeared relieved.

"All right, King. I think I can understand the rest. I hope you have more compulsion to kill the Vietminh than you did Cam. Now … what is your idea?"

"Cam is hiding his main force."

"That was our initial thought," he admitted, "but the force he has committed is about the size of the *gendarmerie*—and well trained. I think we can discount the plantation rabble."

"But not the ancestors … remember?"

His lip curled. "Untrained men."

"They can carry a gun and shoot. From what I gathered, before your concentration camp *führer* put me to bed, there was a convoy of weapons."

He was silent.

"Captain DuPont may be a good officer," I said, "but he has to listen to you. Civilians should never direct wars, but they always do … and foul them up."

Mossard flushed. "Get this straight, King. I am in the rubber business—not in the business of waging war. My concern is to defend this property. If Cam breaks through the outer fencing, then Captain DuPont will deploy his halftracks out the front gate in a skirmishing flank maneuver."

"You should have seen more French movies, Mossard. There is always a shined-up platoon waiting to charge in from the outside where there is no chance of mines."

The corners of his mouth tightened. "Well, King, what do you propose?"

A whistling mortar struck the far end of the *couloir*. Plaster peeled instantly from the walls and the door fell ajar.

We went to the basement.

On the way down I picked up a sunrise-sunset chart from Mossard's office, redeemed my Thompson and had a quick look at the action. My previous fire plan was in effect. The fence was still intact.

"What are those spotlights on the roof for?" I asked the planter.

"They shot out the fence lights. I had portables erected to shine in their eyes."

"Not a bad idea," I admitted. "What about your home guards?"

"Manning all posts in depth behind the Legion—and changing light bulbs," he added lamely. "They are instructed to substitute, if the Legion is deployed outward."

"And your staff Vietnamese?"

"I do not trust them. They are carrying coffee and bandages."

"Casualties?"

"Three dead. Several wounded."

"How is the ammunition supply?"

"Enough for weeks."

"Mossard," I said with finality, "Cam is not attacking. He is playing. His fire is too erratic. That means he does not have ammunition to spare until he mounts his main effort. I doubt if he has committed a tenth of his strength. I might not be so positive, except that he could not afford to strike at the Château unless he thought there was absolutely no doubt of victory."

The planter waved away my theory impatiently.

"Cam is no general," he said. "He would strike without fore-thought and at once—the way the masses tore at the Bastille."

"You forget that he has a diploma from Hue. In addition to poetry and philosophy, there are requirements in political and military strategy."

"You were at least astute while you were harboring him," Mossard said sardonically.

Ignoring the barb, I passed him the sunrise table.

"Whatever Cam may lack as a general, he makes up for with confidence ... and a blind faith in nature."

"Nine minutes past five," the planter read aloud, "... this morning's sunrise. So?"

"At nine minutes past five, the sun comes up *in our eyes* from the east—*to our backs,* the way we are fighting now."

"*Mon Dieu!* The other side." He glanced at his watch.

"An hour and a half from now," I said. "Am I fully pardoned?"

There was a lingering trace of suspicion as he folded the sunrise chart. "I expect to stay close to you, King. If you are wrong ..."

"If I am wrong," I answered softly, "I doubt if it would make any difference."

When we went upstairs to the *rez-de-chaussée,* the bombard-ment from the woods had nearly stopped. A few rifles continued pattering and the occasional tinkle of glass from the bank of spotlights indicated their targets.

"Conserving ammunition," I said. "A broad hint that a good general would not give. I suggest that you keep as much light on the fence as possible and gradually accelerate fire from now until dawn. That will give them the idea that you are expecting a heavy attack there. If Cam has not already thought of the other side, maybe this will put it in his mind."

"What about the other side?" Mossard was anxious.

"I will take care of that. Start the Vietnamese hauling machine guns and belts over here, but quietly and under cover. Send all the boxes of grenades you have up to the rooftops all the way back to the end of the complex. The home guards can carry them up and stay with them. Keep the Legion where they are with plenty of ammunition because there will probably be a strong push on that side as well. And there is always the chance that I could be wrong...."

"What about the machine guns over here?" Mossard motioned to the sunrise side.

I could detect no suspicion in his remark or manner. For the first time in weeks, I felt secure and grinned at him.

"Send me twelve of your best Deutschers—no offense—but I happen to remember that they know this piece by heart."

By a quarter to five, I had defiladed the fence with four fifty-caliber machine guns near each corner and four in the center—all well camouflaged, and pointed inward. The nests were heaped with belts. The Germans, including my guard, were ready for the scythe job.

"Let them get past you," I reminded them, "and go for the ones in front. *Always* the front wave, so the rear will keep coming." I coined a new battle slogan on the spot—" 'Don't shoot until you see the whites of their *rücken!*' "

"*Verrüchter Amerikaner,*" I heard one of the Germans say. He rolled his eyes and tapped his head.

Sending word to the home guards by Mossard's messengers—the French cooks—I told them to wait until the German machine guns opened and then start throwing—no aiming—as fast as they could pull pins and heave.

Toward sunrise Mossard began to get nervous.

"Generals usually go skeet shooting about this time," I told him. "How about some coffee?"

At five o'clock, our battery of supplementary spotlights—Mossard's idea—blinked on and glared at the wreckage along the torn barrier. Our fire was at a peak.

"We win," I said and settled behind my Thompson—aimed toward the reddening sky.

"How do you know?" Mossard asked, gulping the contents of his cup.

"They are not shooting the new lights."

I was not as cocky as I pretended. The front was vulnerable—as was the extreme rear. The minutes ticked by. Sipping my coffee, I watched the glints of the rising sun.

At twelve minutes past five, dynamite charges tore gaping holes all along the sunrise fence. A throaty roar drowned out all other sounds. Cam's main body of troops flooded in—firing, throwing grenades and screaming.

They kept coming until they were all gone. The Vietminh on the other side of the compound charged belatedly against the spotlights at five-thirty. They were repulsed. By six o'clock, Cam's invading horde had been wiped out, or had fled.

Waiting for ten minutes after the last shot, I gulped the chilled dregs of coffee and walked out in the ghastly battlefield. Mossard went to check the Legion casualties.

The sun sparkled on the scarlet swamp of blood that had been the velvet lawn. There were four to five hundred bodies stilled, another hundred squirming and moaning. Chinese rifles lay scattered like matchsticks. The faces of the newly dead wore surprise and disbelief, distorted by the last agony. Wounded peasants moaned as I walked by, some lifting their arms, pleading supplications I did not understand. Hardened as I was to the grisly facts of combat, this was something else. I thrust aside a wave of nausea.

Two of the four Germans in the center nest of machine guns were dead. The two survivors I assigned to disarming the wounded and stacking the captured weapons.

There was no trace of Cam.

Returning from circling the estate, I saw Thi-Tuyet come out of the battle-scarred Château. Holding high the hem of a long tunic, to keep it from trailing in the bloody mire, she began examining the dead. I walked toward her. She turned the other way. I cut across her path and she stopped, avoiding my eyes.

"Have you seen my father?" Her voice was muffled behind a handkerchief held to her nose. The mass of raven hair bowed for an instant. When she straightened, her voice was filled with resignation.

"You have won, King," she said.

So she knew.

"I am not sure it was worth it," I said grimly.

The handkerchief lowered, revealing a brittle face. "Do not waste sympathy with these fools. Any one of them would have rejoiced in squeezing out the balls of your eyes."

"You seemed willing to trust their temper," I said not without irony.

"It was a risk," she admitted. "I did not underestimate you, King. When you refused to kill *patron,* I was not sure of my father's victory."

"Then you should have cried a little harder for Mossard. He was not quite convinced of your innocence."

She regarded me with some apprehension.

"If you know consideration, *chéri*"—her eyes flickered downward—"you will speak to him and confess your lie. You are strong in his favor now. He will believe you."

"And we start all over? Thanks. Look for another cobra."

"You do not understand," Tuyet said impatiently. "My father has blasphemed our ancestors, and they have showed their anger by mortifying him. He dare not return to our village or he will be torn to pieces. Vietnamese can never again be charmed by the opium of his tongue. If I see him, I must turn my back, for he is possessed by the spirits of the *chi-chi* birds."

Mossard emerged from a distant building and began picking his way toward us. Tuyet glanced at him and spoke rapidly. "There are no longer two banyan trees, King. I must look to one for shade. You will speak to him?"

I was aware of a thudding in my chest.

"I already have."

The leaf-shaped eyes tilted upward. "Consideration is not the least of the five essences of joy. If you have proved it, and are not lying, I will be impatient for the love."

"When?" My voice was low.

"Sleep lightly."

She turned to bow as Mossard approached.

The planter was petulant and said, "Go to the house at once, Tuyet. King is busy."

"I was apologizing for the false story," I said.

"It is of no concern to her. You should have apologized to me."

"I just did"—and looked pointedly at the devastation.

Wordlessly, Tuyet glided through the rows of dead toward the Château's *escalier de service*.

Mossard surveyed the carnage with distaste.

"I should get coolies out here to clean up this mess before the sun goes to work."

"There are close to six hundred—practically all tappers."

He grimaced. "They will be hard to replace. Did we get Cam?"

"He and, I would guess, half the *gendarmerie* are missing."

The Frenchman thought briefly.

"*Alors.* I have broken his back, destroyed his myth, and captured his arms. *Il ne peut que dormir.* Nguyen Cam is no longer a determining factor on D'Or Blanc."

"What about the Legion losses?"

His hand dismissed the question. "Negligible."

"Some of these Viets need medical attention," I said.

He deliberated. "Yes, I suppose so."

"And, if you want to be sure of Cam, send some patrols out in the deep timber."

Mossard's lips curved thinly.

"Let us understand one thing, King. You assisted in the battle to pay a debt. The battle is over. Last night's victory was a glorious one for the Foreign Legion—one that will atone for the shame of Dien-Bien-Phu. That is the record—and the one the world will read."

"Cam is still dangerous. He has fifty armed cadres or so."

"It is no longer a concern of yours."

"My congratulations to the Legion," I said. "Should I go on leave when you are passing out medals?"

"Come along," he ordered curtly.

We walked in silence to the swimming pool where Captain DuPont was waiting. Issuing salvage instructions, Mossard seated himself at a terrace table farthest from the wreckage of bodies.

"*Grâce à Dieu,* there is someplace that is not cluttered." He called a passing boy and ordered breakfast.

I was not hungry.

"King," he said, "I let myself be catapulted into bleeding the trees. *Sacrébleu!* Patriotism is the eternal curse of the French. Cam could not have mustered his horde if the tappers had been busy and dispersed. *Alors.* Today we shall visit the mandarins and tell them of our victory. Tuyet will accompany us to dispel the myth of Cam's immortality and to speak for a new 'marriage' of French-Vietnamese endeavor. D'Or Blanc is going back to work."

"I hate to be a killjoy. We were ambushed before by Cam's *gendarmerie.*"

His reply was impatient. "That was before they were defeated. Now, they have the choice of sneaking back to their villages in disgrace or joining one of the armed sects."

"You have not heard the last of him."

"I think we have."

The planter sat in silence for a few minutes surveying the tattered facing of the Château.

"But there are the sects," he said finally. "The Legion, as you know, must eventually leave Viet Nam, in accordance with the Geneva terms. I must have a native *gendarmerie* to replace the D'Or Blanc detachment—ostensibly a police force but actually a mobile battalion well trained in the rudiments of warfare. This is to be your project."

A glow of excitement coursed through me.

"This force must above all be trustworthy—not of the local natives nor subject to any of their orders-of-rule or blandishments. I am told that numerous thousands of Tonkinese in North Viet Nam have asked for refuge in the south as allowed by Geneva. French and American ships are moving to Haiphong to evacuate them to Saigon. They will be looking for employment. More important to us—they will be positively anti-Vietminh.

"You will go to Saigon, screen these refugees as they arrive, select your force and commence training."

The excitement was leavened by a surge of disquiet.

"When does this start?"

Regarding me keenly, he answered, "We are sending the French dead to the capital tomorrow for full military honors. You may go with the cortege."

Trying to hide my growing resentment, I said, "How long will I be in Saigon?"

He shrugged. "A few weeks—perhaps a few months. Until you have seen the bulk of them. I expect you to recruit only the most choice. As for your services here, I think we can dispense with them."

"I thought I contracted to be a bodyguard."

"Your contract is pliable enough to cover this contingency. However, I am prepared to offer an increment. Say—twelve thousand dollars totally."

He considered my silence as a negative reaction.

"Your contract is also subject to termination. You recall the provisions?"

"Fifteen thousand?"

His expression lightened. "*C'est fait.* We shall proceed on the basis of the original. Your performance will determine the amount of the bonus. You are to live at Villa d'Or Blanc and report to Lien-Fat. He is the Chinese *compradore* you met—my business manager. He will arrange for expenses, both on my behalf and to a reasonable extent your own. The change will be good for you, King. As I mentioned before, I have no objection to your returning *encombré*." He laughed.

"I understand." I did.

The boy came running over the scuffed grass and uncovered a tray with coffee, French rolls and a steaming, fragrant omelette. Mossard approached the food with the same savor and delicacy as if he were in Maxim's.

"You should order some buffalo feces to go with that," I said.

He looked at me with disgust. "Is that your idea of a crude joke?"

"The crude joke, as you call him, just walked in."

Roland d'Arbre, legs bent forward painfully, was walking laboriously up the front drive. He fell, lay for a moment in the gravel, and continued more rapidly on his knees.

Mossard cut into the omelette. "Well, well, well . . . ."

He had finished by the time D'Arbre reached us. Wiping his mouth delicately, he said, "What is it you want, Roland?"

The Frenchman's yellow hair was scraggly and the color of rust, his eyes holes of shadow. Through the rips in his tattered calico jacket, I could see dull red welts.

With a pronounced effort, D'Arbre stood up. The movement seemed to bring him excruciating pain.

"You were right, Guillaume," he gasped, tottering, "but that yellow pig had to prove it to me. He was worse..." his knees buckled, but he went on, "... than you ever were. During the strike, we went out... just the two of us. He raised my quota so high... I could not fill it. At night, for punishment... he made me crawl around the top of the village wall... you know the jagged glass they put on the wall... to keep out night animals? I... I went to the mandarin... my old friend. He refused to see me."

D'Arbre pulled up mud-stained trouser legs. His knees and shins were quilts of bloody scabs. His strength gave out and he fell.

Raising himself on an elbow, he continued, "But I got fast, Guillaume... fast the way you wanted." A gouge knife appeared in his hand and flashed through the air. "I left him there...."

From the hate in his expression, there was no doubt as to what he meant.

Mossard was cold. "You did not know of the attack on the Château?"

D'Arbre looked blank. "Attack?"

"Look around you."

The crippled Frenchman lifted his head. "You will have to forgive me, Guillaume. All I have known is the square meter in front of me." Peering out on the destruction, he began to laugh—a racking sort of a sound. "Good for you," he gasped, "... the only way to treat the bastards when they talk back."

Mossard sipped *café au lait.*

"You may have your old job if you want it, Roland."

D'Arbre hobbled forward and clutched Mossard's hand. *"Grace a vous... grace à Dieu."*

"You will need to rest and learn to walk again properly. King, see that he gets priority at the dispensary. Do you remember Thi-Tuyet, Roland?"

The question was savagely calculating.

D'Arbre grunted. "Here...take this knife, Guillaume. I might forget how 'friendly' these natives at the Château are."

Mossard accepted the gouge blade and did not question him further, saying only, as I helped D'Arbre to his feet, "While you are convalescing, Roland, you might review that tapper contract. It may suggest some revisions to you."

CHAPTER NINETEEN

inner was at nine that evening and, following the spectacular train of events that day, a command performance to celebrate the victory. Mossard, Captain DuPont, D'Arbre, Thi-Tuyet and I—dressed formally—sat in our accustomed places.

Miniature French flags jutted from red-white-and-blue floral arrangements on the table. The planter wore a Croix de Guerre on his tuxedo lapel and the Legionnaire captain was in full dress.

D'Arbre, his white dinner jacket ill-fitting in its looseness, boasted a tinge of color in his cheekbones—the mark of emergency shots of multiple vitamins.

Tuyet was sheathed in a furnace-red, Hong Kong dress slashed to mid-thigh, her hair smoothed back and coiled *a la chinoise.* The silk of her dress was not meant to cover lingerie, nor did she spoil the illusion.

I was in my white linen suit.

Lifting a glass of champagne, Mossard rose to toast the occasion.

"We enter upon a new era of prosperity," he said, "thanks to the glorious victory of our Foreign Legion..." and bowed to Captain DuPont. "... To the unstinting loyalty of our civilians"—the glass moved in my direction—"and to the symbol of our new joint effort"—he indicated Tuyet—"whose words moved the mandarins to shame, and whose presence brought cheers in the villages. It is fitting that we observe this day."

We all drank.

"And we have yet another reason to gather together," Mossard continued, "to welcome back our colleague, Roland d'Arbre …"

The foreman crinkled his damask napkin and smiled nervously.

"…and to bid farewell to Mr. Daniel King," Mossard concluded.

Glancing at Tuyet from the corner of my eye, I saw no sign of emotion at his words. She was sitting in rapt attention.

"Mr. King, I might add, after his career in Paris, is unaccustomed to the hardship of celibacy. He is anticipating with delight his new assignment to Saigon. I must warn you, Daniel, that the swimming pool chatter of Asian women—their servility, abandon, or other unique attractions—is highly exaggerated."

Tuyet smiled broadly. Captain DuPont and D'Arbre chuckled.

"Bon appétit, mes amis!" He sat down.

Food came flying from the kitchen. Each servant fumed at the other, vying in efficiency and politeness, in what was an obvious effort to dissociate themselves from sympathy with Cam's cause.

The table conversation accelerated in the brisk atmosphere. D'Arbre, ill at ease, finally spoke to Thi-Tuyet. She returned the inconsequential remark coolly. There was no hint that anything had transpired between them. Relaxing, the foreman joked about his experience with the vitamin syringe.

Having ignored me throughout the daylong ride to the villages, Tuyet gave me the same circumspect attention she awarded the others. To Mossard she catered with an almost smothering concern.

Proposing a toast when it came my turn, I lifted a glass to her and said, "To my last night in the Château. May it be rewarding to you …"

Her amused gaze faltered.

"… and to you." I bowed to Mossard.

There was relief in the quick look she gave me.

"A votre sante!" I said.

"*À la vôtre*," they murmured automatically and drank.

Tuyet leaned to Mossard—taut as a stretching cat in the sheer silk. Pouring his glass full again, she said softly, lifting hers, "*Ce soir, chéri?*"

Flushing, Mossard tilted the glass to its bottom. As he drank, the heavily mascaraed lashes turned briefly to me and widened. Eyes smoldered as her lips repeated the words inaudibly, "*Ce soir, chéri.*"

The wine burned through me like fire.

"If you ever serve rice and *nuoc-mam*, Guillaume," D'Arbre mumbled, his mouth full, "I may borrow back my gouge and go after your cook. *C'est incomparable.*"

Mossard became less attentive with the wine, and Tuyet's glances at me were bolder.

Excusing myself from coffee and cognac on the pretense of packing, I went upstairs to the *couloir*. Breathing the night air, listening to the overwhelming silence and watching the moon flood the cleansed surface of the swimming pool, I fought away from the grip of fever.

With determination to double-lock the door and sleep in the salon where I could hear no one knock, I entered the apartment. Thi-Ba, the little *boyesse*, was still at work cleaning up plaster.

"Oh, monsieur, bedroom not finish yet. *Patron* Mossard give order all Vietnamese work until Château like before."

"Never mind. I am sleeping in the salon."

Thi-Ba leaned forward confidentially, her face wreathed with slyness. "I think you no have worry," she whispered. "Madame come before dinner. Leave word you meet her Nui-Bara when moon straight up. No bother sleep on crooked bed-chair."

Going into the salon, I stretched out on the chaise and stared dejectedly at the ceiling.

CHAPTER TWENTY

The road to Nui-Bara was something else at midnight. The wild beauty had changed to a harsh, breathing, hackle-raising monster. Although I knew the slushing potholes by heart, they rose unexpectedly in unfamiliar shadows. Crashing underbrush and remote screams pierced the high wall of brake on either side of the road. A thick length of bamboo squished angrily under the tires and hissed. Metallic glints swelled in pairs and diminished under the probe of the headlights. The jungle, I was reminded vividly, was the animals' own zoo.

The sound of the falls, hushed and distant, came as a relief. I began to think of Tuyet. There were no fresh tracks in the mud, so I must be ahead of her.

The cascade was precipitate and deadly in the luminous sky. Thunderous plumes spurted before dipping out of sight. Green moonlight wove restlessly between rocks. The area was void of life so far as I could see, but I sought refuge in the cavern. Tiger, python and gaur were notorious water prowlers, I remembered somebody saying. I wished I had brought a gun.

It was nearly two o'clock when a spear of light flashed in the foliage, disappeared briefly and became brighter. The cough of a motor penetrated the roar of the water.

A jeep bounced up behind mine and switched off its headlights. I started toward it and stopped. A familiar voice chiseled the air.

"Tuyet is not coming, King."

Mossard was alone. A shaft of metal glinted dully from a fisted barrel that fixed me like radar. He must have followed, caught her and turned her back. My eyes riveted on the gun—it was steady. Mossard had sobered.

"You are despicable, King. I knew you were attracted to Tuyet, but I did not think you had carried it this far. Just what is your game?"

"I like her ... maybe even love her."

His voice was deadly. "You are lying. She has confessed the entire affair. How, in my absence, you followed her here and raped her, forcing her to silence with the threat of telling me. How, when she would not deceive me again, you tried to undermine her loyalty with your fantastic story of Cam. How today you threatened her once again—to expose her, with possible return to her village, if she did not rendezvous with you tonight."

Tuyet had been caught, I concluded, and was saving her own skin.

"So ... that is what you wrung out of her."

"She came to me voluntarily after dinner—frightened of you."

Suddenly calm, I said, "And, if all this were true, why would I do it?"

"I believe you have designs on the plantation."

Moving close enough to be able to judge his pressure on the gun, I said, "And I believe you are jealous."

Even in the moonlight I could see him blanch. "How dare you!"

"Now I will tell you the truth. We had an affair, yes, but it was as much her idea as mine. More. Cam told me about her plotting against you with D'Arbre. The opium almost worked. Then, she played for me. Got me to cut down Cam—brought me the message to kill you before the attack. Yes, that was true. And tonight, during dinner, she was giving me the eye behind your back. Sent word to meet her when the moon was straight up at Nui-Bara. Ask my Thi-Ba."

"*Boyesses* lie as much as they chew betel."

"You are fooling yourself, Mossard. You believe her story about as much as I do. It is just because you are so damned mad because you cannot keep your hands off her when you are supposed to be thinking of Charlotte … and you take it out on me."

The muscles in his forearm tightened.

Judging the distance, I drop-kicked and fell. The gun spun with an arch into a bank of ferns.

Rubbing his hand tenderly, Mossard said, "I am glad you did that. You may be right about my feelings. I dislike you intensely— yet, I have no reason to kill you for that. Whether your crudities with Tuyet were prompted by ambition or lust, I do not know. But, you have disobeyed me … ."

The springs in Mossard's feet retracted with lightning swiftness. Sliding out of the jeep on the far side, he crashed into the thick fern. Thinking he was going after the gun, I chased him pell-mell. He turned to meet me head on. There was a thick bamboo length parried in his hands.

"… So, I am going to break you, King … just as I broke D'Arbre."

I crumpled to the ground and rolled as the savage whisk skimmed my head. Jackknifing his unbalanced leg, I leaped up as he tumbled, intent with the flash picture of one-two-three-four judo … shin scrape, groin kick, knee mash and stomp.

A hammering at my senses froze the coiling action of my legs. Now it was clear. Tuyet's lying had been calculated to throw us into mortal combat. All else had failed. This was her setting— and I was the executioner. Taking advantage of my hesitation, the planter thrashed through the thicket and sprinted down the rocks to the water's edge.

"Mossard!" I shouted. "Can you see now what she is trying to do? If she wanted you killed, wouldn't she plan it this way? D'Arbre... then me. Everything failed. Think, Mossard... think!"

Back to the falls, he stood poised on the shoals, arms akimbo, bamboo twitching. I looked down at him uncertainly.

"Having second thoughts, King? I am beginning to understand why the American army discharged you."

"I believe I will do Tuyet that favor," I said with cold awareness.

A section of slate rock tore loose in my hand as I slid down the steep slope. Hiding it behind me as I charged, I threw it at his head. The edge caught his shoulder as he whipped the wood and threw him off balance. Ducking under the thrust, I leaped several rocks upstream. Recovering nimbly, he came after me. My footing was unsteady. Trying a jackknife kick under the whipping lance, I slipped, raised a jetty of water in his face and landed on a slimy flat reef. I had time to clamber away—farther out in the rock-strewn torrent.

When I turned, Mossard was upstream and my back was to the cascade. He closed in... the idea was to force me into the brink. Retreating I searched frantically for adjacent footholds. Strong wisps of spray bit at my neck. The rocks trembled from the roar underneath. He jumped closer and poised the lance. I stole a quick backward glance. I had gone as far as I could. With a long uncertain leap, I darted for the bank.

An instant later, my jaw smashed a slimy underwater reef and a shock of pain erupted in my head. The whine of the lance was a distant echo. I felt the uncompromising tug of current and clutched frantically for a hold. My hands slipped on the moss. I grappled a hidden crest in the boiling foam to stop the gravitation.

Mossard stood over me. His teeth gleamed white in that strange light.

"Get up, King. We are just getting started."

The words were barely audible over the roar.

I saw it coming and rolled wildly. A tissue of water jetted in the moonlight and fell in spray. I lost grip on the slimy ribbing and slowly, helplessly, slid toward the churning abyss.

He tendered the end of the lance and I grasped it with the ferocity of the doomed. He dragged me back against the powerful current until I found knee hold on one of the shoals and crouched, panting.

"What are you waiting for, King? I thought you were going to kill me."

Vicious cross welts rent my head and I fell face down to the rocks. Splotches of blood dripped on my hands.

"Get up," Mossard said. "I dislike hitting a man when he is down."

I could not. An agonizing pain bit into my back, causing me to scream out. Somehow, I managed to clamber over the rocks to the bank. Four moons instead of one rotated in a crimson mist. I fell heavily on my face into the slate.

"Up, King!"

I had to blink to see him. Tugging weights held me to the ground.

"So ... you are not going to kill me after all," he mocked.

Some vestigial strength brought me to my feet swaying. I knew the *coup de grâce* was coming. Mossard took his time, watching me like a snake, switching the pole, calculating. I was without power to lift my arms.

"You were lying about Tuyet?"

"No ...."

A soaring bolt riveted me with untold daggers of pain. I was conscious of screaming shrilly and pitching forward. The merciful bed of slate rock smashed into darkness the final engulfing pain.

It was a week later when I recovered sufficient consciousness to realize that I was propped up in my bed at the Château with a nurse in attendance. The major damages were a broken nose, sprained back and cerebral concussion.

Mossard had ordered the nurse and a special doctor from Saigon. I mended slowly.

Three weeks after the nightmare, the planter paid me a visit for the first time. He sauntered into the room, debonair and smiling.

"No hard feelings." He extended his hand.

"No."

"D'Or Blanc is pouring latex, more than ever. Our victory not only impressed the natives—it has calmed the whole country."

He looked at me curiously.

"The refugee ships are beginning to dock in Saigon. Do you still want the job?"

"Yes."

The planter stood silently beside the bed for a few moments, then said, "I am sorry it had to be this way, King. One cannot fight judo by taking chances."

"I understand."

Searching my face, he seemed to register disappointment.

"You must have had beatings or injuries before, King. Surely the girl did not mean that much to you?"

"If she did?"

His lips thinned. "I had not meant to tell you this, but I owe you an apology. You were right about her."

"Tuyet admitted it?" I said with surprise.

"Your *boyesse*."

His air of sociability vanished.

"I cannot fathom Tuyet's purpose in manipulating me now that Cam is neutralized. If it were sexual attraction to you, she would not have compromised you that night. And it is incredible that she seeks power on her own—no Vietnamese woman could long maintain it. Yet she has ingratiated herself in the villages, has even had the mandarins' number one wives here for tea and aracas. She appears to be plotting to make herself absolutely indispensable to the French-Vietnamese union. As her efforts are so successful and seemingly without guile I tolerate them, but I do not trust them."

"I would like to talk to her."

Mossard was on the verge of uttering a cryptic refusal. "Good idea," he said and stalked from the room.

Hobbling to the mirror, I examined my features. The swelling in the nose had gone down. It would be somewhat out of line. The scar across the right cheekbone would be more noticeable. Whatever else, I thought grimly, my usefulness at Tailleur Escorts was finished.

Getting back into bed, I waited.

The door opened and closed.

"You wished to see me?"

Thi-Tuyet's haid was coiffured *à la mode de Rivière*—the style with more on one side than the other. A knee-length French skirt fitted tight across the hips and encased a shirt-type blouse with buckle cuff links in the sleeves. She stood stiffly at the door.

"I just wanted to indulge my habit," I said. "Thanks again."

"You have yourself to thank."

"Tell me about it. I used to listen to the love stories on Radio Diffusion."

"I thought you were a better soldier. Too bad for you—you were not."

She shrugged and patted her hair.

"So?" Her voice was cool.

"You thought I would kill him."

Her eyes widened. "Of course. Did you think I would sit in my room and dream of the love while you were in Saigon with those women? If you had killed him, we would have the love and the plantation. I am angry at you. It was a very great risk for me."

Her expression of honest outrage made me laugh. The pain was intense.

"Unbecoming from such a devoted wife," I said. "The frangipani, I hear, has nestled even closer to the banyan."

"Can you blame me? When I was so stupid to be fooled? I thought because you were clever to win from the Vietminh that you would easily win from *patron*. But, you are soft." Her nose tipped in scorn. "You cannot win from one old man."

"The clothes, I gather, are to make him feel younger?" I questioned, looking her up and down.

She flushed. "Do not think you can worm your way into my favor so that I will take greater risks for the love. The love is dead."

"Not even if I killed Mossard?"

"Ha! You could not kill a *margouilla* without tears falling into your throat."

"I suppose you are right, Tuyet," I said. "Of course, if you had had real love, we could have left Viet Nam together. I seem to remember your offer of money."

"One would spend piasters to run away from gold?" she said contemptuously.

"No ... I guess one would not."

"You have finished with me? *Patron* is looking at his watch."

"Yes, time is running out."

She smiled brightly in agreement and was gone.

Time *was* running out. I wanted the job in Saigon very badly now. Since I had regained consciousness, I had searched for, but had found, no valid reason why I should not kill Mossard or Cam or anybody else, if there were something to be gained.

Thi-Tuyet was no consideration. There were greater stakes. With the *gendarmerie* at my disposal, capturing D'Or Blanc was just the beginning.

Tuyet might be amusing.

Mossard paid me another visit and I confided that I had learned nothing in my talk with the girl.

Two weeks later, I was pronounced recovered and drove with the doctor to the great yellow city of Saigon.

PART TWO

CHAPTER ONE

D irty, lifelessly hot, the city of Saigon sprawls on a delta between the swamplands of rice and the South China Sea. Washed in drab ocher from French paint buckets, it bears superficial resemblance to a Loire provincial town. But the crush of two million Orientals, the hawk of ceaseless vendors, the noise, the filth and the blanket of soupy nauseous air rends the façade and names it the "Yellow Hell of the East."

I walked it every day to strengthen the weakness from my injuries and came to know it by heart.

Thatched huts and tin shacks could not hold all of the people. They backwashed into the coils of the countless arroyos—some dry, some navigable—that wind in scummy necklaces through the city. Floating villages of sampans and junks fattened the sides of the wide canals. Crossing these arroyos from boat to boat by footplank was easier than ferrying.

Saigon traded on man's lowest instincts. Vice, crime and debauchery were major industries—organized the voluntary. Because they made money, they were moral. For what it cost to buy a new shirt, one could spend a week in an opium den, hire a queue of concubines, or send steel vengeance into the heart of a real or pretended enemy.

Knots of Occidentals, diplomats, colonialists and Paris-educated Orientals roped themselves inside the grandeur of the French Quarter of the city—sipped Otard cognac at the Pont de Blageur, took the *apéritif* hour at a sidewalk café on rue Catinat, poised for a dive at the Cercle Sportif, consumed chateaubriand at the Bodega restaurant, lounged during coffee and *pâtisserie* at La Pagode, and occasionally slummed it down the broad, sin-lined Boulevard Gallieni where marriages of any convenience were cheaper than Scotch. This part of the city was called the "Pearl of the Orient."

My favorite stroll was along the dock fronts, where the refu-gees from the North piled off transports in ever-increasing num-bers and the *Produit d'Or Blanc* was hoisted by giant nets and dropped into gaping holds. I could continue to look while enjoy-ing a cool *citron pressé* at the Hotel Majestic Terrace.

There were no piers along the river edge. Ships chugged up the caducean waterway from the South China Sea and pulled in flat against the dock. You could throw an apple from the *ter-rasse* where I was sitting to the nearest deck. I contemplated the Norwegian freighter that was unloading food delicacies and luxury items, earmarked for embassies and restaurants.

I watched for an hour as the boxes pyramided higher and fading daylight gradually clouded the Hong Kong department store label and the stenciled identity of contents—*pâté de fois gras,* caviar, chutney, Pernod, Black and White Scotch, Kleenex, Revlon, mango jam and Lyons coffee.

Strolling over to where the longshoremen were grunting and gabbling, I was propositioned by a fourteen-year-old girl in a too-tight cotton sweater who was leaning against the boxes and scratching herself shamelessly. I brushed her aside and flashed my wallet spuriously to the Vietnamese laborers. They took me for an inspector.

When a fleet of coughing, stubby-nosed trucks wound away from the docks with the merchandise, I followed in a three-wheeled, coolie-driven *cyclo.*

All it cost was the rental of the trucks and generous tipping all around—the rest of the piasters Mossard had given me. Two days later, the booming Bon Marche de Saigon in the native quarter was teeming with glum, well-dressed customers. Even the empty boxes went for a price. I cleared twenty-five thousand dollars in local currency and stuffed it in the *toile à matelas* on my bed at the Villa d'Or Blanc.

I came to know Lien-Fat well. If the huge bulk of the Chinese were squeezed in a wine press, not even the scent of sympathy would have exuded. To the world of white and yellow alike, through his business lenses, he was as ruthless as the marbles of his abacus. But he was fair—even with a sense of humor. One day I heard him speaking faultless French and accused him of hiding his linquistic ability from Mossard.

"Boss Mossard no worry about me," he replied with twinkling eyes, "when I speak like schoolboy with slate."

"And your English?" I insisted, referring to the present conversation.

"English really no good," he grunted and refused to discuss it further.

The *compradore,* that peculiar oriental middleman, I found to be the backbone of every colonialist enterprise from Hong Kong to Rangoon, from Vientiane to Djakarta. It was an envied state of rank, filled for the most part by Chinese of mentality, contacts and reputation. Some of them became richer than the boss.

Lien-Fat was unquestionably the Number Two man in power on D'Or Blanc. To him fell the exacting chores of exporting, importing, warehousing, labor, administration, books, pay and logistic support for the plantation itself. There were two French "overseers" at the Villa—but they were seldom on duty. One liked to hunt; the other liked women. They signed reports.

There was nothing in Viet Nam or in the competing rubber areas of Thailand, Indonesia and Malaya that the *compradore* did not know. The world market was his game of mah-jong and he played to win. When the equatorial plantations burst at the seams with latex, he stored. When the price barometer rose, he summoned ships from the Indian Ocean, the South

Pacific and both China seas within a few days' notice. Cables to Paris, London and New York stacked high on his desk. Lien-Fat accounted for some of the reputation of D'Or Blanc rubber. It always sold higher. He was a ten-percenter on sales. From what I could gather, the company had averaged at least a million dollars annually since 1946.

Also, there was little in Saigon that escaped his ears. The day after the Hong Kong shipment scandal, he called me to his office and commented, "Some American make lots money on food bundles. Not you?"

"Of course not," I answered innocently.

"Then somebody make present of money to you in bed. That very careless thing. I move to safe."

I smiled at him.

"Is best you send America," he continued blandly, "before Mossard make inventory. I say nothing this time because I buy lipsticks and soft papers for young daughter."

"One of these days, I am going to buy you," I said.

He squinted at me with superiority. "I have son in Harvard. Also son in Sorbonne. Older daughter at Vassar. Have married children also in big estates Singapore and Hong Kong. All must have new car every year with top down and many spending money. I very poor man. Work very hard in Saigon. You find oil in Texas. Okay. I come work for you. But, now you in Saigon. Work for me. Too bad. How many men you find now for Mossard army?"

"Out of those scrounges? Not one can lift a gun, much less carry it. They are half-starved."

"That your excuse for several weeks. No rice bowl for flee-ing ones, Mr. King. But muscle grow. I hear port hire many for strong loading. Why you not on ball with hire first?"

"They are not ready."

"Hah!" he scoffed. "You like work sitting on big bottom. Go talk to new dockmen. Port pay very bad. Must gamble with one, two piasters. Can buy only blackest Cambodian woman. You find and play big sport."

He lent emphasis to his seriousness with a fat forefinger jabbing in my direction.

"First, you take to den and offer opium pipe. But, if smoke, leave sleeping and get new applicant. Very important this. No want opium men for army. If no smoke, then take to expensive Palace of Mirrors or House of Five Hundred Girls. If still no want to sign contract, you give drink plenty until hand limber. Then, you make signature mark. I arrange pick up fatigued one, and we send to plantation."

"I could get into trouble," I said cautiously.

"No trouble. I fix with police. If after sign, dockman no want leave Saigon, police put in jail. Stay in jail many long time. Break contract very big offense."

"What about money?"

"You no worry for money," he said smoothly. "I make credit in girl houses."

"Tell me, Lien-Fat, who gets the jack pot from these parish houses?"

He bit rubbery knuckles, contemplating me, and answered, "Binh Xuyen Sect own all five … and police too."

"Who is the boss?"

His eyes were expressionless when he asked, "You like work for D'Or Blanc or Binh Xuyen?"

"D'Or Blanc, of course."

"Okay … then, Mossard your boss. Never mind. That all you need to know."

My talk with Lien-Fat was a good warning. Saigon was a city of informers. Any plans I made would have to be with the utmost secrecy.

Of all the *maisons de joie* that I came to know in the next few weeks, the one that best justified the investment was the House of the Five Hundred Girls. Located by accident or intent near a hospital in the French Quarter, it catered to the imaginative. The girls were carefully classified as advertised. Tonkinese, Annamite, Cochin, Radais, Cantonese, Shanghaiese, Pekinese, White Russian, Cambodian, Laotian, Siamese, Indian, Malayan, Indonesian, Egyptian, Algerian, Filipino, Japanese, English, Polynesian, French, and French-matisse vied with other female oddments of mixture, size, abilities or zest. The house's reputation was supreme throughout the Orient, and not one of my clients could resist. Night after night, as I collected signatures, I watched the production line. The French customers usually chose the dark fluid races, the Sengalese took to the English, the Germans to the White Russians, the Vietnamese to the French, the Chinese to the Japanese, and the Americans to the Chinese.

My own wide-eyed protégés asked for their own kind—the Tonkinese and the Annamite.

I became known in the demimonde of Saigon as "the Shanghai American" after the oriental manner of bestowing identification. The title served to make my recruiting even more difficult.

The musk-drenched, sloe-eyed beauties did not fan my passions. Nor did the pinch-waisted, round-hipped French mademoiselles who had the knack for making clothes look more naked than skin. I was slowly building my *gendarmerie*. Thanks to the port's preconditioning, the choice was good—if restricted. The refugees continued to flood in, but they were even more emanciated than before—some of them had been maimed by the Communists.

After a while, entering the various factories of depravity became as functional as punching a time clock. Vice in Saigon was what conventions are to Chicago, tourists to Paris. From sundown to sundown, the Binh Xuyen methodically crunched out a million-dollar gross in prostitution, opium, gambling, alcohol and assorted business deals. The sect not only owned the police but the port and five thousand army troops to protect its grasp on the city.

Ngo-dinh-Diem made a speech about cleaning up the "Four Vices." With rumors that the Riviera-dwelling Emperor, Bao-Dai, was getting a cut of the million dollars a day, rue Catinat—the gossip street—gave odds that the Premier would be fired by the end of the year.

I took a selfish interest in the political developments.

The South Viet Nam government army was rife with jealously and poor discipline and feeble without customary French leadership. Any two of the sect armies could have ripped it apart but nobody made a move. The Binh Xuyen, considered pro-French, was said to be waiting for the downfall of Ngo-dinh-Diem. The Hoa-Hao was leaning toward Ho-Chi-Minh, while the Cao-Dai's Pope was rumored to be debating the best offer. There were no overt moves for power but the intrigue marts were bustling. Russian and Red Chinese agents were in evidence.

The United States, under the Geneva terms, sent in a few officers and enlisted men to train the appalling government forces. American equipment began to arrive.

Ho-Chi-Minh in the North, the newspapers reported, had consolidated the area above the seventeenth parallel and was massing troops along the border, supported by Red Chinese "volunteers."

The Communist Pathet-Lao, presumably neutralized at Geneva, was poised in Laos at the Thai border—still under Ho's orders.

Indochina was a battleground before dawn; Saigon the pressure head; rue Catinat the tinderbox. One well-placed grenade could have started World War III.

The French Legion began to pull out.

The U. S. military advisors sweated with the sullen Vietnamese in the only army that was considered official. Equipment rusted in the abnormal humidity or disappeared in the black market. Tanks decayed or were disabled by unsure hands. The United States desperately rushed in more arms. Rue Catinat predicted that the army would desert the government, sides would be taken, and the war started.

Ngo-dinh-Diem took to the road in tireless rallies, pleading with the armed camps to stand by him.

Seemingly, the only effective moving thing in the country was D'Or Blanc plantation. As black as the docks were with discharging refugees and American armament, they were blacker still with bales of rubber.

My plan began to jell.

Fifteen thousand workers on D'Or Blanc, plus their families, could build an army—primitive and unwieldy, but an army nonetheless and a balance of power. Such a force could break the deadlock. I could name my price in the fantastic stakes for Indochina. If there were time.

The day came that I had been waiting for. It was a rare crisp sunlit day in November that made one think of Paris.

General Nguyen-van-Hinh balked at taking orders from the Vietnamese Premier. The world held its breath.

The American Ambassador called a press conference. "United States arms and aid," he said, "will only support the legal government and its nominal head, Ngo-dinh-Diem."

Yellow and scarlet striped flags waved from army camps. Pictures of Premier Diem were hoisted everywhere. The troops shouted feverishly, *"Muon Nam Ngo-dinh-Diem!"* (Ten thousand years for Ngo-dinh-Diem) General Nguyen-van-Hinh fled to Paris.

The Americans at the Embassy on Boulevard de la Somme unpacked their bags and put their shirts back in the drawers. I rented a room at the Majestic Hotel, signing the name of Hans Rausch. I bought a one-way ticket to Paris under the same alias, and waited until the neon brilliance of rue Gallieni outshone the moon on Sin Street. Then, taking a pedicab *pousse-pousse,* I

directed my driver to the heart of the Binh Xuyen enterprises—
the dazzling block-long showcase of iniquity called the Grand
Monde.

"The Great Big Wonderful World," as the name was translated, was just that to all people of all yearnings of all means.
Walking down the cobblestoned alley to a side entrance, I passed
the huge circular dance pavilion where the cream of Viet Nam's
femininity was gathering provocatively, and entered the gambling casino.

There were rooms with games for all classes of people. One
piaster or fifty thousand could change hands on a single play. It
was still early and I had the roulette table all to myself. I tossed a
one-hundred piaster note on red. Red paid. I tried a block of four.
The ball hung in number thirty-three. I was touching. Two in a
row. I let it all ride on Double Zero. That was the way I was betting. Leisurely, I watched it waver and click—fifty-six thousand
piasters or two thousand U. S. dollars.

"*Qu'est-ce que c'est, monsieur?*" the croupier asked. He was a
young Vietnamese, stocky but graceful, with inky eyes that hid
below sleek hair. A lazy manner disguised alertness. In French,
he asked why I was staring at him. There was something familiar
about him. Excitement mounted as I remembered. The grenade
attempt on Mossard's life had *not* been coincidental.

"What is your name?" I broached casually, folding five hundred and slipping it into his hand.

"Xuan, monsieur."

"Nguyen?"

"*Oui, monsieur. C'est le nom plus populaire du Viet Nam.*"
His French was schooled.

"I know your father quite well. Also your sister."

His smile faded.

"I am afraid you have made a mistake, monsieur. There are
many who have the name Nguyen. It is derived from an ancient
emperor."

"Have you been riding any bicycles lately?"

His eyes sharpened to cast-iron points and became implacable. In a cool voice he said, "You have won three times, monsieur. Your next play?"

"The name Nguyen was plagiarized by most of its owners," I informed him, "when your ancient emperor decreed that all who wished could select his name. Not many can trace the blood honestly. Those who can should be very proud."

I judged his age to be under thirty. Consternation fought with pride, and youth won.

"Yes, I am Nguyen-van-Xuan. What do you want?"

"If your grenade had found its mark last May, you would have been combed out of hiding and executed. So... we have a bond, *n'est-ce pas?*"

"Who are you?" he asked, breathing unevenly.

"The Shanghai American, I am called."

"Ah yes, I have heard. Please, I do not wish to be recruited for the plantation. Go elsewhere."

"I want you to work for me... here."

His face hardened arrogantly. "Never will I work for Mossard."

"I said for me."

He studied me curiously and silently.

"Are you Communist?" he asked finally.

"No." I placed ten thousand piasters in my open hand and studied the bills casually. "Your first month's salary in advance. You may continue to work here, but meet me at the Majestic Terrace tomorrow just after dark. If I am not there, you are ten thousand ahead."

He accepted the bills and cached them deftly in his trousers.

The floor sentinel strolled toward the table.

"I want to see your boss... the head of the casino," I said quietly to Xuan. "You know who I mean."

His eyes glinted with understanding.

"What is the trouble, sir?" the floorman asked suavely.

"Tell him!" I nodded curtly to Xuan, and proceeded to count my winnings.

A volley of singsong bounced over the table, punctuated by nods and gestures.

The floorman studied me somberly. "If you were short-changed, sir, it was the mistake of our croupier and will show up at the end of the evening. Please come with me."

I closed one eye in Xuan's direction. An argument over mis-counting would excite no notice, whereas a sly visit to the back offices would be noted and become common gossip in every teahouse within hours. I knew that croupiers light-fingered the big payoffs whenever they thought they could get away with it. That was their salary.

I refused all refunds from an assortment of assistants until I was ushered to a poster-spattered office of a thin, spec-tacled Vietnamese whose cigarette extended from a solid gold holder. I was beginning to reach the lower echelons of the sect rulers.

The slight man extended his hand.

"Mr. King, I believe. The Shanghai American. We have fol-lowed your career in Saigon with much interest. Your black-handed tactics have caused our port no little discomfiture, but as you represent its biggest customer, we cannot complain. Now to the matter of the ten thousand which you cleverly employed to gain entrance. What is it that you want?"

"I want to see Ly-van-Vien. I hear he is the head of the Binh Xuyen."

"Ah-hah." His face furrowed intently, before emerging from fanged wisps of smoke. "I am afraid that is quite impossible."

"You are not concerned with Diem's coup of the army? He has vowed to crush your 'Four Vices' and now he has strength."

He broke the smoke blandly by waving a slim, manicured hand.

"We are aware of Monsieur Diem's position. Demagogues, emperors, premiers, dictators—call them what you will—all need money for their soft living. We have it. It is as simple as that."

"The United States is backing Diem. You cannot match that."

"Nonsense. The United States will not dredge in Indochina as it did in Korea. It will abide honestly to the international accords. Three hundred-odd military in the country ... pfft!"

It was not going to be easy.

"There are millions of dollars' worth of weapons arriving ...."

"America's gift to us," he interrupted, "*if* we want them. This is our port. We have already modernized our divisions with your newest weapons and have stockpiled more than we shall ever need. Do not forget, Mr. King, Viet Nam is a wheel that revolves around a hub. The hub is Saigon and the Binh Xuyen controls it. We are perfectly aware of what it requires to continue to control it, and we intend to."

"I have a plan that would guarantee it by putting the tappers at D'Or Blanc under arms. I could work it ... if you supplied the weapons."

He waved his hand impatiently.

"Plans ... plans ... plans. Everybody has plans. Every sect. Every general. Every government. Every *fonctionnaire*. Every *pousse* driver. There are too many plans, Mr. King. Consequently ... stalemate. And, that is exactly what we want—stalemate."

"I also have a plan to take Air France tomorrow, now that you have refused my proposal," I said.

"It is worthy of your character." He laughed. "Never fear, your compromise shall be sealed on my lips. You may continue to work for Mossard with ... shall we say ... unswerving loyalty. The Binh Xuyen needs nothing from D'Or Blanc except continuing tolls. But, it is nice to know that we have a friend at court."

He extended his hand through a fog of cigarette smoke.

"I would like to explain this to Ly-van-Vien," I said.

"Bay-Vien grants audience only to those he calls."

The interview was over.

Despondently, I wound through the warren of rooms and alleys to the casino. Walking through, I felt a tap on my shoulder. The floor manager proffered me a wad of bills. bills.

"I am very sorry, sir," he murmured, "it will not happen again."

I slipped the ten thousand into my wallet.

At the hotel, I sat on the terrace watching the silhouette lights of the restless ships and took stock. The Binh Xuyen were as enmeshed in French interests as their own. France would not abide any halt in the rubber pipeline as, indeed, would the United States. I put at six months' maximum the time before the sheer weight of American arms would force a showdown with the sects and with Ho-Chi-Minh. The Binh Xuyen was confident that it could stall. I doubted it. I had too much knowledge of Uncle Sam's military doggedness. My plan of putting D'Or Blanc under arms was a sound investment for the Binh Xuyen. One day they would wish for it, but who was I to convince them?

My thoughts returned to the *gendarmerie*. I had about half the force I needed. Training them under the watchful eyes of Mossard to be capable of matching the Legion would take several months. I had hoped, if the Binh Xuyen bought my plan, to borrow one of their battalions, effect the coup and commence mass training of the tappers.

Now, there was no alternative to the *gendarmerie*. At least, I had Cam's son. That was better than the daughter.

CHAPTER TWO

Mossard had been so pleased with the first Tonkinese I had sent that he ordered Lien-Fat to recruit apprentice tappers from among the refugees. "For a stablizing influence," he wrote. D'Or Blanc was shy nearly fifteen hundred workers due to desertions during the strike and casualties from the Château attack.

Lien-Fat was surprised when I asked to go along on his daily recruiting pilgrimage to the refugee tent camps outside the city.

"They are getting wise to my tricks," I told him. "The bars empty when they see me coming."

"Okay," he answered, "but is same quality like before. Good for walk under rubber trees but not fight. Besides, I get word from Mossard. He think you have enough and is time to train."

"I have half enough."

"How many soldier bodies you find?"

"One hundred and two," I replied, knowing full well he had the exact number.

"Okay. Start begin train one hundred two. I find rest and send."

"All you would pick out are bookkeepers and gold weighers. Never mind. I will get them."

"You find today or not at all," he commanded firmly. "Mossard want you in new fighting sect village."

"Where is that?"

"Song-Be."

I winced. Song-Be was hot, mosquito-ridden, and too far to sleep in the Chateau.

Lien-Fat chuckled with delight. "Now you know how dock-men feel you tap on head with heavy drink!" The rolls of fat jiggled.

I shrugged. "I will find the rest this week from the camps. There may be a few good ones."

His bowling-pin head retrenched into a dozen chins, which I knew foreshadowed a boiling point.

"Okay...okay, today," I said mollifying him. I wondered if he had gotten wind of last night's venture. Probably not. I would not last an hour in Saigon if he had.

The bleak and muddy tent villages were in the suburbs of the city—a sector called Gia-Dinh—on the road to the plantation. These were thrown up roughly when the refugees who had fled communism exceeded all predictions and threatened to burst the city. The refugees were skeletal—many bore marks of torture from Ho-Chi-Minh's fanatics who had tried to turn them back. Stories were rampant in Saigon about Tonkinese huddled in their northern huts, afraid to attempt evacuation under the Geneva terms, or those who had tried it and been shot.

We drove into the camp of human flotsam and found a queue accepting rice doles in outstretched conical hats. While Lien-Fat talked over a loudspeaker mounted to the Citroën and passed around sample contracts, I scanned the group and automatically looked for the ugliest. That usually meant less family complications, and a hard brawling background.

There were several scarred veterans, still in uniform, who regarded me apathetically. I herded them to one side, filled them in with some teen-agers who were not too weak to play quoits, and signaled another twenty whose faces could only please their mothers. It was a puny lot.

"Want good job?" I spoke in simple French.

They all nodded their heads.

"Job fill opium pipes in den. Plenty free."

Five of the group stepped forward eagerly. I kicked them roughly out of the way.

"This very tough job. Maybe fight. Pay plenty good. Two thousand piasters and rice. No wife. No children. But traveling women—not black or Chinese. Beautiful Tonkinese and Annamite. Free every Saturday."

Four more dropped out.

"What wrong with Chinese?" A stumpy, bird-featured candidate, eyes glittering, stepped up to me with his hand edging toward his frayed pocket.

"Good boy!" I said with considerable surprise. The least I had expected to find was temperament. "We bring Chinese girl just for you. You have all to yourself."

He retreated to the line, but his eyes bored me with defiance.

"Twenty-three," I reported to Lien-Fat.

As the shuffled the pile of contracts, I asked, "Who is the angry one over there, second from the left? Says he is Chinese. What is he doing in this litter?"

The fat *compradore* looked up from his papers.

"Ahhh," he said not without pride, "he Nung. Very good Chinese-Vietnamese race from Far North. Nung very big warrior. Everybody much afraid Nung. All the time fight. You on ball today, King. Get many Nungs. Have best army in Viet Nam."

I searched in vain, but there were no more Nungs to be had in any of the camps. By siesta, I had filled out a round hundred, got them onto trucks and off to the plantation.

It would take a minimum of two hundred expertly trained and toughened soldiers, I had figured, to stand up to the Legion with any hope of winning. Perhaps Mossard had thought of that too ... which would explain the hurry-up call. Well, at least I had the bodies despite his possible misgivings. When he saw them, he probably would not grumble too loudly. Today's batch would take some doing to become hard soldiers, capable of forced marches. Either I would have to plan more time—which in view of Diem's coup was out of the question—or revise my striking force drastically downward.

There was one consolation. Song-Be was isolated enough that I was not likely to get constant supervision. An idea began to build.

"If this is my last night in the city," I told Lien-Fat, "I will take that money from the safe."

He waggled his finger at me suggestively. "Better you sleep in Villa tonight. Otherwise money wake up in different pocket."

Cashing in the Air France ticket, I walked to the Majestic Hotel to renew my room for the night.

Charlotte Mossard was standing in the lobby.

"Good God!" I gasped.

She heard me and turned, the green eyes widened with recognition.

"Why, Mr. ... oh yes, Mr. King, that is it, I remember. The American. How did Guillaume know I was coming? I wanted to surprise him."

"He does not ... and you will."

"*Mon Dieu*, it is hot ... no? I had forgotten the heat of the tropics." She pulled a square of lace and chiffon from her purse and dabbed delicately at her throat. A wisp of perfume reminded me of Orly Field.

Charlotte's expensively cut dress and silver hair dominated the lobby. Curious glances were cast in her direction.

"Actually, it is the cool season now. Take off your nylons."

Looking shocked for only a moment, she rebounded gaily. You are right. This is not Paris. Yes, I remember quite well, Mr. King ... Dan ... *n'est-ce pas?*"

I nodded. That voice—the violin strings—touched something deep. She was something. I had forgotten a woman could be like this.

"I arrived early this morning, but I was so tired I went to bed. This charming young man here"—she rewarded the wizened clerk with a lovely smile—"is being most helpful. You see, I am trying to arrange a car to take me to D'Or Blanc."

The clerk interrupted nervously. "*C'est difficile, madame. La route au nord est fermée. C'est la zone militaire.*"

"I had no idea it would be so difficult." She frowned. "I shall have to get in touch with the Villa. I hate being a nuisance. Guillaume will be furious."

"There is no use to contact the Villa," I said. "Lien-Fat would only warn Mossard, and you wanted to catch him unawares ... did you not?"

Patches of scarlet appeared on her softly molded cheeks.

"I do not understand you, Mr. King."

"That letter I was supposed to write and never did."

Tiny wrinkles compressed the skillful make-up around her eyes.

"*Bonne bête,* I *did* confide in you."

Slipping her arm through mine, she said, "There is a bar in the hotel, is there not?"

She ordered Cinzano. I stirred an *orange pressé,* and thought of the sensation her presence would create at D'Or Blanc. My idea fell into place.

When the waiter had marked the *fiche* and left, her aplomb vanished.

"Is there a woman, Dan?"

I surveyed her with cool detachment. "Of course not."

She searched my face. "You are sure?"

"Well, he has made one trip without me to Saigon and Hanoi. But I doubt it was for the purpose of chasing women."

Her relief was apparent. "If he ... I know that men have different instincts than women ... at least, Frenchmen ...." She smiled to cover her embarrassment and hurried on. "If he occasionally ... well, I mean ... that would not worry me. A mistress is something else."

She continued to study me. "I suppose you would be in a position to know?"

"Unless he is hiding one in the *armoire*."

She laughed with sudden release. The tones were silvery and unrestrained—striking that cord within me again.

"Dan, you must think that I am a terribly suspicious wife. Really I am not. It is just that I have so many friends in Paris and they cannot possibly understand our being separated most of the time. It is"—she shifted uncomfortably—"difficult to convince them that I should be faithful."

"I am driving to the Château tomorrow, if you would like to come along."

Charlotte reached across the table impulsively and squeezed my hand.

"How nice of you. I am so anxious to see Guillaume and our Château. That terrible attack"—her hand flew to her cheek—"and that brave, brave Legion. So thrilling, but I was very frightened. I just had to come and face the danger with him."

"The danger, as you call it, will probably come from Mossard himself... for my driving you to the Château."

She gave me her dazzling smile. "I shall tell him that I ordered you to bring me and would not take no for answer."

I pushed back my chair. "Tomorrow, after siesta then. I shall meet you here in the lobby."

"Ah... siesta! I had forgotten." She pouted delightfully. "But, you are going to take me to dinner this evening? There is such a nice little restaurant near here. L'Amiral. Yes, I am sure that is the name. *Cuisine parisienne!* I will just have time to buy some cotton frocks...." Her voice trailed off provocatively.

I was slow in answering. "I have a business engagement. I am sorry, Madame Mossard. I would like nothing better than L'Amiral."

"*Quel dommage. Alors.* I shall dine in the hotel. If you are finished early, telephone my room. Perhaps we can take a cognac at the Pont de Blageurs and watch the little native boats … or go to Gallieni and dance."

The image and echo of her followed me for the rest of the afternoon. It was dusk before I could shake them off. Converting part of my piasters to American dollars, I had to quicken my pace to get back to the hotel in time to meet Xuan.

The Vietnamese youth appeared promptly at six o'clock. Beckoning him with a stealthy glance, I walked with him to the elevator. I called my floor—the second. Xuan immediately bid *quatrième*. Waiting for him to walk down the two flights, I was pleased that he was discreet as well as bright.

Inside my room, I handed him the sheaf of ten-thousand piaster notes—for the second time.

He appeared relieved. "You know Saigon well for an American."

"You want to work for me, I take it, or you would not have come."

"If it is against Mossard, I would work for nothing."

"I am paying."

"Whom do you represent?" he asked cautiously.

"Myself. Dan King. If I make any alliances, that is my business."

Nguyen Xuan's black eyes glinted with disapproval.

"The Binh Xuyen," he said, "are as bad as the French. In fact, most of them are French citizens with big bank accounts in Paris. They do nothing for our people but bleed them."

He regarded me shrewdly and asked, "What do you want from D'Or Blanc?"

"To make you a general."

His face showed amazement, then skepticism.

"I know nothing of military affairs. You are hiding a fish among the rice, monsieur."

"My plan is to arm and train the workers of D'Or Blanc. Naturally, it has to be seized from Mossard and the French forced out. When that is done, you will assume leadership of the plantation army under my direction."

He regarded me solemnly for a long moment and then said reverently, "You are sent by Ho-Chi-Minh."

"I told you I represent myself."

"Are you one of the Americans who support Ngo-dinh-Diem?"

"No."

He shook his head helplessly. "I do not understand."

"You do not have to understand," I said crisply. "I am a *soldat commerçant*—a soldier of fortune. I plan to sell the army's services to the highest bidder. After the fighting, you inherit what is left."

His jet eyes were full of wonder. "I would be a general?" he asked, relishing the word.

"*The* general. One star or five. Take your pick."

"No," he said slowly. "My father would want to be general. I would have to defer to him."

"Do you know where your father is?"

"He is at the graveyard of our earliest ancestors in Cambodia—Angkor Wat. I send him money."

"I thought his children disowned him."

"All did, except me," Xuan said bitterly. "He was a victim of Mossard's clever magic. I was not fooled."

"Even so…the Vietnamese now despise him."

"That is their stupidity. I continue to accord him obedience."

"Forget Cam," I said impatiently. "Is it a deal?"

He studied me meditatively. "You mean that after you receive money, the army and the plantation would be mine—to dispose to Ho-Chi-Minh?"

"Why would you give it to Ho?"

"Because he is the savior of our people."

"Do you believe that?"

Fanatically he answered, "His motto is Viet Nam for the people. Drive out the foreign imperialists."

I laughed. "He did a good job on your people who wanted to come south, didn't he?"

Xuan was silent—then, "That was not Ho—that was the Chinese."

"You mean those foreign imperialists?"

He reddened. "What my father says is so."

"Only a jungle parrot mocks the cries of the sweetest-sounding birds. Surely, Xuan, your head is not that green."

The room was still as he seemed lost in thought.

Finally he stated, "I will work for you, but not for free. For ten thousand piasters each month ... provided I become a general."

Crossing the room, I dug into my luggage and found a razor blade.

"We seal our pact by the rite of blood. You know what that means?"

He nodded warily.

I scratched the vein on my wrist. The circlet of blood puddled and grew. Reluctantly he extended his arm to me. I clipped it lightly with the blade.

"You swear by your ancestors, as we join our blood, that you relinquish all right to join them in eternal peace unless you obey my every word without question and regardless of circumstances until I release you from this pact, or until I am dead; that you will guard my life and honor it as you would your brother; that no other loyalty will interfere with your carrying out my orders."

"Except my father's," he inserted.

"Except your father's," I assented.

"I swear," he said.

Our blood merged. We held the wrists in union for several minutes.

"Second step," I said quietly. "If you are going to be a successful general in this part of the world, you have to be physically tougher than any one of your troops. I want to see how much training you need. Hit me."

He looked at me with puzzlement. I stuck out my chin invitingly.

"Come on."

Xuan swung half-heartedly.

I dodged and with a vicious clout sent him spinning across the room. He came off the floor, charging me angrily.

"Remember your pledge!" I called.

He stopped uncertainly.

I hit him with an uppercut that lifted him inches from the tiled floor.

Struggling to get up, he stared at me with eyes dazed and confused.

"You are not thinking, Xuan. I gave you permission to hit me."

The youngster had courage. Although he was hopelessly outclassed, he staggered to his feet and rushed me. Sidetripping, I flipped him on the bed and ground his arm back from the joint—away from the shoulder.

He threshed about and tore at the bed clothing, but did not utter a sound. I exerted pressure until the arm was at the snapping point. There was no cry. I released him. He sat back, grimacing and massaging his arm.

"Not tough enough," he panted between clenched teeth.

"It is up to you to get that tough."

When his breathing had quieted, I said, "Listen carefully, Xuan. Perhaps I will not see you for a month or longer, but if I send word for you to come to me, come immediately—no matter where I am."

He nodded.

"Here is twenty thousand dollars in piasters. Go now and buy a Red Cross ambulance—painted and licensed—in good running condition. And buy these weapons: twenty-five M-1

Garand rifles with bayonets and ten boxes of ammunition. Make them open each box and fit the clips so you do not get the wrong size ... and fit the bayonets. Then, twenty-five grenade belts, fully loaded, fragmentary type—not plastic, steel."

I waited until I was sure he had committed the order to memory. "Put it all in the back of the ambulance—but save out five rifles, two boxes of ammunition and five belts. Got that?" Again I paused.

"Hide them. I do not care where—someplace here in Saigon where they cannot rust. If I call for you, take the money that is left over, hire four soldiers and equip them and come running. Do not accept French or Chinese weapons. I want American. Lock the back of the ambulance and park it across from the American Embassy on Boulevard de la Somme. Send the keys here to the hotel by a *pousse* driver."

I took a hotel envelope from the desk drawer and scrawled *Hans Rausch—Hotel Majestic* across the front. "Seal it well," I warned him, "and have the keys to me no later than two-thirty tomorrow afternoon."

He repeated the instructions aloud.

Before I went to sleep, I thought of silver hair, violin strings and perfume, and for a moment I was regretful. But only for a moment.

CHAPTER THREE

That Charlotte Mossard's arrival at the Château would create havoc, I had no doubt. The only thing unpredictable was the turn of violence it would produce within her husband. The other reactions I had calculated.

When the ambulance screeched up to the first bunkered check point above Gia-Dinh, and Madame Mossard displayed her credentials, the Legion insisted upon furnishing an escort for the remainder of the trip.

No one bothered to have a look at the back of the ambulance.

We arrived at the jeweled mansion shortly after dark, just at the time I had planned.

The necklace of lights around the swimming pool and the accompanying *bruit de nageurs* assured me that all of the Frenchmen, except the planter, were out of eye's way. The servants, I hoped, would be so busy chattering about Madame's unexpected arrival that they would not notice.

Parking the vehicle close against the cellar casement window by the "welcoming arms" stairs, I walked with Charlotte into the Chateau.

"It is just the same," she exclaimed happily as we entered. "Oh, my beautiful château! Guillaume! Guillaume! Surprise! *C'est moi* ... Charlotte."

I heard the scuffle of footsteps on the *couloir* and the planter came into view. Gripping the banister for support, he turned ashen.

"Mon Dieu," he gasped. *"Mon Dieu. Qu'est-ce que tu as fait?"*

He seemed carved from the same marble as the stairs.

Charlotte ran up some steps and covered his face with kisses.

"I could not stay away from you another minute," she declared.

Mossard held her in his arms. His eyes found mine.

Shrugging, I shook my head significantly.

"You could have advised me, King," he said, "and let me meet her in Saigon."

"Guillaume darling," Charlotte broke in, "do not blame Monsieur King. He was reluctant to bring me, but I insisted. I wanted it to be a ... surprise!" She hugged him tightly.

Circling her waist with his arm, he said swiftly, "Come, my dear, you are fatigued from the long, hot drive. You must lie down."

"Pas de tout," she protested. "I would love a swim."

She gave him a flashing smile and danced up the steps to the *couloir.*

"Wait here, King," the planter ordered, moving after the servant who was carrying Madame's suitcase. "I shall speak to you in a minute."

He accelerated his pace—two steps at a time. It would be considerably longer than a minute, I thought with humor. He had his hands full.

I went quickly to the cellar.

The word of Madame Number One's arrival had spread to the kitchen. Cooks, *garçons* and *boyesses* were huddled in excited knots. They barely noticed me. Removing the key from a nail in the central corridor, I let myself into the storeroom adjacent to the horseshoe stairs. I could see the shadow of the ambulance through the casement. This was the only glassed-in, air-conditioned room in the entire mansion. Bins of perishable foods from France lay in racks along the walls—potatoes, leeks, oranges, onions, apples and grapefruit. The deep shelves offered good camouflage and with the dehumidified atmosphere, the weapons would not rust.

It took me ten minutes to move the armament from the vehicle into the cellar, another twenty to burrow it well at the bottom of the bins. Xuan had bought exactly what was ordered. Just as I was finishing, the shouts and splashes from the pool diminished sharply. Charlotte must have appeared.

Adjusting the window latch so that it appeared to be locked, but could be opened from the outside, I selected an orange. I was peeling it when I rehung the key on the nail and walked to the *Scène de dénouement.*

Mossard sat heavily at a poolside table, watching Charlotte traverse the length of the pool in graceful strokes. Thi-Tuyet was nowhere in sight.

Sectioning the orange and chewing it, I strolled casually to Mossard's table and sat down.

"I thought I told you to wait for me," he snapped.

"I did until I got hungry. What took you so long?"

He grimaced. "You should have sent some word ahead warning me. It was very nearly catastrophic."

"You handled it well, I am sure, as you do all emergencies. Did you take the swizzle stick to Tuyet?"

Charlotte Mossard waved to us gaily from the pool.

The planter's jaw clamped until his lips were parallel with his eyes.

"Charlotte has agreed to live in Saigon ... with occasional trips to the plantation. She will take an apartment in the city. I shall commute on weekends."

"And Tuyet?"

"Will be confined to her apartment at necessary times ... such as now."

I smiled at his discomfiture. I could count on uninterrupted weekends at Song-Be.

Charlotte emerged from the pool encased in a silver lamé suit. Her figure was all that one might expect from the trimmings—*un corps céleste,* as the French put it.

Mossard projected his voice, "Yes, it is much too dangerous for her to live on the plantation. I will not allow it."

"Do you think so, Dan?" she asked, coming up to us.

"Quite dangerous." I tried to keep *double entendre* from entering my voice.

"*Bonne bête,* I shall be so worried while you are here, Guillaume. The papers in Paris frightened me … the stories about the siege of the Château. Thank God for the Legion."

"Amen," I murmured.

Mossard frowned.

She peeled off her swim cap, shaking loose the dulled platinum hair. It matched her suit.

"Truly, I expected to find everything in ruins. But you are such a genius, darling…." She leaned over Mossard, kissing him lightly on the cheek. Smiling she turned to me and said, "He snaps his fingers and … *voilà!* The Château is put back the way it was."

"Yes, we work just like a team here," I said. "Liberty, equality and fraternity."

Mossard grunted.

"That is wonderful," she exclaimed and then squealed, "Oooo! I had forgotten the mosquitoes." She slapped a shapely thigh and wrapped herself tightly in a turquoise terry robe.

Mossard stood up with relief.

"They are bad during the cool season. Time to go in, I say, and dress for dinner."

"You are joining us for dinner?" Charlotte looked at me. "I think not," the planter interrupted curtly. "It has been a long day for Madame Mossard. We shall dine upstairs and retire early."

"Oh, Guillaume, no," Charlotte protested. "I am not at all tired. I want to enjoy our beautiful dining room, our silver, the damask with the lovely candlelight. Please, I want a wonderfully long dinner with very special guests."

Mossard started to walk away.

"Darling," she said, catching up with him and taking his arm, "we owe it to Mr. King. He turned down my invitation last night at L'Amiral ... to finish whatever it was you wanted him to do."

"How many men did you get, King?"

"A hundred more."

"That was not necessary. I do not want such an unwieldy force. However, it can be pared to a more normal size as training progresses. We shall have guests if it pleases you, *chérie*. Eight o'clock, King."

"No, no," Charlotte said. "Nine. I want to wear my new Balmain, and I need very special make-up. Nine o'clock, please, darling?"

Mossard shrugged with resignation.

Charlotte went on, "We shall invite Roland d'Arbre ... the Commandant ... is there anyone else, Guillaume?"

"Charlotte," the planter said heavily, "D'Arbre cannot come ... he is not feeling well."

"Oh? He looked quite well when I saw him standing on the *couloir* next to your office. But, now that I think of it, he did seem terribly grim. No ... having him is not such a good idea. But, the Commandant ... Captain ... what is his name again?"

"DuPont," I said.

"Yes ... Captain DuPont absolutely! That uniform ... perfect! He is so stiff and correct, and such a hero."

Arms linked together, Madame and Monsieur Mossard strolled across the lawn and disappeared into the elegance of the Château.

CHAPTER FOUR

arking the ambulance in the motor pool, I had a chance
to see how Guillaume Mossard had renovated the estate.
Carpets of grass had been resodded, torn buildings replastered.
New white paint glistened everywhere under the arcs of landscaped light. My Legion defense points were still being manned,
overlooking barbed fencing that had been laid new in double
rows.

Roland d'Arbre stood in the *couloir* breezeway, leaning
against the balustrade in front of Thi-Tuyet's apartment.

He whistled. "King."

I stopped.

Walking toward me, he showed only a trace of awkwardness.
"Guillaume says you are to use his quarters"—he leaned close to
me—"in case the little lynx makes too much noise."

I understood. The connecting door.

"He and Madame Mossard have taken your apartment."

"The rubber business is full of surprises, eh, Roland?"

He saw no humor in my statement. "*Pas de trucs,* King. …" A
long, thin knife appeared in his hand. "The door is bolted. Leave
it that way. If she makes noise, let me know."

The blond Frenchman resheathed the knife and turned—
almost with an air of anticipation—back to his vigil.

It was the first time I had seen Guillaume Mossard's bathroom. Foaming pine-scented water streamed out of sterling-
silver taps into basins of carved pink marble. A white marble

bathtub, supported by gilded mermaids, was long and deep enough to swim in.

As I was dressing, an imperious pounding rattled the bolt of the door leading to Tuyet's quarters. The knob twisted violently. Mossard had good reason and foresight to have moved to the other end of the Château.

I rapped on the door severely and the pounding ceased.

Grooming myself in Mossard's floor-length mirror, I noticed with some satisfaction that the facial scars had blanched almost to the color of my tan. The nose was not as grotesque. Tightening my cravat in a final twist, I saw a movement in the glass.

Thi-Tuyet was walking in from the balcony. Dressed for the pool—a flamingo-red bikini blazed in brevity against her skin. Her face was sulky with anger.

"You ...." She pulled up suddenly.

Grasping her wordlessly by the arm, I tugged her behind me and strode outside. A native ironing plank lay across the space separating the railings of the two private balconies.

"What are you doing?" she said. "Why are you here and why am I locked in my room?"

"Because you make too much noise," I answered and pulled her back into the bedroom.

The purple eyes were murderous. "I am the mistress of this plantation, and I shall make all the noise I wish!" She spun a straight-backed chair over on its side with a thump defiantly. "Where is Guillaume?"

This temperament and familiarity with Mossard's name was new.

"He is engaged with more important matters. Meanwhile, he wants you locked up."

"You are lying. He would not treat me this way."

I propelled her to the door.

"Take your hands off me," she fumed.

Holding her forcibly, I got the door unbolted and pushed her through.

"Guillaume!" she screamed.

Gagging her mouth with my hand, I shoved her forward with a hard slap on the bottom. She turned ferociously, biting.

"You rude animal. This is all your doing. I will tell Guillaume."

"Okay," I grunted. "You asked for it."

My knuckles caught her on the chin and she became limp against me. Motionless for a few seconds, she began to breathe heavily. Her hands wound sinuously behind my neck.

"I know what you want, King. Do not hit me again."

The implication, the closeness of her flesh, the wetness and heat of the struggle, fused my senses. She offered no resistance.

Afterwards, we dressed in silence. Finishing quickly, she sat and studied me morosely. "You must never do that again. Never! Or I shall really tell him."

"You brought that on yourself," I answered shortly, "and please tell him, if it will make you feel more chaste. Now, into your room and no nonsense. I shall lock the balcony doors."

"Why, King?" Her voice was plaintive. "He has never treated me this way before."

She would learn soon enough, I thought. Besides, her vanity needed compressing. I wanted to see her crawl.

"Charlotte is here from Paris," I told her.

Tuyet looked as though I had struck her.

"The first wife ... here?" she whispered.

"In my apartment. Mossard gave up his suite here and has moved into the other wing." I goaded her. "Now, *there* is an exquisite woman. If you want to know what makes up love, forget your five essences of joy, and look at Mossard's face."

Tuyet was not crestfallen nor did she appear jealous. Drawing herself up with *hauteur*, she said, "Then, I am not to meet her."

"Judge for yourself."

I finished dressing.

"You are dining with them," she said with realization.

"I am ... and if you try to get out of your apartment, Roland d'Arbre is waiting on the *couloir.* I have an idea he would like nothing better than to make up for some past grievances."

Deep anger shone from the almond eyes.

"She is replacing me."

"What do you expect?" I said, taking her by the arm. "You are only Number Two."

"The second wife is due honor," she said and there was menace in her voice. "To meet the first wife, to always dine with her, and to serve the *patron* in ways that she is unable. Not to be locked as a bird in a basket."

Anger mounting, she went on, "He has not been husband to me since the day of the attack, so it is clear. He will have only the one wife, Madame Charlotte ... and I am to be locked as a woman in the House of Mirrors ... to be taken by you or any to whom he gives the key. But, I shall not! If that is his plan, then I shall go to the mandarins and speak of the regard the French have for the Vietnamese."

She wrenched free of my hold and dashed away from me.

"Tuyet!" I yelled. "Come back here."

I ran after her through Mossard's *grande chambre* in time to see her opening the exit door.

"D'Arbre!" I shouted in a panic.

The door slammed closed as I reached it. Hurling it open, I saw with dread that she had eluded D'Arbre and was racing down the *couloir.*

CHAPTER FIVE

Guillaume Mossard, fussing with a string tie in front of the mirror, looked up startled. Charlotte, sitting before a vanity clad in a frothy, pale-green half-slip, gasped. Thi-Tuyet sped across the room to Charlotte, knelt before her and kissed the foamy lace edging of the slip. Mossard turned as white as his shirt. His tie slid forgotten to the floor.

"King let her out, Guillaume," D'Abre panted, wavering between Tuyet and me.

Mossard's eyes fastened on me, glinting dully. "So...this is your doing," he said.

The sickening waves in my stomach cleared with the cruel jab that stiffened my back. The knife was only poised, but reacting involuntarily, I spun and with my elbow snapped the foreman's wrist. The weapon clattered to the tile, D'Arbre after it frantically.

"Let it go, Roland," Mossard ordered.

Charlotte had slipped into a negligee, her expression frozen in shock.

"Take Tuyet back to her room," Mossard said quietly to the foreman.

After retrieving the knife, D'Arbre stepped forward.

"Stop it...all of you," Charlotte commanded suddenly. She had put her arm protectively around Tuyet's shoulders. "*Bonne bête*. Have you all lost your manners? This child is hurting no one. Can you not see you have frightened her to death?"

Speaking to the Vietnamese girl, she said, "Now, my dear, what is this all about?"

D'Arbre pulled Tuyet roughly from Charlotte's arm.

"Roland!" Charlotte's face was determined. The foreman's hands dropped.

Turning back to Tuyet, Charlotte smiled and said, "This house certainly shows the lack of a woman's influence. Have you come to welcome me, my dear? That is nice and I am appreciative. And, you are so pretty too. I had forgotten how handsome the Vietnamese are."

Looking at Mossard, Charlotte asked, "Is she one of the servants?"

Tuyet raised her eyes and announced, "I am Guillaume's second wife."

"Get her the blazes out of here, D'Arbre!" Mossard shouted.

Charlotte's sympathy vanished. For the first time she seemed to notice Tuyet's maturity—and costume.

Looking at her husband and then me, she demanded, "Who is this woman?"

Mossard sighed. "You heard what she said."

"Wife?" Charlotte's voice was barely audible.

The silence was affirmation.

Tuyet turned a stunned face to Mossard and said, "But she knew of me, Guillaume. You said she approved."

The planter stiffened.

"All right, Charlotte. You know ... accept it."

She stared at him unbelievingly and when her voice came, it was sharp with rising hysteria. "Accept it!" she echoed. "Not another woman as I suspected. Nothing that simple. A wife!"

Incredulous she stared at Tuyet. "And one of these half-naked savages. Have you lost your mind, Guillaume? What have you done?"

"Do not be so ridiculously dramatic, Charlotte. She is not a half-naked savage. She is the daughter of a mandarin. The union was arranged for political purposes. The native rites are not obligatory under French law. The arrangement has absolutely nothing to do with our marriage and our love."

"Love!" she said scathingly. Her tone desecrated the word. " 'My only love' ... 'I resent each day that separates us' ... 'your faithful Guillaume' ... is this the love you wrote of? Well, you are welcome to it. Do not bother to come back for three months of adultery. Stay with your naked wench. I shall make it very easy for you."

The planter's composure gave way. "Charlotte," he said, "what do you think I am doing here ... serving tea and dancing the gavotte? A war is being fought. France is on the verge of losing every scrap of its rubber and a good bit of blood along with it. If I can use this girl to save it, I will and I intend to. I have told you before, Charlotte, that you do not belong on a battlefield. Now that you are here, you will accept the conditions."

"You plan to see me on weekends in Saigon and live here with her? I am a fool, Guillaume, but I am not a *cocotte*."

"I do not live with her."

Tuyet flared. "That is a lie. I have the room next to his, madame."

Charlotte smiled cynically as her gaze slid over the Vietnamese girl. "You dress her in bikinis for political purposes too, I suppose."

Tuyet twined her fingers around Mossard's arm. "I have worked hard to protect the plantation, madame."

Charlotte laughed unevenly. "Yes ... I can imagine that you have."

The planter shook the Vietnamese girl's hand from his arm. "All right," he said, "I am not a saint. I admit that the union has been consummated—if not recently. So ... if it has. In Paris these things are hidden and thought clever. Here they are open and accepted because there is good reason."

Mossard paced back and forth. Softly, he continued, "What is it you came for, Charlotte—to see me or to taunt me?"

"I do not know you," she said.

"Or did you come here looking for means of divorce?"

Charlotte paled. "I came because I love you and I wanted to be with you."

"Then live up to your intentions."

The Frenchwoman regarded her husband with eyes suddenly tired.

"All right, Guillaume, I will believe your motives and forgive your deception, if only for the sake of our marriage. But, you must put her out. She must leave this house immediately."

Thi-Tuyet interrupted coldly. "I will remain as second wife. Send me to my village and I will tell how the *patron* blasphemed our ancestors with bamboo tricks. I will raise my father to the glory of an emperor."

Perspiration broke through Mossard's shirt.

"Charlotte, be reasonable."

She turned and gave him a long look. "No. I will not share you. I would rather give up everything … and my everything has been you."

Face hard, Tuyet said, "Madame talks like a mouse in a bag of stale rice. Let her go, Guillaume. I will be Number One."

He brushed her aside with irritation.

"Well, Guillaume … ?" Charlotte prodded softly.

The planter's voice was hollow.

"I have explained to you, Charlotte. There are reasons why I cannot send her away."

The Frenchwoman stared at him, her face becoming whiter.

"Please order a car for me to …" and she toppled into a heap on the floor.

Mossard sprang to her side and knelt to hold her tenderly.

Looking up at me he said, "The pieces have fallen together, King—your actions and Tuyet's. Your unreasoning pursuit and now, involvement in this scabrous affair go far beyond consideration of amusement. It is fortunate I awakened before entrusting you with the *gendarmerie.*"

His look at me was venomous. "King," he said, "your contract is terminated now ... without pay. Get off the plantation and out of Viet Nam. If you ever return, I shall hunt you down and kill you."

He turned to D'Arbre, who had been standing by stunned at the turn of events.

"See that he reaches Saigon tonight and is guarded ... until he is on the plane for Paris. Arrange his ticket."

Turning, he snapped, "Tuyet, find the nurse."

Triumph sparkled in the Vietnamese girl's demeanor.

She said to Mossard, "Now that I am Number One, I shall serve you even better."

His hand cracked across her face viciously and she staggered back in pain and surprise. The wall caught her short.

"I told you to get the nurse."

Guillaume Mossard lifted his unconscious wife gently and carried her in his arms to his own suite.

CHAPTER SIX

The next morning when I should have been picking my way over mud slabs to Song-Be, I was sitting in the front-row window seat of a Constellation, winging across Cambodia toward Paris.

When the silver luxury bird landed on the vast cement pasturage of Donmuang Airport in Bangkok, I was the first passenger off. With no little difficulty, I persuaded Air France to refund the remainder of the fare, then bought a one-way ticket on a local flight back to Phnom Penh, and exchanged the thick wad of Siamese baht for Indochinese piasters.

The muddy capital of Cambodia, which mushrooms on stilts along the banks of the Mekong River, was as far as I dared fly. I could not risk Mossard's revenge by being fool-hardly. To arouse the least notice, it was best to go by boat, down the interweaving channels of the Mekong and up the Saigon River to the capital of South Viet Nam. I haggled for an hour, buying a patched-up junk with a two-cylinder Renault CV motor. The deal was settled when I tossed my last piaster on the pile—the Chinese fisherman instinctively knew it.

Two days later, the sluggish stream discharged me into the South China Sea. Heeling the sails clumsily, I applied a well-directed boot to the ancient engine and cut sharp to port. The Mekong and Saigon rivers poured out here in yellow convergence and the sea was rough. The junk pitched, groaned and threatened to burst its ribs. Finally, it slapped clean against the water. Cap St. Jacques hove into view far to the right.

I sputtered into the swampy coils of the Saigon River. This was the home of the Binh Xuyen pirates, some of whom were not so sophisticated as their syndicated brothers in the city. I choked the motor and lay under bamboo rushes until dark.

It was not yet midnight when the lights of the city lit the horizon. I was trying to identify the various docks in order to enter the canal of the Arroyo Chinois when a motor launch purred across the bow. In the dim light, I could see green-bereted sailors—a mark of the Binh Xuyen navy. An automatic fifty-caliber gun mounted on the foredeck fired rapidly. I saw tracers arc in on the port area below the tall Majestic Hotel. A machine gun answered and the fleet launch spun in a wide circle, discharged again, and roared back down the river.

Puzzled, I scratched my new growth of beard. I could not understand the Binh Xuyen firing on its own port. There must have been combat in the city. Finally recognizing the Arroyo bridge near the American Embassy, I drifted under it, and in a matter of minutes was lost in the infinite flotsam of *jonques,* sampans and *paillottes* slewed along the banks. Minutes after I tied onto the Floating City, I got the answer.

Ngo-dinh-Diem's newly loyalized National Army had seized the port from the sect lords. A state of undeclared war existed.

Would Dan King be more welcome now in the top vice councils? Smiling grimly to myself, I suspected that he would.

My neighbors in the watery village, waking early with the heat of the sun, regarded me with lackadaisical interest. I noticed a slim teen-aged girl on an adjoining boat brushing her teeth in the river water.

Using basically simple French that most natives understood, I called, "Is war in whole city, or only in port?"

She gave me a blank look and called her father from the bowels of the thatched scow.

"Feathered Frenchman arrive in dark of night," she explained in singsong French to the wizened face that appeared. "Ask questions beyond my knowledge."

I tried to be casual.

"I come from earliest puddles of mighty Mekong. Hear much wealth of Saigon. High pay for strong backs in rubber gardens. Heard of New Moon Diem, but not of new war. What is thy opinion, Respected One?"

The spiny, betel-toothed Vietnamese coughed laboriously, but appeared pleased.

"The New Moon Diem shines angrily upon the noisy abacus of the Binh Xuyen, hoping to inflict sunstroke. But the moon is not the sun."

"Then he does not roar in steel dragons through the streets?"

"Only at the mouth which feeds from foreign food."

He was referring to the port.

"Does he seize upon the lumps of rubber there to enrich his coffers?"

The old Vietnamese squeezed a lime into a piece of betel leaf, inserted a small black aracas nodule, and gummed the package avidly. Emitting a crimson squirt over the stern, he replied, "Eight tides have passed since the great thunder of foreign firecrackers. The lumps of rubber continue to disappear in the bellies of ships."

"Thank you, Father. May your ancestors accord you special privileges today for your kindness."

Ebony teeth glinted and the warped face screwed thoughtfully.

"Will you stay in our garden of waters?" he asked.

I nodded.

"You may cross our plank bridge, if you like."

"Thank you."

His mouth became a raven crescent.

"May I offer the perfumed coolness of my daughter. She is not yet fifteen, but wise in the ways of the blanket. I am sure she will please you with vigor and adoration."

"I am sorry, Generous One, but I have no money for the prickles of flesh."

"She is not expensive," he pleaded. "Cheaper than the houses. Fifty piasters?"

I shook my head.

"Thirty? She has a mirror and can buy opium if you like."

The eager face of the girl became sullenly blank.

"He does not find me charming, Father."

I bowed graciously across the yard of water.

"My dear," I said, "you are a lotus bud transplanted. Not only am I honored at your father's words, but my skin crawls deliciously at the thought of such a flower. But, I have traveled far and without the luxury of piasters."

The girl grinned widely, and pushed thin breasts into prominence.

"Please, Father," she coaxed.

The old man sighed and broke into a spasm of coughing. He composed himself and growled ruefully, "It is the modern times we live in. She desires a child of whiter skin. Very well. You may take her as you will."

He coughed and spat in disgust.

"Only when I have the piasters to enshrine the feet of such a delectable banquet, will I accept your offer. Until then, I shall fret uncomfortably in my sleep, or leap into the river to cool my fire. Thank you, but one does not steal incense from the community altar."

They were both pleased and smiling.

By noon, the word had seeped along the necklace of rocking boats. I was joined to the Floating Village without question. The Shanghai American had become the Feathered Frenchman.

CHAPTER SEVEN

Christmas 1954 in Saigon, Viet Nam, would have passed unnoticed if I had not been walking along rue Gallieni the night before and heard "Rudolph, the Red-Nosed Reindeer" being slaughtered unmercifully by a Filipino band at the Hoc-Sinh dance hall. Two G.I.s burst out the door and brushed past me.

"What day is this?" I asked abruptly.

They stopped in surprise.

"Why, it is Christmas Eve ... dad. Time to make merry. And, that's just what we're out to do ... if we can find one by that name."

The other one guffawed.

"Whatta town," he drooled. "And to think we're working our balls off to stop all this!"

"Christmas Eve?" I said distantly. "I'll be damned."

"Hey, Mac, you parley pretty damned good English for a frog—I mean Frenchman—no offense."

I grinned at both of them.

"I worked a while for the American Army in Europe."

"No kiddin' ... you did? See, Max, I told you there was some good frogs in this town."

The other G.I. grumbled, "I don't believe it ... I sure as hell didn't see none in France."

"Aw ... listen, this guy's okay. You heard him say he worked with the old brown bag in Europe. Where were you stationed, Mac?"

"I was at Grafenwehr for a while," I said, enjoying the unexpected vignette. "Working with the Big Red One, the Fourth, and Second Armored."

"See?" The larger of the two was vindicated. "He ain't no Communist spy. Well, what d'ya say, Mac? Wanna ball it with us?"

"No, thanks, fellows. I have work to do."

Both looked disappointed. "Sure you won't change your mind?"

"No. But take my advice. Watch your wallets and stay on the main street. If you decide you need a church, there is one two blocks down."

They shifted uncomfortably. "Thanks."

Milling into the crowd, they were quickly lost in the sea of trotting coolies, clawing prostitutes and skeletal drug-bedazed opium men.

I bent my steps in high good humor toward the weather-beaten godown that Xuan had rented on the navigable Arroyo Chinois.

Two flickering bulbs hung from the ceiling of the rotting warehouse and furnished all the light that was to be had. The floor was a field of musty excelsior, browned with age, that rustled incessantly with rats. Dust flew in a cloud as I slammed the sliding door shut. It was insufferably hot.

Xuan walked toward me out of the shadows.

"Did you get the cargo?" I asked.

"Twenty of them," he answered lazily. "All paid for. Their fathers were very glad to receive U. S. money."

I turned to examine the half-nude Nungs clustered against the wall. As I did, Xuan brushed against me, whirled my arm into a whip, and sent me spinning into a crumpled heap.

"I caught you off guard," he said gleefully. "I am studying with a Japanese teacher. Japanese judo is better than American."

I picked myself up carefully. The arm was wrenched but not sprained. "Very good," I commended. "You are an apt student. Did you work your judo on these Nungs?"

He nodded happily. "They would not fight under a Vietnamese until I proved that I was superior."

I looked over the assortment of flesh. The Nungs glared back with hostility.

"On your feet!" I ordered.

None of them moved.

"Where are the weapons?" I asked Xuan.

"Under the planking."

"In oilcloth?"

"Of course. I know that they must not rust."

I stomped on his instep and, as he doubled from the pain, elbowed the pit of his stomach. Timing the involuntary jackknife, I brought my knee up crushingly against his chin. Xuan wavered for a second, blood spurting from his mouth, before toppling helplessly in the straw. He tried to get up and could not.

Dusting my hands, I walked to the score of recruits.

"Up," I ordered, "and get into line."

Wordlessly, they tumbled into a rank. Gone were the traces of enmity. Their eyes burned straight ahead with a rigidity of discipline that would have brought a smile to General George Patton. I slapped their thighs and biceps. There was not a pound of fat in the lot.

I helped the Vietnamese lad up from the floor.

"You have not lost face," I assured him. "They still respect you, but they respect me more. And, until you learn enough to be a general, it is going to stay that way. Now, order the floor swept and distribute the arms. Tonight, we disassemble and assemble M-1s until these Nungs can do it in their sleep."

"But I have gotten the excelsior bags for the bayonet practice."

"The baby crawls before he walks," I snapped. "I want that gun to be like a third arm. When they can strip it with the lights off, we will proceed but not to bayonets. That comes last."

Xuan sopped his mouth with a handkerchief.

"I cannot face them," he said numbly.

"Try it. There is not one of them that could have taken that smash and stood tall a minute later to snap our orders. You are tough. Now prove it."

Trying to smile, but his lips fluttering uncontrollably, he said, "I think we will win," and walked to the line of men. His voice lashed and they scurried.

That is when I noticed the intruder in the godown. Nguyen Cam stood in the dusk of one corner, arms folded. Struts of braided hair fell down his back. He wore a loose, kneelength loincloth after the fashion of Lao mountaineers. Sprouts from his nose covered the telltale scar.

"What are you doing here?" I said striding to him.

"My son called me from Angkor Wat. The great faces in the stone whispered that I should obey."

"What do you want?"

"These men need political inspiration," he said. "I shall give it to them."

"Not to these men."

With an evil smile, he said, "By creating a vision, false though it may be, one may command without fear."

"Spoken like a true son of Mao Tse-tung."

He lifted his eyebrows.

"Communism, as one of the methods of spiritual control, has proved its effectiveness in Viet Nam. Whatever be its fascination, I shall not question it, only put it into practice."

"General Xuan," I called.

Cam's son marched to us and saluted.

"Why is your father here?"

The boy met my condemnation with spirit. "Loyalty to my father is outside of our blood bond. With my great responsibility, I shall need his advice."

"He wants to indoctrinate the men with communism. Do you concur in this waste of time?"

Xuan glanced impatiently at his father.

"It would be unnecessary," the mandarin grumbled, "if you had enlisted trustworthy Vietnamese. But, these Nungs—these Chinese..."

"They are part Vietnamese," the young general said haughtily, "and the best fighters in Indochina. I can vouch for that. I myself went to Phan-Thiet where I know there was a colony. To recruit them, I had to wrestle and win respect from each one of them."

"With experience, they will grow dangerous," Cam warned. "They are twenty against one. You will not be able to handle them."

The boy flushed. "I am the son of Nguyen Cam. I am accustomed to odds. Unless you order it otherwise, Father, I shall train them first as soldiers."

The tall Vietnamese mandarin bowed.

My annoyance at the appearance of Cam began to fade. Although he was of no present use, the Vietnamese tappers would accept him without question if he were installed as the new leader by a *coup d'état*—more importantly so would the National Government. Many of the former Vietminh leaders had changed allegiance in public ceremony from Ho Chi Minh to Ngo-dinh-Diem. Reprisals would be unlikely if Nguyen Cam were the figurehead for a "nationalization" movement—if he could be controlled.

"Let us settle one thing," I said to Cam. "Your advice is not welcome and if you stay here, you do so under my orders. There is a parable that perhaps will make it clearer. 'A cowering cobra does not lose its head.' "

"The affectionate tiger has killed its cub," he said and retreated to his corner.

It was well after midnight when I trudged down the narrow alleyway to the neon brashness of rue Gallieni. The Nungs were showing more promise than I dared expect. They not only had mastered stripping in darkness, but could put the parts back together again. As I left, they were slapping the Garands affectionately and studying the pieces with undisguised interest.

The Nungs were not to leave the godown. They were to eat and sleep on the job—drill an eighteen-hour day. In two more weeks at this pace, I thought optimistically, they could master target sighting, windage exercises, camouflage, crawling, bayonet drills, grenade practice—perhaps even squad exercises.

Sin Street had died in turmoil with the action moving inside. The only signs of the undeclared and still unresolved war were the Binh Xuyen police cars that zipped occasionally along the broad boulevard.

Diem had not moved as he had threatened against the vice halls, but in my book of strategy, it was only a matter of time. It should be clear now ... even to the sect lords. They should be ripe for my offer. I wanted them good and ripe.

As I walked down Gallieni past the Dai-Nam cinema and the Hoc-Sinh dance hall, two soldiers disgorged from *cyclo-pousses* at the curb ... each wrapped in a curvaceous taxi girl. I recognized my two G.I. acquaintances of early in the evening.

"If you haven't lost your wallets by now," I shouted, "You're about to!"

They were thunderstruck.

"Good God!" said one. "It's the missionary."

"Missionary," I echoed. "Me?"

"You aren't a sidewalk Jesus?" the one called Max demanded.

"Come on, big G.I. boy, we dance," the taxi girl chanted, wriggling provocatively in what she imagined to be a jitterbug step. I recognized her as a queen from the Palace of Mirrors.

"In a minute, honey. This here is an ole friend of mine. Well, what d'ya know? We thought … well, you said something about church."

The grumpy one had oiled up considerably in the passing hours. "Hey, it's Christmas Day, Frenchy. You gotta have a drink with your ole buddies. One little ole drink for Santy Claus!"

"American Aid for the clip joints," sang the other. "That's us!"

Feeling secure in the disguise of my beard, I let myself be herded between them to the boisterous lantern-lit interior of the cabaret. I could use some relaxation.

"Rudolph! Where the hell is Rudolph?" the tall one bellowed at the band leader. The slick-suited Filipino smiled suavely, cut the tango, and broke into "Jingle Bells."

"Hey, man … that's it!" Max yelped, closing his eyes. "And lookit what filled my stocking!" He pinched his girl's bottom.

"We dance now, huh baby?" The queen squirmed happily in his lap.

I smelled perfume that reminded me of Orly Field and the Majestic Bar. The platinum-haired waitress serving our table, in the dim light looked like Charlotte Mossard. I scraped back my chair.

"Daniel King," she said, after staring at me intently. Her surprise lacked spirit.

I could hardly believe it was her. "What are you doing here?" I asked.

She continued lifting glasses off the tray and placing them on the table. "What you see."

"Does Mossard know this?"

She shook her head. "I had a month in Paris to think. I could not divorce him, so I came back."

"You could buy this place. Why are you waiting tables?"

She marked the *fiche.* "It is an honest living. The tips are not much, but I am learning what life is like. Perhaps, that is what I need."

One of the G.I.s shouted from the dance floor, "Hey, Frenchy, you wanna swap?"

I ignored his remark.

Max came back to the table, looked Charlotte over, put an arm around her waist and said with a leer, "I dig these madamoiselles. Whatta ya say, baby, you wanna dance?"

Charlotte slipped away from him. I stood up.

"Keep your hands on that slob you're with, Buster." Cold fury filled me.

"He meant no harm, Daniel," Charlotte protested.

"Come on." I took her arm. "We need fresh air."

"I cannot leave yet," she said. "I must work until six o'clock."

"You just resigned." I steered her through the tables.

"Dan, let me go," she pleaded.

"Keep walking." I put pressure on her arm.

A voice drifted over the titillation. "See? What did I tell ya about them frogs … mean as hell, all of 'em. Lemme tell ya about one time in Orleans … man …."

Silently we left the café and crossed the deserted street in the direction of the French Quarter.

Charlotte stopped and said angrily, "If you will please let go of my arm now, I must go back."

"You can learn about life later. The tips at that club depend on the service."

Her eyes under the neat bang of silver were level. "I can take care of myself."

"Not when the Binh Xuyen shops you can't."

"I do not know what you are talking about."

"Did you see that Corsican sitting near the entrance?"

"Yes. He is very nice," she answered tartly. "He offered to take me home last night."

"Home is a room with no windows and a shot of aphrodisiac."

Charlotte recoiled in horror.

"And," I went on, "when he gets through with you, any profession would be a step up."

Her hand, catching mine, was trembling.

"This is not Paris, Charlotte. If you want to play at life, find a French firm with hours from nine to six."

"I had thought of that," she said in a subdued voice, "but I was afraid Guillaume would hear I was back."

"So ... if he did?"

"I do not want to see him."

We had started to walk again slowly up Boulevard Bonard.

She said, "I will look for another job, Daniel."

"Good."

Her hand slipped away. "I owe you an apology. I was the cause of your being let go."

"Not only let go, but deprived of pay, taken under armed guard to the Paris plane, and threatened with death if I ever came back."

She was shocked. "*Fichtre!* That girl has driven Guillaume insane." The bitterness shaded into surprise. "What are you doing here then?"

"Same as you—job hunting."

"That beard will not help you, if he sees you."

"I do not plan to go calling on him."

We walked for a block in silence.

The rich flamboyance and exaggerated naïveté that had been the aura of Charlotte were gone.

"Tell me, why did you come back?" I asked her. "To wait for him to change his mind?"

Her lips tightened. "My friends in Paris ... somehow they heard. It was impossible."

"You could have divorced him."

"I would not subject Guillaume to public ridicule. He is a national hero in France."

We reached rue Catinat and paused. Except for an occasional bistro, the French Quarter was asleep. Carbine-equipped policemen stood at the intersection, alert under green berets. Binh Xuyen.

"But, I had my day," she said, acid in her voice. "I told them I was closing my affairs to return to D'Or Blanc permanently. You should have seen them flock to the plane!"

I took her shoulders gently. "You are in the wrong part of the world, Charlotte, to start learning how the other half lives. If you feel you have been on a pedestal too long...step off. It might do you good. But not here. Out here, the pedestal falls on top of you. Take my advice and buy a oneway ticket...if not to Paris...somewhere."

I was surprised at my vehemence.

Shaking her head stubbornly, she stared up and down Catinat.

"We have walked almost to L'Amiral. I wonder if it is still open?"

"You have expensive tastes for a working girl," I said teasing her.

"I have my tips, monsieur, and if you have some piasters, perhaps we could buy a bottle of champagne."

I hesitated.

"It is Christmas, Dan."

Under the soft glow of the street lamp, I could see a tear glisten on her cheek and fall.

"All right. Champagne and dinner," I agreed. "It's just happens that Santa Claus left me some dollars."

L'Amiral was on the point of closing, but a folded greenback turned on the lights, started recorded French carols, and put a stiff-starched false front back on the sleepy *garçon*.

"Just as it was ... *adorable!*" The sudden music in Charlotte's voice startled me. Spinning a pirouette to the lively shepherd's carol, she slid into the chair held for her.

"*Bonne bête,*" she said breathlessly, "what a nice Christmas after all!"

She surveyed the restaurant with childish pleasure. "Look." She pointed to the tinseled streamers and clusters of bells that hung between each table.

"Order me champagne, Daniel ... lots of champagne." She sang along with the record until it finished.

Retrieving the cork of the Pommery 1947, I spun it on the table top. We watched entranced. Stopping, it pointed to her.

"*L'amour et la chance,*" I said.

The crystal tones of her laughter struck deep within me.

Seizing the cork, she spun it several times until it pointed at me and she said, "Love and luck for you too."

I sipped the topaz bubbles. She drank.

"More music," she called, her breath quick from the champagne.

"Somebody should invent a new meaning," I said, slowly turning my glass.

"Ah, no. There is always luck and love."

"The *garçon* loves us," I said. "Silent Night" began to play.

"And we love him ... *ici, garçon!*" she called.

The waiter came hurrying from the phonograph.

"*Oui, madame?*" He bowed.

From her pocket, Charlotte extracted a wad of crumpled piasters and pressed them into his hand. "*Joyeux Noël!*" She smiled.

"*Merci, madame. Merci beaucoup. Vous-mêmes. Joyeux Noël!*" Beaming, he polished the bottle of Pommery until it sparkled.

We toasted our separate luck, my beard, her pedestal—and finally the empty bottle.

The thought of the training schedule for the morning sobered my soaring reflexes. Beckoning the waiter, I said, "Châteaubriand for two and coffee."

He nodded.

"*Non,* Daniel." She pouted. "Champagne? Lots more champagne?"

"I have an early appointment."

"On Christmas Day? Who would believe that?" Taking my hand in both of hers, she looked at me strangely. "Daniel, you are a very nice man. You are trying to protect me from myself. *Chéri,* I do not want to be protected tonight...."

"Merry Christmas," I said, and ordered the second bottle.

Days passed and I did not know time could speed so quickly. Nor, after the first awakening, did I care. The pent-up bitterness within Charlotte seemed to explode in gay Roman candles that would neither burn out nor fall down.

Dinners lasted until early morning, breakfast was at noon or not at all. We boated in the Saigon River, danced in the penthouse terrace of the Dai-Nam, spent our siestas in Charlotte's modest room on rue Grandière.

There was a frankness that swept us into the clouds and held us tingling, capturing each other's life and breath for what seemed like hours.

If Mossard or Tuyet or D'Or Blanc entered her thoughts, she did not speak of them. In my mind, they gradually dimmed. Drugged by her presence and vitality, the desire for another day with her burned ever stronger.

My dollar supply ran out. Instead of our regular sunset boat ride, we walked the lonesome mile around the vast Palace grounds, holding hands and watching the roaming deer leap over the artificial hills behind the tall wrought-iron fencing.

After a while, I saw only the never-ending barbed wire inside the fencing that sealed the Palace from the street.

"Charlotte," I said, "the fun is over."

She kissed me lightly on the chin. "*Petit trésor,* you have spent your share. Now, it is my turn."

My eyes were on the sentries manning gun emplacements.

"There was a time when I sold myself for those words."

"Silly," she answered, "I do not mean his money. I have jewelry I can sell."

"Is there a difference?"

There was humor in her glance when she said, *"Bonne bête,* one would think that you wanted to leave me."

When I did not answer, the corners of her mouth pinched and the music went out of her voice.

"Daniel, you do want to leave."

"What would you do, Charlotte, if Guillaume asked you to come back to him?"

A look of pain flashed over her face and quickly disappeared.

"With that girl … never!"

"I mean the way it used to be."

"Please, Daniel. You and I know it can never be that way."

"Suppose he decided to … say … leave the plantation and asked you to go back to Paris?"

Moisture loomed in the green eyes.

"I …" Turning her head suddenly, she sobbed, "You are hurting me, Dan. Please do not talk like this. I want to laugh and live and let the years go by. Guillaume is behind me. I want to forget him."

I held her close to me there on the sidewalk until her shoulders became still.

"Do not leave me …." Her lashes were wet cobwebs as they swept up at me. "Promise?"

My voice was husky. "Promise."

We walked back to her room.

"I am going to see about that job I was working on."

Charlotte said in a monotone, "You will not be long?"

"I do not know."

"Tonight?" she pleaded.

With her damp eyes and rounded petulant lips, she looked at me as she had at Mossard that windy afternoon in Paris.

I told her I would come back as soon as I could.

Stopping short at the godown door, I faced the question which I knew was inevitable. Charlotte or D'Or Blanc? It could not be both. I did not go back to her.

CHAPTER EIGHT

I t was a sunny, cool day in mid-January when the young general, Nguyen-van-Xuan failed to report to the godown. Disturbed but not alarmed, I went ahead with grenade practice.

One of the tropical fruits of Viet Nam, *la pomme cannelle*, had a tough, knobby shell that gave it nearly the same grip as the fragmentary explosive. Lacking money, I had had Cam steal a basketful from a street vendor. Lining up several stolen empty barrels at one end of the godown, I placed the Nung troops at the other. With a hundred and eighty hours of elementary training, they were ready to be divided into squads. But each Nung thought that he should be a squad leader. A "grenade in the barrel" contest would work, I thought. By oriental standards, the four winners would be automatically "the best."

The waterfront barn sounded like a bowling alley. I watched their stance and delivery. Any who failed to simulate the pin pulling, heave and cover were disqualified.

Xuan exploded through the door, dodged a zooming *pomme* and pulled up in front of me breathless.

"He wants to see you tonight," he panted.

"Who?"

"Ly-van-Vien, the chief of the Binh Xuyen!"

I stopped the practice. "How did he know where to reach me?"

"I went to the Grand Monde this morning to collect my rice money. They think I am sick, you know, because I have not been coming to the casino. So, I collect the money each week for rice.

The *chef de salle* stopped me and asked if I had seen the Shanghai American. I said I had not but would try to find him if the reward were great enough. He promised five thousand piasters."

"Were you followed, Xuan?"

"I took a Chinese bus. Nobody can follow a Chinese bus." He laughed, and was very proud of himself.

With a deep sigh of satisfaction, I knew that my strategy had succeeded. Five thousand piasters for a "call" in Saigon was urgent.

Exaggerated rumors of impending tragedy never ceased blowing through the catacombs of the vast native market and from café to café on rue Catinat. Last night's hearsay was that Diem was putting out feelers to effect alliance with Pope Tac's Cao Dai Sect. A union of the two armies would be a clear balance of power.

Perhaps the rumor was true and the Pope was interested.

"Go back late this afternoon," I said to Xuan. "Talk to no one until you get into the office of the thin Vietnamese who uses a long, gold cigarette holder. Tell him that I will be waiting in front of the Metropole Hotel in a *cyclo-pousse* at midnight. No other arrangement will be satisfactory. I want to see just how anxious they are."

"Should I come back here," Xuan asked, "and risk being followed again?"

"You will have to. I need part of your reward to pay the *cyclo*."

At just past midnight, a jeepload of green-bereted infantry sloggers in full uniform slowed in front of the Metropole Hotel and flashed lights. Tires squealed in a wild U turn, and the vehicle leapt in high gear back down rue Gallieni toward Cholon. My *cyclo* followed. Veering sharply to the left off the wide boulevard, we bumped through narrow alleys until we reached the upper Arroyo Chinois. The jeep braked to a scorching stop and the soldiers jumped out, facing me. I dismissed the cyclo with a fifty-piaster note.

One of the Binh Xuyen men circled my eyes with a black silk *torchon,* and guided me into the quarter-ton vehicle. Other bodies squeezed in on top of me. We drove for twenty minutes and crossed three bridges. They could have been the same bridge—for all I know—to confuse my sense of direction. Helped from the jeep, I was led for a long walk and finally onto tile flooring.

When the blindfold was removed, I was seated in a foam-rubber chair with a high back. Blinking, I wondered if my eyes were playing tricks. It was pitch-black. The smell of cigar smoke was pungent. As my eyes grew accustomed to the darkness, I saw five coals glowing at intervals circling me.

A crisp, high-pitched voice, belonging to a gesturing cigar, spoke in flawless French.

"We understand you are unemployed, Mr. King?"

I cleared my throat. "I am prepared to deliver fifteen thousand troops in echelons of combat teams to your command within three months," I said.

"Nonsense! I presume you are referring to the labor forces of D'Or Blanc. You are no longer connected with the plantation. You were fired by Mossard, returned to France, and gained illegal re-entry into Viet Nam through circuitous means—posing as the Feathered Frenchman. Whatever influence you may have been able to muster at one time through your peculiar relationship with Guillaume Mossard has been nullified."

Several of the cigars dipped in agreement. I could see the flickering outlines of chins and noses.

"Then, why did you call me here?"

"One of our minor officials was impressed by your foresight. Perhaps we can employ your services."

"In helping to eliminate Pope Tac?"

The coals brightened and faded.

I broke the silence. "You can employ my services in the way I mentioned before … and no other."

"You speak bravely, if rashly, Mr. King. You want us to support a move to coup D'Or Blanc. Is that it? Our interests, as you may know, are not incompatible with those of the French. We have no argument with the Legion or with Guillaume Mossard."

"I do not care about your interests, nor do I need your support to win D'Or Blanc. I am talking about three months from now."

The five tips glowed and the fragrance of cigar smoke filled the room.

"Then, we shall reconvene this discussion if and when you can prove such a boast."

"Agreeable. But, it will cost you more—much more."

The cigars moved centrifugally amidst a low buzz of sing-song Vietnamese.

"Giving you credence only as a hypothesis, what is your definition of cost?" the voice asked.

"I dislike bargaining at a psychological disadvantage. May I have a cigar?"

None of the coals moved, but I heard a shuffle of footsteps. A long, unwrapped Manila was inserted in my mouth. I took my time lighting it, knowing that all eyes were fastened to my face.

"I will furnish manpower as stated, adequately trained, and commit it to combat your direction. The armament, of course, comes from you. The cost of my services, if we deal now, is one million dollars."

The ends of the cigars drew bright in unison.

"You, Mr. King, are mad!" the spokesman stated flatly.

"Possibly," I admitted. "But, I am trying to be fair. It will be worth five million, if I am as good as my boast and then go shopping."

He laughed, a crisp unpleasant sound, lacking in humor.

"You are a cool one. But your *braggadocio* is a sieve. It is impossible to train a combat force of that size in three months."

"I can."

"You are a military man, Mr. King. Surely you do not expect us to swallow a preposterous claim."

I spoke carefully. "If the forces I propose using to conquer D'Or Blanc were fishermen a month ago, and I succeed by the end of this month, would you believe me then?"

"I would." The voice did not hesitate.

"Then, I shall prove it. The choice is yours. If we contract now, I will take a binder of ten thousand dollars and the rest on commitment to combat."

The cigars assembled once more. I slouched comfortably and blew smoke.

The high voice came back, stilling the mumbled chatter. "In a gambling business, Mr. King, one takes as few chances as possible. We dislike taking such a long one with you. How many troops do you possess?"

"Enough." I hoped my tone was nonchalant.

"Ten thousand dollars guarantees our option on the tappers of D'Or Blanc which you agree to train effectively within three months—*if* you are successful without our help in defeating the French and, of equal importance, securing the plantation against reprisals."

"You can deduct it from the million."

The voices slowed until it was sinister. "This contract will, of course, be verbal. If by any chance you succeed, you adhere immediately to our control."

"Correct."

"Then," the implacable voice continued, "let me say this. Ten thousand dollars is a pittance, Mr. King, but few lives in Indochina are worth that amount. Do I make myself clear?"

"Translucent."

The cigar waved a curt pattern.

In a minute, my hand became fat with a sheaf of bills. As the blindfold was readjusted, I stood up.

"*Auf Wiedersehen,* gentlemen. That means—in case you are puzzled—until we *see* each other again."

The jeep, traversing the same number of bridges and taking the same turns in reverse, freed me at the Pont de Y.

Snapping the pad of bills in my pocket, I thought briefly of Charlotte. The end was in sight.

Slowly, I headed for my boat.

CHAPTER NINE

The floating village swayed restlessly in the moonlight, silhouetted against the green curd of the canal. From the huddled shacks along the banks, the smell of joss, burning garbage and urine blended into the overpowering odor that I had become accustomed to. Awakening a sidewalk kitchen vendor who lay sprawled by her shoulder pots, I ate ravenously of rice, fish maws and the strong fermented *nuocmam* sauce, that penetrated the pores to hold off the clouds of hovering mosquitoes.

Tiptoeing across the boards connecting the sleeping sampans, I saw that the young girl in the boat next to mine was awake.

"The moon has thinned and fattened, Feathered One," she said eagerly. "Surely it has brought you luck?"

"The same," I answered. "The piasters fly above arm's reach."

She sighed in disappointment and lay down. I reached into the darkness of the hold and forked her snoring father up by his chest.

"But, the dollars grow on trees. Out, O Sputtering One."

I pushed a hundred-dollar bill into his gaping mouth. His eyes rolled as he saw its value, and he salaamed violently against the deck.

"Praise you, Generous One," he cackled with delight. "Hallowed be your footsteps."

"Idle your tongue, Old Parrot, or we shall have the prying eyes of a thousand neighbors."

Dazed with joy, he fell into a gabble of excitement.

"Tomorrow I sail," I said, "and I will take your Lotus Bud with me."

The young girl's eyes sparkled in the moonlight.

Her wizened father grumbled, "Three thousand piasters is a poor dowry."

"She will be back, ungrateful one—her arms laden with gold and betel. I take her to where Frenchmen are as numerous as the trees and stand just as alone."

Lotus Bud shrieked with joy and in a gust of movement, captured some miserly possessions and bounded to my junk.

Mollified, the old Vietnamese squatted.

"As for you, my Lotus Bud, back to your blanket. You will need to be fragrant and fresh as the early tide."

Reluctantly she returned to her barque where, an orchid mounted over one ear, she sat watching me as I went to sleep.

At the first glint of sun we up-anchored and drifted out into the traffic of the sluggish stream. Within an hour, I had bought two *paillottes*—small, thatch-topped rice barges—and had coupled them on behind the junk. By midmorning, I tied to the mossy quay fronting my decrepit godown.

Xuan was at work with the troops, crawling them in squad competitions that culminated in screaming bayonet charges.

I flashed the sheaf of money under his nose. He gasped.

"When the moon soaks the river tonight, General, you will load these *paillottes* with living sacks of rice and move up the Saigon River to D'Or Blanc."

"But ... I had not expected ..." He began to suffer buck fever.

"Leave the weapons and ammunition here hidden under the floor. The Nungs can pass as rice farmers. If you are stopped at any of the bridges, they will have only rice grains in their hair and calico drawers."

"The Binh Xuyen have agreed," he said, regaining his composure and clapping his hands with satisfaction.

"Yes, but they will not rest until they know where we are and what we are doing. We must evacuate the godown."

"But they are on our side."

"If they knew we had only twenty men, I would float in the river like a balloon for taking money under false pretenses."

His face lit up with understanding, then clouded. "You intend to take D'Or Blanc with…twenty men?" He pointed to the Nungs.

"Twenty-two…counting you and me. Now listen. Sail the junk upriver to Ben-Cat and keep on for another ten kilometers. You should arrive tomorrow night. Hide the boat in the bamboo along the banks and sink the *paillottes*."

"What if the Legion stops me at the guarded bridges?"

"They will not question a rice barge, but keep the men out of sight under the straw matting. If you are boarded, the Nungs are to be asleep. Do you know the small patch of jungle on the Rubber Road north of Hon-Quon?"

He nodded.

"It is a few hours by foot from where you will leave the boat. You will have the night for cover to reach it. You should arrive before the tappers are out in the groves. Bivouac the men and let them sleep all day hidden in the brush. No fires. No noise. I shall be there shortly after dusk with the arms and ammunition. Have the men fed and ready to go to work."

"What will they eat?"

"There is rice in the bottom of those empty barges. The grains can be chewed for nourishment on the way up." Giving him half of the money, I continued, "Buy fifty pounds of raw beef, ground up and salted. Coat it with salt, so it will not spoil. Split it among your squad leaders to carry. But, do not touch it until just before I arrive—that is two days from tonight. Feed them as the sun goes down."

I waited a moment thinking and then continued my instructions. "Get a big can of red paint. Bright red. A new motor for the junk. A Red Cross ambulance—like the one you bought before—and ten or twelve cases of bandage wrappings—the kind with the U.S. seal on them—the double handclasp."

He nodded.

"And find one of the new Diem I.D. cards for me. It makes no difference what the name is—so long as the photo is a Frenchman. Got all that?"

He thought for a moment, then repeated my instructions.

"Good," I said. "Be back here before noon."

He swiftly thumbed through the bills.

"This should be enough."

"And, Xuan ..."

He looked up at me intently, rigid with developed discipline. I let him wait until he frowned.

"I shall bring your general's uniform along in the truck."

Smiling broadly, he departed on his shopping tour.

"Quite a son you have," I remarked to the idling Cam, who had become so morose that I seldom talked to him. His eagle eyes fixed me inscrutably.

"I take it that I am not to go."

Sliding him a hundred-dollar bill, I said, "Select a uniform for your son and a mandarin robe for yourself. You are to ride in the back of the ambulance."

Cam glanced disdainfully at the money.

"It is not enough." His voice was haughty and cold.

"I did not say twenty-two-carat braid. Pack the clothes in a couple of *nuoc-mam* jars—with a shoulder pole. Be waiting for me at the Gia Long market day after tomorrow at noon. If you are not dressed as I prescribe, I shall not pick you up. Nor will I wait if you have dawdled at the mirror."

Accepting the bill with aloofness, he spun on his heel and stalked from the godown.

Calling the Nung squad leaders around me, I looked intently at each face.

"You are good men, so I make you captains. Other Nungs not so good like you, so still privates. When they as good as you, you are majors … they captain. Now look alive!"

The report of their heels, rifling as one, echoed through the hall. The warehouse shook as bodies slammed, rose grimly, slammed again and writhed in rotting excelsior. They were good—for never having fired a shot.

Calling Lotus Bud from the junk, I took her to the narrow babbling corridors of the Saigon silk market. There, I had her fitted in a tight-hipped Red Cross uniform. I specified some alterations. High slashes on each side of the skirt and a built-in brassière. When she tried it on, I had to catch my breath. The old crone saleswoman grinned in toothless appreciation. The next stop was a steam bath and beauty salon.

The *maîtresse de salon* threw up her hands and exclaimed, "*Cela prendra toute la journée!*" I shrugged and left Lotus Bud for the full day's treatment.

When I went to pick her up, I did not recognize her. There, legs crossed tantalizingly as she thumbed through a French comic book, was Lotus Bud.

Her hair trailed in a provocative pony tail. Eye make-up and lipstick were so skillfully applied that she looked to be twenty-one. Her skin glistened with cleanliness.

"Two thousand piasters, monsieur," the *maitresse de salon* said disapprovingly.

I gave her an extra five hundred.

The Frenchwoman beamed. "*Merci! Merci, monsieur.* You are very kind. Bring Madame again."

"Oh, Christ!" I winced, looking at my beauty's red-lacquered toenails. "I forgot to buy you shoes."

Lotus Bud looked even more like a front-ramp pony as she donned silver slippers that I chose from a nearby window assortment. Clinging tightly to my arm, she teetered as we came out on the sidewalk. Curious eyes from every direction turned to look at us.

I registered in a cheap Chinese hotel under the name of Jacques Babineau—the identification on the card that Xuan had gotten for me. Nobody raised an eyebrow at the presence of Lotus Bud. I decided to avoid room solicitations, and paid the double rate.

When we were in the room, the little prostitute said, "I stay here, if you want go. Make plenty piasters with bed so near street."

"You stay here—with me. For two days. And take off that dress, goddammit, before it gets wrinkled."

She stripped obediently.

"Feathered One, two straight days and my back be very tired."

"Take a paid vacation. Go to sleep."

She turned on her stomach, switched her body restlessly and fingered the linen sheets in wonder.

Xuan should be leaving now, I thought. Everything was as planned.

From the window I could see the Red Cross ambulance curbed across from the U.S. Enlisted Men's Club on rue Gallieni. It was in a "restricted" military parking area. It would be safe.

My plan was so fantastic that the only thing that recommended it was its utter boldness. I was going to try to seize the Château with only my platoon of twenty Nungs. Having plotted it out carefully, I felt there was a fifty-fifty chance, if my intelligence were up to date. Pacing back and forth, I decided that I could not risk its being wrong. I opened the door and shouted. A pimply faced adolescent bellboy scurried up and bowed.

"Do you know who I am?" I demanded.

"Yes, mista," he answered in broken English. "You Feathered Frenchman."

I twisted the pearl buttons on his jacket until they matched his eyes.

"Who?"

"I no know," he gasped. "I no see you before in whole life."

I let him down.

"You swear in pagoda, boy?"

His voice cracked with fear. "Yes ... yes, I swear in pagoda."

"You go to Villa d'Or Blanc on Boulevard Norodom. Speak to Lien-Fat. No one but Lien-Fat. Tell him King wants to see him. Alone." I paused.

"Lien-Fat," he mumbled. "Mr. King wants see in secret."

"And, boy, if you are followed back here, I will break your neck."

His face grew white.

Giving him a thousand piasters, I said, "Divide this with the other bellboys." Then I handed him ten hundred-dollar bills and told him, "This is for Lien-Fat."

His eyes popped as he looked at the money. His gaze slid from the bills to Lotus Bud lying on the bed. I slammed the door in his face.

For a thousand dollars, Lien-Fat might bring me up to date about the deployment of forces on D'Or Blanc. In case I was too cheap for him, I put two grenades in my pocket.

Lien-Fat kept the thousand and sent back one word—"siesta."

At noon the next day, as the sweltering mats of humanity disappeared as if by magic from the streets, I hailed a taxi. It never failed to amaze me how Saigon vanished so quickly, or where it went for the two-hour rest. Even the opposing forces in the city—Diem's army and the Binh Xuyen police—were not to be seen—much less heard from.

I held the taxi until the streets were clear. Then we drove through the ghostly city into the French Quarter, past the Palace and onto Boulevard Norodom.

I walked the last block.

The only movements under the scalding sun were fluttering birds and puffs of clouds high in the cobalt sky.

The Villa loomed behind grilled gates. There was no sign of life and no guard.

I opened the gate and walked rapidly toward the portico. Three black Citroëns were parked in the garage. From habit, I scanned the license plates. In the time it took my brain to telegraph the message, I fell flat on the ground, holding my breath, heart pounding. The trunk of the middle Citroën sprang open and the cavity spewed lead. I heard the whistles over me.

Counting anguished seconds, I rolled violently. Just as I did, clogs of turf leaped from where I had lain. I reversed my rolling to the other direction. The burst missed again. I knew that it took seconds to shift the Browning Automatic in order to get a sight. But my luck would not hold forever. The assassin would begin to lead me. I kneeled, cocked a grenade, counted, heaved, and flattened.

Triggered bursts whistled overhead before the rear end of the French car crumpled, sprang incredibly to the top of the port and crunched back down in clattering debris. Smoke swirled from the opening and the bitter stench of powder filled the air.

My hours with the *pommes canelles* had made the throw accurate. Waiting until the rain of metal quieted, I got up cautiously, my second grenade ready. Quiet settled over the smoldering scene. I walked on the balls of my feet to the wreck.

Roland d'Arbre had exploded into fragments. Staring at what was left of the Frenchman, a hot sourness rose in my throat. I spat it out and strode into the villa.

I found the fat Chinese cowering in his bedroom, the pistol in his hand jumping like a Mexican bean.

"Where is Mossard?" I demanded.

"Not here," Lien-Fat quivered in soprano tones.

Looking at him with contempt, I flung open the closets. They were empty.

"Talk fast," I said softly, caressing the grenade.

The gun fell out of his fingers. His English flowed unconsciously, "I did not like it, Mr. King, but was orders from Mossard. If I heard of you, I was to let him know. He sent D'Arbre this morning...."

"Well, at least you are honest," I said, pocketing the grenade.

He sighed with relief and lapsed into his customary manner of speech.

"You very foolish come back Saigon."

"Not foolish. Just not rich enough."

I held out my hand.

Reluctantly he dug in his pocket and came up with the thousand.

"Beard disguise only fool children, Mr. King," he said. "I know you here before, but not report to Mossard until message. That too big risk for me. Also know address of blonde." He held tentatively to the notes.

I took them out of his hand.

"But, Mr. King, I have children in Vassar, Harvard, Sorbonne and—"

Impatiently I broke in. "You have connections with the police." I nodded in the direction of the garage. "Use them ... without involving me."

Wordlessly, he tiptoed out.

"Case of accident," Lien-Fat reported half an hour later. "D'Arbre cleaning gun. Grenade in belt explode. Make one big boom. Very sad. Police sorry."

"A little bald," I answered, "but passable in Saigon."

"Mr. King, you please go away from Saigon. When boss hear D'Arbre fail, he order me make execution. That I not like because I not fail."

"Why, Lien ... you have a heart."

"I no like kill white man. Very bad for business reputation."

I laughed. "When I can afford you, at least I will know I can trust you." I fondled the bills temptingly. His mouth broke into a half-moon.

"Do you know Madame Mossard very well, Lien?"

"I not see her for some years. Before she very beautiful. Hair red … like sunset."

"She is the blonde I have been seeing."

The half-moon set. "Mossard French wife in Paris," he said uncertainly.

"Better shake up your informers, Lien. Mossard's French wife is here. Tell him the next time he comes to town … but not before. Okay?"

"Okay." Pudgy hands swallowed the bills greedily.

Casually I asked, "How is the Legion?"

"Mossard make deal with Diem government. Legion lose only one-quarter soldier bodies. But new ones you pick very good."

"Are they still at Song-Be?"

"Song-Be," he affirmed. "Legion captain train. Finish maybe soon."

I held out my hand to him.

"You are a good man, Lien-Fat. Mossard does not know how good, or he would not have sent D'Arbre. See you someday … maybe in Texas."

He wrung my hand with jellied fervor.

"That very good, Mr. King. But make sure you no in Saigon when Mossard hear about D'Arbre."

I assured him I was leaving.

CHAPTER TEN

I was not sure that my elaborate arrangements for the trip north were necessary, but the barricaded bridges and check points surrounding the city had tightened severely in control of traffic. Free movement had been banned. The French—in reducing forces—had turned over some of the provincial bastions to Diem's army.

Picking up Cam, I took advantage of the siesta period to pack and camouflage the back of the ambulance. We left Saigon promptly at two-thirty in order to mix into the horde of people returning to work, and not create undue attention. North of the Gia-Dinh refugee camps, the traffic thinned, resolving itself into oxcarts, overburdened coolies and occasional military vehicles.

Lotus Bud, restless and provocative in her uniform, sat beside me in the front seat. The five rifles, loaded grenade belts and cases of ammunition rode under excelsior in the back bin, herded by the squatting Cam and his *nuoc-mam* jars. Screening the payload, in case the double back doors were opened, were stacks of bandage boxes liberally displaying the American Aid seal.

We were stopped at the rickety one-way bridge crossing the Rivière Saigon. Armed Vietnamese in lend-lease uniforms approached. I leaped out, saluted and flashed the I.D. card, the one with the photograph of Jacques Babineau that I had ink-daubed with whiskers. Lotus Bud stared haughtily at the guards.

"Ben-Cat Hospital," I announced, and started to open the swinging rear doors.

"Ça va. Ça va. Allez!" Impatiently the sergeant waved us on.

I grinned at my little Red Cross nurse as we clanked over the bridge unchallenged. When we reached the Legion outpost above Ben-Cat, I punched Lotus Bud into readiness. This was the last barrier before D'Or Blanc, and as we drove up, the French guards poured out of the bunker for a showdown inspection. It looked like I might have to play *la petite farce.*

A sour, bandy-legged Legionnaire stepped away from the echelon of troops. He scanned my card with distaste.

"Name?" he rasped.

"Jacques Babineau."

"From?"

"Saigon. I work for the Americans."

"C'est à dire en France!" His language was sharp and liquid. I recognized the Parisian dialect.

"I am from Strasbourg," I replied. My accent was not perfect enough to bluff.

"Half German," he grunted. "It figures that you would work for the Americans. Open up!"

That was the prearranged signal for Lotus Bud.

As I wrestled with the handles of the door, pretending difficulty, she swayed up to him, pressing the rubber contours into silhouette.

"Allo," she said. Flesh showed in triangular slashes well above the knees.

The Frenchman scratched himself and breathed, *"Jesu'*, I like these new uniforms!" His eyes glinted as they lingered on her.

"She is to help distribute the medical supplies in Loc-Ninh." I said smoothly, swinging open the doors of the ambulance.

"Pretty soft," he said sarcastically. "Saigon duty and when you hit the field one night, you bring along a fleshpot. *C'est la guerre civile."*

He handed me the card. I breathed in silent relief.

"Let me see what is inside. Perhaps we can use some of your medicine here."

Methodically, he began to remove the outer cartons.

I signaled urgently to Lotus Bud.

"Oh...oh...." She pressed her head and swayed delicately toward the Legionnaire.

"What is the matter?" he asked and looked at her with interest.

"It is the thin air of the mountains. My head spins like a coin on the street."

She breathed heavily, her fortified bosom a bas-relief of movement. The Frenchman watched it hungrily.

Taking her firmly around the waist, I said, "Into the car. The moving air will make you feel better."

"No, please. I want to lie down." She leaned against the sergeant, her hand lingering as it passed over the lump that was his wallet.

His face diffused.

Languorously, she sighed. "Please, handsome General, tell him I do not have to go to Loc-Ninh."

My face was a thundercloud...I hoped.

"Let me stay with you," Lotus Bud whispered loudly in his ear.

Retrieving the bandage parcels from the ground, I tossed them back into the ambulance. "I should have left you in Saigon," I snapped at Lotus Bud.

In a peculiar tight voice, the Legionnaire said, "I think you should rest here for a while." His arms wrapped around Lotus Bud's eager little frame.

The guards in front of the barrier hooted with bawdy laughter. "Bring her in, Émile," one shouted.

Protesting, I said, "I gave her a thousand piasters to make this trip."

Laughter again.

I slammed the doors and wrenched the handles tight. Glaring angrily at Lotus Bud, I snarled, "Do you want to come with me or not?"

She answered with unmistakable honesty, "I wait for you here. Okay?"

The Legionnaires eagerly hoisted the striped pole blocking the road, and I roared off.

Out of sight, I slowed and drove lazily into the groves of rubber trees. At Hon-Quan, I got a cursory wave-through from the Plantation Detachment and eased up even more. I was ahead of schedule.

The wooded area was dark and deserted when I arrived. Parking in an aisle of trees well off the road near the patch of jungle, I reflected. If Mossard had discovered the arms cache in the cellar, the attack would disintegrate to a slaughter before it commenced. But Lien-Fat had given no indication. Mossard would naturally blame the cache on me—one more grievance. The fat Chinese would logically have been informed. It was a supposition I would have to chance.

Xuan loomed out of the darkness and reported that he had fed the men.

"Any trouble?"

Raking a hand through dust-grayed hair, he grinned.

"The trouble begins now. Our Nungs are not used to raw meat. They will get stomach-aches."

"Not after it digests. Let them lie quiet for a couple of hours. Come on. We have work to do."

We unloaded the godown weapons and the two crates of ammunition.

Cam tumbled out and hobbled back and forth until his muscles loosened. Slipping into his robe, the mandarin drank deeply of the hevea. His shoulders towered erectly.

"If you were as good a mandarin as you are a coolie," I told him, "those statues at Angkor Wat would smile a little broader."

His piercing eyes looked through me. "D'Or Blanc is finished. The white gold has run out for the foreigners. I shall call the plantation Muon Nam—meaning 'Ten Thousand Years'—for the new dynasty."

Turning to Xuan, he said, "Clothe yourself in the uniform, my son, and prepare for the glory that is to be ours."

I glared at him.

Xuan hesitated, torn by the desire to obey. "I shall fight with my men," he said finally. "The uniform would only furnish a bright target."

"Take these supplies into the woods," I ordered Cam, "and wait for us."

His eyes, glittering with hatred, challenged me.

"I mean you. I do not want the Nungs disturbed."

Hefting the guns with silent fury, he strode majestically into the brake.

By nine o'clock, Xuan and I had driven in concentric circles around the patch of woods to a radius of five miles. We scouted up nothing but small game. I had to be sure that our gunfire encountered no human ears.

By midnight, using the beams of the Red Cross truck shining on clay cup targets, the Nungs had rattled through all the clips of ammunition. The taut furrows in my face softened and I could feel anxiety leaving me. They were marksmen. They would not miss.

Each took his turn with the live grenades, arching them between the rubber trees. If one bounced back, I told them, we would be dead. Nobody missed. The red meat was doing its work.

When the weapons had been cleaned, I buried all except one set. Then, in the glaring lights, I laid out branches in a design until I had simulated the contours of the entire Château complex.

"We will pull up here," I said, pointing to the spot by the horseshoe stairs. "There will be a window directly below you. Enter quietly and close the window after you. You should not be observed—if you are quiet. If there is anyone in the basement room, General Xuan, take care of him—silently." I indicated with a slim stick the exact locations of the bins containing the armament.

"Attach your grenade belts, load and lock the M-1s, fill your pockets with clips and fix bayonets. By this time, General Xuan will have opened the can of red paint. Everybody dips his bayonet to simulate fresh blood, and forms into squads. Exactly ten minutes after you have entered—to the second—blast the lock on the door and run.

"Squad One takes cover in the palms around the swimming pool—here."

I placed twigs to indicate the pool and its foliage.

"Squad Two, all the way to this building"—pointing it out for them to see. "It is a long distance, so run low and hard. This is the Legion's arms room and motor pool. Take it and hold it. If necessary, blow it up."

"Squads Three and Four—follow Squad Two, but fork off here. ..." I indicated the buildings containing the Legion defense points. "Three—there; Four—here ...."

I paused for a moment, letting them memorize the locations.

"Get to the top floor of the buildings and destroy the machine-gun emplacements with grenades. If you are fast and quiet, you should effect surprise. Then, from your vantage of height, open fire on the upper windows of these two buildings." I pointed to sticks representing the rear Legion defense points. "You will be accurate. They have machine guns."

I let that sink in and then turned to Xuan.

"General Xuan, you will neutralize the front gate and fall in behind Squad One at the swimming pool. Advance to support the main attack of Squads Three and Four. You will be able to tell by the machine-gun fire which building is the most stubborn. Go after one at a time. Use the walls for shields. Work in close and lob grenades up through the windows. When firing ceases, occupy and demolish. Caution!"

The silence was tense.

"Go after nothing but machine guns. If you do not hear rat-tat-tat, do not shoot. That way you will not be shooting at each other. There will probably be a counterattack from the military barracks in the rear of the compound. Probably twenty or twenty-five men. It will take time for them to organize. The attack will be weak because the arms room is denied to them. By the time they hit, all squads should have seized objectives. General Xuan and Squad One"—I looked at each man in turn—"get them down on their bellies with fire. Squads Three and Four... evacuate your buildings, flank wide to the fence, come in and mop them up."

Xuan repeated the instructions to them in Vietnamese.

For the next three hours, I rehearsed each squad individually in the performance of its action. Only ghostly trees were witness as lithe bodies raced, slammed, wriggled and simulated blade jabs and butt smashes.

When I called it off, the Nungs were disappointed.

"See what red meat and raw blood does?" I said, in grim humor, to Xuan. "Notice a mosquito sometime before he bites. Lazy and slow. Then, let him get a taste—he zips like a fly."

Nguyen Cam's eyes shone in the half-light.

"Ho-Chi-Minh feeds his troops on bat blood. You only copy his methods."

"I expect he learned it when he was working for the U.S.A. during the Japanese occupation of your country."

Cam scowled.

"Half of the meat is left," Xuan said. "Shall I distribute it?"

"In an hour. Let them relax now."

I flicked off the headlights and all of us stretched on the soft turf under the trees. Only Cam, replete in the grandeur of his gilt-crusted robe, walked restlessly. In the deathly quiet, after the thundering bombardment, tensions unfolded up and down the line.

I packed the twenty Nungs and Xuan into the bin of the ambulance like sardines—head to foot and foot to head—until they were squeezed tight against the roof. The springs sagged.

"It will be rough riding and hot, but only for an hour. Xuan, this is your rifle and grenade belt. There are only twenty at the Château."

Cam started to climb in the front.

"You stay here," I told him flatly. "If we win, we will send for you. Meanwhile, stay out of sight."

I slammed the doors and chugged off.

The rubber road gradually filled with plantation jeeps, truck-loads of tappers and roving Legion patrols. I had figured the time of attack carefully at a moment when the armored half-tracks would be spewing out over the loops, and the garrison forces would either be asleep or having breakfast.

The sun rose over the trees.

CHAPTER ELEVEN

began to think of what might go wrong. If the Song-Be recruits had been suddenly brought inside the enclave ... if I could not get the ambulance past the front gate ... if the cache had been discovered ....

Pulling the brake tight, I stopped before the grilled gate. The French Legionnaire came out of his box and regarded me with curiosity.

I had not passed Mossard's Citroen on the road.

"Medical supplies," I said. "Damn stuff is so heavy I broke a spring and had to limp in."

"Attendez un moment," he said evenly. "I will call the dispensary."

He reached for the telephone inside the shack.

"Never mind," I said, getting out. "Let me talk to Mossard."

He looked doubtful, but jiggled the cradle and spoke rapidly into the mouthpiece.

"Allo," the instrument barked metallically. *"Ici Mossard. Qu'est-ce que vous voulez?"*

I took the instrument from the Legionnaire's hand.

"Mossard. This is King."

The phone was silent. For a lifetime of seconds I thought he had hung up. Then, the crisp voice barked back, "I have always admired your fortitude, King—if nothing else. What do you want?"

"To talk," I said. "I am by myself and I have a white handkerchief in my pocket."

"If you are wanting your job back, the answer is 'no.' "

"I am in the mood to deal, Mossard," I said pleasantly. "Maybe the fresh air up here in the mountains has soothed me, but I forgive you for that assassination attempt. Let me put it this way. You have money. I have information that is worth more than you have in the safe. Is it a truce?"

The pause was electric.

"Passez-moi a la sentinelle!"

I passed the telephone to the waiting Frenchman and watched the Legionnaire nod several times in affirmation. He laid down the instrument and frisked me, removing the grenade from my pocket. I did not resist.

Listening warily, I heard him report into the telephone, *"Une grenade… dans sa poche."*

The earpiece burped terse unintelligibles and clicked.

The Legionnaire motioned me into the ambulance, and accompanied me. At the base of the baroque stairs, I backed the ambulance against the window.

"Your post is unguarded, corporal. I know the way in."

His footsteps crunched on the gravel as he double-timed away. Rapping the side of the ambulance sharply, I checked my watch, and ascended the curved steps three at a time.

Mossard was waiting for me on the *couloir*, pistol leveled.

Freezing, I said, "What do you want me to do? Stand on my head and shake myself?"

The planter had aged. Veins threaded a ruddy network over his cheeks. His stance was as square as always, and the shaggy eyebrows had lost none of their menace.

"Lead, motivated by powder, is a trifle quicker than judo," he commented.

"Only when the motivator is cocked," I replied drily.

He examined the pistol, not without surprise.

"During the second it took you to look, Mossard, I could have killed you."

He pocketed the weapon.

"Your new beard conceals not only scars of battle, but adorns an even more agile brain."

We sat in our familiar positions: he in the swivel chair, and I in the overstuffed leather. He sniffed.

"You are usually a harbinger, King, and an ill-fated one at that. This time you smell bad. Please make it brief."

"Your plantation is in immediate danger."

"I have been hearing that for ten years. If your information is worth no more, we can dispense with it and let me finish breakfast."

"We can deal to advantage," I said carefully. "How much money do you have?"

His mouth laughed without influencing his eyes.

"You are stalling, King. I have no need for black-marketed medical supplies, and less for so-called secrets that you have wangled over Chinese teacups. Lien-Fat keeps me informed of your illegal activities. You want me to lift the death sentence from your head, so that you can return to your blond friend on Grandière? Is that it?"

"She is a pleasure I have had to forfeit."

"*Voilà*. That you finally found a woman who sterilizes your attraction to Thi-Tuyet is worth some loss of face to me—platonic as our relation is. I shall retract your sentence. Perhaps your madness was no more significant than the drives of flesh— I am willing to give you the benefit of the doubt. But, possession—no matter for what desire—is the key to peaceful control of D'Or Blanc. I have never underestimated you, King. You have the capability of power, and the possibility of progeny—which I do not. But enough. I have a busy day. Now that you have been reprieved, was there something else behind your trip up here?"

"I might as well take up where Charlotte left off. Which is it to be, she or Tuyet?"

"I do not appreciate your humor. Be careful in mentioning my wife's name, or I may forget my rash of generosity."

"You are getting old, Mossard. Charlotte is in the prime of life. You have made your fortune … a hundred times. You should retire … on the Riviera, in Paris, New York, or someplace. Give somebody else a chance."

The veins in his cheeks became more prominent.

"That is … if you really love Charlotte," I added.

His voice was a whisper. "Your pardon is revoked."

"Just do not try to revoke it by reaching in your pocket."

"You will not leave the Château alive."

"That may be. I told you the plantation is in immediate danger. I was not lying. Surrender it peacefully, or I cannot guarantee your life and the others'."

The planter laughed abruptly. "What gall you have, King. I have never seen it surpassed. I do not find it amusing."

I referred to my watch. "You have less than five minutes to make your decision."

Leaning back in the swivel chair, he said, "There is no combat force within fifty miles of the Legion."

"We shall see."

We sat in stony silence as the minutes ticked off. Through the open balcony doors, only the twitter of birds and the distant sounds of machinery marred the quiet.

"If you think to threaten me with the fear that you have gained control of the *gendarmerie,* that force has been reduced to one hundred, and is equipped only with pistols and carbines— hardly enough to justify your bluff."

I said nothing, but glanced at my watch.

His fingers tapped impatiently on the desk.

"Inevitably you must leave, King, and just as inevitably I must call the Legion guards. Admit your hoax. Your bravery diminishes with each minute you attempt to prolong your life."

I got to my feet and walked toward the *couloir* door. "Last chance, Mossard," I said. "The attack is imminent."

"In your position," he said, his voice perceptibly softer, "I should have tried the same tactic. I have often thought, Daniel, how in most respects we are alike. My only regret is that we could not reach a better understanding. We could have been a Gibraltar of defense. *Alors…* two peas do not melt into one."

Rising from the swivel chair, he came to me, his face strangely emotional. "Defeat is not without its glory—and there is some within you. You do not resort to judo in the desperation of failure—knowing even so that you could not survive the avenging consequences of my death. I thank you for that. As soon as these unholy times are over, I shall bring Charlotte back to me. When I do, it will not be without gratitude."

Mossard grasped my arm in a gesture alien as it was clumsy.

"I wish I could say *bonne chance*."

A muffled thud broke the stillness.

Locking the door swiftly, I pocketed the key.

"I warned you, Mossard."

He stared at me with amazement. "This is a joke."

Rifle fire began to spit. A chatter of machine guns answered in the distance. The *thump-whang* of a grenade sheared plaster and glass. Mossard leaped to the balcony and saw the Legionnaire at the front gate tumble and lie still.

"You cannot possibly succeed," he said tersely, reaching for the telephone.

I covered the instrument.

A thunderous pounding on the *couloir* door reverberated through the room.

"Do not answer, Mossard. There is nothing you can do but sit here and wait."

"The Legion will hang you to the highest tree, King."

"Give me your gun."

The planter made no motion.

"Your gun."

I leaped and snapped his wrist just as the shot fired. The bullet clumped harmlessly into the wall. The pistol skidded along the tile as I forced it out of his hand.

I emptied the gun of its contents and put the bullets in my pocket. I javelined the two bamboo poles, adorning the wall, out of the window.

Mossard came at me savagely with a tackle. Side-stepping, I caught his chin with a short, vicious chop. He went out cold.

Sitting down in the swivel chair, I dipped into a box of Coronas Largas and lit one thoughtfully. Capture of the Château was only the first step.

The gunfire increased in tempo.

Mossard rubbed his jaw and sat up ashen-faced.

"Good cigar," I said.

There was an interminable burst of gunfire, a shattering cascade of bricks, a hideous scream and then silence.

Mossard got slowly to his feet and walked haltingly to the balcony. He stood gazing out over the plantation.

"I wish I could say *bonne chance*," I said.

He ignored me.

The marble stairs of the Château trembled under the weight of pounding feet. The door was tried and beaten.

I arose, snuffed the tail of the Corona and walked the length of the *salon*. It had been a good cigar—a good farewell—if I had lost. My hand was firm as I turned the key.

Xuan bolted in, blood oozing from his shoulder, his face a mask of powder burns.

Three Nungs, their bayonets scarlet and dripping, tumbled in after him. Their faces were distorted in the fury of combat.

"Mossard!" Xuan pointed.

The Nungs went in low toward the stunned Frenchman.

"Stop," I shouted. The Nungs obeyed mechanically, inches short of their target.

"We do not have time for unnecessary killing," I snapped. "Mossard is my prisoner. Xuan, round up all French civilians from the houses back of the Château and put them in the fruit cellar under guard. No more killing—understand?"

"Yes." He sounded reluctant.

"All prisoners and French civilians are to be evacuated safely to Saigon. Get that word to the men fast. How many casualties did we suffer?"

"Six are dead. Some injured."

"How many prisoners?"

"None," he answered proudly.

"The fighting is not over yet. There are Legion half-tracks scattered around the plantation. They may be homing in already, if the defenders thought to get out a radio signal. Split your force. Camouflage half of them around the front gate and dress one in a Legion uniform. In the box. Grenades close up when the half-tracks come in. Send the other half in a Legion truck to Song-Be—dressed in captured uniforms. Surprise them. Surround them and demand surrender. Bring them back intact if you can."

Xuan saluted smartly.

"What about our wounded?" he questioned.

"If they can walk, they are not wounded. If they can throw, put them in the ambush at the front gate. Get that nurse out of the dispensary to patch them up on the run. No relaxing. I want every man deployed within fifteen minutes."

The conquering force trooped out slamming the door.

"How many men did you bring in the back of that ambulance?" Mossard demanded in a tight voice.

"A whole regiment," I said with humor.

"How much money do you want?"

"Money?"

"How much in U.S. dollars will you take to restore this plantation to its rightful owner? One million dollars?"

I studied him thoughtfully. "You know, Mossard, there have been a lot of fortunes made in Indochina. A million is not really very much. Do you realize what D'Or Blanc is worth in international real estate? I do not think you do, because you value it for the trees. What would you say it is worth as a balance of power in the Far East? A man could turn these acres and fifteen thousand men into almost anything he wanted."

The planter grimaced painfully. "He would have to be clever."

"Maybe I am that clever, but I am not going to try. Nor can I accept your offer. I have already been paid for delivering this real estate."

"Who paid you?"

"Nguyen Cam."

Mossard snorted. "How much?"

"Ten thousand dollars."

"And, I am offering a million? Do not take me for an idiot, King."

"The difference is, Mossard, that I can get out safely with ten thousand. With your million, my throat would be cut before I got off the plantation. D'Or Blanc is being nationalized by the Vietnamese."

He looked sadly at me. "I never thought you would be cheap, King."

With those words, he gave up. The hard core of domination which had brought fame to France and rubber to the world became soft and stopped fighting.

He rubbed hands over his face in a tired way, took a deep breath and said, "Thank you for saving my life. I shall be glad to see Charlotte again."

He went quietly to the cellar prison.

CHAPTER TWELVE

That tepid, sun-splashed day in the low plateau of Viet Nam was not to end as I had visualized. The radio signal apparently had gotten out. The first three armored cars of the avenging Legion were demolished by the ambush. Squirting plumes of smoke over the vast green lawn, they choked the driveway. The rest of the outer Legion, apparently anticipating major resistance, pulled back down the Rubber Road toward Ben-Cat. My wounded Nungs at the front gate were wiped out.

The Song-Be expedition fared better. My men brought back Legion prisoners and a hundred reasonably well-trained gendarmes. The North Vietnamese swore immediately over to General Xuan—abetted by a thousand piasters each from Mossard's safe. The Legion instructors from Song-Be went into the cellar stockade.

My plan was to evacuate the French immediately, hoping that they would encounter the retreated Legion on the Rubber Road, and perhaps delay a counterattack. With "nationalization" the prime mover behind the coup, French forces in Saigon would be reluctant to mount reprisal. Cam, as the "agitator," would lend the movement grass-roots plausibility. An "oath of allegiance" relayed to Diem should stop official interference.

I made the "nationalization" announcement to the plantation civilians and described my position as I had for Mossard. They accepted it with hatred and unsubtle clearing of throats. I called Xuan to the cellar. He had donned his dazzling blue-and-gold uniform and was drenched with medals.

"Give them half an hour to pack their effects, feed their babies and so forth—then, get them out of here in trucks. Pick Vietnamese drivers from the staff who want to accompany the French."

"What about my father?" he asked gravely.

"We have our hands full now. You can go after him tomorrow."

Xuan led the internees from the cellar prison, with two of the Nungs herding the flanks. One of the *cocottes* shrieked when she saw the crimson bayonet blades and promptly fainted. Her boy friend slapped her, but she did not move. He threw her over his shoulder.

Guillaume Mossard marched out without looking at me.

The last person in line was Thi-Tuyet—in French clothing.

I caught her by the arm. "Where do you think you are going?"

She shook me off. "I am going with him."

"Sorry. You are the one exception to the volunteer rule for Vietnamese."

She tilted her head arrogantly and said, "You are not the new leader of the plantation. You are only a hired soldier. I will remain with Guillaume."

"There is no more Mossard Dynasty. As a common citizen, he reverts to one wife."

Her mouth flattened over her teeth, making her face ugly.

"If you think that I will stay as your reward, *vous vous bien trompez!*" She used the typical French expression with gallic flair. "I would rather return to my village!"

"That is exactly where you are going."

I snapped at one of the Nungs.

"Take her upstairs, *mais ne touchez pas!*"

A hoarse scream rose faintly from outside and grew in intensity. Hackles speared my back. I raced out of the room and pushed and shoved my way through the mass of humanity. The scream shrilled again.

Close to the swimming pool, two Nungs held the desperately struggling Mossard. Another Nung was extracting a dripping bayonet from his entrails.

Xuan, his face twisted with passion, stood by and commanded, "*Encore....*"

The muscles of the executioner tightened.

"Stop it," I yelled at the top of my lungs. "You goddamned butchers. Stop it...."

As I ran, I saw the long wraith of Nguyen Cam, his face a mask of evil and triumph.

"For the love of God ... oh my God ..." Mossard gasped, head rolling toward me in agony.

The Nung, frozen at the sound of my voice, held the point.

Cam flung his arms in fury and hurled a volley of Vietnamese at his son. Xuan seemed to shrivel. Before I could reach them, the mandarin signaled the executioner.

Mossard split open like a rice bag. The trees seemed to hold and bring back the echo of his death rattle. I flipped the Nung in a whiplash that broke his arm like a dry twig snapping.

The planter sank to his knees. "King...." His whisper was hollow, red bubbles forming on his lips. "My safe ...." He slumped lifelessly into the arms of the men who held him.

I walked quietly toward Nguyen Cam. He slunk back from me. The scar under his nose shone white.

"The French tyrant is dead!" he screamed. "I, Nguyen Cam, have won!"

I measured the distance to a centimeter, stiffened my hand until the forearm was rigid and hard as a pipe, and struck viciously at his neck. Cam flew backward like a giant vulture, flapping its wings. He was dead before he hit the turf.

Winding a dirty handkerchief around my throbbing wrist, I asked Xuan, "How did he get here?"

The muscles in the young general's shoulders bulged. His fists clenched.

"Don't try it, Xuan."

I watched warily until the boy's passion subsided and was visible only in his face.

"How did Cam get here?"

His voice was shaky. "He walked from the woods. The guard let him in."

"Our bond is unbreakable now. If you ever disobey me again, I will do the same to you."

Suddenly, the boy fell to his knees alongside Cam's body. He folded his hands and broke into a singsong wail.

I clapped him hard on the shoulder and commanded, "On your feet!"

He staggered up.

"I want this place cleared within half an hour."

Behind the reluctant salute was repressed hatred.

Turning my back on the scene of death, I tramped past the assembly of stupefied Frenchmen and entered the Château. Slowly, I climbed the marble stairs to the master suite.

CHAPTER THIRTEEN

The moon had emerged from the trees and awakened the calling geckos before I arose from the swivel chair. The French had been evacuated hours before. There had been no renewal of the conflict.

Crossing to the cellarette, I poured myself a generous brandy. The fiery liquid bit into my parched throat, relieving the ache of the day's ordeal. I came out of my trance.

I felt no elation or depression at the victory—except over the loss of Mossard.

I dispatched the *couloir* guard for Xuan. When he reported, he was coldly correct in his posture, his eyes boring past me.

"We have a saying in the West," I said. " 'Thieves hang together, or they hang separately.' Your father, Cam, would not have understood. His proverb was, 'Tigers hunt each other, while they hunt together.' And so ... he died. I take full responsibility. I expect your enmity for my action, but I also expect fulfillment of your bond. Because of your father's stupidity, we many not be able to hold the plantation. Mossard was the last symbol of French strength in Viet Nam. The Legion, from Ben-Cat to Saigon, would like nothing better than to strike at this compound with all of its artillery strength. Shall I tell you what will happen then? The two of us will dangle right from this balcony. No salt in your nose. No prolonged agony. Just the short cracking sound of your neck breaking, and you can start looking for the nearest banyan tree to haunt."

Xuan focused on me with fearful fascination.

"Your father had the prestige to save us from this vengeance—by being the figurehead of nationalism and swearing allegiance to the Diem government. On the verge of becoming a Vietnamese hero, he was too blind and arrogant to realize it, so he falls into ignominy. Now, you are filled with his passion and the same thing will happen to you."

He shifted uncomfortably. "I see now that he was wrong."

I let him squirm.

"There is a chance that the French *fonctionnaires* in Saigon will be afraid to move without word from Paris. If so, that gives us a day's grace. You grew up, Xuan, when your father died. Tomorrow you will have to prove it with men twice your years."

The young Vietnamese general was wary. "What must I do?" he asked.

"You will take the rubber train to Saigon and be at the Palace of Independence by sunup. Present yourself in your father's name, promise allegiance to the new government, take responsibility for the security of the plantation and say that D'Or Blanc will continue to harvest rubber under Vietnamese management."

His resentful manner yielded suddenly to a rush of pompous vanity.

He struck a pose and announced dramatically, "I shall truly take my father's place."

"If you look as absurd as you do now, they will not believe that you can."

Flushing, he avoided my eyes, and I continued, "Your sister … what do you want done with her?"

Adopting a haughty demeanor, he said, "She has forsaken all right to be Vietnamese. Her breath smells of French wine and her skin of French flowers. She flaunts herself in tight French clothes and would shock the most tolerant ancestors … and she is barren. Let her go with the French."

"Too late," I said cryptically. "She can stay where she is until we see if you are capable of deciding more important affairs."

Changing the subject then, I said, "Load the train with whatever crepe is on hand at the siding and be on your way before midnight. Mount an armed guard of gendarmes on the locomotive and tell the engineer not to slow down until he reaches Saigon."

With grave misgivings as to his ability in shrewed political company, I went to bed. Tired as I was, there was no sleep for me in Mossard's broad, velvety throne. Its luxurious depth gave me the feeling of drowning. After tossing for an hour, I tore through the mosquito netting and lay on the cool, hard tiles of the floor. I quickly lost consciousness.

Some sixth sense that fluttered a warning in the back of my head made me awaken. Without moving, I looked across the moon-drenched bedroom. The connecting door to the bedroom was swung open wide. Framed in the emptiness was Thi-Tuyet. She was moving soundlessly toward me.

I sat up.

She stopped instantly. Her voice was soft. "I had hoped you were not yet asleep."

I flicked on a lamp. She was sheathed in a transparent nightgown.

"I did not know of my brother's bond to you," she said. "You are the *patron*. I will stay as your mistress."

"Along with the title and furniture," I said with irritation. "That was Mossard's idea—not mine. I need no second wife, nor even a first one."

Kneeling beside me, she caressed my hair. "We will have time for love, and I will help you with the mandarins even more slyly than I did for Guillaume."

I said coldly, "I do not want you, Tuyet. Xuan will dispose of you, when he has time."

She recoiled as if she had been struck. "You dare say this to me, after what I have risked to encourage you to power."

"Good night."

She sprang to her feet, black ringlets of hair tossing angrily.

"I helped you win. Now, you throw me away. You dare ... dirty as a coolie ... with an ugly beard ... smelling foul ... to throw me away!"

She stamped bare feet near my head. "I would not lie with you now if you begged."

I yawned and turned over.

She was silent for several moments, then—"I shall go to Paris and live among civilized people."

I did not answer.

The heel of her foot jarred my back.

"Wake up and listen," she blazed. "Did you hear me? I said I shall go to Paris."

On my elbows again, I said with exasperation, "Go ahead. But, if you are depending on Mossard's will, he left you nothing."

The temper oozed out of her.

"You are to keep your wardrobe and jewelry. Now, good night."

I turned off the light and closed my eyes.

Her voice held a desperate quality. "I shall ask the French in Saigon to help me."

I did not reply.

She lay down beside me on the floor. The cool of her hand crept across my chest.

"Does not the perfume entering your nose remind you of frangipani, King?"

Her voice was as silken as her touch.

"Have you not longed for, in the dirtiness of your work, a clean woman against your skin?"

I felt her lips against my back.

"I shall draw a bath for you, *chéri*," she murmured.

"If I wanted you," I answered, without turning, "I would take you without bathing. But, get this through your head. I do not.

Now, go back to bed … or to your mother in the paddy … or to France … or to any goddamned place you want. Just get the hell out of here and let me get some sleep."

Her touch vanished and her voice in the dark was tight with fury.

"I despise you, King. I hate you more than I thought I could hate anybody! You would take me without my consent? Hah! I would go through your troops and leave them exhausted before I would have your hand on my thigh again."

I fell into an exhausted sleep.

CHAPTER FOURTEEN

General Nguyen-van-Xuan returned from Saigon in triumph, his train gaily decorated with pictures of Ngo-dinh-Diem and flashing silk banderols of saffron and scarlet. The Legion retreated from the plantation and established its northern outpost in Ben-Cat. We had won.

I concentrated on rubber. The tappers were instructed to do the same things they normally did when the French were watching them. Production dropped off 50 per cent.

Nationalization meant freedom to the tappers and most of them construed it as freedom from work. With some broad hints to the mandarins about an equivalent cut in the payroll, production crawled up to 75 per cent. According to my time-table, if we collected latex for three more weeks, I would have enough to dribble to the port in decreasing amounts while the tappers went into secret training. The political experts in the city would attribute the dwindling trains to poor management—and, without causing alarm, I could "hide" my force. I augmented the *gendarmerie* with the partially trained Tonkinese I had recruited, what remnants of Cam's cadres I could find, and put the lot on eighteen-hour schedule under the Nungs.

Guillaume Mossard was buried in the front garden, and I had his grave surrounded with painted bamboo railings.

Leaving Xuan in command with strict instructions to push production to the highest possible efficiency, I left D'Or Blanc, uncovered the Cambodian junk at the water's edge and floated down the ever-widening coils of the Saigon River to the capital. Unnoticed, I crept into my old niche in the Arroyo Chinois.

Lotus Bud had not returned, but I assured her father that she had struck a rich lode and gave him a thousand piasters to prove it. Unusually responsive, he followed me over the connecting planks to shore, bowing with gratitude.

With dread, I cut across the darkened Grand Marché to rue Grandière and Charlotte Mossard.

"My God!" she whispered thickly, her face drawn in disbelief. "Get out! Get out of here … quickly."

I made no move, nor any attempt to touch her.

"I tried to save him—you must have heard."

"You killed him," she cried. "You planned his murder … even while you were staying with me."

Shivering, she covered her face with her hands. "I feel unclean."

"He asked me to come to you," I said softly, handing her a thick folded paper. "His will. Everything goes to you."

She accepted the legal brief without thanks. Her eyes, pinched by puffy sockets and freshly dry, avoided mine. "Will you please leave now?" she said, holding the door.

There was a newspaper, damp in spots, on the table. I picked it up. A bold three-column picture of Mossard, younger and very handsome, was under a banner headline blazoning the capture. Smaller headlines read, AMERICAN SOLDIER OF FORTUNE ENGINEERS COUP. In the text, I received full and condemnatory credit for the savage murder of fifty-eight French Legionnaires, including Guillaume Mossard—grudging *grâce* for the safety of evacuated civilians.

"This is wrong, Charlotte," I said. "He was being evacuated with the other French. Cam, his old mandarin enemy, got to him behind my back. I was too late…."

The hurt in her face caused me to stop.

"I heard such a rumor," she said. Her voice was resigned. "There is no need to apologize. What is done is done. I did not know you at all, Daniel, and I thought I knew you so well. Now, if you will go ... I have a job and I need my rest."

Suddenly angry, I said, "I did nothing that Mossard himself had not done a dozen times over in building D'Or Blanc. Except I get the publicity. And I am damned. Where do you think the money came from for your minks and alligator bags and miniature Kohinoor diamonds? Because it was the blood of Vietnamese instead of French, does that make it decent and less brutal?"

She trembled, eyes frozen on me.

"You make money in this part of the world, Charlotte, by stepping on people, and if you look back to see how messy it was, somebody will step on you while your back is turned. I am sorry Guillaume got in my way, but I am not sorry for what I have done."

"You make me feel I am at fault, Daniel."

"You had nothing to do with it. It could have been a Marie or Yvette just as easily as a Charlotte who reaped the benefit. You are respectable and beautiful, and the more you are the less questions you ask. Some men buy that way, and some women like it. You seem to be one of them."

A shuddering sob brought no tears. "I loved him."

I continued relentlessly. "You loved your pink cloud. You dreamed up all sorts of excuses to come back to Saigon, but the real one was to be close to your pink cloud. Then, the wind changed. But there was never any pink cloud for Mossard—not for you, or even for the native girl. He had not touched her in months. Mossard was capable of love—for his mistresses, he called them, the trees that gave him their white gold. Before the attack, I offered him the choice of going back to you with his fortune or fighting it out for his life."

Her gaze was steady. "Did he know about us?" she interrupted.

"No."

The will fluttered from her fingers to the floor.

"And you … Daniel? When will you stop?"

Turning to go, I answered, "When I am stopped."

Restraining me with her hand, she murmured, "Nothing I could say would prevent you, but when you buy your beautiful and respectable wife, select one without a heart."

"I do not intend to buy."

Her mouth worked. "Where is he … buried?"

"The garden in front of the Château. I figured he belonged there."

She nodded wearily. "I suppose so. I would like to see his grave."

"That is not possible, Charlotte."

Sighing, she said, "Then I shall return to Paris. There is nothing to hold me here now."

"You will need this." I retrieved the will from the floor and handed it to her. "Your friends will be expecting it."

"I intend to give this to a foundation," she said softly. "The money is not really mine."

Her hand was still touching mine. "I believe what you told me, Daniel, about … how it happened. I do not regret our days together. We are not responsible for what we do in … our pink clouds, are we?"

My throat was knotted.

She smiled faintly and said, "I am glad you came to me. That took courage—the kind I like in a man." Her fingers pressed mine. "*Au revoir.*"

I stumbled out of the apartment.

In the street a blinding spotlight caught and held me. I heard the clatter of hobnailed boots and the rattle of arms. A squad of Binh Xuyen police surrounded me.

"Come," one said, "you are wanted."

I was hustled into the rear of a vehicle and blindfolded. Only a few minutes elapsed before I felt the familiar sponge rubber of the high-backed chair, and opened my eyes to see the ruby glows of cigar tips.

A thin, silver-white strip of light from a gooseneck lamp glared at me suddenly and forced me to squint.

"Mr. King," the same suave voice began, "your taste in women is impeccable, but beautiful baubles extract high tolls … perhaps, *more* than the ten thousand dollars we gave you?"

With irritation I said, "If I had known you owned the Floating City, I would have been more careful. I dislike being tossed about like a coolie basket."

"It behooves us to take a personal interest in our properties, especially when they are on the verge of appreciating. We wanted to be the first to talk to you."

"Your calling card was in exquisite taste.'"

The voice ignored my sarcasm and continued coolly, "We were impressed with the speed and execution with which you contained the plantation. Also, the ambassadorial visit of the boy, Xuan—while crude—seems to have worked. His bragging was ludicrous, but his 'allegiance' was accepted—I am sure only for its propaganda value throughout the country. Be that as it may, time is of the essence now. Why are you wasting it?"

I was contemptuous. "Ten thousand dollars bought an option—not my recreation."

The darkness behind the spotlight seemed amused.

"We have never questioned your motives, other than financial, in deposing Mossard. With Madame in the picture, they could possibly fill a book. So—now that you have attached yourself, a mere million in your future seems inadequate?"

"Forget Madame Mossard. She has nothing to do with the deal—or with me."

"Very interesting …." The voice paused.

I tried to see past the glare to the source of suddenly guarded whispers.

"Frankly, King," he continued aloud, "there are several blocs represented here in Saigon who would find your... new status intriguing. Quite possibly at more than a million. You can understand our concern at your meeting one of them—strictly unintentionally, of course—purely by accident."

There was no mistaking his sarcasm.

"Sure," I said, "lots of people must have spare weapons for fifteen thousand troops."

"I am referring to after our delivery. Saigon is forbidden to you, King, from now on. I have spoken of the exigency of time. The months remaining for you to produce an army at D'Or Blanc do not allow for boudoir activities. Are we understood?"

"I understand when I begin the training. Now I am cutting rubber."

A dry laugh sliced the air.

"The arms you require shall be in your hands a week from today. They will be delivered to you secretly in a manner I shall not discuss. I should not have to warn you of the urgency in maintaining equal secrecy in training. The isolation of D'Or Blanc should not present undue difficulty."

"What arms?" I asked.

"The same that you used in training your Nungs at the Arroyo godown, if you like." The voice was smug in its knowledge.

"Plus mortars."

"That can be arranged. What we desire from you is a frontal assault on the Palace. That will be in conjunction with our own artillery's bombardment and subsequent mopping up. You will be advised of the exact date and time. In lieu of your further visits to Saigon, you may contact us, if necessary, by discreet messenger through the Grand Monde."

"And Ly-van-Vien's million—where will that be? Under the welcome mat at the Palace?"

"With your combat deployment into the Palace grounds, a letter will be sent to Tan-Son-Nhut Airport addressed to you in care of Air France. It will contain the serial of a numbered account drawn on an international Swiss bank. A draft for one million dollars has already been deposited to the credit of this number. It is yours. The letter will contain two tickets to Paris and will be in the possession of Madame Mossard."

I got to my feet. "I do not understand."

"Madame Mossard is to remain under our 'protection' until that time." The high-pitched voice was smooth.

My fists clenched. A powerful hand from out of the dark bounced me back into the cushions.

"I told you she has nothing to do with me. I brought her Mossard's will. I never expect to see her again."

The voice was silken. "We know, Mr. King, all about you and Madame. Never fear for the lovely Madame."

When they released me, I raced toward Charlotte's apartment.

Papers were strewn over the floor and the empty drawers were tilted out crazily. I ripped aside the drapery that covered the closet. Bare hangers clicked together. A pair of high-heeled slippers lay discarded.

The Binh Xuyen had executed its kidnapping ruthlessly and without delay.

Leaving the apartment, I walked the streets. I did not want Charlotte connected with my plans—much less dependent on them. Now, she was deeply involved in them and there was little I could do about it—or was there?

The normally uproarious throngs on the sidewalks seemed more quiet tonight than I remembered—orderly, almost somber. Was it the looming of the inevitable war? Studying faces I passed, I found with great surprise that they were studying me and getting out of the way. A barefoot coolie, toting a long pole of feather dusters over his shoulder, fell in his frantic desire to avoid me.

A squatting hawker, surrounded by pots of poisonous-looking green jelly, grabbed excitedly and pointed at me.

An Indian merchant lounging at the door of his shop spoke surreptitiously to a neighbor. I heard the words "bearded American devil."

The reality broke in on me. My ascension to power in Viet Nam had been so meteoric that I was famous.

Turning into a grimy, one-chair *Hot Toc* shop, I ordered a shave. The whole beard went on the floor. My slacks, shirt and underwear followed. I took a room in a cheap Chinese hotel and scrubbed myself and donned new clothes.

Next morning, nobody noticed me.

At Tan-Son-Nhut Airport, I checked Air France in the possibility that Charlotte had been flown out. She had not been booked, nor had anyone of her description left on the morning flight.

I made arrangements to take flying lessons from one of the private pilots in the commercial hangar. Giving him one thousand dollars in advance, I ordered him to solo me before the end of the week—and to keep his mouth shut. After the grueling lesson, I took a taxi to the Villa d'Or Blanc on Boulevard Norodom.

The elegant terraced *maison* was shuttered. The grilled gates were chained and a Legionnaire paced back and forth in front of the entrance.

"I want to see Lien-Fat," I said, strolling up to him.

He was bored. "La *plantation d'Or Blanc est fermée.*"

"You have the wrong tip, André," I said. "D'Or Blanc is open as it never was before. Tell Lien-Fat that if he will not see me, I shall get an injunction from the new government and confiscate his property."

"Who are you?" he demanded.

"King. Daniel King."

The Legionnaire's face twisted and he growled, "Get moving."

"Better open up before you are in trouble," I said coldly. "I have a record, you know, for showing up the Legion."

Face purple, he dropped the massive chain.

Lien-Fat, spectacles tilted precariously, was in his office poring over a yard-long ledger. When he saw who it was, he throbbed like an accordion, lowering his massive bulk into the chair. In so doing, he cracked a kneecap and let out an agonized yelp.

"Well, Scrooge!" I hailed him cheerfully. "Now that Christmas is over, let us back to squeezing the public."

All he could do was blow out his cheeks and hiss in guttural pain.

Laughing, I sat on a corner of his desk. "Open up! We are in business. Or maybe nobody told you. Let me introduce myself. Dan King—newly appointed adviser to the Vietnamese management of D'Or Blanc. There was a rubber train down last week and another due this week. Stop writing obituaries, and start making us money."

He looked at me in utter amazement and puffed, "I...I...I am resigned!"

"Fine. We shall draw up a new contract. Same salary. Same position. Same winks at the expense account for your children in Harvard, Vassar and the Sorbonne.... Good Christ! Don't they ever graduate?"

"Next year—" he began proudly.

"Never mind. Start writing."

He pulled himself together and scrutinized me. "Maybe you want to kill me?" he queried.

"The best rubber *compradore* in the Far East? Write!"

Lien-Fat opened a desk drawer with alacrity, then screwed his chins doubtfully.

"I think Vietnamese and me work not so good together, Mr. King. French very good. American okay. Vietnamese no good."

I slid off the edge of his desk and asked, "So … what is the matter with the Vietnamese? They have two arms, two legs and two heads—just like you."

He laughed feebly and mopped his face. "You no understand, Mr. King. Vietnamese very jealous of Chinese. Not allow make money. Call all Chinese coolies and treat same. I make plans go Hong Kong next few weeks. Work for English. English very good … same like French, but not pay so good money."

"How much money is in the safe?"

He looked at me with alarm. "What you want? Steal?"

"Is there enough to cover a year's contract for you in advance?"

A flush swept over his face. He scrambled to his feet and clasped my hand. "You very good man, Mr. King. I sorry to help arrange kill you, but you know I got children in Sorbonne, Har—"

"I know … I know. Fill out the contract."

He signed in a flourish, beamed, bowed and shook my hand three times.

"First off," I ordered, "call Legion Headquarters of the French Expeditionary Force and tell them to relieve the guard out front. Tell them you are the General Manager of the Vietnamese National Rubber Company. If they start to sputter, tell them we shall resort to confiscation."

The conversation was lengthy but Lien-Fat hammered the Commandant into submission. The only phrase I caught from the other end of the line was a bewildered *"Mon Dieu! … Quel temps."*

"Good." I said. "Now, give me the payroll cash—whatever is left after your contract. Keep the negotiable credits to use for expenses."

As the rotund Oriental bent over the circular lock in the wall, I said, "Lien, Madame Mossard has disappeared."

He pondered for a moment, turned around and said, "That very bad, Mr. King. Woman go hell fast in Saigon."

"I want to know exactly where she is—by tomorrow. Pay top commission."

A scotch-taped manila envelope crammed with bills lay on my lap as I bit into the wide pasture that was a strip of Tan-Son-Nhut Airport, and pointed the L-5's nose northward. My pilot-instructor breathed with relief as we left the ground.

For five days, I had hovered around the Villa d'Or Blanc waiting for word. Lien-Fat's Chinese tentacles had groped in vain. The platinum-haired girl had been swallowed by the Binh Xuyen as efficiently as she had been kidnaped. I could not afford to wait longer.

As I crossed the unkempt grass leading from the D'Or Blanc strip to the Château, the purring of the pilot's plane faded away in the distance. Mossard's Piper was here in the hangar. Now I could commute at will with little loss of time.

Passing the swimming pool I saw it coated with scum and yellow leaves; a dead gecko floated belly-up in the putrid water. The Château house crew was sprawled indolently around the steps, some nursing babies, others dozing, squatting, and chewing betel. The pristine pavements were stained with red splotches; the "welcoming arms" stair well smelled of urine. A waft of opium floated out of the cellar. Huge flies buzzed around the garbage that had been dumped on Mossard's grave.

Pausing for a moment on the hollow-sounding marble stairs, I heard the gay laughter of dinner parties from the vast dining room, the uncertain clacks of Thi-Tuyet's high heels, the boisterous shouts from the pool, the scuffle of servants bent on orderliness and the stentorian authority of the Master's voice. The balustrade felt icy in my hand. Oddly, I remembered what Tuyet had said once. "You are too late."

The convoy of gray, lumbering trucks came over the Cambodian border and disgorged a mountain of crates. The blank-faced Cambodian border guard, who supervised the delivery, gave me a molded silver bullet. Inside was a tiny scrap of paper with the inscription, *April 1.*

I had a little less than three months to go.

CHAPTER FIFTEEN

The Vietnamese "Year of the Horse" ended in February of 1955. I watched it go along with a trainload of stenciled bales that I had gotten out practically single-handed. The celebration of the New Year—*Fête du Tet*—had thrown me dangerously behind schedule. The entire plantation had taken a week's holiday for celebrating, and there was nothing I could do to stop it.

Xuan had shrugged regretfully, admitted the need for conscientious effort, and then had disappeared into the oriental Mardi Gras.

Amidst the firecrackers, cymbals, dragon dances, gorging and incessant ancestor fires, I fought to train cadres and produce latex. My efforts were as futile as Mossard's had been when the order went out to "bleed." Nothing interfered with the passing of an old year and the greeting of the new.

Rubber production quotas had fallen drastically up to the time of the holiday and then became nil.

Discarding bookkeeping systems, I had conducted a cash pay-off every night at the weighing sheds. Bonus money for top loads. With the mandarins wanting extra money for *Tet,* it had worked—at least enough to get out a train half-filled. But the warehouses were empty. There was no stock for the forthcoming critical weeks.

The Binh Xuyen mountain of weapons had been divided into fifteen hills and trucked to recessed locations in the rubber preserve. But the crates had not been opened. "After *Tet*" was a phrase that had come to rub sorely on my nerves.

At last, the Château was humming with something like efficiency. I had taken care of that with several judicious "transfers" of personnel back to the villages.

The pool water was fresh and invigorating. I swam hard for ten minutes before vaulting out, toweling and sitting under the palms at a table laid for lunch. The boy, in starched white jacket, brought a tray on which steamed Coquilles St. Jacques. His movements were equally deft with the silver wine cooler…into which he slipped a chilled bottle of Vouvray.

My plan was to create three walls of attack—one following the other at intervals—of roughly five thousand each with logistic support in the form of wives, children, oxcarts and water buffalo. The idea was not original. The Russians used it—with infinitely larger masses and waves—to sweep over Poland and Germany.

Clustering the fire of mortars and massing riflemen, even without the keenest accuracy, would put on a good show— at least, against what opposition I had seen around Saigon. Opposing tanks, while formidable, could be blown with home-made plastic grenades. I had already made and tested a plastic antitank grenade that packed about eight pounds of dynamite. They could be strapped to dogs, lured into position by thrown meat, and exploded under the chains with rifle fire.

I had come to the conclusion that Charlotte Mossard meant enough to me that I was going to be on that plane April first.

A jeep plowed up the graveled drive, bounced over flower beds and tracked through the velvet lawn.

"You stupid sonofabitch!" I roared at the wanton destruction.

Xuan, resplendent in glittering uniform, jumped out.

I gritted my teeth. "Your soldiers are the only ones in the world who think that order means something to eat."

With dignity he replied, "Your tone is reminiscent of the French. You sent the driver for me?"

"Yes. Tell him that if I had wanted a road to the swimming pool, I would have built one."

Xuan battled me for a brief second—eyes sullen—then rattled off a vicious command to the offending driver. The jeep whined into reverse and backed off, leaving two more gashes in the nap of the grass.

Between mouthfuls of succulent Châteaubriand, I observed, "The Nungs and the Tonkinese have some brains, but these from Cochin-China are all bone. Do you agree, General?"

Xuan flushed and in a strangled voice said, "They are my people. Please do not talk of them with such derision."

I sighed. "I know. I know. You are Number One and they love you … so long as *I* meet the payroll."

He shifted uncomfortably, and said, "You have become very cruel since the death of my father."

"If I have, it is because you have been listening to shouts of 'Ten Thousand Years' and stuffing yourself into insensibility when you should have been working. Is that nonsense over yet?"

Stiffly he answered, "If you mean *Tet,* it is not nonsense. All Vietnamese must greet the New Year with deference and worship to the departed."

I sighed with resignation. "It is over now. Right?"

He nodded.

"Thanks be to Buddha. Tomorrow, get the *gendarmerie* cadres into every village to conduct physical fitness drills and start picking soldiers. Seal off the Rubber Road with armed guards and get a labor crew breaking down the weapons. But keep the ammunition boxed."

He fidgeted nervously. "My people do not want to fight. I would like to lead them in peace."

I groaned. "Peace! Why do you think they are bowing and scraping all over you? Because all of Indochina is about to explode and you are the closest thing to a general this plantation has. With a platform of peace, you rank after everybody who was born ahead of you, and that is just about everybody. Go and stick your head in the pool, Xuan, and shrink it down to size."

He continued with determination, "I do not like the idea of fighting for the Binh Xuyen, Mr. King."

"So—the worm in the core pushes out its head. What do you suggest doing, General?"

"I should like to side with Ngo-dinh-Diem."

"I thought you were such a rabid Communist?"

"I am sorry that Ho-Chi-Minh turned against his people. The freedom he promised was gold-colored dust. I could not stand to look as they came onto the docks in Saigon. Men wabbling like balloons with no legs to stand on or arms to beg … heads shaved flat of ears. Women with scars where once were proud breasts. Poor … poor people."

His voice was deep with feeling. "Nobody has ever been kind to my people. Nobody except Ngo-dinh-Diem. That is who I would like to lead my country—somebody like him. That is why I should like to side with him."

I stopped eating to ask sternly, "Do you want to offer your men to the National Army?"

He nodded.

"Then, where will you be—the general leading them? They have as many generals sitting around chopping pay vouchers as we have cadres in the *gendarmerie*. Two and three times your age—with years of combat experience in North Viet Nam under the French. Go ahead. Make the offer and see what happens. You will be back rattling roulette wheels at the Grande Monde … and hoping to hell the Binh Xuyen wins."

He regarded me through half-closed eyes.

"Your words are woven like rattan strips," he said, "and I cannot break their strength. After we select the soldiers, what is it that you want me to do?"

"I want them out of the villages and into the rubber where we have stacked the weapons. Start them with basics, as we had at the godown. The women can bring food and stay over Saturday nights, but otherwise—out of the way. Do not disturb the mandarins. Tell them that they will be paid as usual—double if they have no deserters by April first."

"What about the Cao-Dai villages?"

"Leave them alone. We have enough men without them, and I do not want Pope Tac to get suspicious. They can continue to harvest rubber, so we can keep up the semblance of business as usual."

"We are really going to war," he said in half-wonderment.

The Vietnamese general hung around as I finished the steak.

"My sister has been in our village for *Tet*," he said, "and now she is going to Saigon."

"So?"

"Now that she has lost face, the plantation no longer pleases her."

"Does this concern me?"

Xuan was ill at ease. "She said that you had enjoyed her, but did not provide for her as you had promised."

I grunted. "The promise was in her imagination. She was not my wife."

"I am not criticizing you for taking pleasure." His voice was soothing. "She has lost the ways of the Vietnamese. What I mean is … when you fly to Saigon for the new payroll, perhaps you could see that she has money. I would not like … that is … she is of my family."

"Face?"

He reddened.

"Very well, I shall make it a point to see she has money. We cannot have the sister of General Nguyen-van-Xuan reclining in a *maison de tolerance*."

"Thank you, Mr. King."

He turned his back, walked in a dignified manner to the jeep—then, leaping the last few steps, he excoriated the driver.

The vehicle left a cloud of gravel dust to settle slowly over the lawn.

The next day, the rubber train brought back a letter from Lien-Fat. He had located Charlotte Mossard.

CHAPTER SIXTEEN

The minute I touched down at Tan-Son-Nhut Airport, I could sense electricity in the air. Barbed wire was strung everywhere; guards were tense and self-conscious; the formalities of passing through the terminal were tenuous and time-consuming; there were no taxis.

I caught a ride into the city with a truckload of Nationalist soldiers who had just been flown in from Hue, the northernmost garrison of South Viet Nam. Reinforcements.

At the villa, Lien-Fat was scowling. "I make one big mistake stay in Saigon," he complained. "Freighter ships no want come here with big war scare. Also, very inferior rubber bales you send. Much dirt inside. Smell as acid and soft. I think is smart close plantation, Mr. King. Without French, cannot make good rubber."

"Never mind all that." I cut him off. "What is going on here? Has the war started?"

He sighed, removed spectacles and massaged the pinched fat on his nose. "Too many grenades on street. Diem have police now. Binh Xuyen also have police. Every time police meet is grenade and shooting. Many people hurt yesterday at Continental Hotel." He shook his head disconsolately. "Too much police to protect people. I give back money and go Hong Kong. Okay?"

"You will sit here and sell rubber, if you have to mix it with rice and call it *soupe chinois*."

The bulky *compradore* considered me with sad eyes.

"Much rumor, Mr. King, about giant transfer of arms from Binh Xuyen to one of sects. New United Front is formed against government. Cao-Dai and Hoa-Hao men resign from Diem Palace. I feel like fly buzzing between two cymbals. We go Hong Kong? Both go … yes?"

"Neither one of us—no. Where is Madame Mossard?"

"Binh Xuyen made prisoner of silver-hair Mossard wife. Keep alone in luxury villa on rue Grande de la Liraye. Much guard. I pay ten thousand piasters for information. Very secret."

"Do you have the address?"

He nodded.

"Then, get on the telephone with one of your Binh Xuyen contacts—the higher up the better. Tell him I know where Madame Mossard is, and I expect to see her in ten minutes. If they know what is good for them, they will let me in."

He looked at me shrewdly. "You go much trouble for Madame. Maybe later become King wife?"

"Maybe."

He reached for the telephone.

In one of the black Citroëns from the villa garage, I found the gardened, glass-fronted estate on Grande de la Liraye. It lay well back from the street, almost hidden in a riot of Japanese foliage. A vigilant green-bereted guard passed me through the filigreed gates without question.

When I stepped into the *salon,* she was in my arms.

"Daniel," she whispered, and my world became a place worth living.

"I had nothing to do with this," I said after a while. "The Binh Xuyen are using you as a hostage to insure my good behavior."

"I know."

"I told them we meant nothing to each other."

Our eyes locked. Hers were sadder, somehow deeper, steadier. "I would not have believed you either," she said softly. I put my mouth over warm, sweet lips.

"Have they mistreated you?" I demanded in a whisper.

"No. Only I have missed ... people. I was never used to thinking very much, and I am not sure I like it. How much longer must I stay here, Daniel?"

"Another month, darling. No longer. Then, Paris, London, New York—any place you say. We will have enough money for a long while."

She looked at me and a shadow crossed her face. "Have you been stopped, Daniel?"

It took a second to understand her question. "Yes," I said thoughtfully, "I suppose I have."

Her eyes held me, searching. "Then, the time will go quickly for me. I have asked myself so many questions these past weeks. But the one I kept pushing away was, 'He has to take a choice— suppose it is not me?' "

"Silly question."

Her head nestled against my shoulder, the tension seemed to go out of her.

"A letter came this week from the lawyers," she said. "There is a Guillaume Mossard Foundation in Paris now for the education of biochemists and plantologists. There will be a big building with his name on it. It is what he always hoped for."

I kissed the silver mist of her hair.

"Are you going back to the plantation?" she asked softly.

I nodded, still holding her.

"Will you be safe up there? I mean ... there is no chance of ... ?"

"I am safer there than here."

A little laugh of relief brushed my ear. "If we had champagne, I would drink to your lost beard," she smiled, finger lightly touching my chin. "I think I like you best this way."

Lifting my hand in a toasting gesture, I said, "The same for your pedestal."

Her voice was small and there were no violin strings when she said seriously, "I think I will learn to love you very much."

"To love and luck," I answered.

We sat on a flame-pink satin divan until the patches of sun lengthened across the tiled floor. A uniformed shadow appeared significantly in the doorway.

Charlotte's whisper was tense. "You must go?"

"My pact with the Devil," I said, getting up. "No worrying now. The choice is made—like it or not—and I love it."

Her laughter was forced and shallow. "Promise me that you will be careful . . . ."

I held her against me.

"I do not intend to miss my own wedding," I assured her.

Looking at her for a long moment, memorizing her loveliness, I quietly closed the door.

A squad of Binh Xuyen police escorted me all the way to the airport.

CHAPTER SEVENTEEN

The oven of the sun shone brighter and hotter with each March day. Xuan worked at rifle training; I concentrated on mortars. We moved from group to group throughout long torrid days and late into each night. There was no siesta.

The army was sluggish and dispirited. The shock action that worked so well on the Nungs made the Cochin tappers dull and slow. They had trouble with the rudiments of the weapons. Some of them had difficulty in comprehending what the weapons were for. I began to worry less that it was a poor army, and more if it would get as far as Saigon.

Xuan plodded along, obedient but silent. His pride had been hurt because I had failed to find Thi-Tuyet while in Saigon. At least, I thought that was the reason.

When there was a week left, I began to doubt if we would even get past the Legion at Ben-Cat.

"General Xuan, nothing without a tail could be so stupid. What do you suggest we do? Send your troops into the trees and recruit their replacements?"

His face grew red and his eyes flashed with anger.

"My people are not intelligent, but neither are they stupid. They have not the desire to fight."

"Then, create a desire. If they will not fight on your say-so, tell them that if they kill twenty people, they can spread their arms and fly or turn themselves invisible."

He shook his head and argued, "They are wiser than that."

"Then, rally them to freedom. Call yourself a living statue from Angkor Wat. Mix some bat blood with their *nuoc-mam*—but get them off their tails."

Xuan studied the tip of his toe intently.

"I am afraid that is impossible," he announced with finality.

"All right, Xuan," I said, "whatever is on your mind, bring it out."

Head bent, he said softly, "I know you will be angry, but I have written a letter."

Lifting his head and looking directly at me, he continued, "I have written to our Premier, Ngo-dinh-Diem, and signed it Nguyen-van-Xuan, General of the Northern Army of the Plantation Area." He paused, "I presented him the troops under my command." He let his pent-up breath out.

"You ... did ... what?" Dread struck at my core.

He was silent for a moment, probing me with clear brown eyes.

"He has not answered, but I will wait. If he does not accept my offer, then I will fight, as you direct, for the Binh Xuyen."

"So, this is why the army is so bad—blood brother!"

His features filled with pain.

"I am sorry about my oath," he said tightly. "But, it is better that our people gain freedom and happiness, than for one man to know the fullness of Paradise." He "sim-simmed" quickly.

"When did you write?"

"Three days ago."

My mind worked frantically.

"You are not going to hit me?" he asked.

"What good would that do—when you have just signed my death warrant?"

His brown eyes, pools of compassion, remained firm.

"Diem would have accepted your offer by now ... if he wanted you."

Uncertainty was in his voice when he answered, "I thought he would … yes."

"What about our attack date—April first?"

Xuan's eyes glittered venomously.

"If the Premier does not accept me, he will have to fight me."

"Bravo," I said cynically. "With what—tree branches at thirty paces?"

He caught the significance behind my remark.

"My army will be ready."

"Then, see that it is. Distribute the ammunition."

His features narrowed. "Why are you so confident that Diem will not accept me?"

Smiling wryly, I answered, "The condemned man always hopes that the rope will break."

"I am glad you are not angry. I was prepared to fight you."

I cuffed him on the shoulder. "If you want to see me angry, let those troops be as sour as they are now—whether I win or lose."

He clicked his heels sharply and said, huskiness blurring his voice, "You bet on Double Zero once before, I remember." He about-faced and was gone.

I sat staring into space, revolving alternate courses of action. It would take more than courses of action.

An acceptance from the Palace would write *finis* for me and God knows what for Charlotte.

CHAPTER EIGHTEEN

urriedly, I addressed a note to Ly-van-Vien at Binh Xuyen Headquarters, telling him to disregard any rumors about General Xuan's allegiance to Ngo-dinh-Diem, and assuring him that we would attack as scheduled. Encasing the note in candle wax, I routed my courier out of bed and started the locomotive to Saigon. My word should reach the inner circle sometime during the night. All I had to do now was to devise some means to intercept Diem's reply to Xuan.

Next morning I set out on an excursion of the camps, staying as close to the Rubber Road as possible—in the event a message were passed up from the outpost blocking the plantation.

Xuan had gone into action with a vengeance, apparently prepared for the eventuality. Crude signs lettered with talc paint fluttered between trees and hung on sides of trucks—TEN THOUSAND YEARS WITH GENERAL XUAN, VIET NAM FOR THE VIETNAMESE, DRIVE THE IMPERIALISTS FROM VIET NAM WANDERING DEATH FOR THE FEEBLE OF FINGER. X marks for "Xuan" were carved into tree trunks and flowed vividly with latex. Gum had been smeared in crosses on the bare breasts of the soldiers where it oxidized black, giving them a look of grotesque savagery. Occasional bodies swung upside down in the high foliage, the X marks red with spattered blood. They were serving as targets for the infantry. Wincing at Xuan's treatment of the laggard, I could not deny its effectiveness. Sweat poured in agonized intent from every native face. Mistakes were rare. The sound of a dozen mortars burped in unison, and I turned to watch the tracing. Three hevea trees disappeared in dust. When the target cleared, one was standing, its branches bare of leaves.

Returning to the Château at dusk, I was disquietened that the locomotive had not yet returned. A sense of foreboding made me turn on the radio. I sat stunned at the news pouring out of the receiver.

War had been declared at midnight last night, Saigon Radio reported, and the Nationalist troops of Ngo-dinh-Diem had smashed into the Binh Xuyen strongholds along rue Gallieni and in Cholon. They had attacked the vice dens, bombarded patrol cars and had set fire to the sect's police headquarters. The Binh Xuyen had struck back in heavy street fighting. The French Foreign Legion—partly in process of evacuating—had been sent into the fray to drive a wedge of armor between the conflicting forces. Casualties were in the hundreds. Hospitals were jammed beyond capability.

When I flipped off the set, I knew with certainty that Xuan's pledge giving Diem an overwhelming balance of power had prompted the Premier's long-delayed strike.

The whistle of the locomotive interrupted my savage mood. Racing to the depot, I met the courier halfway. He handed me two letters. Ripping open the first, I read:

MR. KING:

Your secret presentation of the army to Diem, through the boy, Xuan, has been uncovered. I have a copy of the letter.

Yours, received 29 March, 02:00, is herewith returned without comment.

We warned you as to the consequences of duplicity. You may expect that they will be exacted without possibility of failure.

L.V.V.

The letter was on Grand Monde stationery, and the initials encircled with the sect seal.

Twisting the courier by his coat collar, I asked, "What took you so long?"

"There was fighting," he stammered with difficulty. "I could not get through to the Grand Monde until this morning. and then, it was smashed. I was given an address in Cholon. I did not sleep, Mr. King."

I let him go.

"Mr. Lien-Fat gave me the other letter," he said.

The second letter in my hand was addressed to Nguyen-van-Xuan and bore the official stamp of the government. I tore it open. It was written in Vietnamese.

"Can you translate Vietnamese?" I demanded of the waiting courier.

"Yes, sir."

I handed the letter to him. Appearing surprised, he began slowly, "Monsieur: The Provisional Government of South Viet Nam appreciates the offer of troops from the Plantation d'Or Blanc. It would be glad to enlist any volunteers into the regular National Army. Recruiting stations may be found in Saigon, Bien-Hoa or Ben-Cat. The allegiance expressed to Ngo-dinh-Diem is acknowledged and favored."

It was signed by a military *fonctionnaire*. I had him read it again, disbelief fading to a volt of soaring hope.

The government had no idea as to the extent of our army. How could they, the plantation having been sealed? The Binh Xuyen had jumped to the conclusion that I had been bargaining surreptitiously with the Palace and the letter they had intercepted and copied was the final commitment.

"Come along," I said crisply to the courier.

We found Xuan at a camp in the Upper Loop training relentlessly under the lights of trucks.

He read the letter twice and spoke rapidly to the courier—then, turning to me, his eyes smoldering black fire through the mask of dust, he said grimly, "I am sorry. You have lived more years than I, and are wiser in the ways of men. I will never question you again. My army has improved. It will be ready by the first. I will fight as you direct… for any cause you say."

"I am flying to Saigon," I told him. "Unseal the plantation. Roll your battalions in order of battle with the family wagons behind. Let them roll over the Legion at Ben-Cat to get some practice. Then, hold and wait word from me. Make the Château your headquarters. I will be in touch with you."

He saluted smartly.

"If anybody comes near with a white flag," I added, "smash them."

Tan-Son-Nhut Airport was deserted when I landed. So was the villa on rue Grande de la Liraye. Vaulting over the jagged glass-topped wall, I tried all the doors. *Jalousies* were bolted tightly. I called. I knocked. I shouted. There was no answer, nor any sign of Charlotte.

A taxi refused to take me to the Grand Monde until I bribed him. We were stopped by the French Legion as we approached the market area. All intersections to Boulevard Gallieni and Cholon were blocked.

It was impossible to get through.

CHAPTER NINETEEN

Lien-Fat grimaced sourly as I charged into the office.

"Maybe now you listen. No market in world for mud you send on last train. Cost me five thousand piaster to dump in canal. Checks I write on Paris bank bounce back with better rubber. We now broke."

"Never mind that," I said impatiently. "Do you know where the Binh Xuyen took Madame Mossard?"

Squinting eyes frowned. "I have no time watch snowhaired Mossard wife. I look find buyer for Villa and go Hong Kong quick."

"You try and get out of Saigon," I said evenly, "and I will have you thrown in jail for breach of contract."

He sighed. "New government have jails plenty full Binh Xuyen police. No have room for Lien-Fat."

He scratched his nose and regarded me accusingly.

"We finish business, Mr. King. You no good rubber man."

"The hell with rubber. Can you reach the Binh Xuyen?"

He shrugged fat shoulders. "When soldier bodies shoot each other, hit mostly telephone wire."

"Try it."

Bleeps and metallic static rewarded his effort. Waiting several minutes, he cradled the receiver and sat regarding the instrument.

"Get somebody through the truce line to Cholon," I said, "and arrange a meeting with the Number One for me."

He shook his head in amazement.

"You crazy, Mr. King. Top boss never see anybody."

"Then, a little boss will do. Just mention the name King."

His eyes guarded the strong box jealously. "That cost much money."

"Lien," I said flatly, "I have an army at D'Or Blanc…a big army. Fifteen thousand men and they are on the march right now to attack the Palace. Will you please get word to the Binh Xuyen?"

His mouth fell open and his eyes popped.

"You…speak…truth?"

"You will read it in the newspapers when they run into the Legion at Ben-Cat."

"I never think you so clever, Mr. King. Is also secret of Chinese success, you know. 'Wise mandarin hide jewels in foolish cloth.'"

"Will you stay on the job?"

Looking suspicious, he asked, "Have something to do with money in safe?"

"You win. Here is my deal…and you will never get a better one. I will sign over the plantation to you right now as the sole owner. In return, you stay on one more week, carry out my orders and spend all the money that is needed."

His eyes glazed in appraisal.

"That is very bad bargain. Winner of war take plantation."

"But you will have a claim. It has already been nationalized from the French, and I am empowered to sign for the Vietnamese. As of today, it is the best title you can find."

The fat Chinese shook his head slowly.

"Too many war in Indochina. New proud owner of plantation soon be dead."

"Lien," I argued, "the war will be over sooner or later—with my army probably sooner. Look what you will have then."

The chins poised in thought. His fingers moved on an imaginary abacus. "Okay," he said finally. "Is a deal. I work for you seven days. I no like take wild chance, but have grandchildren who grow up soon and want go Harvard, Vassar and Sorbonne like father and mother!" He grinned.

I signed over the title and Lien-Fat tucked it away carefully in the safe.

"Now, get on your dragon and get through to Number One Binh Xuyen, and if it costs to get through, pretend you are spending Mossard's money. Tell the Number One my promise is still good for April first, and I want a guarantee of Charlotte Mossard's safety."

"Okay, seven-day boss. I arrange see him tonight."

Disregarding the vice sect's threat over my life, I left the Villa and walked openly down rue Catinat. I hoped I would be spotted and reported ... to give credibility to Lien-Fat's message. The sooner the better for Charlotte's sake. The thought of the empty villa filled me with an unshakable apprehension.

Somewhere in the distance, the *pham-pham* of a grenade broke the noise of the traffic. No one paid the slightest attention. Women in rainbow silk paused in front of expensive shop windows. Music blared. The grill-front sidewalk cafés were crowded.

Marking time, I looked over the selection of Moi cloth offered by a strolling Hindu, eyed a bare-midriffed French mademoiselle who crossed her legs invitingly in my direction, and turned down an offer to change American money. When the bells of the Saigon Cathedral tolled nine o'clock, I returned with quickening pulse to the Villa d'Or Blanc.

Lien-Fat was still out. When he came in at ten, I met him at the door. The Chinese was haggard and wet with sweat. Something in his expression made me forget the discomfort of the hot night—made me freeze.

"Come to office please, Mr. King."

I followed him. Seating himself behind the desk, he stared at me somberly.

"For God's sake, Lien, what is it?"

"Binh Xuyen say you double-cross and sell army to Diem. Not believe me what I say…even when I swear on Confucius. They want kill you. Ask where you are. I lie. Say not know."

I could hear the thuds in my body.

"And…Madame Mossard?" the words came out with difficulty.

He was silent, but the creaking chair was evidence he had heard the question. His eyes held pity and his chins quivered.

"You deal with very bad men, Mr. King. Madame Mossard is put in house of prostitution."

"My God …" I whispered. "Where is she?"

"Not certain. Is probably in red-light shacks along Cholon canal. Is custom put first women in cheapest house until broken good."

The torrent came.

"The dirty bastards. They took it out on her. Well, I will take it out on them. They will know soon enough who the power is in Viet Nam. They will know when Saigon begins to shake and tremble. And then, they had better tremble too!"

I did not know it, but I was sobbing. I towered over the Chinese.

"I want her out of that house, Lien-Fat, and here in one hour's time, or so help me God, I will smash through Saigon tomorrow and hang every Binh Xuyen to the cross on the church down the street. Tell them that I will not stop at the Palace. I will smash through the Legion and run them right into the sea. *I want her here within the hour. Here!*"

Falling into the chair again, I buried my head in my hands. I was not conscious of time passing. It must have been after midnight when I heard footsteps and turned my head woodenly.

She tottered in front of me. Her eyes, in their delicate frames, burnt and vacuous, looked at me without recognition. Her jaw was bruised. A hank of misty hair had been torn out. The fingers of her hand twitched convulsively. Her dress was splotched with dirt, sweat and stains ... and torn in spots.

"Charlotte!"

There was no recognition. Her mouth worked silently and I could see a tooth missing. Mechanically, she shrank to the floor and started pulling up her dress.

I cried, "Get her to a hospital, Lien-Fat."

The Chinese shifted uncomfortably. "No hospital take white slave woman."

"I ... said ... get ... her ... to ... a ... hospital." I moved toward him with purpose.

"Is very expensive, Mr. King," he whined. "Even so, maybe not possible with wounded soldier bodies."

My hand was close to his throat.

"If it takes every damned cent of that hundred thousand, get ... her ... to a ... hospital."

I twisted the pleats of fat viciously.

"Okay. Okay. I do. I do!"

Distastefully, he unraveled a handkerchief, wrapped his hand and with it guided her from the room.

Hours later, I heard the sound of his bearlike step crunching the floor overhead. I caught him just as he was going into the shower connecting with his room.

"Is okay," he said defensively. "Madame Mossard in hospital. Cost me five thousand dollars."

"What did they say?"

"No say." He shrugged.

"What I like about the Orient," I sneered, "is the love of one for his fellow man."

"You please go away now, Mr. King." He tried to push me toward the door. "I very sleepy."

Standing firm, I watched his face fall. "No sleep for you. Does the Binh Xuyen believe me now?"

"They not sure I think. Give up Madame because already broken."

My laugh was harsh. "You tell them mistakes cost money. The price of my army—if they want it—has gone up to five million dollars."

Sleep vanished from Lien-Fat's eyes. His mouth made a circle of respect.

"I will give them until tomorrow to let me know. I can be contacted at the Hotel Majestic. Now, get moving."

I slept fitfully until the sun came up and then fell into a deep slumber. Late afternoon, I went to the de luxe hotel that overlooked the Saigon River. The lobby was crawling with people anxious for rooms. The International Control Commission, created by the Geneva Accords to inspect North and South Viet Nam, was using the Majestic Hotel as headquarters for its Canadian, Polish and Indian delegations.

I elbowed a tawny-complexioned and overpressed Cambodian out of the way, and planted both hands firmly on the desk.

"I want a room facing the river."

The clerk sniffed and, without looking up, rattled, "Booked up. Sorry. No rooms available."

"My name is King. Dan King."

The face jerked up and the supercilious jelly of his expression froze. His eyes darted to a pile of newspapers stacked on the counter. Black print blared.

D'OR BLANC ARMY THREATENS SAIGON CRUSHES
TWO VILLAGES SOUTH OF PLANTATION LEGION
RETREATS FROM BEN-CAT TO BIEN-HOA

I got a room on the top floor with a view of the river.

When the bellboy had gone, I called the floor steward and pressed his hand full of piasters.

"I want the room across from this one," I said.

"Very sorry, sir. That room is occupied."

"Get them out. Put them somewhere else … without calling the desk. You have ways. I want both of these rooms."

I equaled the amount of money in his hand.

"Yes, sir. Yes, Mr. King."

"The desk is not to know … understand? I am in the room overlooking the river. That is my only room."

"Room four hundred two—yes, Mr. King."

Waiting until he had moved the surprised but not displeased American couple into an air-conditioned suite reserved for French V.I.Ps, I went into room four hundred one—the vacated one—opening on an air shaft, and left the door slightly ajar.

Spreading the journal, I read that an entourage of government vehicles was proceeding to Ben-Cat to swear over the unexpected army. Little trouble was anticipated. Nguyen-van-Xuan, the youthful general, was described as loyal to Ngo-dinh-Diem, and the Premier was praised for drawing on this show of power at a critical moment.

There was some speculation about the size of the D'Or Blanc army and its weapons arsenal. I received cursory mention as a "battle-scarred veteran from European campaigns" who, as military adviser, was "allegedly in the pay of the Americans."

I heard a knock at the door across the hall.

Tiptoeing to my vantage point, I saw the back of the little Cambodian that I had knocked out of the way in the lobby. Opening the door noiselessly, I seized him in a half-Nelson, and with the other hand searched him for weapons. He was unarmed. Gasping at the sudden clamp, he smiled when he saw it was me. I stepped back to let him in.

"My name is Shranisouk," he said, when he was seated. "I do not waste your time or mine. You have an army. I have money. Do we talk?"

Taking my time, I pulled up a chair opposite him.

"How much money?"

"How much army?"

His expression was professionally pleasant.

"Counting wives, warriors, pie-dogs and water buffaloes, enough to drag this city clean by the end of the week."

"One division? Two divisions?" He was curt. I did not like his attitude.

"No divisions. I do not fight that way."

He watched me, digesting my last words.

"I have fifteen thousand combat soldiers."

He whistled—then, his eyes shrank into blank pockets. "Where is Nguyen Cam?"

I smiled in answering. "I thought Moscow ran better intelligence than that. He is dead."

The swarthy Cambodian frowned. "How do you know whom I represent?"

"From the honesty that radiates from your face—the mark of free men everywhere."

He grimaced. "What is the price?"

"More than you have," I told him evenly.

"I will pay one million dollars on a Hong Kong bank."

"Tip it to the bellboy."

"How much do you want, King?" His pointed shoe swung elegantly and easily.

"Say … the top floor of that Hong Kong bank."

"Ten million?"

"You talk big—very big for a Mekong cadre."

He was on his feet in a flash.

"Both Moscow and Peiping know about your army. They are not asleep as decadent nations. If you sell to us, I will have a letter of credit in your name within three days."

"For how much?"

Without hesitating, he said, "Ten million—in any currency convertible in Hong Kong."

"What else?"

"What do you mean?"

"No stainless-steel Stalin medals?"

The Cambodian reseated himself smoothly and tapped out a gold-tipped cigarette.

"I think I understand," he said suavely. "Since you are American, if you turn against the policies of your government, you may not be able to enjoy your gain. Is that it?"

"I have a U.S. passport."

"Ahhh...." His brow furrowed into damp wrinkles. "I am sure I can obtain for you ... sanctuary ... is that what you call it? Yes, sanctuary ... in a northern province of China—your own province, if you like, with a palace, or a *dacha* near Moscow, if you prefer."

"And protection against ... 'taxation'?"

He shrugged. "The tax is thirteen per cent. In our savings banks, at three per cent a year, you can redeem your slight loss in four years."

"You must want that army bad," I said. "If this ground means so much, why does Ho-Chi-Minh stall around?"

"You may be a good military man, Mr. King, but as a politician, you are naïve. Aggression is old-fashioned. It is much better to have people in a target country riot for liberation. Then, Ho-Chi-Minh can come down through Cambodia to protect order. After that ..." He spread his hands.

"What do you want my army to do, tie itself in chains and start singing the 'International'?"

He edged to the front of the chair.

"Attack Diem. Occupy the city. Set up a new government. Declare Ho the father of all Vietnamese people. When the dissident elements fight back, Ho-Chi-Minh will march to unite the true spirit of the country."

"All figured out," I observed thoughtfully. "And it would probably work, too."

The Cambodian arose and ceremoniously extended his hand. "Welcome," he said.

"To what?"

"To the inevitable cause of communism!"

"Better not count on your promotion yet," I said, ignoring his hand. "I will consider your offer."

He was not in the least disappointed.

"We shall talk further when I can deliver your letter of credit."

Bowing slightly, the Cambodian departed.

I could understand now why the Binh Xuyen had been so suspicious, had leaped to conclusions, and even now did not believe my loyalty. What woman according to their bureau of standards was worth the difference between one and ten million dollars?

Charlotte ... ? The hurt returned. Love and luck.

Closing the door to the barely perceptible crack, I heard heavy muffled footsteps on the carpet outside. They paused. A stentorian knocking echoed from room four hundred two.

Peering, I could see the outline of three men with bulky coats. I froze, motionless.

The pounding repeated and I heard the doorknob being tried. The quiet of what seemed to be an endless pause was shattered suddenly by carbine fire, multiple and constant. The sound diminished abruptly in a rapid patter of running feet.

Cracking my aperture to thumb width, I saw the room across as bellboys and stewards opened the door and rushed in. Windows and mirrors were shattered, furniture splintered and smoking, the bed and carpet sieves of torn fabric.

Closing the door, my knees buckled. The intense heat of the tropical spring seemed suddenly to penetrate my skin and roll through me. I retreated to the bed, drenched with sweat and shaking. The consistent chopping of the overhead fan finally lulled me into a fretful sleep.

I awoke with my skin on fire and when I saw myself in the mirror, I was yellow. I telephoned for a doctor. Shivering and burning alternately, I awaited his arrival. The French hotel physician came shortly after siesta.

"Hepatitis," he pronounced immediately. "The trouble with you Americans is that you do not take the lettuce here. You think to avoid amoebic dysentery from the vegetables—and so end up with hepatitis."

He looked me over skeptically while lighting a black, foul-smelling cigarette. "Also, you have not had enough rest."

"Lettuce, hell!" I snapped at him weakly. "Too damned much rich French food. I should have stayed with rice and *nuoc-mam* when I was ahead."

He shrugged his shoulders and curled his lip.

"*N'importe.* Now you have only to stay in bed and eat what the hotel serves. I shall look in on you again in a few days."

"Save your gasoline. I will not be here."

"No," he agreed coldly, "you probably will not." Packing gadgets back into his bag, he snapped it closed and left without a backward glance.

I forced myself to walk around the room. Other than a faint giddiness and dead weight of body, I did not feel too badly. I telephoned a food order. Rice, fish sauce, bat cooked in its own blood, and durion—the tropical fruit that smelled like decomposed human flesh, but tasted delicious once past the nose.

I dieted ruthlessly on the native food, avoided all liquids, and felt the strength pour back into my body. If my liver was not healed, at least it was swathed in bandages.

A brief newspaper account of the shooting mentioned my name in connection with the room, and that the bullets had eluded me. However, I was not too concerned over another attempt—not immediately.

The same issue blazoned the news of the government delegation's disaster. Approaching the D'Or Blanc forces at Ben-Cat, the "allegiance" party's flag-bedecked vehicles had been pulverized by an artillery barrage. Five were dead. The remainder, after identifying themselves, barely succeeded in fleeing reddened bayonet points. One surviving witness likened the array of forces to the army of Genghis Khan. He was prayerful that he had not been pursued further. Xuan was officially denounced.

I folded the newspaper. The Binh Xuyen now had its proof. I decided to sell to the highest bidder.

CHAPTER TWENTY

It took all the will power I could muster to look at the medical report the nurse handed me.

I did not recognize my voice when I asked, "How is she?"

The spic and span mademoiselle in starched white answered coldly, "As well as could be expected, monsieur."

"What do you mean?"

"This is a respectable hospital—not a clinic for prostitutes. We gave your ... friend ... treatment because she is French, and that is all we can do. Beds are scarce. When the prescribed series of injections are completed, she will leave."

"When will that be?"

"Five more days."

"Where is the doctor who got the five thousand dollars to admit her? Playing tennis with Bao Dai?"

"I do not know what you are talking about," she answered stiffly.

"What is all this scribbling on the report?"

"Undiagnosed form of shock. We do not have the facilities, time or doctors to treat it, monsieur."

"Are you fixing her teeth?"

"No."

"Nice work, angel."

For the first time, she seemed to become human. "Please do not be angry with our hospital. We do our best. It is hard to be merciful as one wants during these times, and even harder to keep up a reputation."

"Your reputation is doing fine."

"Would you like to see her?" The nurse was cold again.

"Why do you think I came?"

Briskly she walked away, her rubber heels making no noise on the tiles. When she returned, she appeared disconcerted.

"I am sorry, monsieur. Madame refuses to see anyone."

"That sounds better, Nurse. See that you treat her like Madame. Fix her teeth. Do something with her hair, and if five thousand dollars will not diagnose that shock, tell your doctor he will have a shock all of his own."

The nurse turned her head. "I will speak to him," she promised distantly.

"I have a native army that is going to overrun this town. If Charlotte Mossard is not still here in this hospital and getting excellent attention when I bring them through, I may just turn a few of them loose—in your office, Nurse. Some of them have never seen a white woman."

She stared at me in horror. "I will give the doctor your message."

The line of *pousses* in front of the hospital bobbled like swaying gondolas when I walked out. A dozen voices called for my business. I selected an olive-skinned coolie whose leg muscles bulged with the promise of speed that would work up a breeze in my face. I directed him to the Villa d'Or Blanc.

It was padlocked and shuttered. The call button raised nothing but a horde of disturbed insects from the portico roof. I swore in disgust. Lien-Fat had not waited seven days. He had already gone to Hong Kong.

There was a letter in my box at the hotel desk. As I accepted it, a New England accent inquired politely at my elbow, "Mr. King?"

I turned. The young-looking, middle-aged man was slim and wiry, with horn-rimmed glasses. Hair clipped in a bristle, he wore PX loafers with a high polish. An English briar lay cradled in the curve of his hand.

Ignoring him, I opened the letter and read it.

My intentional rudeness did not disconcert him.

"I would like to talk to you in your room, Mr. King," he said quietly.

"After you," I said, gesturing and folding the envelope. "Obviously, you know which one it is."

We rode the *ascenseur* in silence.

"Mr. King," he said, when we were seated and his pipe was drawing nicely, "your activities in Viet Nam have become a concern not only to the government of this country, but to the United States as well."

"Why? Are they running short of Master Sergeants?"

"I do not believe I understand you?"

"G.I. joke."

"Oh yes, you used to be in the army, I believe."

"Don't you know?"

"Well, yes, as a matter of fact, I do," he said reluctantly. "It is no secret that we have a dossier on you, Mr. King. Are you overseas on a U.S. passport?"

"Why? Are you thinking of extraditing me?"

"We have no control over you as a private American citizen. Of course, we could ask the Vietnamese government to request that you report to the Embassy for passport examination. However, that is not the purpose of my visit. I shall get to the point. You are reported to be the war lord of certain armed forces assembled north of Ben-Cat—the former plantation workers of D'Or Blanc. Apparently, they are not loyalists. What are your intentions?"

"I have not decided yet."

The agent frowned. "To have reached such a position in this most delicate of all international situations, you must have an inkling of the political ramifications. Your country's interest is in backing Ngo-dinh-Diem."

"Really?"

Leaning forward in anticipation, he saw the expression on my face, coughed and struck a match to his pipe.

"Then, I am to take it that you are a mercenary?"

"Look, let's get down to four-letter words. I have an army. You want it for Diem. What is your deal?"

He flushed slightly. "I am in no position nor am I authorized to negotiate for your alleged force, Mr. King."

"Then, what are you here for?"

"I am concerned with your intent."

"It makes no difference then whether I fight for Diem, Ho-Chi-Minh, the Binh Xuyen, or myself—so long as you can file a historical report. Right?"

The pipe went in and out of his mouth, until clouds obscured the angry contours of his face. When the smoke cleared, his voice was ill-disguised in its contempt.

"A patriotic appeal would be wasted on you, I can see."

"Try me. I like the Declaration of Independence and Lincoln's Gettysburg Address especially."

That got him. He arose uncertainly, distaste written all over his face.

"King, I do not mind saying that you are a most loathsome kind of American and that, in my own personal opinion, the country is better off with you outside its borders."

"Better not say that in your report." I countered easily. "If I were home, you would not have such a problem."

His eyes, brimming with animosity, finally glared.

"You want to discuss intent?" I asked. "All right. Let's discuss intent. My top general is disillusioned with Ngo-dinh-Diem. The United States will not pay. The Binh Xuyen put my fiancée into white slavery. So, that leaves the Communists."

I shook out the inserts of the envelope I had picked up at the desk and handed them to him. He examined them quickly and in silence.

"What would you do, Mr. Political Expert?"

He returned the letter of credit and the land grant deed without comment.

"What would you do, if you were stuck in this Godforsaken acre of the world without money, with no family, with a girl you love who is forced to pull up her dress when somebody calls her name and who has gone all to hell mentally from the horror of it, and a diplomat telling you your country is better off without you?" I knew my voice was shaking with bitterness.

The agent's face was pale as he scanned my face intently.

"I think that answers all my questions, King."

"All but one."

"Which is?"

"What am I going to do?"

"That apparently has been settled," he commented bitterly.

"You give up too easily."

"I told you before that I am not authorized to make a counter offer or even an offer. Furthermore, I do not think Washington would ever consider such a proposition."

Striding thoughtfully up and down the room, he flicked the stem of his pipe against his teeth in tiny rattles.

"I wish it were possible, King. I would resent every taxpayer's penny that went into your pocket, but as strongly recommend it. The edge that your army would give to Ngo-dinh-Diem—now this is my own personal thinking and not official—would turn the tide in this part of the world."

"There is an original thought. Better classify it."

His face reddened. "King, your flippant attitude is forcing me to words which I may regret. But, if I may say so, you are living in a fool's dream. The Communists will no more honor this paper than they have a thousand other agreements in the past. What value are you to them, once your army has been turned over? This is the way they entice, not only individuals and groups, but entire governments. And then, when the coup is struck, their memories become conveniently short. That bank in Hong Kong may or may not honor that letter of credit. It is a Communist-owned bank. If not, where would you make your claim—in Peiping? That palace they offer you—does it exist? What recourse do you have, if it does not? Once you are behind the Bamboo Curtain, you belong to them...body and soul. They will tell you what you can have or not have and if you do not like it, there is nothing you can do—not even get out. There are Americans still being held there in prisons, if you doubt my words. Not even international law nor your government's protests have been able to extricate them. Think well, King, of the consequences—if not to your country, to you personally."

The emotion-charged speech left him panting.

"Bravo," I said quietly. "Tell the Ambassador you earned your money today."

"What are you going to do?"

"I may take over Viet Nam myself."

He sputtered and strode angrily to the door, then paused to light the cold pipe.

Turning around, he asked, "Who did you say your top general was?"

"I didn't. But Xuan is his name. If you want to know how to spell it, look in the newspapers."

He sucked thoughtfully, started to shake hands and changed his mind. There was a knock on the door. He stood quickly to one side and motioned for me to open it.

The bellboy handed me another letter. I ripped it open and scanned it hurriedly.

The agent held out his hand for the letter. I shook my head smiling.

He shrugged with exasperation and was gone.

I reread the cryptic message.

Today. Grande de la Liraye. Five million dollars.

The same initials, L.V.V., were encrusted with the sect seal.

I was the only man in the world who, at that moment, held a total of fifteen million dollars plus a mandarin palace, without cash to cover the hotel bill....

As my taxi sped up rue Catinat, I could see through the rear window a black Chevrolet and a *cyclo-pousse* start up after me. I was not surprised. My movements from here on could shake stock markets. I ordered the driver left in front of the bomb-shattered Opera and we drove into the Charner traffic circle by the GMC Department Store. The taxi moved slowly until the sleuthing vehicles fell in line behind. I told the driver to speed up and keep going around. Pretty soon, the three of us were racing around the landscaped fountain, and crowds of people stopped to gape at us. A police whistle blew frantically.

In the melee, I got a good look at my shadows—the Cambodian Communist in the *cyclo-pousse,* and a young American at the wheel of the Chevrolet. Directing the taxi out of the circle, I stopped him suddenly, leaped out, and entered one of the twin entrances of the Passage Eden, a twisting shopping arcade that went through the block. As the others came charging into the cool, dark tunnel, I stepped out of the other entrance, re-entered my taxi and continued unobserved to the Binh Xuyen villa on Grande de la Liraye, where Charlotte had been kept prisoner.

It bore the semblance of being shuttered as tightly as before, but the grilled gate swung open at my touch. The villa door was ajar. Walking into the darkened *salon,* the memory of Charlotte—perfume and violins—overwhelmed me.

"Dirty bastards," I said aloud.

"We do not pretend to be anything else," an amused voice said, and the thin, bespectacled Vietnamese from the Grand Monde stepped gracefully out from behind the heavy draperies.

"Haunting houses must pay better than I thought."

He gave me an oily smile. "Precautionary, my sedentary friend—in case you brought company."

"Trusting to the end, I see. I expect your Zurich bank is on a vacant lot."

"No. It has a cement foundation—as you may have, unless you keep us better informed."

"Like telling you which room at the Majestic I am staying in?"

"All right, King. We made a mistake. Do not expect apologies … or for Madame Mossard. We are not running a debutante school. The world is full of *jeunes filles* and with our new offer, you can buy a whole harem."

He fitted a cigarette into the gold holder and continued, "The point is that we admit we were premature in judging your intentions. We are now ready to discuss finalities."

He sat down in a dusty chair, crossing his legs negligently.

"Direct your forces to the west, as if you were planning to engage the Cao-Dai. It will look in Saigon as if you have either made a pact with Ho-Chi-Minh for a double-pronged envelopment of Indochina, or else you are preparing to swallow the sect armies before tangling with Diem. The Nationalists will shift their defenses to the west. By pivoting your forces diametrically, you can in an overnight march retrace your ground and effect surprise by attacking from the north."

"You have been reading up on Rommel," I observed.

"The new date is April twenty-ninth—without fail."

"And the new money?"

Ash from the cigarette was tapped languidly into a massive crystal tray.

"Your Swiss account has been increased." Again he tapped the cigarette. He was nervous under the calm exterior.

"Your technical strategy is not bad. As a matter of fact,

I have been offered ten million dollars to start out that way. Nobody would ever know, until the twenty-ninth of April, whether I was going to cut back to Saigon for you, or keep going to Bangkok."

Hooded eyelids flickered.

"Charlotte Mossard," I continued, "is one woman you are not going to forget."

"Five," he said quietly, "is the top."

I lifted my shoulders in a shrug.

His eyes were intent behind the glittering spectacles.

"You will recall, King, that we were reluctant to do business with you from the beginning. Not that we did not respect your military ability. We did not trust you. We suspected that you would not stop at one million, and we were prepared to go as high as five. Let me warn you of something, in case that Communist offer intrigues you. We are one of the richest syndicates in the world. No matter what happens to our interests in Saigon, we will continue to operate. We have long ... very long arms. You will not be safe anywhere in the world, not even in that remote Chinese province."

He must have sensed my surprise.

The cold menace softened. "Do you agree, Mr. King, that we settle at five?"

"Ten ... and one provision. I want Madame Mossard made completely well—physically *and* mentally. You may have to fly in a medical staff from Paris to do the job."

"Our influence in Saigon has been temporarily disrupted, you know."

"Tough. I won't worry about China, if you can't reach across five miles."

We stared at each other for a long moment.

"Eight?" he suggested.

I started walking toward the door.

"Ten is agreed," he said crisply. I knew from his tone that was his authorized limit.

"Plus the medical services for Madame," I said evenly. "Tell your Number One I will loft just one mortar shell into the Palace, then hold up until I get—first, *not* the number of some Swiss bank account, but a certified cashier's check for ten million dollars, which you will leave at the desk of the Hotel Majestic; second, a look at Madame Mossard. If both are not as promised, I shall forget the Palace and come after the Binh Xuyen."

"Fair enough," he said calmly, and sauntered out of the house.

At the window, I watched him climb into my waiting taxi and drive off.

The room and its memories pressed in on me again.

Tearing up the Communist letter of credit and the land grant, I left them in pieces strewn on the floor.

My legs wobbled as I turned out into the street, and I felt my face alternately flushing with fire and numbing with cold. I held onto a tree for support.

CHAPTER TWENTY-ONE

It was the time of evening before the city lights came on. The horde of cruising *pousse* drivers slowed and shouted, "*Cong Gai! Cong Gai!* Young girl for Monsieur!" In each hooded carriage was a girl with only her legs showing, skirt slitted high, or draped diaphanously in the Vietnamese fashion. I realized what had happened to the vast multitude of Saigon's female charmers. Thrown out of business by Diem's crackdown, they had gone mobile. The Binh Xuyen was still grinding out profits.

An empty *pousse* stopped and I got in. The warm, ever-damp night air whipped into a breeze by the hard-pedaling coolie choked my breathing. I felt a pounding in my head.

I vomited over the side of the careening carriage, and everything went black.

When I came to, it was to the sound of jostling tin being battered by hordes of insects. Opening my eyes, I saw lamp shades strung overhead—lit saucers moving restlessly under the brunt of the attacking bugs. I was lying on the ground in the open air, the *pousse* driver bending over me anxiously. A long, quiet queue of people stretched behind him and out of sight. A smell of sickness and the faint odor of disinfectant reached me. I recognized the Hong Thap Tu Clinic in the Gia-Dinh native quarter.

A nurse in a Red Cross uniform was giving shots. Shapely enough from the rear in the trim white uniform, her profile, when she turned, was bent with fatigue and her stomach distended slightly, as I had seen natives afflicted with parasites.

"Okay, you?" the kneeling coolie asked apprehensively.

"Okay." I tried to find my pocket.

"No mind. No mind," he said. "I take you to nurse." His scrawny arms shoveled under my back.

The diamond-shaped face of the girl twisted into view and purple eyes regarded me gravely. It was Thi-Tuyet.

The shock pumped adrenalin into me. Lurching forward on my knees, I took a deep breath and managed to stand upright.

She said in an impersonal voice, "This clinic is for the poor. There are hospitals for the French ... and the Americans."

The soft molding of her chin was gone. The cascading ringlets had been clipped, leaving uneven edges. Her roundness had disappeared into purposeful lines that rippled the cotton of her uniform as she worked. Scarlet and saffron ribbons crossed in a pin attached to her nurse's cassock.

I spoke weakly. "I was brought here."

My Vietnamese coolie launched into a stream of Tonkinese with gestures.

A scabby mandarin stepped up, dropped his trousers in front of Tuyet and bent over with a wheeze. She placed a *piqure* in what little flesh there was exposed and helped him to his feet when he tumbled.

Turning to me, she said, "All right. But you should go to a doctor for examination and diagnosis. I can give you a shot of beef extract. It is no cure, but it will make you feel stronger."

She could have been a total stranger.

I followed the mandarin into position as her nimble fingers prepared the syringe.

"I am glad you ... found work," I said.

"It was not easy."

I grunted from the jolt of the needle.

"Please rest for an hour." She pointed to the ground. "I am sorry we have no beds."

I lay and watched her as the long line gradually dissipated. Finally, the trunk of Red Cross supplies was belted, locked and chained under a small thatched pavilion. The lights were turned off.

"You are still here?" she asked in surprise. "I think you can get up now."

I tried and could.

Tuyet swept off the white cassock and pulled a black tunic over her head until the twin hems swirled about her pantaloons. Her movements were deftly familiar.

"I have finished my work for the evening," she said. "I will help you find a doctor, if you like."

"He would have to be pretty good to match you."

She shrugged, but pleasure in my remark softened her face.

"You may have hepatitis. It is very common during the hot season. If so, King, you will need attention."

I tested my legs. "I feel like walking."

Her eyes measured me questioningly. She took my arm. We moved in silence along the broken macadam, pressed close to the open sewer by oncoming traffic.

"You have succeeded in becoming a power in Viet Nam," Tuyet said.

"I could use a little more—in my legs."

She reflected. "Who are you and Xuan going to fight?" she asked.

"If I told you, you would run and tell Ngo-dinh-Diem."

She smiled.

"I have never seen him … but yes, I should like to run and tell him."

"Why?"

In the darkness I could see her eyes sparkle.

"He believes that we should be one people," she answered, "and own our own country. I never thought of Vietnamese that way. We were always like the gray elephants who must work in the forest, while the white one is dressed in silver bangles and lives at the palace. Diem says we are to be proud of our race—that the lowest coolie is as important as the highest mandarin, and that all are entitled to the same dignity as the foreigner."

"The French must have let you down with a bang."

Her jaw tightened. "There were other reasons for my becoming a nurse."

"Like the ones I told you at the Château?"

She stopped, anger congealing in her face. "I am going to have your baby, King."

I looked at her in amazement. The slight bulge that I had seen was pronounced by a curved back and tightness of *poitrine*.

"You have a nerve," I said coldly, "pretending it is mine. Do not forget … I know this city."

"So do I," she answered, starting to walk. "But the nicer people in it." The implication sank in.

"You are not like Americans I have met, King—at the French Library and the culture center. I thought that in …" Glancing at me abruptly, she stopped. Her voice was calm when she continued, "Let us talk of other things."

"Then why did you bother to tell me about the baby?"

There was a wistfulness that escaped her solemn manner. "I thought that you might care."

"If you are using wiles because of my army, it will take more than a baby."

She shrugged. "God will take care of your army."

"God! Don't tell me you are throwing firecrackers in church."

A smile flitted over her face.

"I have been to church once or twice. I want him"—her hand touched her stomach—"to believe differently than I was taught. Our religion was what our fathers learned from their fathers. Most of it, I think, was vanity. My father must get down on his knees, like everyone else, before the Creator of the Universe." She looked intently at me. "Are you tired?"

As we had walked the traffic had thickened.

"I am all right," I answered gruffly.

"Then," she said, "I will show you something."

We were approaching the Gia-Dinh market place on rue Paul Blanchy. Thousands of people were packed around it. Over the turret of dirty market stalls, there was a huge screen projected against the sky. Pictures flashed. The crush of spectators became silent and awed. A newsreel showed the grim Communist take-over in Haiphong, the National Army overrunning the Binh Xuyen's rue Gallieni, cranes disgorging American-aid supplies at the Saigon port, Diem making a speech, and President Eisenhower's press conference on the Saigon crisis.

The viewers were perched on bicycles, in trees and atop the market stalls—squatting and standing. Their eyes were frozen to the magic spectacle of light and movement. A USIS documentary on American government followed the newsreel. There were scenes from the Revolutionary War, the Declaration of Independence, the War between the States, a dour picture of Lincoln maintaining "of the people, by the people, and for the people." Clips of crude wilderness changed to a montage of steel-towered cities, miles of waving grain, superhighways, a plateau of shiny cars and the family—healthy, happy, prosperous.

The message was clear.

The crowd applauded vociferously.

A still projection of Ngo-dinh-Diem and the national colors signified the end. Thousands of people broke into a throaty roar that held long after the screen went blank.

"Your army may be strong," Tuyet said simply. "But it cannot defeat this."

She took my hand gently. "Come home with me."

We lay for a long time in the *boyerie*—the servants' quarters of a bomb-shattered villa that had been deserted. I stole a glance at her, the once-arrogant mandarin's daughter, sleeping on the crumbled floor. My hand crept over the swell of her abdomen exploring gently. He was too young to have a heartbeat yet. *He.*

CHAPTER TWENTY-TWO

awoke with the sun in my eyes. Sticky with perspiration, I staggered up to wash myself from an urn of rusty water. Tuyet appeared with a newspaper, a book and a large package of meat and bread.

"Get back in bed," she commanded sternly. "You are not to get up until the doctor says."

"What are you talking about?"

"You have been sick for two weeks. You almost died."

I stared at her dumfounded.

"What day is this, Tuyet?"

She handed me the newspaper. It was April twenty-fifth, nineteen hundred and fifty-five. I was due to attack on the twenty-ninth.

Feverishly, I searched the front page. There were no banner headlines. The conflict was stalemated. The uneasy truce, forced by the French Legion, was still effective. But the Legion had withdrawn its wedge.

"I am glad to see you better," Tuyet said, unwrapping the meat. "It was fortunate that I could get our doctor to come and see you."

I lay back on the blanket to gather my wits.

Tuyet lit the charcoal brazier and fanned furiously.

"The doctor told me about Charlotte Mossard," she said over her shoulder.

I snapped like a rubber band. "What about Charlotte Mossard?"

Her eyes appraised me. "Every doctor in Saigon has been called in to see her."

Turning back to the brazier, she said, "She talks to Guillaume all the time."

A crisp, sizzling sound filled the open-air room. She was frying a filet steak.

"If you are cooking that for me," I said rudely, "I eat rice and *nuoc-mam*."

"You will eat this Japanese beef"—her voice brooked no argument—"after I walked all the way to the *bon marché* and spent a week's salary for it. Steak and rest, the doctor says, is the best cure for *la hépatique*."

I laughed bitterly. "Talking to Guillaume."

She came over to the blanket and slid arms around my neck.

"I have liked taking care of you, King, and was frightened that you would die. Does … that mean anything to you?"

"You will be paid for your trouble."

Tuyet regarded me somberly. "It is not money that makes the five joys. I used to think that it was. My father thought so, and Guillaume. And look at Madame Mossard … ."

I pushed her away. "What do you want from me?"

"You," she answered humbly. There were tears in the downcast eyes.

"You want a father for your baby. If a paddy coolie had raped you, you would be standing there with the same tears in your eyes. If you want an American so badly, strap in your stomach good and tight and let some G.I. pick you up. The army will make him take care of it—even if it is born prematurely."

Convulsions worked her slim throat.

"I am trying hard not to be angry." Her voice shook.

"Do not try so hard."

Heaving myself up from the blanket, I started for the street.

"See you around," I threw back over my shoulder.

"But, King … your steak," she cried desperately.

"The two of you enjoy it."

As my plane floated toward the blue mountains rising in the distance, the quilt of rubber trees rushed up underneath.

Tuyet really knew how to work me. How well I knew, by bitter experience, what happened to the compassionate in Indochina.

One bit of information I had gleaned in my overextended visit to Saigon was that the National Army liked carbines. They looked fearsome and spat lead profusely, but they discouraged marksmanship. A well-aimed Garand could knock one out, before getting in range. I hoped Xuan had not wasted too much ammunition in target practice.

I followed the splashing Song-Be mountain stream over the unbroken jungle until Nui-Bara loomed ahead. The waterfall was a silver chain against the green wilderness. Dropping altitude, I veered the stick and in a few minutes was over the Château. I circled it wide twice. Something about it seemed different and I could not place what it was. Circling again, I shook off the uneasy feeling, and let down on the runway.

Xuan came walking from the shadow of the trees to meet me. Nothing seemed to have changed in his stance or mannerism. I scanned the Château critically.

A flagpole had been mounted on the summit—a Nationalist banner waving from its height.

My eyes swept the grounds for traces of an ambush. I saw none.

Xuan saluted. We waited—each for the other to speak.

"Where did you get the flag?" I said finally.

"Oh, that...." He seemed uncomfortable. "I...well, I had a visit. It was an American airplane. A Beechcraft...you should have seen it come in...pfff...just like that!" He made a sharp diving arc with his hand.

"Get to the point."

His uniformed figure tightened until he was ramrod erect.

"The Premier was on the plane. Ngo-dinh-Diem. He told me he had not seen my letter, and apologized to me for the mistake. He appointed me to the Vietnamese General Staff with full pay and privileges." Xuan paused, eying me warily. "I swore to obey his orders."

"Which were?"

"To stand ready. There will be a public manifestation soon to impress the other sects. He wants to avoid an all-out war."

"And neutralize you out of the glory until he can replace you."

Xuan's lips tightened.

"*N'importe,*" I continued. "Your allegiance to me comes first. Alert the army. Tomorrow we swing it around facing Cambodia. By noon, I want us within shouting distance of Pope Tac's Temple. But no engagement with the Cao-Dai—even if they shoot."

"Is your object a deception to drop the guard of the National Army?"

"It is."

"And you are determined to fight in the interests of the Binh Xuyen?"

"Of course."

"Then, my army will not follow your orders." He folded his arms defiantly. "If you insist, you will have to kill me."

"Like father, like son," I said with sudden menace.

He circled away from me, assuming an alert position.

"You are better at judo than I, but I shall do my best to kill you."

I regarded him incredulously and asked, "You would give your life for a cheap promise?"

"Make the first move," he said tonelessly.

"Your dramatics are childish, Xuan. If you mean what you say, you could have had a squad cut me down the minute I got off the plane."

"I could have, yes," he said, without relaxing his guard. "But, that is the dirty way of the imperialists and the Communists.

If we are to ever grow into a decent civilization, the manner of getting there is as important as the goal. I wanted to be fair with you, King, and give you a chance to side with our cause, as your country already has."

"And there is an execution squad in the barracks, in case you start to lose."

"There are no troops within sight or call," he answered stiffly.

"I can see one in the window—over there."

His eyes never left mine. "You see, Mr. King, I have learned well. We Vietnamese have an expression—'It is a foolish student to challenge the teacher.' But I am ready."

"There is a better one—'When the leech sucks a body dry, it moves to a fresh one.' "

"And, there is yet another one. 'The affectionate tiger kills with compassion.' "

I could feel my blood draining. "What do you mean?"

A dry smile carved his face and he looked suddenly old. "My father told me of the affectionate tiger who had killed the moral spirit it was nursing because the spirit would not strike to kill in cold blood. When you did not kill me after I wrote the letter, as I expected, I began to doubt the wisdom of the proverb. I think I can understand now. One may learn from the animals in the jungle. But man is not the same. If he were, he would have four legs and a tail."

We challenged each other silently—a dozen feet apart.

"It is a risk to doubt my father's wisdom, I will admit. But I think I am right. You would kill—yes—in anger because of injustice. That I have seen. But, without anger, for the side of injustice, I do not believe it."

I tried to get angry—to think of the ten million dollars hanging in the balance, of Xuan's duplicity, of the Binh Xuyen's parting threat. Maybe I was too tired. Maybe it was Charlotte. Maybe the money was not that important. Maybe ... Xuan was right.

"You win."

Xuan leaned forward impulsively, eyes glistening.

"You are not going to fight me?"

His voice was eager with boyish relief.

I shook my head.

"No trick?"

"No trick."

He came running and kissed me on both cheeks.

"I was afraid," his voice shook with emotion, "and was preparing to join my father in Paradise."

"There was a time when you might have," I said slowly. "Your father was right as far as he went, but the tiger became domesticated."

He eyed me seriously for a moment. "I think, rather, the man became compassionate."

I turned to climb into the plane.

"King, will you direct my army for Ngo-dinh-Diem?"

"No. It is your show from here on. But watch your step. You are in high-level politics now, Xuan. You will not last long unless there is a wall behind you when you start dealing, and at least a few riflemen the rest of the time."

Through the blur of the revolving propeller, I could see him grin.

"There is something you can do for me, Xuan," I called. "Keep Mossard's grave clean and the marker up."

He shouted back, "All right. And, if you have a chance, find my sister."

It was my turn to grin.

As I left the ground, I could see him standing on the strip, his arm waving ceaselessly. I flew over the Château for one final look. It was the same as I had first seen it a year ago—in May 1954. Only two things were different. The green mound in the front lawn, and the red and yellow flag flying from the steep Château roof.

CHAPTER TWENTY-THREE

I hung around Tan-Son-Nhut Airport until I found a buyer for Mossard's airplane. With the money, I went to the hospital.

The same nurse, chalky when she recognized me, hurried to explain that a Parisian psychiatrist had arrived and was administering the *Méthode Castellane* to Madame Mossard, a system which had been used with effect in excessive shock cases. Madame could not receive visitors, the nurse chattered, unless the doctor approved.

Doctor Marcellin, a wizened, petulant man with constantly slipping eyeglasses, shrugged and said it would be a matter of weeks before the *Méthode* results could be decisively evaluated. He asked numerous questions about Guillaume Mossard, and I filled him in on the grim details of the incident. He was reluctant to take my money—a matter of several consultations, according to his fee—but accepted when I told him that the current paying client "might" become discouraged. He advised against visiting Charlotte until there was some evidence of advancement.

Returning to the *boyerie*, I found Thi-Tuyet gone, fell onto the blanket and dropped into exhausted sleep.

A U.S. Navy officer with a round mirror on his forehead was peering at me when I awoke. Vaguely, I could see Tuyet's anxious face over his shoulder, silhouetted in the moonlight.

"Leave me alone, for Christ's sake. Does it take a doctor to prescribe a night's sleep?" Threshing about, I turned my back on them. He proceeded to take my temperature, pulse, various specimens, and to probe until I grunted with pain. Leaving abruptly, he returned several hours later with tubes of medicine. I sat up in disgust. "Now what?"

"From the looks of you," he answered shortly, "I should have brought a priest. How many times have you been up, since you have had this infection?"

"A few," I grunted. "Forget it. All I need is some uninterrupted sleep."

"You are on the way to a good, long one. Your hepatitis is infectious. If that does not impress you, it is about as serious as double pneumonia was before they discovered penicillin. Unless you have absolute bed rest for at least a month, strict protein diet and proper medicine, you had better appoint a new commander in chief for your army."

I looked at him with interest.

"Your bedside manner is touching, Lieutenant. Did the Embassy send you?"

Tuyet caught my hand. "I asked him to come, King," she said. "He was helping at the clinic. When I came home and saw you, I went back for him."

"Treating the enemy is not the good old tradition it used to be," I said. "You must be bucking for Ensign."

Ignoring me, and in a voice deep with fatigue, the naval officer said, "I shall try to check you again in a few days. The nurse here has offered to administer the medicine and diet and to keep me posted on your condition."

I regarded him critically. "You will be too busy in a few days to worry about me. Just so you can arrange your blood bank, the Binh Xuyen plans to attack on the twenty-ninth—with my help, they think. But, my army is going with Diem. You might pass that along, Lieutenant, to a fellow in the Embassy with a crew cut surrounded by pipe smoke."

The Navy officer put instruments back into his bag without replying. Then, at the door he paused to say warmly, "Welcome home!" and disappeared into the night.

On April twenty-ninth, the Binh Xuyen began the attack by shelling the Independence Palace from howitzer emplacements across the Saigon River. The bombardment continued until the fearsome half-naked soldiers of General Xuan—in waves of fire, black crosses, and lumbering oxcarts—smashed into the city.

Leaving buildings wrecked and white X marks on trees in their wake, they rolled around the Palace and converged on the Binh Xuyen's infantry divisions.

The National Army, in a simultaneous movement, struck at the sect's strongholds along the river, and swept over Cholon.

At the end of five days, the remnants of the sect's forces had been driven into the swamps bordering the China Sea.

Saigon-Cholon belonged to Ngo-dinh-Diem.

Thi-Tuyet brought me newspapers. The National Army continued to press forward into the waist-deep swamps, but Xuan's army was halted and disbanded—the tappers sworn to government allegiance, and integrated into Nationalist training camps. There was a picture of the youthful general emerging from the Palace with a scowl on his face.

The lord of the vice sect, Ly-van-Vien, was reputed to have escaped and set up a command post near the sea.

Known Binh Xuyen agents and spies in Saigon were being rounded up by the government.

The last item pleased Tuyet. "You will be safe now," she said. "And, in another few months, if you are not foolish, you will be well. We can go to America."

The Vietnamese girl was tireless. In addition to her job at the clinic, she cooked and cared for me, brought the doctor on regular visits, forced me to take medicine, and prepared for the May monsoon by building a bed of crisscross rattan and raising a thatch over it. Out of money she had somehow saved, she bought chairs and a table. When I tried to help her, she flew into a rage.

The Navy doctor, in his last examination, admitted I was improving but cautioned me against premature activity. He also told me that Doctor Marcellin was still in Saigon. Charlotte Mossard was responding, at last, to the treatment.

Restless, I took to pacing the floor when Thi-Tuyet was absent.

What had appeared to be an overwhelming victory in Indochina turned once more into the familiar powder keg. The National Army was making little, if any, progress against the Binh Xuyen survivors, who were allegedly getting support from the French along the coast. General Xuan was in the provinces inspecting training camps. The Cao-Dai and Hoa-Hao sects announced a new United Front against the government and their armies began bristling along the Cambodian border and south-west of Saigon.

I regaled Thi-Tuyet with my theories on how the war could be won in three weeks. She listened quietly, preparing my usual dose of buffalo steak and salad.

"You are getting better, King," she said with a wide smile. Her eyes dropped to the prominent mound, ill-concealed in the thin Vietnamese tunic. "I think it is time we got married," she said softly.

We had never discussed marriage.

"Yes," I answered, "soon." Perhaps it had to be that way.

There was a trace of sadness in her face. "You have not the love for me, do you, King?"

"Love?" I said with a rude laugh. "What is that?"

She puttered about with the food. "I think that you know about love," she said. "You have it for Charlotte Mossard."

I was startled. "What do you mean by that?"

"I can tell from your eyes whenever she is mentioned." Tuyet added hastily, "But I am not jealous, King... only sad for you."

"Suppose I were in love with Charlotte. Would that change your mind about our marriage?"

"Oh, no," she answered confidently. "After a while you would forget about her, and begin to have love for me." She patted her abdomen. "And for him."

It was a week later when I was alone in the *boyerie*—Tuyet having gone to the clinic—that I heard my name being called. The soft, musical voice brought me to my feet, stunned. I ran out into the court. There stood Charlotte.

Half-dazed, I approached her.

She retreated a tiny step. Twin flames burned in her cheeks.

"Please," she said. My outstretched arms dropped.

"I came to thank you, Daniel, for the money. I brought my jewels to repay you—at least some of what you spent."

"My God," I cried in anguish, "you owe me nothing. It is I who owe … I mean … for what you went through …."

She absorbed the implication of my words with a slight shudder.

I bit my tongue and waited for her to speak.

There was a stately beauty in the lift of her chin, a loftiness, almost a condescendence.

"Guillaume helped me. He gave me his strength. Doctor Marcellin showed me how such a thing is possible. Now, I can face people who know …."

My voice was shaky. "Thank God that you are finally well."

She continued as though she had not heard me, "You told me once, Daniel, that Guillaume was incapable of love. That was not true. Perhaps, he did not show it during his lifetime, but it was there … when I needed it the most."

"What about us, Charlotte?" I asked softly.

She trembled. "There is no more physical ability in me, Dan … for you or anybody. Please understand …."

"I do," I said and took her hand gently. It was cold and unresponsive. "I do because I love you in a way I have never loved any person … or ever could again. That kind of love never works. People are bastards."

"I have been to his grave." Her eyes searched mine and a slight warmth stirred in the hand I held. "Thank you." She sighed and added, "I am sorry about … us." She extricated her fingers and pulled at them nervously.

"You will not take the jewels?"

"Only when you come with them," I answered lightly.

She did not smile.

"Good-by, Daniel."

I watched until she turned the corner at the end of the block. There was so much that we had not said, so many ways that I had wanted to apologize, so many plans that I had thought of for the future. I did not even know what she was doing now that she was out of the hospital, or how she had learned my whereabouts. Only as these thoughts occurred did I become concerned that she might have been followed. Detecting no loungers or waiting *pousses* within the area, I dismissed the idea. The rest of the evening I spent hardening my decision.

When Tuyet returned from the clinic, I said nothing until we had eaten.

"Well, I guess I must tell you … and I might as well get it over." The words came from her. I was surprised because they had been on the verge of my own lips.

Looking at her questioningly, I said, "Tell me what?"

"I saw Charlotte Mossard today."

My chair scraped.

"She is working in a department store on rue Catinat." Thi-Tuyet watched my face closely.

"How is she?" I kept my voice casual.

"She looks fine," Tuyet answered, and with some reluctance added, "As before—blonde and very beautiful."

"Did she speak to you?"

"She waited on me. I invited her to come to see you. There is no use postponing the inevitable. You must decide if the love is to be me or her."

The Vietnamese girl stared straight ahead.

"Tuyet," I said, reaching for her hand across the table. "Tuyet, look at me."

She looked up, searching my face.

"You do not want to see her?" she asked.

"I have you, and that is all I want."

"Eat your steak, Dan," she commanded gently, and made it impossible by pressing my hands against her cheek.

CHAPTER TWENTY-FOUR

We set July twentieth as the day of our wedding. With her tiny savings, Thi-Tuyet bought a length of white French lace and sat up, after the clinic, sewing it by candlelight. With the doctor's cautious approval, I began to use this time for strolls around the block—the streets being deserted and the light poor. There were stories in the newspapers that Ngo-dinh-Diem's Sureté had cleaned out the last vestiges of the Binh Xuyen agents. The trouble was that the same story kept cropping up every week.

I had to get a job—something out of the country—somewhere remote. I thought of going to the American Embassy, but decided against it. I would be spotted. By the time they got around to flying me out, it might be feet first.

Thi-Tuyet could not understand my worry.

"The Binh Xuyen is finished," she said. "I think you can start taking walks during the day."

I answered, "You do not know those cutthroats the way I do. The name Dan King will be on their list for a long time."

"*Tiens!* My brother will run them up on his sword."

No more stories of a similar nature appeared.

On the day of our wedding, Tuyet was gone when I woke up. By noon I was beginning to prickle with apprehension. Peering constantly out the shattered casement, I finally walked boldly down the street to rue Paul Blanchy, one of Saigon's main arteries. I noticed it had been renamed Hai-Ba-Trung in a neat, blue-lettered sign.

The sun was hot and I felt it pouring iron into my pallid skin. Some of the gaily colored shop fronts were shuttered, but others were open. With a start I realized that it was siesta time. A few private cars whizzed by. More people were promenading than I ever remembered seeing during the rest hours. They were neatly dressed. The street was incredibly clean.

I absorbed a feeling of peace and well-being. Several of the Vietnamese strollers nodded and spoke. I had never seen them before in my life, and was surprised. I was suddenly aware that their courtesy was being extended because I was American.

Returning to the *boyerie,* I waited out the daily downpour of rain with nerves relaxed. Tuyet was planning some sort of surprise and was keeping me in suspense.

At six o'clock, I heard the snarl of military vehicles and the whine of fast brakes. I got out of my chair to see soldiers vaulting from the high bin of *camions* and forming stiffly into facing ranks. I recognized them as my old platoon of Nungs. All of them wore officer insignia of the National Army.

A shining black Citroën, emblazoned with flags and stars, pulled up behind and discharged the smart, erect figure of General Nguyen-van-Xuan. He was in tan cloth, trimmed with red and gold. Waving a baton jauntily, he marched crisply through the double ranks, kissed me formally on both cheeks and broke into a boyish grin.

"*Mon capitaine!*" he said huskily, and embraced me emotionally without regard for the honor guard who were cheating ramrod stances to get glimpses of our meeting.

My arm around his shoulder, my voice strangely raw, I said, "I knew that bride of mine was up to something."

We walked through the line of soldiers, and I slapped each back reminiscently. Their faces defied any attempt at discipline.

At the end of the ranks, and filling the whole gap, was a sight I could not believe. Lien-Fat, in a massive white shroud of a linen suit, stood beaming blisters of gold. Nodding like a Buddha, he kept repeating, *"Hai ... Hai ... Hai ... Hai. ..."*

I enfolded him in my arms.

"Lien ... Lien! This *does* make the day complete."

"I fight with new general over who is best man. I win because bigger! Besides," and he grinned shrewdly, "must have soldier body to give away bride."

He blew mightily into a handkerchief and kept clapping me on the back.

"I find not so happy in Hong Kong ... away from business of rubber in Viet Nam. So, I make new start. No all French owner this time. I sell into tracts. Some French. Some Vietnamese. Some Chinese. All work very good I think. Try to beat each other. Have lady tappers from ox army who very happy go home from bullets. Good, huh?"

His grin was constant and contagious.

"Do you have a job for me, Lien?" I asked.

"Always a job for you, Mr. King. You make plantation possible. Government very happy. New owners happy. I am happy. Even France not too sad." He laughed hugely and shook all over.

"When do I start?"

"Plenty time think about that. You have new wife worry and honeymoon first. Here!"

He shoved an envelope into my hand.

"Present from Co-operative Management of Viet Nam Rubber," he announced with gusto.

I opened it. There were fifty thousand piasters and two Air France tickets marked *Saigon-Paris-Saigon*.

The whole scene blurred in front of me. After a minute, the only thing I could say was, "My God. ..." I said it again and again.

Suddenly, I came to. "Where is Thi-Tuyet? Where is the bride?"

"She is at the hotel," Xuan answered eagerly. "She would not let you see her in the wedding gown until the ceremony. We have planned a big party on the roof and, after that, you take the *chambre nuptiale.* Tomorrow morning you take the plane for Paris. Okay?" His face was shining with pleasure and excitement.

"It is wonderful," I answered. "What are we waiting for? *Allons!*"

The street lights blinked on, dimming the stars, as we rounded the twin-spired cathedral, and roared into rue Catinat. I noticed that the street had been renamed Tu-Do—meaning freedom. The motorcycle escort in front of us opened its siren. I saw a roadblock near the Opera House, with people crushed against the barrier.

"What is it?" I asked Xuan, a feeling of uneasiness creeping through me.

"A manifestation, probably," he answered easily. "This is the anniversary of the Geneva Accords."

"Damn! I had forgotten. July twentieth ... no wonder I pulled that date out of the hat for our wedding!"

"You will have a good reminder," he laughed. "No excuse to forget."

We slowed to a halt. I saw the silver-helmeted motorcyclist gesturing with a policeman.

Xuan leaned forward. "A lot of people do not like the ICC," he said, "the North-South Control Commission created at Geneva. They feel that it strangles our independence." His tone was conversational, but rocklike ridges jutted from his face. He barked invective at the harassed policeman.

The police used their sticks to beat back the surging mob. Our convoy inched through.

In a flash, I felt my body turn to ice. I found myself pointing with frenzy. Silhouetted against the murky blue sky at the end of rue Catinat was a tinge of pink framing the Hotel Majestic.

Xuan paled. *"Allez!"* he grated at the military chauffeur.

The car lurched forward, crunching a bicycle, and raced down the street.

Humanity milled at the base of the five-storied hotel. There were banners denouncing the ICC and its Majestic Hotel head-quarters. Tongues of flame licked out of the upper windows. Smoke rose above the building like hair on end. Tinkling sounds of destruction and brawling shouts came from the interior.

Xuan was out on the street before the car stopped, shouting at the Nungs. They leaped to the concrete, fixed bayonets, and formed a V. I had to run to keep up with them.

The clog of people evaporated magically in front of the grue-some red bayonets, and we gained the entrance.

The lobby was a shambles. Paper littered the floor; the recep-tion desk was turned upside down; ceiling fans, contorted out of shape, scraped feebly against the plaster; smoke wisped out of the elevator shaft.

I found a clerk cowering in the rubble.

"What room is she in?" I shouted.

"Who?" he chattered.

"Tuyet … Tuyet … Tuyet. Nguyen-thi-Tuyet!"

"There is nobody here with that name."

"Goddammit! Give me the book!" I tore the register out of his shaking hands, and looked at the page marked *July twentieth, nineteen fifty-five.* The first entry, in neat French script, was writ-ten *Mr. and Mrs. Daniel King. Four hundred twelve, Four hundred fourteen. Four hundred sixteen.*

"Mrs. King," I shouted at the clerk. "Is she upstairs, or has she left?"

"Nobody has been hurt," he said soothingly. "The demon-strators are only making damage."

I lifted him a foot off the floor. "I said is Mrs. King still upstairs?"

"I think so," he sputtered, eyes popping. "Our guests have been advised to stay in their rooms."

I let him drop with a bump.

We took the circular stairs by threes and ran headlong into one of the brawling groups carrying signs and torches. They were trying to fire the carpet runner.

"Get them out," Xuan ordered the Nungs. Uncompromising steel pinched the demonstrators, and they slithered over each other clambering down the steps.

"She is all right, I am sure," Xuan called over his shoulder, as we rushed through the acrid air. "One of our political parties organized this. It is out of hand, that is all."

I said nothing. We slammed open the door of the bridal suite. There was no smoke inside. Nor was there any answer.

I saw the telltale chips of plaster on the floor and the ugly gaps in the wall … and I knew we were too late. Fragmentation. M-1.

She lay in a frilly white heap in front of the shattered mirror of the dressing table, slivers of glass shredded over her, a lipstick pinched tight between her fingers. Somehow the merciless steel had missed the beautiful diamond face, frozen in horror. The velvety purple eyes stared at me and there was nothing in them.

"I will bury them alive in rice." Xuan spoke in shock.

"The Binh Xuyen," I heard myself saying and repeating. "They used the demonstration for cover. They thought I was in the room."

Clumsily, I picked Tuyet up. The weight was cold and ungiving. The swelling that was my child was hard and still. My lips touched her throat and clung. I began to sob.

Xuan bowed his head and turned away from me.

"I will take her," I said.

I do not remember how long I carried her, or where it was I left her. What Xuan said to me, or any of the others, is only dim memory. I can only remember with any distinctness that I wanted to be alone with the thought of her. In *our* home. The shabby little room in the *boyerie*.

All night long, I sat in the chair she had bought, ran my hands through the dresses she had worn, fondled the handle of the skillet that had cooked my steaks, and cried into the little thatched roof that had covered our bed.

When the early cathedral bells tolled finally in my consciousness, I struggled to my feet. It was time to go. I put the Air France ticket marked with her name in the pocket of the Red Cross cassock and, without looking back, began the long, final walk to the airport.

CHAPTER TWENTY-FIVE

So many things have occurred in the year since that July night, it seems incredible that I lived it, or when I dwell back on it, as I sometimes do, it seems as remote as earlier tragedies. One of my fellow Americans, James Russell Lowell, whose writings I have gotten to know better during this past year, once said, "Joy comes, grief goes. We know not how."

I have not enjoyed the year, nor have I gone home to the United States. But certain things have helped. My job, for instance, in a small commercial bookshop near the Sorbonne, has kept me busy, and forced me to read. Lien-Fat's son, the one who is finally going to graduate, is my good friend. And there is a French *écrivaine,* a diminutive brunette who works at the Mossard Foundation. One evening a week, I help her in writing the history of France's most famous rubber man. I am not in love with her. She is just pleasant company.

The fifty thousand piasters from Lien-Fat helped me in the beginning until I found a steady job. There is not much salary at the bookshop, but my needs, then as now, are modest.

After my first revulsion at news coming from Viet Nam, I began to read avidly all incoming reports and question new students from Indochina who happened to visit the bookshop.

The ill-fated Majestic fire was, in reality, a political demonstration against the ICC which the Binh Xuyen agents abetted to get out of control. General Xuan was finally placed in charge of an army to stamp out the sect in the swamps. He smashed it into oblivion and, although I do not know with certainty, I suspect that he kept his promise made in the hotel room, with a vengeance. Xuan distinguished himself later in battles with the Cao-Dai and in the mop-up of the last rebels, the Hoa-Hao sect. The war ended just this month—July nineteen hundred and fifty-six—with the execution of the Hoa-Hao leader, Ba Cut.

The Premier, Ngo-dinh-Diem, was elected president last October over the absent Emperor Bao Dai. Ly-van-Vien, the head of the Binh Xuyen, whom I never met face to face and hope I never will, is now in Paris, according to the newspapers. I do not know if he was the one with the high-pitched voice or not. I am sure the sect—if it still exists—knows where I am and what I am doing. Perhaps they have come to realize that whether Dan King existed or not, the dice would have rolled the same.

A few months ago, on one of the rare evenings when I splurged at Maxim's, I thought I heard a familiar voice from a nearby table. There were several Vietnamese, heads huddled together over cognac, all smoking cigars. I squinted until I could see only the red dots glowing in the darkness.

On the way out, I stopped to look at them carefully. They were total strangers. One of them said, *"Qu'est-ce que c'est?"* The other shrugged. So did I. It could have been my imagination.

In my walk-up room on the Left Bank, I have tacked on the wall just two momentos of Viet Nam. One is the Air France ticket back, which expires next week—and the other is a letter Lien-Fat's son gave me recently. It was from his father, written in clear, well-expressed English.

So, Mr. King has become a friend of yours. That is very nice. I always liked Mr. King very much. Too bad he had such a sad experience here. He loved the poor girl who died in the hotel. So please to say nothing to him. Yesterday, I met in a store Madame Mossard. She asked me about Mr. King. I thought at one time he loved her. She is very beautiful, as before, when she smiles, but

I think she smiles not often. She has the sad eyes of a gazelle too deep in rice paddy. She asked me if Mr. King was to come back to Viet Nam ....

The letter and ticket propped before me on the desk, I stared longest at the ticket.

Perhaps it is time to go back.

ABOUT THE AUTHOR

H UNTON DOWNS *is an officer in the U. S. Foreign Service and currently Cultural Editor of the Voice of America. About* The Compassionate Tiger, *his first novel, he writes, "It was three years in the writing. To gather material I traveled upcountry through the jungles of Viet Nam and west to Cambodia by jeep. I was one of the few westerners to see the sacred waterfalls at Nui-Bara and actually saw a Moi chief crossing the rocks at the crest as Nguyen Cam does in the novel. I did further research in Hue at the Palace of the Mandarins (near the 17th Parallel separating North from South Viet Nam). I interviewed hundreds of Vietnamese, French, Chinese, American, British, Philippine and Indian people who were in Indochina during the years covered by the story."*

www.ingramcontent.com/pod-product-compliance
Lightning Source LLC
Chambersburg PA
CBHW031342070726
47496CB00017B/1419